LUNA

Also by Ian McDonald from Gollancz:

Necroville
Brasyl
River of Gods
Cyberabad Days
The Dervish House

LUNA

NEW MOON

Ian McDonald

GOLLANCZ

LONDON

The right of Ian McDonald to be identified as the author
of this work has been asserted by him in accordance with
the Copyright, Designs and Patents Act 1988.

First published in Great Britain in 2015
by Gollancz
An imprint of the Orion Publishing Group
Carmelite House, 50 Victoria Embankment,
London EC4Y 0DZ
An Hachette UK Company

A CIP catalogue record for this book
is available from the British Library

ISBN 978 1 473 20223 8

1 3 5 7 9 10 8 6 4 2

Typeset at The Spartan Press Ltd,
Lymington, Hants

Printed and bound by CPI Group (UK) Ltd,
Croydon, CR0 4YY

The Orion Publishing Group's policy is to use papers that
are natural, renewable and recyclable products and made
from wood grown in sustainable forests. The logging and
manufacturing processes are expected to conform to the
environmental regulations of the country of origin.

www.orionbooks.co.uk
www.gollancz.co.uk

To Enid

Luna: Character List

For terms relating to lunar marriage customs and corporate titles, see the glossary on page 393.

CORTA HÉLIO

Adriana Corta: founder and choego of Corta Hélio
Carlos de Madeiras Castro: oko of Adriana (d)
Rafael (Rafa) Corta: oldest son of Adriana. Hwaejang of Corta Hélio
Rachel Mackenzie: oko of Rafa Corta
Lousika Asamoah: keji-oko of Rafa Corta
Robson Corta: son of Rafa Corta and Rachel Mackenzie
Luna Corta: daughter of Rafa Corta and Lousika Asamoah
Lucas Corta: second son of Adriana. Jonmu of Corta Hélio
Amanda Sun: oko of Lucas Corta
Lucasinho Corta: son of Lucas Corta and Amanda Sun
Ariel Corta: daughter of Adriana Corta. Prominent lawyer at the Court of Clavius
Carlinhos Corta: third son of Adriana Corta. Surface work manager and zashitnik for Corta Hélio

Wagner 'Lobinho' Corta: fourth (disowned) son of Adriana
Corta. Analyst and moon wolf

Marina Calzaghe: Corta Hélio surface worker, later assistant to
Ariel Corta

Helen De Braga: Head of Finance Corta Hélio

Heitor Pereira: Head of Security Corta Hélio

Dr. Carolina Macaraeg: personal physician to Adriana Corta

Nilson Nunes: Steward of Boa Vista

MADRINHAS

Ivete: host mother to Rafa Corta

Monica: host mother to Lucas Corta

Amalia: host mother to Ariel Corta

Flavia: host mother to Carlinhos, Wagner and Lucasinho Corta

Elis: host mother to Robson and Luna Corta

MACKENZIE METALS

Robert Mackenzie: founder Mackenzie Metals; retired CEO

Alyssa Mackenzie: oko of Robert Mackenzie (d)

Duncan Mackenzie: oldest son of Robert and Alyssa Mackenzie,
CEO of Mackenzie Metals

Anastasia Vorontsov: oko of Duncan Mackenzie

Rachel Mackenzie: youngest daughter of Duncan and Anastasia,
oko of Rafa Corta and mother of Robson Corta

Apollonaire Vorontsov: keji-oko of Duncan Mackenzie

Adrian Mackenzie: oldest son of Duncan and Apollonaire; oko to
Jonathon Kayode, Eagle of the Moon

Denny Mackenzie: youngest son of Duncan and Apollonaire: head of
Mackenzie Fusible, the helium-3 subdivision of Mackenzie Metals

Bryce Mackenzie: younger son of Robert Mackenzie, Head of Finance for Mackenzie Metals, father of numerous 'adoptees'

Hoang Lam Hung: adoptee of Bryce Mackenzie and briefly oko to Robson Corta

Jade Sun-Mackenzie: second oko of Robert Mackenzie

Hadley Mackenzie: son of Jade Sun and Robert Mackenzie; zashitnik to Mackenzie Metals. Half-brother of Duncan and Bryce

Analiese Mackenzie: dark-amor of Wagner Corta in his dark aspect

Eoin Keefe: Head of security at Mackenzie Metals; replaced by Hadley Mackenzie

Kyra Mackenzie: Moonrunner

AKA

Lousika Asamoah: oko to Rafa Corta, later member of the Kotoko

Abena Asamoah: Moonrunner

Kojo Asamoah: Colloquium colleague of Lucasinho Corta and Moonrunner

Ya Afuom Asamoah: party-goer at Twé

Adofo Mensa Asamoah: Omahene of the Golden Stool, head of the Kotoko

TAIYANG

Jade Sun: oko to Duncan Mackenzie

Amanda Sun: oko to Lucas Corta

Jaden Wen Sun: owner of Tigers of the Sun handball team

Jake Tenglong Sun: CEO of the short-lived *Smallest Birds* design house

Fu Xi, Shennong, the Yellow Emperor: the Three August Ones: high level AIs developed by Taiyang

VTO

Valery Vorontsov: founder of VTO, has spent the last fifty years in free fall aboard the cycler *Sts. Peter and Paul*

Nicolai 'Nick' Vorontsov: commander of the VTO moonship fleet

Grigori Vorontsov: (briefly) amor and shelterer of Lucasinho Corta

LUNAR DEVELOPMENT CORPORATION

Jonathon Kayode: Eagle of the Moon: President of the Lunar Development Corporation

Judge Kuffuor: Senior Judge on the Court of Clavius and Ariel Corta's law teacher

Nagai Rieko: Senior Judge of the Court of Clavius and member of the Pavilion of the White Hare

Vidhya Rao: economist and mathematician, White Hare and Lunarian Society member, independence campaigner. Developed the Three August Ones with Taiyang for the Whitacre Goddard corporation

SISTERHOOD OF THE LORDS OF NOW

Irmã Loa: Confessor to Adriana Corta

Madrinha Flavia: joined the Sisterhood after her exile from Boa Vista

Mãe-de-Santo Odunlade Abosede Adekola: Matron of the Sisters of the Lords of Now

MERIDIAN/QUEEN OF THE SOUTH

Jorge Nardes: bossanova musician and amor of Lucas Corta
Sohni Sharma: researcher at the University of Farside
Mariano Gabriel Demaria: director of the School of Seven Bells, an assassin's college
An Xiuying: trade delegate from the China Power Investment Corporation
Elisa Stracchi: freelance nanoware designer for Smallest Birds

THE WOLVES

Amal: leader of the Meridian Blue Wolves pack
Sasha Volchonok Ermin: leader of the Magdalena pack from Queen of the South
Irina: light-time pack amor of Wagner Corta

NEAR SIDE of THE MOON

ONE

In a white room on the edge of the Sinus Medii sit six naked teen-agers. Three girls, three boys. Their skins are black, yellow, brown, white. They scratch at their skins constantly, intently. Depressurisation dries hide, breeds itches.

The room is tight, a barrel barely large enough to stand up in. The kids are wedged on benches facing each other, thighs pressed against their neighbours', knees touching those opposite. There is nowhere to look and nothing to see except each other but they are shy of eye contact. Too close, too exposed. Each breathes through a transparent mask. Oxygen hisses where the seals are inexact. Just below the window on the outlock door is a pressure meter. It stands at fifteen kilopascals. It has taken an hour to bring the pressure this low.

But outside is vacuum.

Lucasinho leans forward and once again looks through the small window. The gate is easily visible; the line from him to it is straight and open. The sun is low, the shadows are long and profound, thrown towards him. Blacker on the black regolith, they could conceal many treacheries. *Surface temperature is one hundred and twenty Celsius,* his familiar had warned. *It will be a fire-walk.*

A fire-walk, an ice-walk.

Seven kilopascals. Lucasinho feels bloated, his skin taut and

1

unclean. When the meter reads five the lock will open. Lucasinho wishes his familiar was with him. Jinji could have dialled down his racing heart, stilled the twitching muscle in his right thigh. His eyes catch those of the girl opposite him. She is an Asamoah; her older brother sits beside her. Her fingers twist the adinkra amulet around her neck. Her familiar will have warned her about that. Metal can flash weld to skin out there. She might wear the mark of Gye Nyame as scar tissue forever. She gives him a fractional smile. There are six naked, good-looking teenagers pressed thigh to thigh but the chamber is a sexual vacuum. Every thought is turned to what is beyond the lock. Two Asamoahs; a Sun girl; a Mackenzie girl; a scared Vorontsov boy, hyperventilating; and Lucasinho Alves Mão de Ferro Arena de Corta. Lucasinho has hooked up with all of them but the Mackenzie girl. Cortas and Mackenzies don't hook up. And Abena Maanu Asamoah, because her perfection intimidates Lucasinho Corta. Her brother though; he gives the best blowjobs.

Twenty metres. Fifteen seconds. Jinji has burned those numbers into him. The distance to the second lock. The time a naked human body can survive hard vacuum. Fifteen seconds before unconsciousness. Thirty seconds before irreversible damage. Twenty metres. Ten strides.

Lucasinho smiles at handsome Abena Asamoah. Then lights flash red. Lucasinho is on his feet as the lock opens. The last breath of pressurisation shoots him out on to the Sinus Medii.

Stride one. His right foot touches the regolith and drives every thought from his head. Eyes burn. Lungs blaze. He is bursting.

Stride two. Breathe out. *Out. Zero pressure in your lungs*, Jinji said. No no, it's wrong it's death. Breathe out or your lungs will explode. His foot comes down.

Stride three. He exhales. The breath freezes on his face. The water on his tongue, the tears in the corners of his eyes are boiling.

Four. Abena Asamoah streaks ahead of him. Her skin is grey with frost.

Five. His eyes are freezing. He daren't blink. Eyelids would freeze shut. Blink is blind, blind is dead. He fixes on the lock, ringed with blue navigation lights. The skinny Vorontsov boy passes him. He runs like a madman.

Six. His heart is panicking, fighting, burning. Abena Asamoah throws herself into the lock, looks around as she reaches for the mask. Her eyes go wide, she sees something behind Lucasinho. Her mouth opens in a silent cry.

Seven. He looks over his shoulder. Kojo Asamoah is down, tumbling, rolling. Kojo Asamoah is drowning in the oceans of the moon.

Eight. As he lunges towards the blue lock lights, Lucasinho throws his arms out and breaks his headlong flight.

Nine. Kojo Asamoah struggles to find his feet but he's blind, dust frozen to his eyeballs. He waves his hands, lurches, stumbles forward. Lucasinho grabs an arm. Up. Up!

Ten. The red pulses in his eyes: a circle of light and consciousness focused on the circle of the entry lock. A circle closing in with every pulse of the red in his disintegrating brain. Breathe! his lungs shriek. Breathe! Up. Up. The lock is full of arms and faces. Lucasinho throws himself at the circle of reaching arms. His blood is boiling. Gas bubbles in his veins; each bubble a white-hot ball bearing. His strength is failing. His mind is dying but he doesn't let go of Kojo's arm. He hauls that arm, hauls that boy; agonised, burning. He feels a shock, hears a shriek of blast-pressurisation

In the tiny circle of sight he has left he sees a tangle of limbs, skins, asses and bellies, dripping with condensation and sweat. He hears gasps turn to laughs, sobs to insane giggling. The bodies quiver with crazy laughing. We did the moon-run. We beat Lady Moon.

Another flash of vision: a splatter of red on the centreline of the outlock door: weird red on white. He fixes on it, a red bull's-eye that draws all his awareness into a line between him and it. As his consciousness slips into the dark he understands what the red spot is. Blood. The outlock door has slammed shut on Kojo Asamoah's left big toe, smashing it to a smear of flesh.

Dark now.

The winged woman soars out of the top of the thermal. Early light turns her to gold. She scrapes the very roof of the world, then arches her back, tucks in her arms, flicks her feet and stoops into a swallow dive. One hundred, two hundred metres she plummets, a black dot hurtling out of the false dawn, past factories and apartments, windows and balconies, cableways and elevators, walkways and bridges. At the last instant she flexes her fingers, spreads nanofibre primary feathers and pulls out of the dive. And up, sweeping high, her wings flashing in the brightening light. In three wing-beats she is a kilometre away, a fleck of gold against Orion Quadra's monumental canyon-scape.

'Bitch,' Marina Calzaghe whispers. She hates the flying woman's freedom, her athleticism, her perfect skin and tight, gymnastic body. Most of all she hates that the woman has breath to waste on recreation and Marina must fight for every sip of air. Marina has dialled down her breathing reflex. The chib on her eyeball shows Marina's increasing oxygen debt. Every lungful costs. She is overdrawn at the breath-bank. She remembers the feeling of panic when she first tried to blink the new chib out of her eye. It wouldn't go. She prodded it with a finger. It remained bonded to her eye.

'Everyone wears one,' the LDC Induction and Acclimatisation agent had said. 'Whether you're a Joe Moonbeam straight off the cycler or the Eagle himself.'

The status bars for her Four Elementals had ticked into life: water, space, data, air account status. From that moment they measured and charged every sip and sleep, every thought and breath.

By the time she gets to the top of the staircase her head is swimming. She leans against the low railing and fights for breath. Before her, the terrifying, crowded void, brilliant with thousands of lights.

4

Meridian's quadras are dug a kilometre deep and obey an inverted social order: the rich live low, the poor live high. Ultraviolet, cosmic rays, charged particles from solar flares bombard the naked face of the moon. The radiation is readily absorbed by a few metres of lunar regolith, but high-energy cosmic rays spark off a firework cascade of secondary particles from the soil that can damage human DNA. So human habitats dig deep and citizens live as far from the surface as they can afford. Only the industrial levels are higher than Marina Calzaghe and they are almost completely automated.

Up against the false sky bobs a single silver child's balloon, trapped.

Marina Calzaghe is going up to sell the contents of her bladder. The pissbuyer nods her into his booth. Her piss is scanty, ochre and grainy. Does she see tinges of blood? The pissbuyer assays her minerals and nutrients and credits her. Marina transfers the funds to her network account. You can turn down your breathing, pirate water, scrounge for food, but you cannot beg bandwidth. Hetty, her familiar, coalesces out of a spray of pixels over her left shoulder. She's a basic free skin, but Marina Calzaghe is back on the network again.

Next time, she whispers as she ascends again, up to the fog trap. *I'll get the pharma next time, Blake.*

Marina climbs the last few steps on hands and feet. The web of plastic was a choice scavenge; snatched and secreted before the salvage bots of the Zabbaleen could recycle it. The principle is ancient and trustworthy. Plastic mesh slung between support beams. Warm moist air rises and in the cool of the artificial night forms brief cirrus clouds. The mist condenses on the fine mesh and drips down the strands into drinkable amounts of water in the collecting jar. A sip for her, a sup for Blake.

There is someone at her trap. A tall, moon-thin man drinks from her collecting jar.

'Give me that!'

The man looks at her, then drains the jar dry.

'That's not yours!'

She still has earth-muscles. Even with no air in her lungs, she could take him; big pale fragile moon-flower.

'Get out of here. This is mine.'

'Not any more.' There is a knife in his hand. She can't beat a knife. 'I see you back here again, I find anything gone, I'll cut you up and sell you.'

There is nothing she can do. No action, no words, no threats or clever ideas can change anything. This man with a knife has crushed her. All she can do is skulk away. Every step, every rung is wracking shame. At the small gallery from which she saw the flying woman she falls to her knees and retches with clenching anger. Dry and heaving and unproductive. There is no moisture, no food left inside her.

Up and out of the moon.

Lucasinho wakes. A clear shell lies over his face so close his breath mists it. He panics, raises his hands to beat the claustrophobic thing away from him. Dark warmth spreads through his skull, the back of his head, down his arms, his torso. No panic. Sleep. The last thing he sees is the figure at the foot of the bed. He knows it isn't a ghost because there are no ghosts on the moon. Its rock rejects them, its radiation and vacuum dispel them. Ghosts are fragile things, vapours and tints and sighs. But the figure stands like a ghost, grey, hands folded.

'Madrinha Flavia?'

The ghost looks up and smiles.

God would not punish the woman who thieves in desperation. Marina passes the street shrine every day on her way from the piss-buyer: an icon of Our Lady of Kazan attended by a constellation of pulsing biolights. Each of those blobs of jelly contains a mouthful of water. Quickly, sinfully, she jams them into her backpack. She will give four of them to Blake. He is thirsty all the time.

It's only been two weeks but Marina feels she has known Blake a lifetime. Poverty stretches time. And poverty is an avalanche. One tiny slippage knocks on another, knocks loose yet others and everything is sliding, rushing away. One cancelled contract. One day the agency didn't call. And those tiny digits on the edge of her vision kept ticking away. Sliding, rushing away. And then she was climbing up the ladders and staircases, up the walls of Orion Quadra. Climbing up from the weft of bridges and galleries, up above the avenues of apartments, up the ever-steeper staircases and ladders (for elevators cost, and to those highest levels, the elevators don't go at all), up towards the overhanging stacks and cubes of Bairro Alto. The thin air smelled of fireworks: raw stone still fresh from the construction bots, sintered glass. Walkways lurched perilously past the door-curtains of stone cells, lit only by what light fell through their doors and unglazed windows. One false step was a slow scream down to the neons of Gagarin Prospekt.

Bairro Alto changed with every passing lune and Marina wandered far before finding Blake's room. *Apt to share; per diems pooled,* read the ad in the Meridian listings.

'I'm not staying long,' she said, looking round the single room at the two memory-foam mattresses, the empty plastic water bottles, the discarded food trays.

'They never do,' Blake said. Then his eyes bulged and he doubled over into a wracking, sterile cough that shook every rib and spar in his sparse frame. The hacking cough kept Marina awake all that night; three dry, almost petulant little coughs. Then three more. Three more. Three more. The cough kept her awake every subsequent night. It was the song of Bairro Alto: coughing. Silicosis. Moon dust turns lungs to stone. Behind the paralysis comes tuberculosis. Phages treat it easily. People who live in Bairro Alto spend their money on air, water and space. Even cheap phages are a distant hope.

Marina. It's been so long since her familiar spoke to her that she falls off the ladder in surprise. *You have a job offer.* The fall is a handful of metres; nothing in this crazy gravity. She still has flying dreams: in them she is a wind-up bird orbiting a clockwork orrery. An orrery spinning in a stone cage.

'I'll take it.'

It's catering.

'I cater.' She'll do anything. She scans the contract. She's bid herself low, but the offer is barely adequate. It's her air-water-carbon-network, and a little more. There's an up-front payment. She'll need a new uniform from the printers. And a bath in a banya. She can smell her hair. And a train fare.

She has an hour to be in Central Station. Marina blinks up a signature. The contact lens scans and transmits her retinal pattern to the agency. Familiars handshake and there is money in her account. The joy is so sharp it hurts. The might and magic of money is not what it allows you to own; it is what it allows you to be. Money is freedom.

'Take it up,' she says to Hetty. 'Restore defaults.'

Instantly the tightness in her lungs releases. Exhaling is wonderful. Inhaling is an exaltation. Marina savours the Meridian perfume: electricity and gunpowder and sewage tang and mould. And when she gets to where the breath should end, there is more. She draws deep.

But time is tight. To make the train she will have to take the West 83rd elevator, but that is in the opposite direction to Blake's place. Elevator or Blake? There is no decision.

Again Lucasinho wakes. He tries to sit up and pain drives him down on to the bed. He aches as if every muscle in his body has been pulled away from its bone or joint and that space filled with ground glass. He lies on a bed, dressed in a pressure skin, the same kind he would wear for a sane, safe, ordinary walk on the surface. He can move his arms, his hands. His fingers walk up and down his body, stocktaking. The abs, the armour of muscle across his belly, his thighs tight and defined. His ass feels fabulous. He wishes he could touch his skin. He needs to know his skin is good. He is famous for his skin.

'I feel like shit. Even my eyes hurt. Am I getting drugs?'

The mu-opioid clusters in your Periaqueductal grey are under direct stimulation, says a voice inside his head. *I can adjust the input.*

'Hey Jinji you're back.' No mistaking the picky, butlerish speech of his familiar. Familiars have problems with ambiguity. He's aware of the chib in the bottom right corner of his vision. Cortas don't need to notice those numbers but he's glad to see it. The chib tells him he's alive, aware, consuming. 'Where am I?'

You're in the Sanafil Meridian medical facility, Jinji says. *You've been moved from a hyperbaric chamber to a compression skin. You've been in a series of medically induced comas.*

'How long?' He tries to sit upright. Pain tears along every bone and joint. 'My party!'

It's been rescheduled. You're due another induced coma now. Your father is coming to see you.

White articulated medical arms unfold from the walls.

'Wait, no. I saw Flavia.'

Yes. She came to visit you.

'Don't tell him.'

He has never understood why his father banished his madrinha, his host-mother, from Boa Vista the morning of Lucasinho's sixteenth birthday. He just knows that if Lucas Corta learns that Madrinha Flavia has been here, his father will hurt her with a hundred spiteful-nesses.

I won't, says Jinji.

A third time Lucasinho wakes. His father stands at the foot of the bed. A short man, slight; dark and haunted as his older brother is broad and golden. Poised and polished, a pencil line of moustache and beard, no more; perfect but always scrutinising to keep that perfection: his clothes, his hair, his nails are immaculate. A cool, judging man. Above his left shoulder hovers Toquinho. His familiar is an intricate knot of musical notes and complex chords that occasionally resolves into half-heard, whispered bossa-nova guitar.

Lucas Corta applauds. Five clear claps.

'Congratulations. You're a Runner now.' It's known inside the family and out that Lucas Corta never made the moon-run. The reason is his secret: Lucasinho has heard that people who pry are punished, badly. 'Emergency room team; ophthalmics, pneumothoracic specialists; hire of hyperbaric chamber, hire of pressure skin, O_2 charges...' his father says. Lucasinho swings off the bed. The medical bots have removed the pressure skin. The white walls open around him; robot arms unfold with offers of fresh-printed clothing. 'Transfer from Meridian to João de Deus...'

'I'm at João de Deus?'

'You've a party to go to. A homecoming for a hero. Make an effort. And try to keep your cock out of someone for five minutes. Everyone's here. Even Ariel's managed to tear herself away from the Court of Clavius.'

Before anything else: the essentials. Metal studs and spikes slip into the careful holes in his flesh – each one the record of a heartbreak. Jinji shows Lucasinho himself so he can comb up the quiff to its full low-gravity magnificence; a deep-sea wave of glossy thick hair. Killer cheekbones and you could breaks rocks on his belly. He's taller than his father. Everyone in this generation is taller than the second-generations. He is so freakin' hot.

'He'll live,' Lucas says.

'Who?' Lucasinho hesitates between shirts before choosing the soft brown marl pattern.

'Kojo Asamoah. He has twenty per cent second-degree burns, ruptured alveoli, burst blood vessels, brain lesions. And the toe. He'll be all right. There's a delegation of Asamoahs waiting at Boa Vista to thank you.'

Abena Asamoah might be there. Maybe she would be so thankful she would let him fuck her. Tan pants with two-centimetre turn ups and six pleats. He snaps the belt shut. Spider-silk socks and the two-tone loafers. It's a party so a sports jacket will be right. He picks the tweed, feels the prickle of the fibres between thumb and fingers. That's animal-stuff, not printed. Insanely-expensive animal stuff.

'You could have died.'

As Lucasinho slips the jacket on, he notices the pin on the lapel: Dona Luna, the sigil of the moon-runners. The patron saint of the moon: Our Lady of Life and Death, Light and Dark, one half of her face a black angel, the other a naked white skull. Lady Two-Face. Lady Moon.

'What would the family have done then?'

How did his father know he'd pick the jacket with the pin on it? Then the arms take the rest of the clothing into the walls and he notices that every jacket has a Dona Luna pin on it.

'I'd have left him, if it had been me.'

'It wasn't you,' Lucasinho says. Jinji shows Lucasinho the total effect of his choices. Smart but not formal, casual but classy and on the season's trend, which is European 1950s. Lucasinho Corta adores clothes and adornment. 'I'm ready for my party now.'

'I'll fight you.'

Ariel Corta's words carry clear across the court. And the room erupts. The defendant bellows: you can't do that. The defence counsel thunders abuse of process. Ariel's legal team – they are seconds now that the trial by combat has been agreed – plead, cajole, shout that this is insane, Alyaoum's zashitnik will cut her apart. The public gallery is in uproar. Court journalists clog the bandwidth as they stream live feed.

A routine post-divorce custody settlement has turned into the highest drama. Ariel Corta is Meridian's – and therefore the moon's – leading marriage lawyer, both making and breaking. Her nikah contracts touch every one of the Five Dragons, the moon's great dynasties. She arranges marriages, negotiates terminations, finds loopholes in titanium-bound nikahs, bargains buy-outs and settles swingeing alimonies. The court, the public gallery, the press and social commentators and court fans, have the highest expectations for Alyaoum vs Filmus.

Ariel Corta does not disappoint. She peels off the gloves. Kicks off the shoes. Slips off the Dior dress. In sheer capri tights and a sports top, Ariel Corta stands before the Court of Clavius. Ariel claps Ishola her zashitnik on the back. He is a broad, bullet-headed Yoruba, a kindly man and a brutal fighter. Joe Moonbeams – new immigrants – with their Earth muscle mass, make the best court-room fighters.

'I'll take this one, Ishola.'

'No senhora.'

'He won't lay a finger on me.'

Ariel approaches the three judges.

'There is no objection to my challenge?'

Judge Kuffuor and Ariel Corta have old history; teacher and pupil. On her first day in law school he taught her that Lunar law stands on three legs. The first leg is that there is no criminal law, only contract law: everything is negotiable. The second is that more law is bad law. The third leg is that a fly move, a smart turn, a dashing risk is as powerful as reasoned argument and cross-examination.

'Counsel Corta, you know as well as us that this is the Court of Clavius. Everything may be tested, including the Court of Clavius,' Judge Kuffuor says.

Ariel purses the fingers of her right hand and dips her head to the judges. She turns to face the defendant's zashitnik down in the pit. He is muscle and scars, the veteran of a score of trials that have gone to combat, already beckoning her to come on, come down, come into the fighting pit.

'So let's fight.'

The courtroom roars approval.

'First blood,' shouts Heraldo Muñoz, Alyaoum's counsel.

'Oh no,' roars Ariel Corta. 'Death, or nothing.'

Her team, her zashitnik are on their feet. Judge Nagai Rieko tries to make herself heard over the tempest of voices. 'Counsel Corta, I must caution you ...' Through the tumult, Ariel Corta stands poised, powerful, the calm at the heart of the storm of voices. Counsels for the defence confer, heads dipped, eyes flashing towards her and then back to their fast, low talk.

'If the court please.' Muñoz is on his feet. 'The defendant withdraws.'

Not a breath is taken in Courtroom Three.

'Then we find for the plaintiff,' says Judge Zhang. 'Costs against the defendant.'

A third time the court erupts and this time is the loudest of all. Ariel drinks down the adulation. She makes sure the cameras get every angle. She slides her long, slender titanium vaper out of her bag, snaps it to length, locks and lights and exhales a thin stream of white mist. She slings her jacket over her shoulder, hooks her shoes on a finger and stalks out of the court in her fighting gear. The applause, the faces, the hovering cloud of familiars: she devours them. All trials are theatre.

An outside view costs; entertainment costs even more so Marina sits in her bottom deck, centre-section seat and makes faces at the kid peeking at her between the headrests. It's only an hour by high-speed train from Meridian to João de Deus. Amusing a kid is entertainment enough. This is the first time Marina has been out of Meridian. She's on the moon. She's on the surface of the moon, racing across it on magnetic rails at a thousand kilometres per hour, and she's blind inside a metal tube. Plains and crater rims and rilles and escarpments. Great mountains and vast craters. All out there, beyond this warm, jasmine-scented, pastel-coloured, chattery interior. All grey and dusty. All the same, all short of magnificence. She's missing nothing.

Hetty has full network access so when the kid is told to quit bothering the lady in the row behind, Marina passes the time with music and pictures. Her sister has uploaded new family photographs. There's her new niece, and her old nephew. There's brother-in-law Arun. There's her mother, in the chair, with the tubes in the backs of her hands. She's smiling. Marina's glad she can't see the airless mountains, the harsh empty seas. Against the treasury of leaves, the soft dove skies, the sea so green and full she could almost smell its depth; the moon would look like a white skull. In this train Marina can pretend she's home on Earth and she will step out among the trees and volcanoes of Cascadia.

Mom starts a new course Tuesday. Kessie would never openly beg for money but the ask is there. Mom's medical bills sent Marina to the moon. The Big Boom on the Moon! Everyone has their hands out. Everyone, every second of every day. Marina bites back the anger. It's not the lunar way. If everyone acted how they felt, the cities would be morgues by nightfall.

The train slows into João de Deus. Passengers collect belongings. Hetty's instructions are to present to security on Platform 6, from which the private tram will take her to the site. Marina feels a kick of excitement; for the first time she's thought about what lies at the end of that private line: Boa Vista, the legendary garden-palace of the Cortas.

Outside Courtroom Three the entourage descends. Ariel Corta is never without admirers, clingers, potential clients, potential suitors of all genders. *Attractive* is the first thing people say about Ariel. The Cortas have never been deep beauties but no Brazilian has ever been ugly and every child of Adriana commands the eye with some grace. Ariel's attraction is her bearing; she carries herself with poise and assurance, a cool confidence. Attention flows to her. Her colleague Idris Irmak pushes through the kisses and congratulations.

'You could have died in there.'

Insect-sized cameras swarm above Ariel's head.

'No I couldn't.'

'He would have cut you open.'

'You think?'

Ariel's hands move and grip Idris's forearm. She locks his elbow. Her slightest pressure will pop the joint like a bottle cap. The entourage gasps. The cameras dart lower for a tighter angle. This is sensational. The gossip webs will be squealing for days. And release. Idris shakes out his agonised hand. All Corta children are taught Gracie jiu jitsu. Adriana Corta believes that every child should know a fighting art, play a musical instrument, speak three languages, read an annual report and dance a tango.

'He'd have cut me to ribbons. Do you think I would have risked it if I didn't know Muñoz would capitulate?'

Idris spreads his hands. Explain the trick.

'The Alyaoums were clients of the Mackenzies until Betake Alyaoum insulted Duncan Mackenzie by not marrying Tansy Mackenzie,' Ariel says. The entourage dotes on her words. 'The Mackenzies withdrew their support. Without it: if Alyaoum had so much as scratched me, it would have been vendetta with the Cortas, without House Mackenzie behind them. They couldn't risk that. All the way I was forcing a trial by combat, knowing they had to concede.' She stops at the door of the Counsel Room to address the entourage. 'Now if you'll excuse I have a moon-run party for my nephew and I simply can't go like this.'

Judge Nagai and a bottle of ten-botanical gin wait for Ariel in the Counsel Room.

'Pull a trick like that in my court again, and I will order the zashitniks to gut you,' the judge says. She's perched on the edge of the washbasin. Counsel chambers are small and stuffy.

'But that would be clear dereliction of due diligence,' Ariel says. She dumps her armful of business suit into the deprinter. The hopper swallows it and reduces the fabric to organic feedstock. Beijaflor, Ariel's familiar, has already picked out her party frock: a 1958 Balenciaga, shoulder straps, asymmetric cut, black floral print on deep grey. 'The court failing to protect the interests of a contracted party?'

'Why can't you just mine helium like your brothers?'

'They're such dull boys.' Ariel kisses her on each cheek. 'Lucas has a negative sense of humour.' Ariel studies the gin: a gift from her client. 'Custom printed. What a nice touch.' She tips the bottle towards Judge Nagai. A shake of the head. Ariel fixes herself a martini, blisteringly dry.

Rieko touches her left forefinger between her eyes: the accepted gesture to speak without familiars. Ariel blinks Beijaflor away: a half-seen hummingbird, a spray of iridescence constantly changing hue to match Ariel's fashion. Rieko's familiar, a blank sheet constantly folding itself into new origami models, blinks out.

'I'll not keep you,' Judge Nagai says. 'To be brief, you may be unaware that I am a member of the Pavilion of the White Hare.'

'What's it they say? Anyone who says they're a member of the White Hare—'

'—isn't,' Judge Nagai finishes the aphorism. 'There's an exception to every generality.'

Ariel Corta takes a debonair sip of her martini but every sense is alert and vibrant. The Pavilion of the White Hare, the council of advisers to the Eagle of the Moon, inhabits a place between myth and truth. It exists, it could not possibly exist. It hides in plain sight. Its members confirm and deny their membership. Ariel Corta does not need Beijaflor to tell her her heart rate has increased, her breath quickened. It takes all her concentration to keep her excitement from rippling across the surface of her martini.

'I am a member of the White Hare,' Judge Nagai says. 'I have been for five years. Every year the White Hare drops two members. I am part of this year's rotation. I would like to nominate you for a seat.'

Ariel's belly tightens. A seat at the round table and here she stands in her underwear.

'I'm honoured. But I do have to ask...'

'Because you are an exceptionally gifted young woman. Because the White Hare is conscious of the increasing influence of certain elements among the Five Dragons on the LDC and desires to offset that influence.'

'The Mackenzies.' No other family is as nakedly ambitious for political power. Adrian Mackenzie, the youngest son of CEO Duncan, is oko to Jonathon Ayode, Eagle of the Moon, Chair of the Lunar Development Corporation. Robert Mackenzie, clan patriarch, has long campaigned for the abolition of the LDC and full lunar independence, free from the paternal oversight of Earth. *The moon is ours.* Ariel knows the political arguments and the players but has always remained disinterested. More than any other kind of law, lunar matrimonial law is a chaotic terrain of fierce loyalties, hissing resentments and unending grudges. It's a volatile mix with LDC politics. But a seat at the hand of the Eagle... She may never have smelt moon dust on her skin, but Ariel is a Corta, and the spirit of the Cortas is power.

'There are figures close to power who feel it's time the Cortas gave up their isolation and became participating members of the lunar polity.'

Of all her family, Ariel has flown closest to political power. Rafa, bu-hwaejang of Corta Hélio, has economic power: Corta Hélio lights the night of Earth; Adriana, founder, matriarch of Corta Hélio, has moral power. But the Cortas are not universally adored among the older families. The Fifth Dragon; they are regarded as upstarts, crooks made good, grinning assassins, carioca cowboys. Cortas smile as they cut you. Carioca cowboys, helium hellions no more. This is their invitation to the table of power. This is the Cortas' acceptance as a noble house. Mamãe will be scornful – who needs the approval of these degenerates, these soft parasites? – but she would be pleased for Ariel. Ariel has always known she was never the favourite, never the golden child, but if Adriana Corta is hard on her daughter, it is because she expects more of her than the sons.

'So do you accept?' Judge Nagai says. 'Only I'd quite like off this wash-hand basin.'

'Of course I accept,' Ariel says. 'What did you think I would say?'

'You might have given it due diligence,' Judge Nagai suggests.

'Why?' Ariel's wide-eyed surprise is open and sincere. 'I'd be a fool not to accept.'

'Your family might have an opinion...'

'My family's opinion is that I should be back at João de Deus getting dusty and sweaty in a sasuit. No.' She raises her martini glass. 'Here's to me. Ariel Corta, White Hare.'

Judge Nagai brushes her brow with her right forefinger. *We may return to the recorded world.* Ariel blinks Beijaflor back. The judge's familiar Oko reappears. Judge Nagai leaves. The printer chimes. The Balenciaga party dress is ready. Beijaflor is already changing colour to match it.

Little Luna Corta is in a peony-print bubble dress. The dress is white, gathered at the hem, with a bold print of crimson flowers. A Pierre Cardin. But Luna is eight years old and tired of smart clothes so she kicks off her shoes and dashes barefoot through the bamboo. Her familiar is also Luna: a lime-green luna moth with great blue eyes on its wings. *Luna moths are North American not South American,* Grandmother Adriana told her. *And you really shouldn't give your familiar your own name. People mightn't know who they are talking to.*

Butterflies break from cover and swirl over Luna's head. Blue, blue as the false sky, and wide as her hand. The Asamoah kids brought a party box and released them. Luna claps her hands in delight. She never sees animals in Boa Vista: her grandmother has a horror of them. Won't allow anything furred or scaled or winged into Boa Vista. Luna chases the ribbon of slow-flapping butterflies, running not to catch them but to be free and floating like them. Air eddies, bamboo breaks whisper, carrying voices and music and the smell of cooking. Meat! Luna hugs herself. This is special. Distracted by the smell of grilling meat she pushes her way between the tall, waving canes of bamboo. Behind her, slow waterfalls cascade between the huge stone faces of the orixas.

Three and a half billion years ago magma burst from the living heart of the moon to flood the Fecunditatis basin; glugging slow in rilles and levees and lava tubes. Then the moon's heart died and flows cooled and the hollow lava tubes lay cold and dark and secret, ossified arteries. In 2050 Adriana Corta came rappelling down from the access tunnel her selenologists had bored into the Sea of Fecundity. Her lights flashed out over a hidden world; an intact lava tube a hundred metres wide and high and two kilometres long. An empty, virgin universe, precious as a geode. *This is the place,* Adriana Corta declared. *This is where I will create a dynasty.* Within five years her machines had landscaped the interior, sculpted faces of umbanda gods the size of city blocks, set up a water cycle and filled the space with balconies and apartments, pavilions and galleries. This is Boa Vista, the mansion of the Corta family. Even on this celebration day the rock trembles to the vibrations of excavators and sinterers working deep in the walls, shaping rooms and spaces for Luna and her generations.

Today is Lucasinho's moon-run party and Boa Vista has opened its green heart to society. Luna Corta weaves between amors and madrinhas, family and retainers, Asamoahs and Suns, Vorontsovs and even Mackenzies and people from no great family at all. Tall third-generations and short, squat first gens. Dresses and suits, turn-ups and petticoats, party gloves and coloured shoes. A dozen skin and eye colours. Wealth and beauty. Friends and enemies. Luna Corta was born to this, to the sound of falling water and the murmur of artificial wind through bamboo and branch. She knows no other world. On this special day, there is meat.

The caterers have set up electric barbecues under the overhang beneath Oxum's bottom lip. Chefs poke and turn skewers. Greasy smoke rises up towards the skyline, set today for a bright blue afternoon with passing clouds. A bright Earth afternoon. Waiters ferry large plates of skewered meat to the guests. Luna places herself between a woman waitress and her destination.

'Hey that's a pretty dress,' the waitress says in very bad Portuguese. She is short, not much taller than Luna, and square. She moves too much for the gravity. A Jo Moonbeam, fresh off the cycler. Her familiar is a cheap skin of unfolding tetrahedrons.

'Thank you,' Luna says, switching to Globo, the simplified English that is the common tongue. 'It is.'

The wait-woman offers Luna her tray.

'Chicken or beef?'

Luna takes a greasy, juicy beef skewer.

'Careful not to get that on your lovely dress.' She has a norte accent.

'I would never do that,' Luna says with immense gravity. Then she skips down the stone path beside the stream that runs through the heart of Boa Vista, pulling at chunks of bloody beef with her small white teeth. There is Lucasinho in his party clothes with his Dona Luna pin and a Blue Moon martini in his hand. His moon-run friends surround him. Luna recognises the Asamoah girl, and the Sun. Suns and Asamoahs have always been part of the family. It is easy to recognise the weird, pale Vorontsov boy. Like a vampire, Luna thinks. And that must be the Mackenzie girl. All gold.

'You have beautiful freckles,' Luna declares, butting in on Lucasinho's group. She looks the Mackenzie girl full in the face. They laugh at her boldness, the Mackenzie girl most of all.

'Luna,' Lucasinho says. 'Go and eat that thing someplace else.' He makes it sound like a joke but Luna hears better. He's pissed off at her. She is getting between him and Abena Asamoah. He probably wants sex with her. He is such a user. There is a line of upturned cocktail glasses at his feet. A user, and drunk.

'Just saying.' Cortas say what they think. Luna wipes her mouth with the back of her hand. Meat, and now she hears music. 'I got freckles too!' She touches a finger to her Corta-Asamoah cheeks, then runs on again. She darts over the stepping stones in the river in search of the music. She splashes up the river, kicking up slow-falling spray. Party guests coo and shriek and move away from the flying water but their faces are smiling. Luna knows she is irresistible.

'Tio Lucas!'

Luna runs up to him and throws her arms around his legs. Of course he would be near the music. He is talking with the immigrant woman who served Luna the meat. She now bears a tray of blue cocktails. Luna has interrupted him. He ruffles Luna's dark curly hair.

'Luna, coração, you run on now. Yes?' A little touch on the shoulder, turning her. As she slides away she hears him say to the waiter, 'My son is not to be served any more alcohol. Understand? I'll not have him drunk and ridiculous in front of everyone. He can do what he likes in private, but I won't have him disgrace the family. If a single drop goes near him for the rest of the day, I will have every one of you back in Bairro Alto begging for second-hand oxygen and drinking each other's piss. Nothing personal. Please convey this to your management.'

Luna loves her Uncle Lucas, the way he gets down to her level, his little games, his tricks and jokes that are just between them, but there are times when he is tall and far away, in another world that's hard and cold and unkind. Luna sees the look of pale fear on the immigrant woman's face and feels horrible for her.

Arms sweep her up, lift her high, throw her up into the air.

'Hey hey anzinho!'

And catch her as she falls soft as a feather, her peony dress up around her face. Rafa. Luna presses close to her father.

'Hey hey, guess who's just arrived. Tia Ariel. Shall we go and find her?' Rafa squeezes Luna's hand and she nods her head vigorously.

In her killing dress Ariel Corta steps out of the station into Boa Vista's great garden. The layers of her 1958 Balenciaga float in lunar gravity like petals. A murmur passes through the throng of guests. Ariel Corta. Everyone has heard of Alayoum vs Filmus. Luna bounds up to her tia. Ariel snatches her niece up in mid-bound, swirls her around while Luna shrieks in delight. Now her madrinha, Mônica, arrives. Warm embraces, kisses. Amanda Sun, Lucas's wife. Lousika Asamoah, Luna's mother. Rafa himself, snatching his sister up into the air so that she begs him to mind the dress. His other oko, Rachel Mackenzie, is in Queen of the South with their son Robson. She never sets foot in Boa Vista. Ariel is glad Rachel is not here. There is legal between them, and Mackenzies hold grudges. Next: moon-run boy himself. He's awkward, gawky with his tia in a way he never is with his friends. Her finger rests a moment on his Dona Luna emblem, drawing his eye to the matching token on her corsage: *imagine me naked, frosted, running across the bare moon.*

Next the family retainers: Helen de Braga, head of finance – she has aged since Ariel last came to Boa Vista – and old, upright Heitor Pereira, head of security. Last of all, Lucas arrives. He kisses his sister warmly. She is the only sibling Lucas considers his equal. A whisper: he wants private words. Ariel's gloved hand effortlessly snares a Blue Moon from a passing tray.

'And how is Meridian this season?' Lucas says. 'I just can't get the time to make it up there.'

Ariel knows that her brother thinks her disloyal for choosing the law over Corta Hélio.

'Apparently I'm famous. Briefly.'

'I heard something like that. Gossip and rumours.'

'More rumours than oxygen, more gossip than water.'

'I've also heard that a delegation from the China Power Investment Corporation is coming in on the *Saints Peter and Paul*. The rumour is a five-year output deal with Mackenzie Metals.'

'I've heard similar myself.'

'I also heard that the Eagle of the Moon is throwing a welcome jamboree for them.'

'He is. And, yes, I am invited.' Ariel knows her brother's information network is powerful enough to have found about her counsel chamber chat with Judge Nagai.

'You always had a skill for social politics. I envy that.'

'Whatever it is Lucas, no.'

Lucas throws up his hands in mea culpa.

'I merely repeated a few rumours.'

Ariel laughs like silver but Lucas is tenacious, Lucas is steel, Lucas has her trapped. Then, in a gust of peppery moon dust, a saviour arrives.

Maybe more meat. Maybe juice to drink. Lucas has cornered Tia Ariel. Uncle Lucas is boring when he talks with his face so close to another person. Then her eyes, her mouth go wide. She gives a squeak of excitement.

A figure in a sasuit strides down the ravine. His helmet is under his right arm, his left hand carries his LS pack. His feet are booted and the skin-hugging sasuit is a bright patchwork of logos and hi-visibility strips, navigation lights and race badges. His familiar rezzes, pixel by pixel, as he enters Boa Vista's network. He sheds dust; a slow-settling trail of silvery black.

'Carlinhos!'

Carlinhos Corta sees his niece rush to hug him and steps back but she bangs into him, grabs his legs, sends up a huge cloud of dust that settles on her beautiful peony dress like soot.

Two steps behind Luna comes Rafa. He trades play-punches, knuckle-touches with his kid brother.

'You came cross-surface?'

Carlinhos holds out his helmet in evidence. In his patchwork sasuit and bearing the spicy, gunpowder smell of moon dust, he's a pirate at a cocktail party. He dumps his LS pack and snatches a Blue Moon, downs it in one.

'Tell you something, after two hours on a bike, drinking your own piss...'

Rafa shakes his head in appreciation of lunacy.

'It's going to kill you, that dumb biking. Maybe not today, maybe not tomorrow, but some day the sun's going to flare and you'll be out on the surface on a dust-bike five hours from anywhere. And it will fry. Your. Carioca. Ass.' Each emphasis driven home with a prod to the shoulder.

'And when was the last time you were up on the surface?' Carlinhos play-punches his brother in the stomach. 'What's that I feel? Belly. You're out of condition, irmão. You need to get surface-fit. You've been to too many meetings. We're helium miners, not accountants.'

Oldest and youngest Corta boys adore sport. Carlinhos's passion is dust-biking. He's a pioneer of the extreme sport. He developed the bikes, the customised suits. He's cut trails all over the Imbrium Apennines and established the cross-Serenitatis endurance race. Rafa's sport is safer and more enclosed. He owns an LHL handball team. They're standing high in the Premier League. Rafa shares the mania with his brother-in-law Jaden Wen Sun, owner of the Tigers of the Sun. They compete with humour and ferocity.

'You staying around after the party?' Rafa asks,

'I've awarded myself a furlough.' Carlinhos has been out for three lunes on Tranquilitatis, winning helium.

'Come to the game. You should see what we're doing.'

'Losing, is what I heard,' Carlinhos says. 'Where's moon-run boy? I

24

heard about the Asamoah kid. That was good work. If he ever wants a job on the outside, I could use him.'

'That's not in Lucas's life-plan.'

Two steps behind Carlinhos is a second young man in a sasuit, dark as Carlinhos is fair, with beautiful cheekbones and narrow, hunter eyes.

'Wagner, irmão,' Rafa says. A second volley of knuckle-touching. Wagner, youngest brother, smiles coyly.

Luna clings to her Uncle Carlinhos's leg, smudged and smutted with moon dust.

'Let me see you!' Ariel declares, arriving with her entourage. 'Beautiful boys!' She bends to kiss but does not touch. No smuts on this dress.

Lucas has arrived, tactically late. He greets Carlinhos politely but routinely. He gives his attention to Wagner. 'I love parties. All those distant relatives we never see.'

'Wagner's here as my guest,' Carlinhos says.

'Of course,' Lucas says. 'My house is your house.'

Naked hatred arcs between Wagner and Lucas, then Carlinhos takes Wagner by the elbow and whirls him away into the party.

'Luna, run on with Madrinha Elis,' Rafa says.

'We'll get some of that dirt off you,' Madrinha Elis says. She is a strong-faced, strong-built Paulistana, a head shorter than the moon-born generations. Earth bodies make strong hosts. The Cortas let none but Brazilians bear their children. She takes sooty little Luna by the hand and leads her away from grown-up talk to look at the musicians.

'Lucas, not here,' Rafa says softly.

'He's not a Corta,' Lucas says simply.

A hand touches the back of Lucas's hand. Amanda Sun is at his side.

'Even for you, that was rude,' she chides. Amanda Sun is third-generation; moon-tall, taller than her husband. Her familiar is zhen:

'Shake', in deep red. The Suns traditionally skin their familiars in hexagrams from the *Book of Changes*.

'Why? It's the truth,' Lucas says. Society was surprised when Amanda Sun moved from the Palace of Eternal Light to still-raw Boa Vista. The nikah hadn't specified it. The marriage was powerfully dynastic. Checks, balances, annulment clauses were in place. Yet Amanda Sun came to Boa Vista and has lived there for seventeen years. She seems as much a part of it as the peaceful orixas, or the running waters. Society – some parts of that still care – think she is playing the long game. The Suns were among the first settlers; with the Mackenzies, they consider themselves old stock, true lunar aristocracy. For over half a century they have battled the hegemony of the Peoples' Republic, which would use the House of Sun as their bridgehead to dominate the moon. All agree that the Suns never marry without consideration.

For the past five years, Lucas Corta has lived in his apartment in João de Deus.

The music – soft bossa-jazz – stops. Glasses halt on their journeys to lips. Conversations die; words evaporate; kisses fail. Everyone is transfixed by the small woman who has stepped out from a door between the enormous, serene faces of the orixas.

Adriana Corta has arrived.

'Won't they be looking for you?'

Lucasinho has taken Abena Maanu Asamoah by the hand and led her far from inhabited ways, along corridors lit by gleams of light from other rooms – construction bots need light – through new-cut chambers and rooms that still hum with the vibration of digging machines.

'They'll be kissing hands and making speeches for ages. We've plenty of time.' Lucasinho pulls Abena to him. Heat-lamps lift the permanent minus-twenty sub-surface cold but the air is chilly enough for breath to hang in clouds and Abena to shiver in her party frock.

The moon has a cold heart. 'So what is this special thing you want to give me?' Lucasinho moves a hand down Abena's flank to rest on her hip. She pushes him away with a laugh.

'Kojo is right, you are a bad boy.'

'Bad is good. No, really. But come on – we're moon-runners.' His other hand strokes Abena's Lady Luna, moves like a spider up to the bare upper slope of her breast. 'We're alive. More alive than anyone on this rock, right now.'

'Lucasinho, no.'

'I saved your brother. I could have died. I nearly did die. I was in a hyperbaric chamber. They put me in a coma. I went back and I saved Kojo. I didn't have to do it. We all know the risks.'

'Lucasinho, if you go on like this you will kill it.'

He lifts his hands: surrender.

'So what is this thing?'

Abena opens her right hand. Silver there; a glinting tooth of metal. Then she snaps her hand to Lucasinho's left ear. He cries out, claps a hand to unexpected pain. There is blood on his fingers.

'What did you do? Jinji, what did she do?'

We are outside Boa Vista camera coverage, Jinji says. *I can't see.*

'I gave you something to remember Kojo by.' It may be the red glow of the heat-lamps, but Lucasinho sees a light in Abena's eyes he's never known before. He doesn't know who she is. 'Do you know what they say about you? That you put a pierce in for every heart-break. Well, with me it's different. That pierce I put in your ear is a heart-make. It's a promise. When you need the help of the Asamoahs – really need it; when you have no other hope, when you're alone and naked and exposed, like my brother; send the pierce. I will remember.'

'That hurt!' Lucasinho whines.

'Then you'll remember it,' Abena says. There is a smear of Lucasinho's blood on her forefinger. Very slowly, very gracefully, she licks it off.

Adriana Corta is slight and elegant as a bird among her tall children and taller grandchildren. Age lies lightly under lunar gravity; her skin is smooth and unlined, her body is unstooped by her seventy-nine years. She bears herself with the poise of a debutante. She is still head of Corta Hélio, though she has not been seen outside Boa Vista for months now. She is as rare a sight to many of Boa Vista's residents. But she can still muster a show for family. Adriana greets her children. Three kisses for Rafael and Ariel. Two for Lucas and Carlinhos, one for Wagner. Luna breaks free from Madrinha Elis and runs to her Vovo Adriana. Gasps about the smudges on Adriana's Ceil Chapman dress. Adriana doesn't wear a Lady Luna pin. In her wild-catting years she drank more vacuum than all the moon-runners in Boa Vista.

Lucas falls in behind his mother's shoulder as she works the line of grandchildren, madrinhas and okos and guests. She has a word for everyone. Special minutes are spent with Amanda Sun and Lousika Asamoah, Rafa's keji-oko.

'Now, where is Lucasinho?' Adriana Corta says. 'We must have the hero.'

Lucas realises that his son is absent. He bites back rage.

'I'll find him, Mama.' Toquinho tries to call but the boy is off-network. Adriana Corta tsahs in disapproval. Protocol will not be proper until she has congratulated the party-boy. Lucas goes down to the band; a small ensemble of guitar, piano, double bass, soft-shuffling drums. 'Do you know *Aguas de Marco*?'

'Of course.' It's a standard, a classic.

'Play it sweet. It's my mama's favourite.'

Guitarist and pianist nod to each other, count in the subtle off-beat. *Waters of March*: an old and lovely song that Adriana Corta sang to her children when their madrinhas brought them and set them on her knee, sang over them in their cots. It's an impressionistic autumn song about the rain and sticks and tiny living things, about the universal in the hand-sized, at once joyful yet spiked through with saudade. Male and female voices exchange lines; snapping up each other's cues; vivacious and playful. Lucas listens closely, passionately. His breath is shallow, his body tense. Tears haunt the folds of his eyes. Music has always moved him powerfully, especially the old music of Brazil. Bossa-nova, MBP. Elevator music; MOR blandout. Smooooth ball-less jazz. The ones who say that don't have ears; don't listen. They don't hear the saudade; the sweet sorrow of the fleetingness of things that makes all joys sharper. They don't hear the hushed despair, the sense that beyond the beauty and the languor, something has gone terribly, terribly wrong.

Lucas glances at his mother. She nods to the sidewinding rhythm, eyes closed. He has distracted her from prodigal Lucasinho. Lucas will deal with him later.

The song's highlight is the two voices playing capoeira over single words, cutting in on each other; tumbling and dodging. The man on guitar, the woman on piano are very good. Lucas had never heard of this combo before but he is delighted to have heard them. The song ends. Lucas chews back emotion. He applauds loud and clear;.

'Bravo!' he cries. Adriana joins him; then Rafa, Ariel. Carlinhos, Wagner. The applause ripples out across the party. 'Bravo!' Drinks come round again, the moment of embarrassment forgotten, the party rolls on. Lucas steps in for a word with the pianist. 'Thank you. You have bossa, sir. My mamãe loved it. I'd like it if you were to come and perform for me, in my own apartment in João de Deus.'

'We'd be honoured, Mr Corta.'

'Not we. Just you. Soon. What's your name?'

'Jorge. Jorge Nardes.'

Familiars exchange contact details. And then the waiter, the norte Jo Moonbeam with the cocktail tray, makes a sudden lunge at Rafael Corta.

*

29

She likes the rough texture of the scab on Lucasinho's ear. She enjoys tugging at it, undoing the healing, letting a little fresh blood seep. It gets Abena wet inside her Helena Barber ballgown. Now they're back in Boa Vista's network, Jinji has shown Lucasinho her gift; a chrome fang curving through the top arc of his right ear. Looks good. Looks hot. But she won't let him even slip an arm around her waist.

Before they reach the window they both know something is wrong. No music, no chatter, no splashing of bodies in the waterfall pool. Shouting voices, orders snapped in Portuguese and Globo. The pupil of Xangô's stone eye overlooks the length of the Boa Vista's gardens. Lucasinho sees Corta security escoltas guarding groups of guests. The band and the wait staff have their hands on their heads. Security drones scan the sculpted walls; their lasers rest a moment on Lucasinho and Abena.

'What's going on?' Lucasinho asks. Jinji answers in the same instant as Abena's face turns to shock.

There has been an attempt on the life on Rafael Corta.

The edge of the knife lies against Marina Calzaghe's throat. If she moves, if she speaks, if she takes too deep a breath, it will part her flesh. The blade is so insanely sharp it is almost anaesthetic: she would not feel the slitting of her windpipe. But she must move, she must speak if she is to live.

Her fingers tap the stem of the cocktail glass clamped upside down on the tray.

'The fly,' she hisses.

Flies didn't move like that. Marina Calzaghe knows flies. She worked as a flycatcher. On the moon, insects – pollinators, decorative butterflies like the ones the Asamoah kids sent wafting through Boa Vista, are licensed. Flies, wasps, wild bugs threaten the complex systems of lunar cities and are exterminated. Marina Calzaghe has killed a million flies and knows they don't fly like that, in a straight attack line for the exposed soft skin in the corner of Rafael Corta's jaw line. She lunged with the glass, caught the fly millimetres from its target and clapped the empty martini glass to the tray. A cocktail prison. And in the same instant, a knife whispered out of a concealed magnetic sheath to her throat. At the end of the knife, a Corta escolta in a tailored suit with a perfectly folded square in his breast pocket. He still looks like a thug. He still looks like death.

Heitor Pereira squats stiffly to examine the thing in the glass. For a first-generation, he is a big man, square built. A big ex-navy man peering into an upturned cocktail glass would be comedy but for the knives.

'An assassin bug,' Heitor Pereira says. 'AKA.'

In an instant blades ring Lousika Asamoah. Their tips are millimetres from her skin. Luna wails and sobs, clinging to her mother. Rafael hurls himself at the security men. Men in suits pile on him, pinion him.

'For your own safety, senhor,' Heitor Pereira says. 'She may be harbouring biological agents.'

'It's a drone,' Marina Calzaghe whispers. 'It's chipped.'

Heitor Pereira looks closer. The fly batters itself against the glass but in its moments of stillness a pattern of gold tracery is clearly visible on its wings and carapace.

'Let her go.' Adriana Corta's voice is quiet but the tone of command makes every security man and woman flinch. Heitor Pereira nods. The knives are sheathed. Lousika scoops up the howling Luna.

'And her,' Adriana Corta orders. Marina gasps as the knife is removed from her throat and realises she has not inhaled since security grabbed her. The shaking starts.

Lucas is shouting, 'Lucasinho? Where is Lucasinho?'

'I'll take that now.' Heitor Pereira places his hand on top of the glass. He takes a pulse-gun from a small holster. The device is the size of his thumb, a silly, camp weapon in his huge hand. 'Shut down your familiars.' Up and down Boa Vista familiars wink out of existence.

Marina blinks off her own Hetty. That camp little gun possesses enough power to take down the whole of Boa Vista's network. There is nothing to see or hear, but the little wired fly goes from moving to still and dead.

Lucas Corta leans close to his Head of Security and whispers to him.

'They tried to kill my brother. They got into Boa Vista; into our home, and they tried to kill my brother.'

'The situation is under control, Senhor Corta.'

'The situation is that an assassin came within the thickness of a cocktail glass of killing Rafa. In front of guests from every one of the Five Dragons. In front of our mother. That doesn't strike me as a situation under control, does it?'

'We'll analyse the weapon. We'll find out who's behind it.'

"Well that's not enough. There could be another attack any moment. I want this place secured. This party is over.'

'Senhors, senhoras, there has been a security incident,' Heitor Pereira announces. 'We must secure Boa Vista. I have to ask you to leave. If you could make your way to the tram station. It's now safe to relog your familiars.'

'Find my son!' Lucas orders Heitor Pereira. Lucasinho's friends mill, lost and overshadowed. Their moon-run, Lucasinho's saving of Kojo Asamoah, are eclipsed. Boa Vista security shepherd guests out of the gardens towards the station. A guard escorts Corta grandees indoors. Lucas Corta considers Marina Calzaghe with ice and iron. She is shivering with shock.

'What's your name?'

'Marina Calzaghe.'

'You work for the caterers?'

'I work at what I can get. I am – I was – a Process Control Engineer.'

'You work for Corta Hélio now.'

Lucas offers a hand. Marina takes it.

'Talk to my brother Carlinhos. The Cortas owe you.'

And gone. Still numb with shock, Marina tries to work out what happened. The Cortas try to slit her throat, now she works for them. But: the Cortas. Blake, it will be all right. I can get you meds. We'll never be thirsty again. We can breathe easy.

TWO

Luna Corta: small spy. Boa Vista is rich in hiding places for a bored girl. Luna discovered the service tunnel following a cleaning bot one long Boa Vista morning. Like all moon kids Luna is drawn to tunnels and crawlspaces. No adult could fit it and that is good because hiding holes and dens must be secret. The shaft has grown tight since Luna first crawled in and realised she could look down into her mother's private room and, if she held her breath, hear. Tucked up behind the eyes of Oxossi, Luna squirms, a constriction in a sinus in the head of the hunter and protector.

'They put a knife to my throat.'

Her father says something she can't make out. Luna twists closer to the ventilation grille. Dusty light-rays strike up around her face.

'They put a knife to my throat, Rafa!'

Luna sees her mother brush fingers against her neck, touching the remembered edge of the knife.

'It was just security.'

'Would they have killed me?'

Luna moves again to fit both of her parents into her narrow slot of sight. Her father sits on the bed. He looks small, diminished, as if the air and light has gone out of him.

'They were protecting us. Anyone who wasn't a Corta was suspect.'

'Amanda Sun isn't a Corta. I didn't see a knife at her throat.'

'The fly. Everyone knows you people use biological weapons.'

'You people.'

'The Asamoahs.'

'There were other Asamoahs at the party. Abena Maanu for one. I didn't see a knife at her throat. My people, or just some of my people?'

'Why are you doing this?'

'Because your people, Rafa, put a knife to my throat. And I don't hear anything from you that says they wouldn't have cut me.'

'I would never let them do that.'

'If your mother gave the order, would you have stopped them?'

'I'm bu-hwaejang of Corta Hélio.'

'Don't insult me, Rafa.'

'I'm angry our security put a knife to your throat. I'm angry that you were a suspect. I'm raging, but you know how we live here.'

'Yes. Well maybe I don't want to live here.'

Luna sees Rafa look up.

'I know how we live in Twé. It's a good place, Twé. It's a safe place. With *my people*, Rafa. I want to take Luna there.'

Luna gasps. The shaft is so tight she can't press hands to mouth, to try and call back the noise. They might have heard. But then she thinks, Boa Vista is full of sighs and whispers.

Rafa is on his feet. When he is angry, he gets close, breath-close. Spit-in-my face close. Lousika doesn't flinch.

'You're not taking Luna.'

'She's not safe here.'

'My children stay with me.'

'Your children?'

'Didn't you read the nikah? Or were you too eager to jump into bed with the heir apparent of Corta Hélio.'

'Rafa. No. Don't say this. This is beneath you. This is not you.'

36

Rafa's anger is stoked now. Anger is his sin. It is the other side of his affability: easy to laugh, to play, to make love. Easy to rage.

'You know? Maybe your people planned...'

'Rafa. Stop.' Lousika presses her fingers to Rafa lips. She knows his anger is as quick to ebb as to flow. 'I would never, ever plot against you – not me, not *my people* – to get hold of Luna.'

'Luna stays with me.'

'Yes. But I won't.'

'I don't want you to go. This is your home. With me. With Luna.'

'I'm not safe here. Luna's not safe. But the nikah won't let me take her. If you'd once said you were sorry that your escoltas put a knife to my throat, it might be different. You were angry. You weren't sorry.'

Now her father speaks but Luna can't hear his words. She can't hear anything but a rushing noise inside her head that is the sound of the worst things in the world arriving. Her mamãe is going away. Her chest is tight. Her head rings with the horrible hissing, like air and life leaking away. Luna wriggles free, pushes herself down the shaft away from the hidey-hole where she overheard too much. She has scuffed her shoes and torn her Pierre Cardin dress on the raw stone.

The rain has swept the dead butterflies into floes and flotsam. Their wings form an azure scum around the lips of pools. Luna Corta sits among the corpses.

'Hey hey hey, what is it?' Lousika Asamoah crouches beside her daughter.

'The butterflies died.'

'They don't live very long. Just a day.'

'I liked them. They were pretty. It's not fair.'

'That's how we make them.'

Lousika kicks off her shoes and sits down on the stone beside Luna. She swishes her feet in the water. Blue wings cling to her dark legs.

'You could make them live longer than a day,' Luna says.

'We could, but what would they eat? Where would they go? They're decorations, like flags for Yam Festival.'

'But they're not,' Luna says. 'They're alive.'

'Luna, what happened to your shoes?' Lousika says. 'And your dress.'

Luna looks at the floes of butterflies slowly drifting downstream.

'You're going away.'

'What makes you think that?'

'I heard you say it.'

None of the questions Lousika could ask have any meaning here.

'Yes. I am going back to Twé, back to my family. But only for a while. Not for always.'

'How long?'

'I don't know, love. No longer than I have to.'

'But I'm not going with you.'

'No. I would love to, more than anything – more than myself – but I can't.'

'Am I safe, Mama?'

Lousika hugs Luna to her, kisses the top of her head.

'You're safe. Papa will keep you safe. He'll tear the head off anyone who tries to hurt you. But I have to go until things are clear. I don't want to, and I will miss you so much. Papa will look after you, and Madrinha Elis. Elis will not let anything hurt you.'

The words burn Lousika Asamoah's throat. Madrinhas, host mothers. Hired wombs, who become nannies, who become unofficial aunts, become family. For small corporations like the Cortas with a business to build and no time for pregnancy, birth, early infancy, Lousika could understand the arrangement. Not for the next generation, not that the coven of demure, ever-present madrinhas should become tradition. She resented tall, Brazilian-cheek-boned Madrinha Elis carrying her child, birthing her baby. She had been shocked when Rafa had presented the surrogacy as a done thing: the Corta way. Put it in me, plant it in me, let me grow it and carry it and press it into the world. I don't need Madonnas of Conception to mix your sperm with my egg and pronounce, *let there be life*. I don't need to watch your gyno-bots slide the embryo up into sleek, smiling Elis and watch her every day grow bigger and fuller. I don't need to see the reports, the scans of her uterus, the daily posts of how her pregnancy is progressing. And I did not need to lock myself away in my room howling and smashing things as Elis went under the knife. It should have been me, Luna. It should have been me they brought you to. My smiling, exhausted, teary face the first thing you saw. An Asamoah. Life flows and spurts and gushes in all our fluids and juices. I am fit, fertile, everything works naturally, brilliantly, fecundly. But it's not the Corta way.

I love you Luna, but I cannot love the Corta way.

Lousika wraps Luna up in her arms, rocks as much for her own comfort as for Luna's. One assassin-fly has cracked her world. This is not a garden of gods, a palace of waters. It's a tunnel in the rock. Every one of her family's light-filled agraria, every city and factory and settlement, is a scrape, a fragile bivouac of rocks against the vacuum sky and the killing sun. Everyone is in danger, all the time. Nowhere can you escape, or even hide.

'Your papa and the contract and everyone may say you're a Corta, but you are an Asamoah. You're an Asamoah because I am an Asamoah because my mother is an Asamoah. That's our way.'

Lucas Corta sweeps his hand across the board table and scatters the virtual documents.

'I haven't time for this. Where did it come from? Who made it?'

Heitor Pereira dips his head. He is a head shorter and a decade greyer than everyone at the board table except Adriana Corta and her Finance Director, Helen de Braga, the dark will of Corta Hélio.

'We're still analysing—'

'We have the best R&D unit on the moon and you can't tell me who made this?'

'They've gone to remarkable lengths to hide anything that might identify the drone. The chips are generic, we've nothing on the printer pattern.'

'So you don't know.'

'We don't know yet.' Everyone around the table hears the tremble in Heitor Pereira's voice.

'You don't know who made it, you don't know who sent it, you don't know how it got through security. You don't know if, right now, another one of those things is coming for my brother, or me, or, God save us, my mother. You're head of security, and you don't know this?'

Lucas holds the stare. Heitor Pereira's face twitches.

'We are in a total security situation. We're monitoring everything over the size of a skin-flake.'

'What if they're here already? That drone could have been planted months ago. Have you thought of that? There could be a dozen more waking up right now. A hundred more. They only need to get lucky once. I know what modern poisons do. They make you wait. They make you wait in hours of pain, knowing each breath is shorter than the one before, knowing there's no antidote, knowing you're going to die. You spend a long time looking at death. Only then do they let you die. And I know that someone tried to use one of those poisons on my brother. That's what I know. Now, tell me, what do you know?'

'Lucas, enough.' Adriana Corta occupies the head of the board table. For months her seat has been empty, her only presence the large, clumsy portrait of her in a sasuit, Our Lady of Helium, looking down the length of the table. An immediate and lethal threat her children has brought her to the board room in all her authority. Rafa is seated at her right hand, Ariel to her left. Lucas sits to the right of his brother.

'Mamãe, if your head of security can't keep us safe, who can?'

'Heitor has been a faithful agent of our family for longer than you have been alive.' No one can mistake the sting of authority.

'Yes, Mãe.' Lucas dips his head to his mother.

'Isn't it obvious?' Rafa fills the stinging silence.

'Is it obvious?' Ariel says.

'Who else has it ever been?' Rafa leans low over the table. His anger smokes. 'Bob Mackenzie has never forgiven Mamãe. He's slow poison. Not today, not tomorrow; not this year or even this decade, but some year, some day. The Mackenzies pay back three times. They're striking at the succession. They want you to see everything you've built come apart, Mamãe.'

'Rafa . . .' Ariel begins.

'Kyra Mackenzie,' Rafa interrupts. 'She was at the party. Did anyone search her, or did we just wave her through, because she was one of Lucasinho's friends?'

'Rafa, do you think the Mackenzies would risk all-out war?' Ariel says. She draws long on her vaper. 'Really?'

'If they thought they could break our monopoly, they might.' Lucas says.

'It's starting again, can't you see that?' Rafa says.

Eight years before, Corta Hélio and Mackenzie Metals fought a brief territory war. Extractors fallen in tangles of metal, trains boarded and shipments hijacked, bots and AIs crashed under bombardments of dark code. Dusters fought hand to hand, knife to knife in the tunnels of Maskelyne and Jansen and out on the stone seas of Tranquillity and Serenity. One hundred and twenty deaths, damage in the millions of bitsies. In the end, Cortas and Mackenzies agreed to arbitration. The Court of Clavius ruled for Corta Hélio. Two months later Adrian Mackenzie married Jonathon Kayode, Eagle of the Moon, CEO of the Lunar Development Corporation, the owners of the moon.

'Rafa, enough,' Adriana Corta says. Her voice is thin, her authority is incontestable. 'We fight the Mackenzies through business, we beat them through business. We make money.' Adriana rises from the table, stiff and worn in face and limb. Her children and retainers bow and follow her from the board room.

Carlinhos stands, purses the fingers of his right hand and bows to his mother. He has not spoken a word at this board meeting. He never does. His place is out in the field, with the extractors and refiners and the dusters. He's the duster, the fighter. Rafa can outshine him with his charm, Lucas bludgeon him with his arguments, Ariel tie him up with her eloquence but none of them can walk the dirt the way he does.

Lucas detains Heitor Pereira a moment.

'You made a mistake,' Lucas whispers. 'You're too old. You're past it, and you're gone.'

In the lobby outside the board room Wagner Corta waits. Adriana and her retainers pass without looking at him, then Lucas and Ariel. Ariel nods, a tight smile. Carlinhos claps his brother on the back.

'Hey brother.'

Wagner is the conspicuous absence at the board table.

'I want a word with Rafa,' Wagner says.

'Sure. You want to bike back to João?'

'I've something else planned.'

'Catch you later, Lobinho.'

'A word about what?' Rafa says. He perches on the inside lip of Oxala's right eye. Behind him water tumbles slowly.

'The fly. I want to take a look at it.'

Rafa has made sure that Wagner received Heitor Pereira's schematics. Rafa makes sure Wagner receives all data from every board meeting.

'You've got everything.'

'Respect to Heitor and even your R&D, but there're things I'd see he wouldn't.'

Rafa knows that Wagner's life is complicated and lived in the shadows on the edge of the family and that his contribution to Corta

Hélio is solid but hard to quantify, but he is an outstanding engineer of the small and intricate. Sometime Rafa envies his two natures; the dark precision, the light creativity.

'Like what?'

'I'll know it when I see it. But I will need to see it.'

'I'll let Heitor know.' Socrates, Rafa's familiar, has already sent the notification. 'I've told him not to let Adriana know.'

'Thank you.'

Wagner has been the shadow in the family so long his siblings have evolved an alternative social gravity, informing him, including him while keeping him invisible, like a black hole.

'When will we see you around, miudo?' Rafa says. Adriana is looking back, waiting for him.

'When I have something to say,' Wagner says. 'You know me. Keep breathing, Rafa.'

'Keep breathing, Little Wolf.'

'Ariel.' Lucas calls to his sister down the length of the Oxala steps. Ariel turns. 'Going back already?'

'I have business in Meridian.'

'Yes, the reception for the Chinese trade delegation. I couldn't ask you to miss that.'

'I told you clearly at the party.'

'It's family.'

'Oh come on, Lucas.'

Lucas frowns in puzzlement and Ariel sees that he cannot understand what she is saying. He believes absolutely that his every act is for the family, only the family.

'If the positions were reversed, I would do it. Without a thought.'

'Things are simpler for you, Lucas. People are taking an interest in my career. My skin has to be airtight. I have to be clean.'

'No one's clean on the moon. They tried to kill Rafa.'

'No. Don't you ever do that.'

'Maybe not the Mackenzies. But someone did. We're Corta Hélio: we're good, but we're good at only one thing. We extract helium. We keep the lights burning down there. That's our strength but it's also our vulnerability. AKA, Taiyang; they're everywhere, doing everything. They've got more than one place to go. Even Mackenzie Metals is diversifying – into our core business. We lose the business, we have nowhere to go. We lose everything. The moon does not suffer losers. And mamãe. She's not what she was.'

Ariel had been glancing away from Lucas, breaking his powerful eye contact. Even as a child, he won every staring-game. Now he says five words and she can't look away.

'Even you must have noticed,' Lucas says. Ariel takes the barb. It is months since she was at a Corta Hélio board meeting.

'I know Rafa's been managing her public engagements.'

'Rafa Corta. The Golden Boy. He'll run this business into the dust. Help me, Ariel. Help me, help mamãe.'

'You're a bastard, Lucas.'

'I'm not. I'm the only true son in this entire place. I need something on those Chinese, Ariel. Not much. Just a tiny edge. They'll have something. A little loose skin I can tear.'

'Leave it with me.'

Lucas bows. As he turns away from his sister, a smile breaks on to his face.

One light for doors locked, two for undocking. Three for departure. A small tremor in the rock as the induction motors levitate the car. And the tram is gone. It is only five kilometres from Boa Vista to João de Deus station. From Rafa's hugs, farewells, and, yes tears, it might be worlds.

Lucas observes his brother's bare emotion with discomfort. The corner of his mouth twitches. Everything is big with Rafa. It always was. The biggest bully, the loudest laugher, the charismatic boy, the golden light; as profligate with his anger as his pleasure. Lucas has grown up as his shadow: restrained and precise; honed and holstered like a taser. Lucas feels as profoundly and intensely as his older brother. Emotion is not emotionalism. One is script, the other performance. Lucas Corta has room for emotion but it is a private room, windowless, white and airy. White rooms, without shadows.

Rafa hugs his brother. This is undignified and embarrassing. Lucas huffs in pain.

'She'll come back to you.' It's the kind of platitude that is expected in situations like this.

'She doesn't trust me.'

Lucas cannot understand his brother's emotional incontinence. This is what marriage contracts are for. Trust and love are no architecture for a dynasty.

'While Luna is here, she will come back to you,' Lucas says. 'She understands. I'm keeping Lucasinho here until the security situation improves. He'll hate it. It'll be good for him. Give him something to work against. He has it all too easy.' Lucas claps Rafa on the back. Make light of it. Get over it. Let go of me.

'I'm going to get Robson back.'

Lucas suppresses the sigh of exasperation. This, *again*. When Rafa is frustrated, in business or sport or society or sex, he falls back on the enduring injustice of his son and first born. It has been three years since Rachel Mackenzie took Robson back to her family. Contracts were broken, flagrantly and deliberately. Lawyers are still arguing what is effectively an act of hostage-taking. Ariel has negotiated a steel-bound access agreement but every time the tram takes Robson back to Queen of the South or Crucible, Rafa's scabs tear and bleed. In such moods, not even Lucas can talk his brother down.

'You do what you have to.' Lucas respects his mother in all things, except in her blind adoration of Rafa. Golden Rafa, the heir apparent. He's too emotional, too open, too soft to run the company. Hearts can't decide the fate of dynasties that keep Earth's lights burning.

Lucas hugs Rafa again. His mission is clear. He will have to take control of Corta Hélio.

Two jumps from Queen of the South to João de Deus. Rafa and his escoltas wait in the private arrivals area of the BALTRAN station. Until now Rafa's guards have been electronic. Today they are close and biological: two men, one woman, armed and alert.

The capsule is in the elevator tube, Socrates informs him.

Green lights. Doors open. A boy charges out; brown-skinned, mane of dreadlocks; all legs and arms. He crashes into Rafa. Rafa scoops him up, swirls the boy around, laughing.

'Oh you you you you!'

Behind the boy comes the woman: tall, red-haired, white-skinned. Green-eyed like her boy. With infinite poise she stalks up to Rafa and slaps him hard across the face. Bodyguards' hands flash to the hilts of knives concealed in well-cut suits.

'We have trains, you know.'

Rafa cracks into great golden laughter.

'You look stunning,' Rafa says to his wife. And she does look fantastic, for a woman who has been bucketed across the moon in a converted cargo can like a load of ore. Make-up immaculate; every hair, every pleat and fold: immaculate. And she is right. The BALTRAN is outmoded since the high-speed rail network has been linked up: it's crude, but it is quick. The BALTRAN is a ballistic transport system. On an airless moon, ballistic trajectories can be calculated with precision. A magnetic mass-driver accelerates a capsule. Throws it up. Gravity brings it down. A receiving end of the target mass-driver catches the capsule and decelerates it to rest. In between, twenty minutes of free fall. Repeat as necessary. The capsules can contain cargo, or people. It's tough but endurable; fast and only hair-raising if you think about it too much. Rafa used to enjoy it for the freefall sex.

'I want him to catch the game. He'd miss it if he came by train.'

Then to the boy: 'You want to see the game? Moços versus Tigers. Jaden Sun thinks he's got us beat but I say we kick Tiger ass all over the stadium. What do you say?'

Robson Corta is eleven years old and the sight of him, the presence of him, his magnificent hair, his face, his great green eyes, the way his lips part in excitement, fill Rafa's heart with a joy so great it is pain, and at the same time a loss so deep it is a nausea. He crouches to kid level. 'Game day. What do you think, eh?'

'Oh for God's sake, Raf.' Rachel Mackenzie knows, Rafa knows; their respective sets of bodyguards, even Robson knows that this is not about a handball match. The terms allow Rafa access to his son at any time. Even if that means lobbing him like a handball across the moon. Throw and catch. Throw and catch.

'We can have this in front of him if you want,' Rafa says.

'Robbo, honey, could you go back to the capsule? It'll only be a couple of minutes.' A nod from Rachel sends one her blades with the boy. He glances back once at his father. Killing green eyes. He will break hearts. He is breaking one now.

'Robbo,' Rafa says with contempt.

'I had nothing to do with what happened at the party.'

' "What happened at the party." What happened at the party was someone tried to stick me with a neurotoxin-armed fly. I'd've been spasming and pissing and shitting myself for hours before I suffocated.'

'Classy, but it's not our style. Mackenzies like you to see our faces before they kill you. You should look to your friends the Asamoahs. Poisons, assassin bugs; that's more their game.'

'I want him back.'

'The terms of the settlement...'

'Fuck the settlement.'

'Leave this to the lawyers, Raf. You really don't know what you're talking about.'

'He's not safe with you. I'm invoking the security clause. Please send Robson to me.'

'Not safe with me?' Rachel Mackenzie's laugh is like mining tools on stone. 'Are you insane? Raf, I don't care how they kill you, or even if they kill you but I know the moon and they won't stop at you. Root and branch, Rafa. Let you take Robson? No fucking way. Rob stays with me. Mackenzies look after their own.' She turns to her guard. 'Lay in a new BALTRAN jump. We're going to Crucible.'

Rafa roars in inarticulate rage. Knives whip out from magnetic sheaths: escoltas and blades.

'You know, your brother's right,' Rachel Mackenzie says. 'You are shit-stupid. You want to start a war with us? Stand down lads.' The Mackenzie blades open the capsule. Rachel Mackenzie says as the lock closes, 'I tell you something; your sister scares me more than you do. And she's got more balls.'

The capsule is in the elevator, Socrates says. *The mass-driver is powering up.*

Rafa punches concrete, hard. Blood sprays from his knuckles.

'I know it was you!' he bellows. 'I know it was you! You want to put him in the chair of Corta Hélio!'

On her return to Meridian Marina Calzaghe buys a window seat, top deck. Mountains and craters, great and dusty, short of magnificence, as she thought. She watches a telenovella on the entertainment channel. It makes no sense, it makes all sense. Love, betrayal and rivalry among the elite. This elite are rare-earth miners. It's stupid and repetitive and badly acted. She watches it because she can. She sends a message home. *Mom, Kessie: news news news. I GOT A JOB! A proper job. With Corta Hélio. The fusion people. Five Dragons. I can get that money to you.* Hetty out-boxes it, then Marina goes into the train shopping menu to find a new skin for her familiar. Cute robot monkeys are cute but so very obvious. God with swords. Steam witch. Cyborg orca. Yes. She blinks buy and Hetty's default form reformats into lithe liquid metal and black. Marina lets out a little ecstatic squeak. Money makes you free. She looks out the window again at the soft grey mountains and rilles, patterned with tyre and foot tracks, tries to imagine her feet out there with Carlinhos Corta and his dusters. The Cortas scoop up great buckets of dust, sift, sort it, extract the helium-3 and throw the rest away. Dirt work.

Talk to Carlinhos, Lucas Corta had said. Marina ran. Post-crisis promises are forgotten if not redeemed instantly. Carlinhos brought her tea and sat her down under the dome of one of Boa Vista's many pavilions to explain herself to him and Wagner.

'So what's your business?'

'My postgrad degree was computational evolutionary biology in process control architecture.'

There was a thing Carlinhos Corta did when he didn't understand a thing. His lower lip sagged, just a millimetre, and the tiniest vertical line formed between his eyebrows. She thought it was cute. But when Wagner made that same frown, it meant he had dug deep beneath her words.

'That's making manufacturing more like biology,' Wagner said.

'Put very simply. I was studying how a solar-rich energy environment like the moon is analogous to a terrestrial photosynthetic dryland ecosystem like a tall-grass prairie, and how that might generate new manufacturing paradigms, and increase efficiency. Technology will always converge with biology.'

'That's interesting,' Wagner said with tilt of his head, as if the weight of ideas had shifted him off balance. *That's your cute thing,* Marina thought.

'So have you any surface experience?' Carlinhos interrupted.

'I've been here eight weeks. I haven't seen anything except the inside of Meridian.'

Both Corta brothers still wore their sasuits. The hi-visibility beading followed the lines of their musculature. Marina inhaled their perfume of gunpowder moon dust and recycled body-fluids. Sweat of the moon. The boys were relaxed and easy in their dirty pressure skins. They filled her with hurt and longing in that same way snowboard gear and goggles made her soul tighten. Her friends, they boarded; up at Snoqualmie and Mission Ridge. They were snow kids. They had offered once to take her and teach her but a paper was due. Not an impossible paper, but a troubling one. It needed time. So she stayed in the apartment while they loaded the car and cried with loneliness when it drove away. She completed the paper but she would always be the Girl Who Missed Snowboarding. The offer never came again. Every time she saw goggles and gloves and gear in the stores, when the weather reported first falls up in the ranges; she ached with want and loss. Someone out in a parallel universe, snowboarder Marina existed; fresh and joyful. The decal-plastered sasuits, the helmets; they called her like rumours of snow. The opportunity is back again. Do not be the Woman Who Missed the Moon.

'I want to work on the surface. I want to be up there. I can learn it.'

'You need to learn a whole set of physical skills,' Wagner said.

'I'll teach you,' Carlinhos said. 'Report to the Corta Hélio Extractions Facility in João de Deus.'

'I can do that.' A subvocal whisper set Hetty on the task of finding accommodation.

'Learn Portuguese,' Carlinhos called as a farewell. Security was escorting huddles of guests and catering staff to the station. 'And thank you.'

Marina leans back in her window seat. The job, the apartment, the complete transformation of her life, is reflected in one tiny, imperceptible movement: she flicks up her chib in the bottom right corner of her vision and sees the O_2 gauge in gold. She's breathing on the Corta account. Marina is nearing the bottom of her second mojitka as the train pulls into Meridian and the airlocks seal with the doors. The escalators bring her up into the roaring, chaotic cathedral of Orion Hub. Every tea and water stall, every shop and outlet, every street food stand and service kiosk is brilliant with things she can *buy*. Then she remembers Blake, up there in the roof of the city, coughing his lungs up gobbet by gobbet. Orca-Hetty puts out bids to farmacias, contracts a price for a course of phage therapy. Multiply-resistant tuberculosis is a recent invader from Earth despite the strict quarantine, and not long finding a lodging, clinging like white mould to the damp, stagnant high ribs of the quadras, up among the poor. The stall prints out twenty white tablets. Little white tablets.

Three bitsies for the express elevator. One bitsie for the escalator; riding up through the flat roofs and staircases and alleys of the West '80s and '90s. Beyond 110 nothing mechanical goes. She runs the rest of the way up into Bairro Alto, great tireless earth-leaps; whole stairways at a time. Here is the pissbuyer, here is our Lady of Kazan, still lightless and loveless. Here is the balcony from which she had envied the flying woman.

The room is empty. Everything is gone: mattress; water bottles, Blake's scraps and orts of things. Plastic spoons and plates. Empty to the last fleck of mucus, the last grain of dust. Skin flakes are precious organics.

Surely she has come to the wrong house.

Surely Blake has moved.

Surely this can't be.

Marina leans against the door frame. She can't breathe. Can't breathe. Hetty adjusts her lung function. *Breathe*. She shouldn't breathe, oughtn't breathe. Breathing undeserved air, while Blake is gone.

'What happened?' she shouts to the curtained doors and empty windows of the jostling cubicles. On the ladders and corridors, Bairro Alto turns backs to her. 'Where were you?'

I have footage, Hetty says and Marina's lens overlays the empty room with bodies. Zabbaleen with their robots. Scavengers. She glimpses a foot, ankle turned out, at the end of a mattress. The Zabbaleen close around it and shut it out from view. The video has been snatched from a street camera so the angle is obtuse and the magnification grainy. The Zabbaleen come out with a hefty metal cannister in each hand.

'Take it away take it away!' she screams. Hetty kills the feed just as Marina sees the machines covering the door and window in vacuum plastic. Every last skin flake. Every last drop of blood. And there is nothing to be done. No appeal to be made. Blake is dead but, on the moon, death is no release from debt. The Zabbaleen sill collect on Blake's chib accounts by viciously recycling every part of his body into useful organics.

Coughing yourself to death, listening for the scritch-scratch of the Zabbaleen bots around your door, waiting for the coughs to fall silent.

'Why didn't you do anything?' Marina shouts at the door and windows. 'You could have done something. It wouldn't take much. A couple of decimas from everyone. Would a couple of decimas have killed you? What kind of people are you?' The empty doors, the turned backs, the shoulders hurrying away from her are her answer. People of the moon.

The tram denies him. Refuses him. Defies him.

Nothing has ever defied Lucasinho Corta before. For a moment the sheer affront paralyses him. He orders Jinji to open the lock again.

Access is denied to you, Jinji said.

'What do you mean, denied to me?'

Access to the tram has been restricted from the following list of people: Luna Corta, Lucasinho Corta.

He had thought his father was joking when he told Lucasinho that Boa Vista was under lock down. Protect the children.

'Over-ride it.'

I'm not able to that. I could inform security. Do you wish me to inform security?

'Leave it.'

Lucasinho had liked the idea of hanging around Boa Vista and João de Deus a while. Live the way you're meant to live. No hurry about getting back to the university: his colloquium will fill in what he missed. That's what it's for. Now his father has locked him down and he has to get out. This is claustrophobia. Boa Vista is a stone intestine. He is locked in the gut of the beast, being slowly digested. He raises a fist to strike the defiant metal of the gate. Stopped. Has a sudden, brilliant, better idea.

Carlinhos and Wagner came in through the surface lock. He can go out through it. And when he is through that lock, he can go anywhere. Everywhere. Away. Fuck lock-downs, fuck family security. Fuck family. Maybe not fuck his vo. She is old and not what she was, but she can still burn fierce and Lucasinho admires how she commands respect as naturally as breathing. And maybe not Carlinhos, though Lucasinho never quite knows what to say to his uncle, how to tell him that he thinks he's all right. Lucasinho has feared for years that Carlinhos thinks him a dick. The kids aren't even worth considering. The rest, fuck them.

Especially fuck his father.

The emergency suit-liners were not designed for third gens and it takes Lucasinho five minutes wrestling to pull it on. There is no room in the suit shell's pressure pouch for his clothes. No loss. He can print new gear in João de Deus. He unpins his Lady Luna and packs her in the pouch. The emergency suit is a bulbous sci-fi robbie-robot, hi-viz orange, with flashers. Roomy enough inside for Lucasinho to move around. Jinji copies into the suit system and powers it up. On the surface he will be out of range of the network. Clamps clunk. Seals lock. Pressurisation hisses and fades.

'Let's take a walk,' Lucasinho breathes. Jinji marches Lucasinho into the outlock. Lucasinho remembers his last outlock. Naked bodies. Knee to knee. Naked Abena Asamoah opposite him. The sweat evaporating on her perfectly curved breasts as the pressure reduces. He will have those breasts. Out there in the world. He will find them. He's owed them. She has drawn his blood.

He does not think about the inlock. The tangle of bodies, pulsing in and out of consciousness. The pain the red the black the pain. The scream of emergency repressurisation.

The outer door slams open.

Jinji controls the hard-shell's servos and pushes the suit into a fast, loping run. Security will know a lock has been opened, a suit taken. They won't know who had taken the suit, where it was going, how fast. They will work that out, but by then Lucasinho will be in, repressurised, out of the shell suit and lost among João de Deus's crowds.

You're not so smart, Pai.

Lucasinho steps out of the João de Deus lock and rides the elevator downtown. The suit will cycle out and jog back to Boa Vista under its own power. Emergency suits are too valuable to leave scattered around the Sea of Fecundity. A life might depend on it one day. It is almost as tough to pin the moon-run token through the pressure weave as it was to pull the skin-tight suit-liner on. He's ruined its integrity. He hopes a life won't depend on it one day. Hopes his life won't depend on it. No: that was the last time Lucasinho Corta intends be on the surface.

João de Deus is a half-made town; raw rock and low lintels, its prospekts and quadras tight and lean. Safety doors spasm and jerk, the sunline flickers. It smells of shit and body odour and environmental systems straining at their performance limits. The water tastes of batteries. Too many people, scurrying people. Always someone in front of you, in your way. Elbows and breath, ghosting through floating hosts of familiars. The signs and names, the handbills and graffiti are all Portuguese. João de Deus is Helium-ville, a frontier town. A company town and that is why Lucasinho is not staying here.

'If you were my father, what would you do?' Lucasinho asks Jinji.

I would freeze your cash accounts.

So Lucasinho heads to the station, not the fashion printshop.

Suit-liners are commonplace in João de Deus, even acceptable. In Meridian Main Station, twenty heads have turned by the time he gets to the main escalator and up on to Gagarin Prospekt. Got to get out is this suit, even if he does wear it well? Could he persuade everyone it's a new micro-trend? 1950s is so last lune. Surface-worker chic. Blue collar is the thing: so honest and *now*. He starts to walk a little big. Lead from the package, the lower belly. Swagger. He feels good. He's done a thing. Because Boa Vista couldn't hold him and family couldn't keep him. Because he ran away, by his own cleverness and cool. Because he's free. Because he is back. That's not just a thing. That's *things*. Lucasinho Corta feels more than good; he feels great.

The waiter can't hide the stare as Lucasinho orders a vaper and mint tea and stretches out in the café chair. Is it the suit or the muscles inside it? Lucasinho arches his back to tighten his stomach muscles opens his legs to show off the thighs. He likes to be looked at. I'm a rich kid in a suit-liner. I make this thing look good, but you can't afford me.

Lucasinho flicks the end of the vaper and inhales. THC coils cool in his throat. He feels the unwinding inside, the inner smile. He sips a glass of tea and has Jinji flash up the Boy de la Boy catalogue on his lens. By the time he has put a wardrobe together he is nicely high. Jinji flicks the order to a printshop. The order bounces back.

Payment declined.

Lucasinho falls off his high. It's a long fall, and the hit at the bottom is hard.

Your account has been frozen, Jinji says. A sick pit opens in Lucasinho's stomach, full of wheels of rotating teeth. He looks around to see if anyone has noticed him jolt, gasp. The motos whir by, the crowds push along Gagarin Prospekt beneath the trees. No one one knows that in an instant he has gone from Dragon to beggar. No money, he has no money. He has never had no money. He doesn't know what to do with no money.

Lucasinho's fingers find the plug Abena Asamoah put through his ear. *When you need the help of House Asamoah; when you have no other hope, when you're alone and naked and exposed, like Kojo...* He turns it, enjoying the small pain of its tug on the scab. No. He is not that desperate yet. He's Lucasinho Corta; he has charm, looks and hotness. These he can parlay.

The four digits in his chib are huge and brilliant. They are the whole world: air, water, carbon, data. They can't cut off the Four Elementals. Paying for air and data is a thing people who have to work do. Cortas have these things arranged. He can breathe, he can drink, he is connected, he has his carbon allowance. From that plan your next move. He can't go to the apartment. His father's escoltas are probably there already. He has friends, he has amors, he has places he can go. He needs clothes, somewhere to stay.

He needs to go dark. Yes. This. His father can trace him through the network. So Jinji must go. That does make Lucasinho's belly and balls tighten with fear. Off-network, disconnected. He hesitates to whisper the words that will shut Jinji down. This is social death. No, it's survival. His father may already have identified his location from the failed payment. Contract security may already be on their way.

He needs to pay for a vape and a tea.

No he doesn't need to pay for them. Like he did at Boa Vista and João de Deus, he can just walk away. What is the waiter going to do? Stab him? Raise a mob? He's still a Corta. Lay skin on one Corta and all Cortas will cut you. There are no crimes on the moon, no theft, no murder. There are only contracts and negotiations.

Lucasinho eases out of the chair and strolls across Gagarin Prospekt. Even in his fluorescent pink suit-liner, he disappears into the push of people and vehicles and bots. A few steps more and he is under trees. Don't look back. Don't ever look back. As he walks he strips out commands and routines from Jinji, severs connections and clicks off utilities until he is left with an empty skin hovering over his left shoulder. People get suspicious if they can't see a familiar in their augmented vision.

The walls of Orion Quadra rise on either side of him; tier upon tier, level upon level, lights and neons; Roman and Cyrillic and Chinese neons. Disconnecting Jinji has removed a layer of augmented advertising from the world but there are still physical screens and cute kawaii animations, looking down on him. Alone in Meridian without a bitsie to his thumbprint. Like poor people. Except he has friends up there, among the lights in the walls of the world. So, not like the poor people really. Fuck poor. He needs to get moving.

All the moon is in love with Ariel by the time she arrives at the reception for the Chinese trade delegation. The LDC has hired an open belvedere on the eightieth level of the rotunda, the central axis where the five Prospekts of Aquarius Quadra meet. Vistas stretch for kilometres. Vertical gardens drop curtains of climbing plants over the open arches. Beyond them, lights drift across the voids.

Ariel wears a Ceil Chapman cocktail dress. Every eye turns to her. Every human wants to orbit her. She can hear the whispers, see the heads nodding together. Attention is oxygen. She takes a draw on her long titanium vaper and advances into the party.

The guests from the Five Dragons: Yao Asamoah from the Golden Stool; a reluctant, shy Alexei Vorontsov; Verity Mackenzie cradling a beautiful pet angora ferret, a biological one. It draws admiring attention. Wei-Lun Sun, orbiting at aphelion from the Chinese.

The Chinese mission, all men, still ungainly and exaggerated in their movements. They make no effort to tune their bodies to the demands of lunar gravity. They don't intend to be here that long. They bow and smile and shake Ariel's hand and have no idea who she is except that she seems to be greatly celebrated. Ariel enjoys a small, sexual lower-belly prickle of excitement. She is the spy in the Ceil Chapman dress.

The LDC grandees. Company managers and finance directors. Lawyers and judges.

Judge Nagai Rieko nods over from across the room. Nods to the Eagle of the Moon. *I've mentioned you to the Eagle,* she says through her familiar. *He approves.* Ariel lifts a cocktail glass in answer. Welcome to the Pavilion of the White Hare.

And there is the Eagle of the Moon. Jonathon Kayode, Chief Executive of the Lunar Development Corporation; King, Pope and Emperor, in reality a figurehead, a brightly-plumaged cage-bird. His familiar is the lunar eagle itself. Only he is allowed to bear this skin. At his shoulder, his oko Adrian Mackenzie, careful to be always one shade drabber than the resplendent Eagle. His familiar takes the shape of a raven.

'The famous Ariel Corta,' the Eagle of the Moon says. He is big for an Earth-born; a giant Igbo from Lagos. He stands shoulder to shoulder with even the second generation moon-children. 'I can trust you not to start a fight here?'

'In this frock?' Ariel says flirtatiously, but still turns her empty cocktail glass upside down; the sign that she will fight the entire party. The Eagle of the Moon does not know the sign but his husband, an Australian, understands the joke. His smile is thin.

'I made on you in the Celebdaq,' the Eagle whispers. He flashes his eyes at his oko. 'We have these little competitions. They keep us sane. He is a terribly bad loser.'

'Even on the moon the only way a girl can get noticed is by taking her clothes off.'

The Eagle of the Moon guffaws. His laugh is huge. The room freezes, then little aftershocks of humour ripple across the party; people laughing because more important people are laughing.

'Too true. Alas, too true, what?' He playfully slaps Adrian Mackenzie in the ribs. Adrian winces, chews resentment. The rumour is that Adrian Mackenzie has been manoeuvring the Eagle of the Moon into making his office more political, more powerful, more presidential, while settling it deeper into the pockets of Mackenzie Metals. 'Your family has quite a facility for the public eye. You pull off a spectacular *coup du tribunal* in your underwear. Your nephew saves that Asamoah boy on the moon-run. And then your brother, well; shocking. Quite shocking.'

'It seems we have compounded one security breach with another.' Ariel sends a spiral of vapour up to the lights.

Jonathon Kayode pulls down one eyelid.

'The eye of the Eagle,' he quips. He guides Ariel out through hibiscus curtains to an outside balcony. A glance tells Adrian Mackenzie to remain inside. The balcony is high, stirred by air currents spiralling up from the lower levels. The light moves into sundown. Long golden light, mauve shadows, indigo rising from the floor far below; whole districts coming alive with lights, twinkling in the dust. Jonathon Kayode says in a deep, intimate whisper, 'I am delighted to have you on my advisory panel.'

'It's an honour.'

'Speaking personally, I think it's high time the Cortas kicked the dust off their boots and took their proper place in political society. It's not a dirty word, politics. However, we are disturbed by the assassination attempt. It is like some ghastly throwback to the sixties. Duels and vendettas and assassinations – we've moved on from that. Of course, the Eagle has no authority to intervene, but we can advise and warn. It would be a shame if an opportunity for the Cortas were stymied by the behaviour of the few bellicose brothers.'

The Eagle of the Moon dips his head. Ariel Corta purses her fingers. The audience is over. Jonathon Kayode brushes through the hibiscus curtain. Loose petals powder the shoulders of his agbada. Adrian Mackenzie links his arm.

Ariel lingers, leans on the stone balustrade. The riding lights of drones and pedicopters, the sparkle of fliers, the jewelled abacus of the elevator cars and cable gondolas: she is immersed in light, breathing it as a fish breathes water. Bubbles of exhaled light.

She draws on her long vaper and reviews the brief conversation. Two things. The LDC knew about the assassination attempt, and also Rafa's certainty that it was a flare-up of the old Mackenzie-Corta feud. And the Eagle of the Moon had left the conversation on-record; overheard by familiars. She was meant to relay it to Boa Vista, with all its promises and threats. We can be kings of the moon like we are kings of helium but we must act like kings, not wild bandeirantes. The Eagle of the Moon had tasked her with restraining her impetuous brother.

The party beckons and she will flirt outrageously tonight, but there is one last piece of work; Corta work. Bandeirante work. She tilts her head to the man who has been hovering at the edge of her vision all evening. The man comes out on to the balcony and stands a moment beside her, looking out at the constant movement.

'An Xiuying,' he says without a look or an acknowledgement.

And he's gone. He's a middle-ranking Lunar Development Corporation civil servant in a suit better than his salary, who hired a nikah advocate better than his salary, to allow him to marry the Sun boy he loves with all his generous, weak heart.

'Lucas,' Ariel murmurs to Beijaflor. Her brother is on instantly. He's been waiting for this call all night.

'An Xiuying,' Ariel says.

'Thank you.'

'And don't ask me for any more favours Lucas,' Ariel says and breaks the connection. She straightens her back, uncoils the day's tensions and tightness. Confidence is the most alluring necklace. She suits the sexy jewels of power. She suits them so well.

Movement, noise at the door. A figure in pink beyond the bots and the obdurate human security. Some want, some grudge, some hope. Some petition. The Chinese are looking now.

'Senhora Corta?' Ariel did not see the aide approach. All of a sudden a voice is at her ear. That is what aides are supposed to do, approach inconspicuously. An eagle pin on the upper breast of her

Suzy Perette dress identifies the aide's allegiance. 'Do you know a Lucas Corta Junior?'

'My nephew.'

'He would like to see you. Outside, if you would be so kind. His dress is not appropriate.'

The figure in pink recognises her. What is that, a suit-liner? But there is no mistaking the handsome big lunk. No mistaking those love-god cheekbones, that big heart-melting grin.

'Tia, he says in Portuguese. 'I've run away from Boa Vista. Can I stay at yours?'

Cake and mint tea wait for Ariel in her tiny, unused kitchen space.

'I made you cake,' Lucasinho says. 'To say thank you. For the hammock.' Ariel's apartment is very small. Living for one. She sent Lucasinho there from the door of the Chinese reception. A hammock was waiting for him in the printer hopper. By the time she returned he was lolling in it, deeply unconscious, mouth open, limbs loose and sprawling in deep sleep beneath the wall-sized print of Richard Avedon's full-face photograph of Dovima. It's her only decoration: bleached-out face, soft dark eyes and mouth, holes for nostrils.

'You won't tell Papai?' Lucasinho says.

'Lucas will find out,' Ariel says. She takes a slice of the cake. Lemon, light as a breath. 'If he hasn't already. He will ask me.'

'What will you say?'

'My brother owes me.' Lucas would have been awake all night, calling in debts, tapping up allies, marshalling his agents biological and informational down on Earth. All his resources he would bring to bear on An Xiuying, but most of all his deliberate, relentless intelligence, that would never rest or relinquish until Lucas Corta had what he wanted. Ariel is almost sorry for the poor man. Lucas will play the coercion sudden, sharp and impossible to escape. 'So I can say what I like.' This time. But she isn't clean. A seat in the Pavilion of the White Hare and she has already betrayed privileged information;

under the eyes of the Eagle of the Moon himself. Lucas has never approved of her seeking a life and career outside the family. Now, making this one, tiny betrayal for family, she has given her brother an edge. Not now. Not soon. But some day, when he needs it most. For the family. Always for the family. 'This cake,' Ariel takes another bite. 'Where did you learn this?'

'Where does anyone learn anything? The network.' Lucasinho slides the cake towards Ariel for her inspection. 'I'm good at cake.'

'You are.'

'It was kind of tricky. You don't have much stuff in your kitchen. Actually, just water and gin.'

'Did you order it in?'

'Ingredients, yeah. Stuff I couldn't print. Like eggs.'

'Then you're very tidy too.'

He grins and his pleasure is plain and guileless.

'Ariel; can I stay?'

Ariel imagines him a fixture in her apartment. Something bright and funny and unpredictable amid the severe whites and pure surfaces, the bespoke gin and the pure water in her cooler, the vast face of a long-dead 1950s model, eyes closed, teeth catching lower lip. Something cute and kind.

'He doesn't owe me that much.'

He shrugs.

'Okay. I understand that.'

'Where will you go?'

'Friends. Girls. Boys. My colloquium.'

'Wait.' Ariel slips into her room and takes paper from her bag. 'You'll need this.'

Lucasinho frowns at the bouquet of grey slips in his hands.

'Is this?'

'Money.'

'Wow.'

'Cash. Your father's frozen your checking account.'

'I've never . . . Wow. It smells funny. Kind of hot. And like pepper. What's it made from?'

'Paper.'

'That's . . .'

'Rag fibre, if that means anything. And yes, it's not LDC sanctioned, but it'll get you where you need, and beyond there, where you want.'

'How did you get it?'

'Clients are often imaginative in settling accounts. Try not to blow it all at once.'

'How do I use it?'

'You can count can't you?'

'I made you a cake. I can count. And add. And take away.'

'Of course you can. Hundreds, fifties, tens and fives. That's how you use it.'

'Thanks Ariel.'

That great heart-melting smile. Ariel is seventeen again; out from under her mother's wing, blinking in the light of a big world. The University of Farside had just opened its first colloquium in Meridian and Ariel Corta was first name in the study group. Farside was a geeky warren, João de Deus a dirty mining outpost, Boa Vista little more than a cave. Meridian was colour, glamour, ardour and the best legal minds on the moon. She took the BALTRAN. Nothing could take her away from Corta Hélio fast enough. She ran away, she stayed away. Lucas won't let that happen to his son. Lucasinho's future is laid out like a boardgame: a chair at the table in Boa Vista, a family job tailored to his talents and limitations. Where is there a place for cakes made with love? The same place as his father's love for music. Suborned to the needs of Corta Hélio.

Love this small escape, kid.

'One note: I spent a lot of carbon on printing those clothes. The least you can do is wear them.'

Lucasinho grins. He is magnificent, Ariel thinks. Muscles and metal and dancer's poise. And the cake is so very good.

Handball! Game night! Handball! João de Deus Moços versus the Tigers of the Sun Men's.

Estádio da Luz is a colosseum; steeply banked seats and boxes carved from raw rock, tier upon tier so that the uppermost levels look almost vertically down on the court. The only things higher than the cheap seats are the lights and the robot blimps in the shapes of cute manhua icons, carrying advertising on their bellies. The fans sit close; a player on the court, if he could spare the moment of attention, would see a wall of faces, tier upon tier. He would feel like a gladiator in a pit. The players have yet to make their entrance. Cameras flit across the banks of fans, beaming their faces into everyone's lens. Down in the court jugglers perform tremendous stunts of skill, cheerleaders strut and thrust, beautiful boys and girls of startling gymnasticism. The fans see it every game but it is part of the rubric. Music and lights. The blimps, fat as gods, manoeuvre into new formations. Jeers and whistles: the LDC has of course increased the O_2 price for the game. But the betting is still ferocious.

The people of João de Deus live in tunnels and warrens, but they have the best handball stadium on the moon.

Rafa Corta opens the glass wall of the director's box and escorts An Xiuying on to the balcony. His right hand is enclosed in a healing glove. He was stupid. Stupid and hasty. Stupid and hot-tempered and emotional. Robson should be here with him, in the box, high above the rows of fans: your team, son. Your players. He played it wrong. Wrong from the moment he saw Rachel Mackenzie step flawless and magnificent out of the BALTRAN pod. He remembered everything he adored about her. The poise, the pride, the intelligence and fire. A dynastic marriage. A truce between Cortas and Mackenzies, sealed with a son. Robson was the central term of the marriage contract, and the thing that had split them apart, like ice cracking rock. At the baptism – one for the Church, once for the orixas – he had seen the Mackenzies cooing around the baby like a flock of scavenging pigeons. Vampires. Parasites. Each time Rachel took him to visit her family – each visit longer than the one before – the mistrust and dread would hollow out his bones. Inside the glove his wounded hand throbs.

But it's game night. Game night! And he has a guest from Earth. There is the game, and then there is the other game. The one that really matters in this arena tonight.

Turn off your heart, Rafa.

The sounds, the sights, the sensations momentarily stagger An Xiuying as he steps out on to the balcony. Rafa raises a hand to the galleries. The fans respond with a roar. The Patrão is here. Rafa sees Jaden Wen Sun in the next box and bounds over to greet and rib his friend and rival, leaving his guest to soak in the game-night atmosphere. The Earth man grips the rail with both hands, vertiginous with noise and gravity.

Now the stadium announcer is reading out the team list. The fans can get this information instantly on their familiars but it doesn't have the commonality, the moment, the emotion. Each name is greeted with a wall of noise. The loudest roar greets Muhammad Basra, the left ringcourt recently signed from CSK St Ekaterina.

'This is very exciting, Senhor Corta,' An Xiuying says.

'Wait until the teams run out.'

Fanfare! The visitors run on to the court. The away supporters go crazy down at their end of the court, waving banners and blowing airhorns. In the adjacent box Jaden Sun punches the air and yells himself hoarse. His Tigers of the Sun snap a few balls between each other, practise their leaps and drives and shoulder charges. The goalkeeper hangs a tiny icon in the back of the tiny net. This is what makes handball the moon's great team sport: gravity may be free but the net is tight.

Music! *The Kids are Back.* The Moços theme. Here come the boys, the boys, the boys! The fans rise. Their voices become something more than noise. The closed colosseum of Estádio da Luz throbs with it. Rafa Corta bathes in it. It washes him clean of anger and hurt. This moment he loves even more than winning; the moment where he opens his hands and the magic bursts out. See what I give you? But I'm selfish; I give it to myself as well. I'm a fan, just like you.

The team starts its on-court warm-up. An Xiuying leans forward on the rail. Rafa can see in the movements of his contact lens: his familiar is zooming in. Muhammad Basra's back. His name, his number, the sponsor's logo.

'It's the first run out in those game-suits,' Rafa says. 'New deal. Golden Phoenix Holdings.' The same name is on the back of every João de Dios Moço.

An Xiuying steps back from the rail. His hands are shaking. His face is pale and sheened with sweat.

'I don't feel very well, Senhor Corta. I'm not sure I can finish the game.'

And Lucas is behind him. His shirt so crisp, his creases so sharp, his pocket-square so precise.

'I'm sorry to hear that Mr An. It's quite a sight. Has our choice of shirt logo upset you? An interesting company, Golden Phoenix. I found it surprisingly hard to pin down what they actually did. From my research, it seems to exist solely to redirect infrastructure development funding through a series of shell companies registered in tax havens – many of them here on the moon – in a pattern even I found difficult to unravel. If you don't want to watch the game – the Tigers will win, Rafa's boys have been on terrible form all season – maybe we could have a talk about your connection with Golden Phoenix. You see, I can disclose it. Your government seems to be going through one of its periodic clamp-downs on corruption. The penalties are quite harsh. Or I can conceal it. Rafa can retire those shirts. Your decision. We could also talk about the China Power Investment Corporation's future helium-3 requirements. Corta Hélio is eminently capable of meeting those. The game lasts an hour. I'm sure that's enough time to make a deal.'

A hand on the shoulder guides An Xiuying back into the director's box. Before he closes the door, Lucas nods to his older brother.

Rachel was right, Rafa thinks. You are smarter than me. Then the whistle blows and the ball goes up. Game on!

One hour, plus time-outs. The Tigers win; 31-15. A trouncing. Jaden Sun is jubilant, Rafa Corta despondent. Lucas is never wrong about the outcome of games.

The tram will carry one passenger. Boa Vista security has been notified. Surveillance will be discreet. Under no circumstances may the passenger be searched. She comes at the personal invitation of Adriana Corta.

The car pulls into Boa Vista Station. The woman who steps on to the polished stone is tall even by lunar standards; dark of face and eye and blade-thin. She wears voluminous white: a many-skirted dress, a loose turban. Colours: a woven stole in green gold and blue; string upon string of heavy beads around her neck, gold hoops at each ear and around each finger. Her loose clothing accentuates her height and thinness. The woman wears no familiar; an absence like a lost limb. The guards straighten their backs. Charisma crackles from her. They would not dream of searching her.

'Irmã,' says Nilson Nunes, steward of Boa Vista. She acknowledges him with the least inclination of the head. In the garden of the Cortas the woman stops. She looks up at the sky panels and blinks in the false sunlight. She takes in the great stone faces of the orixas, mouths the name of each one.

'Irmã?'

A nod. Onward.

Adriana Corta waits in the São Sebastião Pavilion, a confection of pillars and domes at the highest point of the sloping lava-tube. Waters rush from between its columns. Two chairs, a table. A samovar of mint tea. Adriana Corta, dressed in lounging pants and a soft silk blouse, rises.

'Irmã Loa.'

'Senhora Corta. I bring you the fondest greetings of the sisterhood and the blessings of the saints and orixas.'

'Thank you, sister. Tea?' Adriana Corta pours a glass of mint tea. 'I do so wish we could grow coffee on this world. It's almost fifty years since my last arabica.'

The woman sits but she does not touch the glass.

'I'm sorry for your family's recent trouble,' she says.

'We survived.' Adriana says. She sips her mint tea and grimaces. 'Vile. You never stop worrying for them. Rafa will not give up on Robson. Carlinhos is fretting to get back in the field. Ariel has gone back to Meridian. Lucasinho has run off. Lucas has frozen his account but that won't stop the boy. He is more like his father than Lucas realises.'

Irmã Loa lifts a cross from amongst her cascades of beads to her lips and kisses the crucified man.

'Saints and orixas protect you. And Wagner?'

Adriana Corta brushes over the question with another.

'But you; your work is secure now?'

'Saint and sinner both pay breath tax,' Irmã Loa says. 'And Catholicism still objects to us. On the other hand we had our most successful Assumption Day festival. Your patronage is a constant blessing to us. It is so rare to find someone who thinks as we do, in centuries.'

'You invest in people. I invest in technology. Our long-term goals will inevitably meet. Best if they meet now, so they will recognise each other when they meet up again, hundreds – thousands of years from now. So few people think in the long term. The truly long term. We're both dynasty.'

Splashing up through the rivulets, drawn by voices; Luna: barefoot in a red play-dress.

'Who are you?' she says to the woman in white.

'This is Irmã Loa of the Sisters of the Lords of Now,' Adriana says. 'She is taking tea with me.'

'She's not drinking her tea,' Luna declares.

'What's that over your shoulder, a moth?' Irmã Loa says. Luna nods, still a little afraid of the thin woman in white, despite her smile. 'She is drawn to the light. But because she is so single-minded, that makes her easy to distract. The moth is so fragile, but she is the daughter is Yemanja. She is filled with intuition, the moth. She is drawn to love, and others love her.'

'You don't have a familiar,' Luna says.

'We don't use them. They clutter us up. They get in the way of our communications.'

'But you can see mine.'

'We all wear the lenses, anzinho.' Irmã Loa reaches into the folds of her turban to press a small object into Luna's hand: a tiny print-plastic votive of a mermaid with a star on her brow. 'Our Lady of the Waters. She will be your friend and guide you to the light.'

Luna presses the deity in her fist and skips off down through the tumbling waters.

'That was kind of you,' Adriana says. 'I think of all my grand-children, I love Luna the most. I fear for them. Havaianas to Havaianas in three generations. Do you know that saying, Sister? The first generation rises from poor people's shoes. The second generation builds the riches. The third generation squanders the riches. Back to poor people's shoes again. Long term projects, Sister.'

'Why have you asked me here, Senhora Corta?'

'I want to make a confession.'

Surprise on Irmã Loa's still face.

'With respect, you don't strike me as a woman with much of a sense of sin, Senhora.'

'And the Sisters are not a religion with much of a sense of sin either. I am an old woman, Sister. I am seventy-nine years old. No great age biologically, but I'm older than most things in this world.

I wasn't the first, but I was among the few. I came from nothing – a girl from nowhere – and I built all this, up in the sky. I want to tell that story. All of it. The good and the bad. Did you really think that funding was a donation?'

'Senhora Corta, simplicity of spirit is not naivety.'

'You will come here once a week, and I will make my confession to you. My family will enquire – Lucas needs to protect me – but they are not to know. Not until...' Adriana Corta breaks off.

'You're dying, aren't you?'

'Yes. I've kept it secret of course. Only Helen de Braga knows. She has been with me through everything.'

'Is it far advanced?'

'It is. The pain is under control. I know I am laying a burden on you. What you tell Rafa, or Ariel, but most of all Lucas, is up to you. But Lucas especially will pick and pick and pick away. Your lies must be airtight. If my children learn that I am dying, they will tear each other apart. Corta Hélio will fall.'

'I should like to pray for you, Senhora Corta.'

'Do as you wish. Then I will begin.'

THREE

My name. Begin with my name. Corta. It's not a Portuguese name. The word is Spanish: it means a cut. It's not really a name in Spanish either. It's a sound that has rolled around the world, from country to country, language to language and become a word and then a name and finally washed up on the shores of Brazil.

When you apply to go to the moon the LDC insists on a DNA test. If you plan on staying, if you plan on raising children, the LDC doesn't want chronic genetic conditions showing up in later life, or in your descendants. My DNA is from all over Earth. Old World, New World; Africa, eastern Mediterranean, western Mediterranean, Tupi, Japanese, Norwegian. I'm a planet in one woman.

Adriana Corta. Adriana after my Great-aunt Adriana. My clearest memory of her is that she played the electric organ. She lived in a tiny apartment and there in the middle of the room was this huge electric organ. It was the only thing of any value she owned. It was theft-proof: no one could have got it out of the apartment. She would play and we would dance around it. There were seven of us. Byron, Emerson, Elis, Adriana, Luiz, Eden, Caio. I was the middle kid. The worst place to be, the middle kid. But you get away with things when you're in the middle. Your brothers and sisters are your camouflage. There was always music in the house. My mother couldn't play

71

any instruments but she loved to sing and a radio was always on somewhere. I grew up with all the classics. I brought them with me. When I worked on the surface, I'd play them in my helmet. Lucas is the only one who has my love of music. It's a pity he has no voice.

Adriana Arena de Corta. My mother was Maria Cecilia Arena. She was a health worker for a Catholic social charity. Childcare and no contraception. I'm being unfair to her. She worked up in Vila Canoas; when she retired the whole favela turned out. My father burned his hand welding a car one day. He went to my mother to have it treated and ended up welded to her. She was a big, slow-moving woman; stiff in the hips and after Eden she gave up work and rarely went out of the apartment. She couldn't hope to catch all of us so she shouted. She had a great booming voice that always found exactly whichever one of us was meant to hear it. She was so kind. Papa adored her. She had bad circulation and a sickly heart. Why are health workers always the least healthy?

I miss her still. Of all the ones back there, I think about her most.

Adriana Mão de Ferro Arena de Corta. Mão de Ferro. Iron hand. What a name, yes? All of us were Iron Hands, as was my father and all my uncles. It was the nickname of my grandfather Diogo, from Belo Horizonte. He died before I was born, but he worked in the iron mines from the age of fourteen until they laid him off because he was a danger to himself and others. Ten million tons he shovelled. I've shovelled more than that. A thousand times more than that. Ten thousand times. If anyone is Iron Hand, it's me. Mining and metal. My father was a car dealer. He could strip and rebuild an engine before he could drive. He came to Rio when a recession hit Minas Gerais and he got a job in a cut-and-shut shop – you take two insurance write-offs, cut the front of one, the end off the other and weld them together. New car! He never liked the work – he was a very honest man, my father. Any news of corruption or graft on the news and he would shout at the screen. In Brazil in the tens and twenties he was shouting all the time. That graft on the Olympic stadiums! Working people can't afford to ride the bus! He got into dealing cars – whether that is more honest than building ringers is a moral hair I can't split. But he worked up quickly to a dealership, then gambled and bought a Mercedes franchise. It was the best decision he ever made – after marrying Mãe. My father, it seemed, had a gift for business. He moved us to Barra de Tijuca. Oh! I had never seen anything like it! A whole floor of an apartment block just for us. I only had to share a room with one sister! And if we leaned out of the window, and craned around, there, down between the other apartment blocks we could see the sea!

Adriana Maria do Céu Mão de Ferro Arena de Corta. Mary of Heaven. Our Lady of the Starry Skies. My mother worked for the Abrigo Cristo Redentor and sent us all to catechism and mass but she was very far from being a good Catholic. When we were sick she would light a candle and slip a holy medal under the pillow but she also bought herbs and prayers and icons from mãe-do-santo. Double insurance, she called it. The more deities on the case the better. We grew up with two invisible worlds overlapping us; saints and orixas. So I was named after a Catholic saint who was also Yemanja. I remember my mother taking us down to the beach at Barra for Reveillon. It was the one time of the year she would go to the beach. The ocean scared her. We spent the week after Christmas making costumes – blue and white, the holy colours. Mãe made fantastic head-dresses out of wire and old pairs of tights – Pai would spray-paint them in the back of the workshop. That for me is the smell of New Year – car paint. Mãe would dress all in white and everyone treated her with great respect as she walked down to the beach. I felt so proud – she was like a great ship. Millions went to Reveillon up at Rio but we weren't so shabby down at Barra. This was our festival. Everyone hung out palm fronds on their balconies. Cars drove up and down Avenida Sernambetida playing music. There were so many people milling around they could only drive slowly so it was safe even for very small kids. There were DJs and lots of food.

All the things that Yemanja loved. Weed. Flowers. White flowers, paper boats, candles. We went down to the edge of the water with the ocean at our toes. Even Mãe, ankle deep in the breaking waves, sand running out from under her toes. Flowers in our hair, candles in our hands. We were waiting for the moment the edge of the moon rose over the sea. And there it was – the tiniest edge of moon, as thin as a fingernail clipping. It seemed to bleed over the horizon. Huge. So huge. Then my perceptions moved and I saw that it wasn't rising beyond the edge of the world; it was forming out of the water. The sea was boiling and breaking and the white of the waves were being pulled together into the moon. I couldn't speak. None of us could. Still we stood, thousands of us. A line of white and blue along the edge of Brazil. Then the moon rose clear and full and a line of silver reached across the sea from it to me. The path of Yemanja. The road the Lady walked to reach our world. And I remember thinking, but roads lead both ways. I could walk out along that road to the moon. Then we threw our flowers into the water and the waves drew them out. We set our little tea-lights in the paper boats and put them in to follow the flowers. Most drowned but some were drawn out along the moon path to Yemanja. I have never forgotten the tiny boats bobbing out along the line of the moon.

Mãe never believed that people had walked there, up on the moon. It was inconceivable. The moon was a person, not a stone satellite. People could not walk like fleas on the skins of other people. She still did not believe that people were walking there, years later, before I left, when I took her down to the beach. By then she could hardly move. I hired a car and drove the couple of hundred metres to the beach. Pai had lost the dealership. We weren't car people any more. We had the apartment because Pai had paid off the mortgage early. It was full of us again: Byron, Emerson, Elis, Luiz, Eden, Caio. Adriana. All the birds back to roost.

Mãe was huge as a moon by then, but all the people down for Reveillon paid her respect and the cars on the Avenida hooted their horns to her. She was great and holy. I took her by the hand down to the water and we saw the moon seem to form out of the sea and I said, *I'll be there soon.* She laughed and could not believe it, but then she said, well, it'll be easy for me to go on to the balcony and wave to you.

Adriana Maria do Céu Mão de Ferro Arena de Corta. A Outra. Outrinha. The other one, the little other one. Average Jane. That's my final name. That's the name that has shaped my life the most. The average one. Not the best looker, not the brightest and most outgoing. Not the one vovo gave the Easter money to first. Average Adriana. I had good legs but my body was too short and my nose and ears too big. Little slitty eyes, and my skin was too dark. My parents thought they were doing me a favour. They didn't want me to have any illusions. They said, you'll never be a looker, you'll never be the golden one, the lucky one, so don't expect the world to fall into your hands like a peach. You'll have to work for it. You'll have to use every one of your strengths and talents to get what others get because of their looks, their smiles. The Other One. No one has called me that in fifty years. You are the only person on this world knows that name. And I can feel my jaw setting hard. My teeth are clenching. All because of that name. Fifty years on this world, and still that name! That name!

So: I was born without grace or favour. So: my nose was too big and my skin too dark. I would make myself exceptional. I would be the one who would do anything, dare anything. I knew I would never be caught. In school I was the kid with her hand up first. I was the girl who wouldn't shut up when the boys were talking. I was the one who hacked into the school network and changed exam results. The obvious geek boy did it. I asked Baby Norton, the futsal star all the girls worshipped, to slip his hand down the front of my skirt. And he did and everyone was so shocked. I wore the camouflage of the pretty around me. I was never again picked for the girls' futsal team.

So be it: I found my own sport, Brazilian jiu jitsu. My mother didn't approve at all. Pai loved MMA on the cable and he found me a dojo. I was small and sneaky and dirty and could throw boys twice my age. I was in secondary school then. Oh I was bad. I beat the pretty girls to the guys because they knew I would do anything. I did, but not as much as the pretty girls thought I did. The legend was enough. The pretty girls cut me out of their social cliques and parties. Big loss. They tried schemes and stings to humiliate me but none of them could dream up a social scam worth a damn. They put stuff about me on Facebook; I hacked them back ten times. I could code better than all of them put together. And they didn't dare try to physically bully me or throw battery acid at me; I was quick and I was hard and I could throw them around like Barbie dolls. Secondary school was war. Isn't it always, everywhere?

The guys were mostly okay, by the way. They talked anal but guys always talk anal. A blow job and they were satisfied. They were as scared of me as the girls.

Isn't this scandalous? A lady of my years talking about anal and oral sex.

Papai was delighted when he heard I was going to study engineering. Extraction engineering: I was a true daughter of Minas Gerais. A true Iron Hand. My mother was ten types of horrified. Engineering was a man's thing. I would never marry. I would never have children. I would eat with my fingers and have dirt under my nails and no man would look at me. And in São Paulo. That dreadful dreadful city.

I loved São Paulo. I loved the scary ugliness of it. I loved its anonymity. I loved its banality. I loved the endless vista of skyscrapers. I loved that it didn't compromise. Compared to the moon, it's an angel of beauty. There is no beauty on the moon. São Paulo was like me; nothing to look at but bursting with energy, ideas, anger and spit.

I found a good group of friends. Guys most and first – it was still unusual to find a woman studying extraction engineering and I knew better how guys worked than girls. Men were simple and straightforward. I found I could have girls as friends. I found out what how the friendship of women differs from the friendship of men. I found I could like girls. I found I could love them. I was an opportunist, I was flagrant. I knew tricks. I think of that young woman and her boldness and brashness and I adore her. She wasted no opportunity. I had only just moved on to the campus when I painted myself in the national flag, head to toenails and went on a naked bike ride through the streets of São Paulo. Everyone looked at me, no one saw me. I was naked and invisible. I liked that very much. Oh, the body I had then. So much more I could have done with it!

I will tell you now about Lyoto. He is a name trawled up from deep – do you know what trawling is? I sometimes forget that there are old world words and ideas the new generations have no reference for. Animal similes – my grandchildren just frown. Luna has never seen a cow, or a pig, or even a chicken, alive and clucking.

Lyoto. I can't see him clearly any more, but I remember his voice. He had a southern accent – he was from Curitiba. I think he was my first love. Oh, you smile. I didn't flirt with him, tease him, seduce him, play sexy games with him so it must have been love. I met him on the jiu jitsu team. Sports teams, they're all sex sex sex; everyone is doing it all the time. We were at a competition – I was on the women's team, Light class, Purple belt. He was Heavy, Black Fifth. I remember his weight and his belt, but not his face.

Papai would borrow the flashiest Mercedes from the showroom and drive to home competitions. It was a long drive but he enjoyed it. Afterwards he would drive me through Jardins and take me out to dinner somewhere expensive. I would step out of that big car and feel like a millionaire.

Then one time he drove up and I didn't get in the car and go with him. I wanted to go drinking beer with Lyoto and then on to a party. I remember the sad look on Papai's face that we wouldn't be driving down Rua Barão de Capanema again checking off the menus on the car screen. I think I made him feel like a millionaire too. He still came to the tournaments, right up until I went to Ouro Preto for post-grad. It was too far for him to drive and I was losing interest in the fighting by then. Year after year, tumbling about on a mat, to advance by a Dan here, a belt there.

Lyoto had been dead two years by then. We had been lovers for over a year. I wasn't there when he was shot down in the Praça da Sé. I was working on a term paper when the word came. I never was the political one. I was an engineer, he was a literature student. An activist. I was just a natural capitalist who had never taken a position because I had never really thought about politics, he told me. I had pragmatism. He had theory. I could never debate with him because he had everything thought out; argument after argument like a colonial army. When one line fell, the next would advance, firing. The world order was rotten. Diseased with social injustice, racism, sexism, inequality and bad gender politics. I thought that was just the natural state of Brazil. But even I could see the number of helicopters that flew over USP campus increasing every day: the limousines of the hyper-rich, the people who lived up there among the tower-tops and never touched the ground. The changes fell like micro-meteors, like hundreds of tiny impacts. The bus and metro fares going up again. My friends tagging their bicycles, because theft was going up, because fares were going up. Shops buying full shutters because more people were sleeping in shop porches. More cameras on the streets, because of the street sleepers. Surveillance drones. In São Paulo! Maybe in some European state, or the Gulf, but it is not the Brazilian way. Where there are drones, there will always be police. Where there are police, there will always be violence. And every day the price of bread went up, up, up. If there is one thing that will bring people on to the streets, it's the price of bread.

Lyoto was committed. He went down to Praça da Sé and painted placards and occupied spaces. He thought I was uncaring. I was caring, but not about people I didn't know. Not about Chinese companies buying up whole provinces and driving people off the land. Not about refugees from the country, who even favelados looked down on. I could only care about what I knew. My family, my friends, the family I would have some day. Family first, family always.

I was scared for him. I watched Youtube. I could see how the protests were escalating. Shouting to stones to petrol bombs. Each step the police responded: riot shields to tear gas to guns. I told him I didn't like him going down there. I told him he could get arrested, or go to jail and get his CPF pulled and he could never get credit or a proper job. I told him that he cared more about strangers than he did about people who cared for him. About me. We split up for a while. We still had sex. No one ever really splits up.

At first I didn't know what had happened. All at once a dozen messages came up. OMG. Police shooting. People shot. Shots fired. Lyoto wounded, Lyoto okay, Lyoto shot. Messages coming in, one on top of the other. There was jerky camera feed: a body dragged into a shop door. Then sirens, ambulances arriving. All jerky, all shaking. Nothing in focus. In the distance, gunshots. Have you ever heard gunshots? I suppose not. No guns on the moon. They sound small and mean. All this information bombarding me, but I couldn't pick the truth out of it. I tried calling him. No signal. Then the rumours started to coalesce. Lyoto had been shot. He had been taken to hospital. Which hospital? Can you imagine how helpless I felt? I called round everyone I knew who knew Lyoto, who knew any of his activist friends. Hospital Sírio-Libanês. I stole a bicycle. It took me seconds to hack the tracking chip. I rode like a madwoman through São Paulo traffic. They wouldn't let me see him. I waited in the emergency room – there were police everywhere, and news cameras. I said nothing and sat at the back. The police would have asked me questions, then the news people. I listened and listened but I couldn't hear anything about how he was. Then his family came. I had never met them, I didn't even know he had a family but I could see at once who they were. I waited and waited, trying to overhear.

Then the word came that he had died in the emergency room. The family were devastated. The hospital staff kept the police away. The news people got all the right shots. There was nothing to be done. Nothing to be taken back. Death keeps everything. I crept away on my stolen bike.

Lyoto died, and five others. He wasn't the first to be shot, so no one remembered his name. No one sprayed it on walls and buses: remember Lyoto Matsushita. No one remembers the second man on the moon. I remember I was shocked; numb; terrified, but my chief emotion was anger. I was angry that he thought so little of me to put himself in danger of death. I was angry that he died in such a stupid way. I remember the anger, but I can't feel the sickness, the set of the muscles, the pressure behind the eyes, the feeling of dying inside over and over again. I'm old. I'm a long way from that engineering student at USP. Does anger have a half-life?

I wonder, if he had lived, what Lyoto would have thought of me? I'm rich and I'm powerful. With a word I can switch off every light on Earth and plunge the planet into darkness and winter. I'm not even the one per cent; I'm the one per cent of the one per cent; the ones who left Earth.

Within a week we had forgotten about Lyoto Matsushita, the second martyr. There were new riots, new deaths. The government made promises and broke them all. Then came the first of a series of crashes, each one bringing the country and economy lower until it hit the ground and broke beyond any repair.

I didn't know then that Lyoto was one of the first casualties in the class war. The great class war; final class war: the hollowing out of the middle class. The financialised economy didn't need workers and mechanisation was driving the middle classes into a race to the bottom. If a robot could do it acceptably and cheaper, the robot got your job. The machines made you bid against them. The machines even supplied the apps you used to bid against them and against each other. If you were cheaper than a machine, you ate. Just. We always thought the robot apocalypse would be fleets of killer drones and war mecha the size of apartment blocks and terminators with red eyes. Not a row of mechanised checkouts in the local Extra and the alco station; online banking; self-driving taxis; an automated triage system in the hospital. One by one, the bots came and replaced us.

And here we are, in the most machine-dependent society humanity has ever produced. I've grown rich, I've built a dynasty on those very robots that beggared Earth.

My father didn't remember the North Americans landing on the moon, but he told me old Mão de Ferro did. He was drinking in a bar in Belo Horizonte. The television was switched to the football and Mão de Ferro almost started a fight insisting the bar owner switch over to the moon landing. This is history, he said. We won't see a greater thing on our time. Faked, the others in the bar shouted. Shot on a Hollywood sound stage. But he stood in front of the television, staring up at the black and images, daring anyone to turn it back to the football. And I remember when the Mackenzies put robots on the moon. I too was in a bar, with my study group. I had gone back to the homeland, to Minas Gerais, and DEMIN, the mining institute, for post-grad. I was even more of an oddity in Ouro Preto. No: I was unique. I was the only woman. The men were over-polite and clubbish. I would not let them leave me out, so I was drinking beer with them in that bar. The bar owner was flicking between sports channels when he dropped for a moment on to the news. I saw the moon, I saw machines, I saw wheel tracks. I shouted at the bar man – hey hey hey, leave it. I was the only person in that bar watching the screen, watching history happening. The Australian Mackenzie Mining Corporation had sent robots to the moon to prospect for rare earth metals for the IT industry. Why aren't you watching this? I wanted to to shout to my group. Why can't you see what I see? Call yourself engineers? Watching that screen I felt a flash of understanding, a brilliance in my head. I felt as if my breath were catching, as if my heart were skipping every third, fourth beat. It was feeling of the impossible becoming not just possible, but achievable. By me. Then the news item moved on – it was far down the news, no one was interested in space and science. News was what telenovella stars and models did. I went out of the bar into the beer garden and sat on the wall under the dusty trees and looked up into the night. I saw the moon. I said to myself, there are things up there, making money.

My father came to see me. He came on the bus. I knew instantly the news was bad. Ouro Preto was a long way but my father would have made an adventure out of the drive. He had lost the dealership. No one was buying high-end Mercedes any more, not even in Barra. He'd been careful: bought out the apartment and my education was safe. As long I delivered in the next two years and did not fill the fridge with beer on a weekly basis. But the business was over and at his age there was no hope of him re-skilling for the machine-code economy, let alone finding another job. He was sorry yet proud – he had done everything he could the best he could. The markets had failed him.

Then Our Lady of Tuberculosis came and knocked his plans off the table. Caio, boy-baby; kid brother. Caizinho: the runt of the litter we called him. He had never moved out, perpetually thirteen years old it seemed. As jobs collapsed and marriages failed and families imploded, the rest of Mamãe Corta's seven babies moved back in. All but me. The learner, the keeper. Then Caio breathed in bacillus of TDR-tuberculosis – a bus, a classroom, mass. There were three types of tuberculosis then. MDR, XDR, TDR. Multiply Drug Resistant, Extensively Drug Resistant, Totally Drug Resistant. MDR resists the first-line antibiotics. XDR resists even the second-line drugs, which are basically toxic chemotherapy treatments. TDR: you can guess that. The White Lady we called it, and she wafted into Caio's lungs and grew there.

Mamãe turned a room into a sanatorium; sealed it up with plastic. Papa engineered an air-conditioning unit. They couldn't afford the hospital, they couldn't afford the drugs. They bought experimental treatments on the black market – experimental Russian phages; chemo-hecked generic pharmaceuticals. I came home. I saw Caio through plastic. It wasn't safe to go into the room. Mãe slid his meals in on trays my siblings stole from McDonalds, in through two layers of heavy plastic. Caio double-bagged the refuse. I saw him, I saw Pai tired to the marrow, I saw Mãe talking to her saints and orixas. I saw my brothers and sisters and their children scraping a réal where they could: scrap dealing here, buying and selling there, running an animal lottery there. Caio would die but I couldn't begrudge my family saving every centavo in hope. They could not afford my completing my post-grad. There was a way I could finish. The advertisements had been appearing in the professional journals and sites, within weeks of the Mackenzie landing.

I applied to work on the moon.

My adviser of studies helped me with the loan application. My paper on solar distillation of rare earth elements from lunar regolith marked me as a valuable asset in lunar development. I got a contract with Mackenzie Metals. My application was approved, I got the loan.

I went home that weekend. I could afford to fly. I went down to Barra and I saw the grass sprouting through the Niemeyer cobbles. Shrubs had taken root on apartment rooftops and empty windows. Avenida Sernambetida was lined with stalls and shelters and every apartment block was webbed in water pipes and electricity cables like strangling figs. Every traffic circle held a cluster of water tanks and solar panels. The football stadium, the Olympic park, the uprooted seating, roofs half missing since the last storm. The city was failing. The planet was failing.

The apartment was crammed full of people but I was given my own room. Caio was still in his plastic cave. He was on oxygen now. Caio and I, in our chambers: the dying prince and the homecoming princess. Television day and night, people coming and going day and night, husbands and wives and partners and their relatives, family members who were not family members. And my mamãe, so big she could only waddle, ruling them all with her shout. I went out on to the balcony that night and I saw the moon. Yemanja, my goddess: only she was not forming out of the sea; she was far beyond the world, and the world was turning to her. The world was turning and bringing me under her gaze, and all the water in the ocean was drawn to her. And me with it. Oh, me with it.

I loved training for the moon. I ran, I swam, I did weights and cross. I was lean and purposeful and so so fit. I adored my muscles. I think I was very much in love with myself. I was not just the Iron Hand, I was the Iron Woman.

The South American training centre was in Guiana, near the ESA launch facility. Out running, I would hear the roar of the Orbital Transfer Vehicle engines powering up. They shook me until I couldn't hear. They shook Earth and Heaven. Then I saw the vapour trail, curving upwards and the tiny dark needle of the spaceplane at its tip, powering up. Up, away from the world. It made me cry. Every time.

The thing about training for the moon: you aren't training for the moon. You're training for launch. The moon had no need for my fantastic body. The moon would eat it, slowly. The moon would change me to itself.

I wasn't the only woman, but almost. The Korou facility was DEMIN, on steroids. The moon would be like a giant college football team, in space. I realised that the moon was not a safe place. It knew a thousand ways to kill you if you were stupid, if you were careless, if you were lazy, but the real danger was the people around you. The moon was not a world, it was a submarine. Outside was death. I would be sealed in with these people. There was no law, no justice: there was only management. The moon was the frontier, but it was the frontier to nothing. There was nowhere to run.

It took three months to make me ready for the moon. Centrifuge training, freefall training – up in an ancient A319 over the South

Atlantic and me throwing up every single time we went into the dive. And the suit training – the suits were huge clunking things compared to the sasuits we have now: try threading screws in those gauntlets! I was good at it. Good fine motor skills. Low pressure training, zero-pressure training. Low-gee manufacturing, vacuum manufacturing, robotics and 3D-print coding. Three months! Three years wouldn't have been enough. Three lifetimes.

And then it was three weeks to launch day. I went back home. Papa threw a party on the roof. He always leaped at any chance to hold a churrasceria. Everyone told me how hot I looked. It was a great party, joy shot through with saudade. It was a wake for the dead. Everyone knew I would never come back.

Caio died three days before launch. And my thought wasn't loss or grief. My thought was, why couldn't you have waited? A week, even five days? Why did you have to give me something to feel, when all my feeling is taken up by that big moon up there, and that star in the morning sky that grows a little brighter every day – the cycler, approaching Earth – and most immediately, that black bird waiting to roll out from Hangar 6 on to the strip.

So anger, then guilt. I asked for compassionate leave. I was refused. I couldn't risk infection so close to launch day. Any bug would rip through the confined spaces of the cycler and the facility. The moon was an enormous clean room. We were checked daily for viral infections, parasites, insects. No vermin on the moon.

So they burned Caio to kill the White Lady as I was driven out in the pressurised bus to the spaceplane. We had practised embarkation a dozen times in the hangar, but we still pressed to the darkened windows for our first glimpse of the OTV, black and glinting naked under the sun. The sense of power, of human ability, was so strong. Many of the men cried. Men are so easily moved.

We strapped in, suited and helmeted, no windows, the screens off. We had done it twenty times before but I still fumbled with the straps, the safety checklist. I wasn't ready. No one could be, for a thing like this. I couldn't stop thinking about the hydrogen tanks before and behind me, the oxygen tank under my feet. I was rigid with fear. Then I found there was a place beyond that fear – not calm, not beautiful, nor resigned or helpless, but firm and resolute.

Then the OTV rolled out and it went cunk cunk cunk over the strip where its tyres had developed flat spots from the standing. Fifty years and I remember it all so clearly. I felt us turn on to the strip, I felt the spaceplane pause, then the engines fire. Oh my! The power! You won't have felt anything like it, not even if you've gone by the BALTRAN. It's like every part of you, yelling. And I found out what was beyond the resolution beyond the fear. Excitement. Pure excitement. This was the sexiest thing I had ever done.

The engines cut out. A slight shock: the payload pod had unlatched. We were in free fall. I felt my stomach begin to unravel, the acid bile burning up my throat. Vomiting in your helmet is not just vile. It can drown you. Then I felt centrifugal force tug at the base of my stomach and I knew the tether had us and was swinging us up into a transfer orbit to the cycler. The gees peaked, the blood rushed to my toes. Freefall again. The next touch of weight I would feel would be in the centrifuge arms of the cycler.

A judder. A lurch, loud clunks and clangs and servo whine. We had docked with the cycler. Our belts released. I pushed myself free towards the open lock. It looked far too small even for small me. But I was through, we were all through, all twenty-four of us.

I stayed a time in the lock, clinging to a stanchion, fighting nausea, looking through a tiny window at the spaceplane hanging against the huge blue Earth. It was too big, too close to reveal the movement of the cycler, rushing away from it. But I felt it. I was out on the moon path, me: Adriana Maria do Céu Mão de Ferro Arena de Corta.

FOUR

Two kisses for Adriana Corta, one for each cheek. A small gift, wrapped in Japanese print paper, soft as fabric.

'What is it?'

Lucas loves to bring his mother gifts when he visits. He is assiduous: at least once a week he takes the tram to Boa Vista and meets his mother in the Santa Barbra pavilion.

'Open it,' Lucas Corta says.

He sees delight dawn across his mother's face as she carefully unwraps the paper and catches the tell-tale perfume of the gift. He loves the management of emotion.

'Oh Lucas, you shouldn't have. It's so expensive.'

Adriana Corta opens the tiny jar and breathes in the full aroma of the coffee. Lucas sees years and hundreds of thousands of kilometres roll across her face.

'I'm afraid it's not Brazilian.' Coffee is more expensive than gold. Gold is cheap on the moon, valued only for its beauty. Coffee is more precious than alkaloids and diamorphines. Printers can synthesise narcotics; no printer has ever produced a coffee that tasted of anything other than shit. Lucas doesn't have the taste for coffee – too bitter, and it is a liar. It never tastes the way it smells.

'I will keep it,' Adriana says, closing the jar and for a moment pressing it to her heart. 'Something special. I'll know the time. Thank you, Lucas. Have you called Amanda?'

'I thought I might pass on it this time.'

Adriana passes no comment, not even a look. Lucas's marriage to Amanda Sun has been etiquette for years now.

'And Lucasinho?'

'I cut off his money. I think Ariel gave him some. Dirty cash. What does it say about the family?'

'Let him have his head.'

'At some point the boy will have to take some responsibility.'

'He's seventeen. When I was that age I was running around with every boy and girl I could lay my hands on. He needs to run wild. By all means cut his money off – it's good for him to live on his wits. It showed initiative, that trick with the escape suit.'

'Wits? He's not been graced with many of those. He takes after his mother.'

'Lucas!'

Lucas winces at the rebuke.

'Amanda is still family. We don't put the bad mouth on family. And you have no right to be displeased with Ariel. Her seat in the White Hare isn't even warm, and you're compromising her position.'

'We got the Chinese deal. We beat out the Mackenzies.'

'I enjoyed that very much, Lucas. The handball shirts were a nice touch. We're indebted to you. But sometimes there are bigger issues than family.'

'Not to me, Mamãe. Never to me.'

'You're your father's son, Lucas. Your father's true son.'

Lucas accepts the praise, though to him it is bitter, like coffee. His father he has never known. He has only ever wanted to be his mother's son.

'Mamãe, can I speak in confidence?'

'Of course, Lucas.'

'I'm worried about Rafa.'

'I wish Rachel hadn't taken Robson to Crucible. And so soon after the assassination attempt. One could mistake it for conspiracy.'

'Rafa's convinced it is.'

Adriana purses her lips, shakes her head in frustration.

'Oh come now, Lucas.'

'He sees the Mackenzies' hand in everything. Rafa's said this to me. You know Rafa: good old Rafa, fun Rafa, party-boy Rafa. Who else might he say it to in an unguarded moment? Can you see the danger to the company?'

'Robert Mackenzie will want payback for losing the Chinese deal.'

'Of course. We'd do exactly the same. But Rafa will see it as another piece of Robert Mackenzie's personal vendetta.'

'What are you asking for, Lucas?'

'Cooler heads, Mamãe. That's all.'

'Do you mean, Lucas Corta's head?'

'Rafa is bu-hwaejang, I have no disagreement with that. I wouldn't want any diminution of his prestige. But maybe delegate some responsibilities?'

'Go on.'

'He's the face of Corta Hélio. Let him be the face. Let him be the figurehead. Let him take the meetings and the pitches. Let him continue to sit in that chair at the head of the board table. Just, very subtly, move him out of making the decisions for the company.'

'What do you want, Lucas?'

'Only the best for the company, Mamãe. Only the best for the family.'

Lucas Corta kisses his mother goodbye: twice, for family. Once on each cheek.

Twenty kilometres downline from Crucible, Robson Corta-Mackenzie's familiar wakes him with a song in his ear. The boy runs to the observation blister at the front of the car and presses his hands against the glass. To an eleven-year-old, the first glimpse of the capital of the Mackenzies never ages. The railcar is a Mackenzie Metals private shuttle, running out across the Ocean of Storms on the slow east line of Equatorial One: six sets of three-metre wide track; pure and shining with reflected Earth light, reaching out around the shoulder of the world, all the way around the world. A fast express, inbound from Jinzhong, seemingly leaps out of nowhere and is gone in a blur of light. Rachel finds the view from the front end of the shuttle nerve-wracking. The boy loves it.

'Look, a Ghan-class hauler,' Robson says as the rail car skims along the flank of the long, ponderous freight train on the slow up-line. It's quickly forgotten for, on the eastern horizon, a second sun is rising; a dot of light so brilliant and piercing that the glass darkens to protect human eyes. The dot expands into a ball, hovering like a mirage on the edge of the world, never seeming to grow closer or brighter.

We will be arriving at Crucible in five minutes, the familiars announce.

Rachel Corta shields her eyes. She has seen this trick many times: the dot will dance and dazzle, then at the last instant, resolve into detail. It never fails to awe. The dazzle fills the entire observation bubble, then the rail car moves into the shadow of Crucible.

Crucible straddles the four inner tracks of Equatorial One. The bogies run on two separate outer tracks; old-fashioned steel, not maglev. The living modules hang twenty metres above the line, studded with windows and lights, casting perpetual shadow on the track beneath. Above them are the separators, the graders, the smelters; higher than all of them, parabolic mirrors focus sunlight into the converters. Crucible is a train ten kilometres long, straddling Equatorial One. Passenger expresses, freighters, repair cars run under and through it as if it's the superstructure of a colossal bridge. Forever moving at an inexorable ten kilometres per hour, it completes one orbit in one lunar day. The sun stands at permanent noon above its mirrors and smelters. The Suns call their glass spire on the top of Malapert Mountain the Tower of Eternal Light. The

Mackenzies scorn their affectations. They are the dwellers in endless light. Light bathes them, soaks them, enriches them; leaches and bleaches them. Born without shadows, the Mackenzies have taken darkness inside them.

The rail car passes under the lip of Crucible into shadows and spotlights. Half-seen highlights become a freighter, disgorging regolith through a battery of Archimedes screws. The rail car slows: train and Crucible AIs exchange protocols. This is the bit Robson likes best. Grapples lock on to the railcar and lift it from the line to dock into a slot in the rack of MacKenzie Metals rail shuttles. Hatches meet, pressure equalises.

Welcome home, Robson Mackenzie.

Blades of light stab down through the roof slots, so bright they seem solid. The approach to the heart of the Crucible is guarded by a palisade of light; shards from the mirrors that focus the sun on the smelters. A thousand times Rachel has made the progress down the hall and every time she feels the weight and heat of thousands of tons of molten metal above her head. It is danger, it is wealth, and it is security. The molten metal is Crucible's only shield from the punishing radiation. It's a constant awareness for the people of Crucible: the molten metals above their heads, like a steel plate in a fractured skull. Balanced, precarious. One day a system may fail, the metal will fall, but not this day, in her days, in her life.

Robson runs ahead of her. He's seen Hadley Mackenzie at the lock to the next compartment, his favourite uncle, though only eight years separate them. Hadley is the son of patriarch Robert from his winter marriage to Jade Sun. An uncle then, but more like an older brother. Only sons are born to Robert Mackenzie. *It's the Man in the Moon*, the old monster still jokes. Through selective abortion, embryo mapping, chromosome engineering the joke has become a truth. Hadley scoops Robson up into the air. The boy flies high, laughing and Hadley Mackenzie's strong arms catch him.

'Result with the Brazilian then,' Hadley says. He kisses his step-niece on each cheek.

'I really think he's the child,' Rachel Mackenzie says.

'I hate the thought of Robbo growing up there,' Hadley says. He's short, wire and steel, knots of wrought muscle and sinew. Blade of the Mackenzies; deeply freckled from sessions in sun-rooms. Spots upon spots; a leopard of a man. He picks and scratches constantly at his pelt. Too long under the sun-lamps, working on his vitamin D. 'That's no place for a kid to learn how to live right.'

Message from Robert Mackenzie, announces Cameny, Rachel's familiar. Hadley and Robson's expressions tell Rachel that they are receiving the same communication. 'Rachel, my love. I'm glad you've brought Robson home safe. Delighted. Come and see me.' The voice is soft, still accented with Western Australian, and unreal. Robert Mackenzie hasn't sounded like that longer than any of the three people in the lobby have been alive. The image in the lenses isn't Robert Mackenzie, but his familiar: Red Dog, the symbol of the town that birthed his ambition.

'I'll take you up to him,' Hadley says.

A capsule takes Rachel, Robson and Hadley to the head of Crucible; ten kilometres upline. The maglev drive of the capsule seems to Rachel to amplify the gentle but ever-present tremor of movement. The slow rock of the Crucible on its tracks is the heartbeat of home. Rachel Mackenzie was a reading child, and on those screens, among those worlds built of words, she sailed oceans of water with dire pirates and swashbucklers. In her world of stone seas, this is the closest she can imagine to being on a sailing ship.

The capsule decelerates abruptly and docks. The lock opens. Rachel breathes green and rot, humidity and chlorophyll. This carriage is a great glass conservatory. Under constant sunlight and low lunar gravity, ferns grow to stupendous heights; a green vault of fronds against the curved ribs of the greenhouse. Dappled light, tiger-stripe light: the sun stands unmoving, a hair off the zenith. The ferns all lean towards it. Among the ferns, bird-calls and bright flickers of plumage. Something is whooping somewhere. This is a paradise garden but Robson takes his mother's hand. Bob Mackenzie dwells here.

A path winds between pools and softly gurgling streams.

'Rachel. Darling!'

Jade Sun-Mackenzie greets her step-granddaughter with two kisses. The same for Robson. She is tall, long-fingered, elegant and delicate as the fronds around her. She looks not a day older than the one on which she married Robert Mackenzie, nineteen years ago. None of Robert Mackenzie's offspring are deceived by her appearance. She's wire and thorn and tight, sinewy will. 'He can't wait to see you.'

Robson's hand tightens on his mother's.

'He's been in a foul mood since the Cortas stole that Chinese output deal,' Jade throws over her shoulder. She sees Robson glance up at at his mother. 'But you'll sweeten it.'

Robert Mackenzie waits in a belvedere shaped from woven ferns. Budgerigars and parakeets keep up an insane gossip of chirps and whistles. Robot butterflies flap lazily on wide iridescent polymer wings.

The legend is that the chair keeps Robert Mackenzie alive but one look tells the truth: it is the will that burns in the back of his eyes. Will to power, will to own, will to hold and let nothing be taken, not even his husk of a life. Robert Mackenzie stares down death. The life-support system towers over his head like a crown, a halo. Tubes pulse, pumps hiss and spin, motors hum. The backs of his hands are blotched with slow-healing haemotomas where needles and cannulas pierce the flesh. No one can bear to look more than an instant at the tube in his throat. The perfume of fern, the smell of fresh water, can't hide the smell. Rachel Mackenzie's stomach lifts at the taint of colostomy.

'My darling.'

Rachel bends to kiss the sunken cheeks. Robert Mackenzie would notice any hesitation or revulsion.

'Robson.' He opens his arms to embrace. Robson steps forward and lets the arms enfold him. A kiss from the hideous old mummy, on both cheeks. Robert Mackenzie was forty-eight years old when he chose Mare Insularum over Western Australia and committed family and future to the moon. Too old to go to the moon. He would never survive the lift to orbit, let alone the slow gnaw of low gravity on his bones and blood vessels and lungs, the steady sleet of radiation. Leave it to the kids and the robots. Robert Mackenzie came and sunk the foundations of the moon's million-strong society. This thing in the life-support chair can rightly claim to be the Man in the Moon. One hundred and three years old, a dozen medical AIs monitor and maintain his body, but its fuel is the same will in his pale blue eyes.

'You're a good kid, Robson,' Robert Mackenzie breathes in the boy's ear. 'A good kid. It's good to have you back where you belong, away from those Corta thieves.' The papery claw hands shake the boy. 'Welcome home.' Robson tears himself free from the frail claws. 'They won't steal you back.'

'My husband has been thinking,' says Jade Sun. She stands behind him, one hand on the old man's shoulder. The hand is slim, refined, nails lacquered, but Robert Mackenzie seems to sag under its tiny weight. 'Is there any reason why Robson shouldn't be married?'

Hi Mom, hi Kessie. Kids, if you see this, hi. I've been kind of quiet for a while. I have an excuse. So: as I said in my really rushed mail, I am working for the Dragons. Corta Hélio. The helium-3 miners.

I'm working for Corta Hélio. I just thought I'd say that again so you can appreciate it. What it means right up front is, no more worrying about oxygen or water or carbon or network, which is why I can send you this. I don't think I can make you understand how it feels not to have to worry about the Four Elementals again. It's like winning a lotteria, where you get to keep breathing rather than winning ten million dollars.

I can't tell you too much about how I got the job – it's a security thing: the Five Dragons are like the Mafia, always at each other's throats. But I can say that I am under the personal watch of Carlinhos Corta. Kessie, sister. You should emigrate. This rock is full of hot bodies.

I'm in a surface activity induction squad. Moon-walking. There's a lot to learn. The moon knows a thousand ways to kill you. That's rule one and it rules everything. There are ways of moving, reading signs and signals, being in or out of communications, analysing data from your suit and you need to know them or the one tiny thing you've overlooked will cook you or freeze you or asphyxiate you or shoot you full of radiation. We spent three whole days on dust. There are fifteen kinds of dust and you need to know the physical properties of each one from abrasion to electrostatic properties to adhesion. Like Sherlock Holmes learning his fifty types of cigar ash? There's battery recharge times, lunar navigation – Jo Moonbeams misjudge the horizon and think everything is much further away than it is. And they haven't even taken us up on the surface yet. And the sasuits. I know they're meant to be tight, but are they sure they've got the size right? Took me ten minutes to get into the thing. Wouldn't want to do that in a depressurisation. Put it on wrong and you get bruising where the seams pinch. Mind, if the environment deepees, bruising is the least of your worries.

I'm probably scaring you to death. But you get used to it. No one could live with that level of constant dread. But if you ever once get sloppy, it will have no mercy. Carlinhos tells me we usually have at least one death each induction squad. I'm being extra careful that it's not me.

My squad: Oleg, José, Saadia, Thandeka, Patience and me. I'm the only Norte. They look at me. They would say things about me but the only common language is Globo and I'm a native anglophone. They

95

don't like me. Carlinhos works more or less one to one with me and that makes me different. The special one. So the trainers think I'm a Corta spy and class thinks I'm teacher's pet. The one who dislikes me least is Patience. She's originally from Botswana but, like the rest of the squad, she's been in universities and corporations all over the worlds. Jo Moonbeams must be the most educated immigrants in history. Patience will talk to me and share tea. José wants me dead. If he could engineer it without him getting caught I think he might. He interrupts everything I have to say. I can't work out if it's because I'm a woman or a North American. Probably both. Asshole. The squad mentality is like a college football team. Everything in your face in your face in your face. Every breath you taste testosterone. It's not just because it's extractive industries; everyone is young, smart, ambitious and very very motivated. At the same time, this is the most sexually liberal society that has ever existed. Lunar Globo doesn't even have words for straight or gay. Everyone is on the spectrum somewhere.

I'll tell you what's hard. Learning Portuguese. What kind of language is this? You have to make yourself sound like you have a permanent head-cold. Nothing sounds the way it spells. At least Portuguese reads logically. But the pronunciation . . . There is Portuguese pronunciation, and then there is Brazilian Portuguese pronunciation. And then there is Rio Brazilian Pronunciation. And last of all there is the Lunar Variant Rio Brazilian Portuguese pronunciation; and that's what Corta Hélio speaks. I suggested Hetty translates everything: the looks I got. So, it's time to learn Portuguese. Which means, adeus, eu te amo, e eu vou falar com você de novo em breve!

Lucas Corta spirals down as light and fragile as a dream through pillars of leaves. Water drips and runs, trickles and riffles, through the runnels and pipes that connect the tiers of grow-tanks. He spirals around the central column of mirrors, reflecting sunlight on to the stacks. Glances up: the green goes up forever until it merges with the blinding sun-coin of the farm cylinder cap. The agriculture shaft is a kilometre deep. The Obuasi agrarium contains five such shafts, and Twé lies at the centre of a pentagram of seventy-five such agraria. Lettuces, salad vegetables, packed so tight a beetle could not crawl between them. If there were beetles on the moon but there are none, nor aphids, nor chewing caterpillars: no insect pests. Potato plants the size of trees; climbing beans reach a hundred metres up the support lattices. The fronds of root vegetables; verdant banks of calaloo and aki. Yams and sweet potatoes; gourds and cucurbits: pumpkins the size of Meridian motos. All nurtured by the run and trickle of nutritionally enriched water, crossplanted and symbiotically managed in self-sustaining micro-ecosystems. Obuasi has never lost a harvest, and it crops four times a year. Now Lucas looks down. Far below, on the catwalks over the fish tanks, are two insect-figures. Ducks gabble, frogs belch. One of those tiny figures is him.

'The audio quality is extraordinary,' he says, blinking out of the vision on his lens.

'Thank you,' says Kobby Asamoah. He is a vast man, tall and broad. Lucas Corta is a pale shadow next to him. He lifts a hand and the fly lands on it.

'May I?'

A thought sends the fly from Kobby Asamoah's hand to Lucas's. He lifts it to eye-level.

'You could kill us all in our sleep. I like it.' Lucas Corta throws the fly up into the air and watches it climb up the shaft of light and green and dank chlorophyll until it is lost to vision. 'I'll buy it.'

'Unit life is three days,' Kobby Asamoah says.

'I'll need thirty.'

'We can deliver ten and print the rest up.'

'Deal.'

Toquinho takes the price from Kobby Asamoah's familiar and flashes it up on Lucas's lens. It is quite obscene.

'Authorise payment,' Lucas orders.

'We'll have them for you at the station,' Kobby Asamoah says. His big, wide open face works again. 'With respect, Mr Corta, isn't it a rather excessive way to keep an eye on your son?'

Lucas Corta laughs aloud. Lucas Corta's laugh is deep, resonant, like chiming music. It quite startles Kobby Asamoah. The ducks and frogs of Obuasi agrarium tubefarm five fall silent.

'Who says it's for my son?'

Heitor Pereira lets the fly run over his hand, tiny hooked feet tickling his dark, wrinkled skin. Whichever way he turns the hand, the Asamoah fly stays uppermost.

Lucas says, 'I want twenty-four-hour surveillance.'

'Of course, Senhor. Who is the target?'

'My brother.'

'Carlinhos?'

'Rafael.'

'Very good, Senhor.'

'I want to know when my brother fucks, farts or finances. Everything. My mother is not to know. No one is to know, except you and me.'

'Very good, Senhor.'

'Toquinho will send you the protocols. I want you to handle it personally. No one else. I want daily reports, encrypted, to Toquinho.'

Lucas reads the distaste on Heitor Pereira's face. He is a former Brazilian naval officer, cashiered when Brazil privatised its defence forces. He fell from grace with the sea and left it for the moon where, like so many ex-military, he set up a private security company. Those days when Adriana was tearing Corta Hélio from the ribcage of Mackenzie Metals were bloody days, of claim jumping and duels of honour and faction fights, when legal disputes were more quickly and economically ended with a knife in the dark. Lives pressed up close against each other, breathing each other's air. Heitor Pereira has stopped many a blade for Adriana Corta. His loyalty, his bravery and honour are beyond question. They are just irrelevant. Corta Hélio has moved around him. But the loathing Lucas sees is not for that, not even the surveillance fly. Heitor hates that his lapse at the moon-run party has led him into a yoke and harness. Lucas can ask anything of him, forever more.

'And Heitor?'

'Senhor?'

'Don't fail me.'

An archipelago of dried semen lies across the perfect hollow of Lucasinho Corta's left ass cheek. He gently lifts Grigori Vorontsov's arm and slides out from the boy's embrace. He stretches, tightens muscles, cracks joints. The Vorontsov kid is heavy. And demanding. Five times he had been tottering on the edge of sleep when he felt the prickle of beard against his cheek, the whisper in his ear – *hey, hey* – the throb of hardening penis against his inner thigh.

Lucasinho has always known that Grigori is hot for him – mad hot, Afua in the study group had said, in one of those girls' games where you are never told the rules but are punished horribly if you break them – but not that he was such a consummate fucker. He could fuck for hours. Steady, deep, hard. A relentless fucker. And generous with the reach-round. He had hardly been able even to moan. Who would have known the passion inside the guy across the table, when they met up at their weekly in-person colloquium seminars? It was great, tremendous, the best sex he has ever had with a boy, but no more now, right? No more.

For such as Lucasinho Corta has received, what shall he give? Cake. Since his father cut him off he has little else to give. While Grigori snores Lucasinho searches the cooler. Almost as bare as Ariel's, but there's enough to bake up a batch of flourless brownies. Two batches. Lucasinho is thinking of his next bed. He can't stay another night in this one. He can't take it. Lucasinho drips a little of Grigori's stash of THC juice into the mix. They had vaped it last night, sprawled across each other on the couch, sharing smokes and kisses. He glances back at Grigori spread like a star across the bed. So hairy. They say that about the Vorontsovs. Hairy and weird. Touched by space. Lucasinho knows the legends. House Vorontsov descends from Valery, the original patriarch, an oligarch who invested in a private launch facility in Central Asia. Wherever that is. They built the orbital tethers, the two cyclers that loop constantly in a figure of eight between moon and Earth; the BALTRAN, the rail network. Space has changed them. They have bred strange: weird, elongated things born to freefall. No one has seen a cycler crewperson for years. They can never come down. Gravity would crush them like decorative butterflies. But none so strange as Valery himself – still alive, a monster grown so huge, so bloated that he fills all the core of a cycler. The legends can never agree whether it's *Sts Peter and Paul* or *Alexander Nevsky*. That's how you know it's true. Stories are always too neat.

Lucasinho waves his hand over the cooker panel to clear the glass, peers in at his batches. He glances anxiously at Grigori. This is not the time for the beast to wake. A few minutes more. And out and cooling. Lucasinho feels the shadow on his skin before the press of Grigori's hair and muscles.

'Hey.'

'Hey.'

'What are you doing?'

'Baking.'

'What, like?'

'Brownies. They're good. They've got hash in them.'

'Do you always bake like this?'

'Like what?'

'Like no clothes.'

'It connects me.'

'I think it's hot.'

Lucasinho's heart sinks. Grigori is close and tight against him, getting hard. Is this boy made of cum? Lucasinho picks of a crumb of cooling brownie and turns to slip it between Grigori's lips.

'Sweet.'

Then they go back to it again.

Marina has a balcony. It's small but quite addictive. At the end of each day she returns from her training group bone-weary and aching from the new things her body must learn for Corta Hélio and goes to her balcony.

The apartment Corta Hélio has assigned her is on the West 23rd of Santa Barbra Quadra so the drop from the balcony to the street, while not as high as the one from Bairro Alto to Gagarin Prospekt, is an overhang. The vertigo attracts her. And the sounds. João de Deus's Portuguese-speaking streets have a different timbre from Meridian. Shouts and greetings; the look-at-me cries of teenagers, the voices of children buzzing up and down Kondakova Prospekt on big-tyred tri-cycles. Different voices. The hum of the moto engines, the elevators, the escalators and moving walkways, the airplant; different noises. The light of the skyline is brighter, the spectrum more yellow than Meridian. The colours of the neons cluster around blue green and gold, the colours of Old Brasil. The names, the words are exclusively Portuguese. Different, exciting. João de Deus is a compact city; eighty thousand people in three quadras, each eight hours out of phase with its neighbours: mañana, tarde, noche. In many ways João de Deus is an old-fashioned place, sculpted from the lava tubes that thread the skin of Mare Fecunditatis. Santa Barbra Quadra is three hundred metres in diameter and feels cramped to Marina. The roof feels close and heavy. She is a little claustrophobic. But there is not enough airspace for fliers and for that Marina is thankful. She hates those fit, arrogant aeronauts.

'O bloqueio de ar não é completamente despressurizado,' she says. She tries to speak Portuguese around the apartment. Hetty has been programmed not to respond to Globo.

Daqui a pouco sair para a superfície da lua, Hetty responds. *Seu sotaque é péssimo.* Her familiar not only speaks better Portuguese than her, she does so in a perfect Corta Hélio accent.

Hetty breaks off her lesson.

Carlinhos Corta está na porta, she says.

Hair good, face good, straighten clothing, check teeth, fold unmade bed back into wall. Within twenty seconds Marina is ready to receive her boss.

'Oh.'

Carlinhos Corta is dressed in a pair of shorts, footgloves and coloured braids around his elbows, wrists, knees and ankles. That's all. He greets her in Portuguese. Marina barely hears him. He is a beautiful sight. He smells of honey and coconut oil. Beautiful, intimidating.

'Get dressed,' he says in Globo. 'You're coming out with me.'

'I am dressed.'

'No you're not.'

Senhor Corta está acessando a sua impressora, Hetty says. The printer dispenses shorts (short) a bra top (skimpy) and footgloves. The instruction is clear. Marina slips them on in her washroom. She tries to pull the top down, the shorts up. She feels nakeder than naked. In her room is her boss and she doesn't know what he is doing, why he has come, who or what he is really.

'For you.' Carlinhos scoops handful of green braids from the printer. 'I'm giving you the colour of my orixa, Ogun.' He shows her how to tie them around her joints, how much of a tail to leave hanging. The footgloves feel as if they are sucking her toes. 'You can run, can't you?'

Marina follows him down ladeiros. The staircases are narrow and shallow, difficult to jog. Passersby press in to the walls and nod greetings. She runs at Carlinhos's shoulder along Third, parallel to the central Prospekt but three levels higher. Bicycles and motos whirl past. Marina smells grilling corn, hot oil, frying falafel. Music beats from tiny five-seater bars carved into naked rock. The skyline dims towards purples and reds. Carlinhos takes a left on to a cross-passage. Marina is now under artificial lights. From a T-junction main tunnel ahead she thinks she hears chanting voices. Then she sees a body of runners sweep past along the tunnel, their familiars a hovering choir. Bare skin glistens with oil, sweat, body-paint. Tassels and braids stream from elbows and knees, wrists and throats and foreheads. Singing. They are singing. Marina almost stops dead in surprise.

'Come on pick it up,' Carlinhos says and adds half a metre to his stride. Marina lunges after him. She is not a runner but she still has Earth muscle and she catches him easily. Carlinhos turns into the intersecting tunnel, a wide service way curving gently to the right. Marina is unfamiliar with this part of João de Deus. Ahead is the pack of runners, tightly bunched, a peloton. Under lunar gravity they surge and lunge like running gazelles. A rolling sea of movement. Marina hears drums, whistles, the chime of finger cymbals over the chanting. Carlinhos catches up with the back markers. Marina is two steps behind him. The runners part to admit them and Marina falls in easily with the pace.

'Pick it up again,' Carlinhos calls and pulls ahead. Marina kicks and follows him into the heart of the pack. Beats engulf her, their rhythm the rhythm of her heart, her feet. The chanting voices call to her voice. She can't understand the words but she wants to join them. She is expanded. Her senses, her personal space overlap with the runners close around her, yet at the same time she is radiantly conscious of her body. Lungs, nerves, bones and brain are a unity. She moves effortlessly, perfectly. Every sense is tuned to its highest possible note. She hears the drums in her knees, her heels. She smells the sweat of Carlinhos's skin. The play of the tassels across her skin is erotic. She can distinguish every hovering dust mote. She recognises a shoulder tattoo at the head of the pack and, as if her look was a touch, Saadia from her squad turns and acknowledges her. A wave of undiluted joy breaks through Marina's entire body.

The words. She knows them now. They are Portuguese, a language she doesn't fully understand, in a dialect she can't comprehend, but their meaning is clear. *St George, lord of iron, my husband. Saint strike boldly. St George has water but bathes in blood. St George has two cutlasses. One for cutting grass, one for making marks. He wears robes of fire. He wears a shirt of blood. He has three houses. The house of riches. The house of wealth. The house of war.* The words are in her throat, the words are on her lips. Marina has no idea how they got there.

'Pick it up, Marina,' Carlinhos says a third time and together they move through the press of bodies and familiars to the head of the pack of runners. There is nothing in front of Marina. The tunnel curves away forever before her. Air eddies cool on her skin. She could run like this forever. Body and mind, soul and senses are one thing, greater and more perceptive than any of its elements.

'Marina.' The voice has been calling her name for some time. 'Drop back.' They peel from the lead position and drop down the side of the pack. 'Take this right.'

It's physical pain to leave the runners for the cross tunnel, but the emotional hurt is crushing. Marina comes to a halt, hands on thighs, head bowed, and howls with loss. She hears the voices and drums and chimes of the runners disappearing into the distance and it is like she has been cast out of elf-land. Beat by beat she remembers who she is. Who he is.

'I'm sorry. Oh God.'

'Better to keep moving or you will lock up.'

She coaxes her body into a painful jog. The cross tunnel opens on to Third Santa Barbra Quadra. The skyline is dark, the quadra glows with low pools of street light and ten thousand windows. Marina is cold now.

'How long was I...'

'Two complete circuits. Sixteen kilometres.'

'I didn't notice...'

'You don't. That's the idea.'

'How long...'

'No one really knows, but it's been going on all my life. The idea is that it never stops. Runners drop in, runners drop out. We cycle through the saints. It's my church. It's where I heal, where I disappear for a time. Where I stop being Carlinhos Corta.'

Now the weight of those sixteen kilometres descends on Marina's thighs and calves. She had only ever been a reluctant runner in pre-launch training. This is different. Part of her will always be out there, running in that ever-circling wheel of praise. She can't wait to go back.

'Thank you,' she says. Anything more would tarnish the moment. 'So what do we do now?'

'Now,' says Carlinhos Corta, 'we shower.'

Analiese Mackenzie descends the spiral staircase from the bedroom into the entrails of a fly; exploded, expanded, enhanced and annotated. Wings unfold into vanes, eyes disintegrate into their component lens, legs and pulps and proboscis, nanochips and protein processors whirl around her head. At the centre sits Wagner, back turned, naked as he likes to be when he is concentrating, summoning and dismissing, enlarging and superimposing images in their shared sight. It's dazzling, it's dizzying, it's four thirty in the morning.

'Ana.'

She made no sound she's aware of but Wagner has picked her out of the apartment's background of hisses and hums and creaks. It starts with heightened sensitivities, restlessness, a boundless energy. This insomnia is something new.

'Wagner, it's...'

'Take a look at this.'

Wagner leans back his chair, slips an arm around Analiese's ass. His other hand spins dismembered fly around the room.

'What is this?' Analiese asks.

'This is the fly that tried to kill my brother.'

'Before you jump to any conclusions, it wasn't me, it wasn't any of us.'

'Oh I'm sure of that.' Wagner reaches out, pulls a knot of protein circuit out of the exploded fly and dismisses everything else. 'See?' He twists his hand, enlarges it until it fills the small room; a brain of folded proteins.

'You know I've got no eye for this kind of thing.' Analiese works in custom meta logics and plays sitar in a classical Persian ensemble.

'Heitor Pereira wouldn't have known what to look for. Not even the R&D guys. It took me a while to find it but the moment I saw it, I thought, that has to be it, and I blew it up and it was, I mean, it's written all over the molecules, it's like she scrawled her tag all over it but you have to know what you're looking for, you have to know how to see.'

'Wagner.'

'Am I talking really fast?'

'Yes you are. I think it's starting.'

'It can't. It's too early.'

'It's been getting earlier and earlier.'

'It can't!' Wagner snaps. 'It's a clock. Sun rises, sun sets. You can't change that. That's astronomy.'

'Wagner...'

'Sorry. Sorry.' He kisses the hollow of her belly and he feels the muscles tighten beneath the honey skin, a thing he loves so hard, because it's not tech or code or math; it's physical and chemical. But he can feel the change, like the sun beneath the horizon. He had thought it was the fascination, the dedication that drove his mood, but he realises it's the change driving his fascination. When the Earth is full, he can work for days on end, burning. 'I have to go to Meridian.'

He feels Analiese pull away from him.

'You know I hate it when you go there.'

'It's where the woman who made this processor is.'

'You never had to make excuses before.'

He kisses her strong belly again and she slips a hand behind his head, lacing her fingers through his hair. Analiese smells of vanilla and fabric-conditioned sheets. Wagner breathes deep and pulls away.

'I got some more work to do.'

'Go to bed, Analiese,' Analiese says.

'I'll be up later.'

'You won't. Promise me, you will be here in the morning.'

'I will.'

'You didn't promise.'

When Analiese has gone Wagner opens his arms and pulls his hands together in a slow clap, summoning the exploded elements of assassin-fly. He set them in slow orbit around him, looking for other clues to its builders but his concentration is broken. On the edge of his hearing, on the edge of every sense, he can hear his pack calling across the Sea of Tranquillity.

For the Pavilion of the White Hare, Ariel Corta wears a reprint 1955 Dior in chocolate with a Chantilly cap-sleeve blouse, deep plunging, ruched. A pillbox hat with a brown silk rose, gloves to mid forearm, complementing bag and shoes. Co-ordinating, not odiously matchy-matchy. Professional but not starchy.

A receptionist takes Ariel up to the conference suite. The hotel is tasteful, the service discreet, but it is far from the most expensive or opulent Meridian offers. In the elevator Ariel switches off Beijaflor as instructed. There is a level of political and social life where constant connectivity is a liability. Nagai Rieko greets Ariel in the lobby where the counsellors socialise in the lobby drinking tea, taking sweet-bean baozi from trays. Fourteen, including the outgoing members. So many exquisite dresses, so many bare shoulders. Ariel feels as if she has been admitted to a secret louche sex party: improper, a little scandalous.

Rieko makes the introductions. Jaiyue Sun, head of development at Taiyang; Stephany Mayor Robles the educationalist from Queen of the South. Professor Monique Dujardin from the Faculty of Astrophysics at the University of Farside. Daw Suu Hla, her family allies of the Asamoahs by blood and business, Ataa Afua Asamoah of the Kotoko trying to keep an over-lively pet meerkat under control. Fashionable chef Marin Olmstead: Ariel blinks at his presence: *Everyone does that,* he says. He's been in the White Hare for four years. Pyotr Vorontsov from VTO. Marlena Lesnik from Sanafil Health, the major medical insurers. Sheikh Mohammed el-Tayyeb, Grand Mufti of the Queen of the South Central Mosque, scholar and legalist, famous for his fatwa excusing the necessity of the Haj on the lunar acclimated. Outgoing Niles Hanrahan, and V. P. Singh the poet, his replacement. Six women, five men, one neutro: all successful, professional, moneyed.

'Vidhya Rao.' A small, elderly neutro shakes Ariel's hand vigorously. 'A pleasure, Senhora Corta. Your family's presence in the White Hare is long overdue.'

'Pleasure is mine,' Ariel says but she is already scanning the room, smart as the meerkat, seeking social advantage.

'Long overdue,' Vidhya Rao says again. 'I was a doctor of mathematics at Farside but for the past ten years I've been on the board at Whitacre Goddard.'

Ariel's attention snaps back to the neutro.

'The Rao forward.'

Vidhya Rao claps er hands in pleasure.

'Thank you. I'm honoured.'

'I'm aware of the Rao forward, but I don't really understand it. My brother speculates regularly in them.'

'I would have thought Lucas Corta was far too canny to gamble on the forwards market.'

'He is. It's Rafa. Lucas insists he only use his own money.' Rafa has explained Rao forwards several times – too many times. They are financial instruments, a variant of a futures contract that exploits the 1.26 second communications gap between Earth and moon: the time it takes any signal, travelling at the speed of light, to cross 384,000 kilometres. Time enough for price differentials to open between terrestrial and lunar markets: differentials traders can exploit. The Rao forward is a short-term contract to buy or sell on the LMX exchange at a set price. If the lunar price drops, you are in the money. If it rises, you are out. Like all futures trading, it is a guessing game; a good one, adjudicated by the iron law of the speed of light. That is where Ariel Corta's understanding ends. The rest is voodoo. To the AIs that trade in milliseconds on the electronic markets, 1.26 seconds is an aeon. Billions of forwards, trillions of dollars, are traded back and forth between Earth and moon. Ariel has heard that the Vorontsovs are considering building an automated trading platform at the L1 point between moon and Earth, setting up a secondary forwards market; time delay .75 of a second. 'Lucas believes that you should never invest in something you don't understand.'

'Lucas Corta is a wise man,' says Vidhya Rao with a smile. The doors to the suite open. Inside are low tables, deep sofas upholstered in vat-grown leather, tasteful art works.

'Shall we?'

'Shouldn't we wait for the Eagle?' Ariel asks.

'Oh, he's not invited,' Vidhya Rao says. 'Marin is our liaison.' E nods at the celebrity chef.

'It's all very informal,' Judge Rieko says at the door. With Niles Hanrahan she remains outside as Ariel follows Vidhya Rao into the room. Then the hotel staff close the doors and the Pavilion of the White Hare is in session.

*

'Hey.'

Kojo Asamoah lies facing the wall. Medical bots flit and dart around him. At the sound of Lucasinho's voice he rolls over, sits up in surprise.

'Hey!' A wave of the hand banishes the medical machines. They flock in the corners of the room; digitally concerned. Access to the medical centre had not been so easy now that Lucasinho was Kid Off-grid. Grigori Vorontsov had swung it. He had always been the best coder in the colloquium.

'What are you wearing?'

Lucasinho shows off in the suit-liner. The clothes Ariel printed are top-marque, of the mode, but he tried them on once and then consigned them to the backpack. He likes the look of the suit-liner now. It turns him into a lean rebel. People notice. Eyes catch him as he swings past. That's good. He might even become a fashion.

He kisses Kojo on the mouth, like a boy.

'How are you?'

'Bored bored bored bored bored.'

'But you are all right?'

Kojo leans back, arms behind head.

'Still coughing up bits of lung but at least I can lie on my ass now.' He lifts his left foot. It's enclosed in what looks like a sasuit boot, with tubes running from it into the base of the bed. 'They're growing me a new toe. They printed a bone out, and the stem cells. It'll be back in about a month.'

'Brought you something.'

Lucasinho takes the seal-pack from his bag and opens it. The medical bots flutter in distress as their sensors register chocolate, sugar, THC. Kojo props himself up on his elbow and takes an offered brownie, sniffs at it.

'What have you got in this?'

'Fun.'

'That's what I heard you were having with Grigori Vorontsov.'

'Where did you hear that?'

'Afua.'

'This time she's right.'

Kojo sits up in the bed. His face is puzzled.

'What happened to Jinji?'

'I'm not wearing him.'

Not wearing a familiar is like not wearing clothes. Or skin.

'Afua said you'd run out on the family. Your father cut you off.'

'She's right about that too.'

'Wow.' Kojo studies Lucasinho closely, as if looking for sins, or parasites. 'I mean, you can breathe all right?'

'He'd never do that. Grandmother would never forgive him. She loves me. Water is okay too, but he has frozen my carbon and data accounts.'

'What do you do for money?'

Lucasinho spreads a fan of cash.

'I have a useful aunt.'

'I've never seen this before. Can I smell it?' Kojo riffles notes under his nose. He shudders. 'Just think of all those hands that have touched it.'

Lucasinho sits on the bed. 'Kojo, how long are you going to be in here?'

'What do you want?'

'Just, if you're not using your place...'

'You want my place?'

'I saved your life.' At once Lucasinho regrets playing his ace. It's unbeatable, it's low.

'Is that the reason you came here? Just to hide out at my place?'

'No, not at all...' Lucasinho backtracks. No words will convince. He offers a brownie. 'I made these for you. Really.'

'I'm not supposed to have anything recreational until the toe grows back,' Kojo says and takes a brownie. He bites. He melts. 'Oh man these are great.' He finishes the brownie. 'You're really good at this.'

Halfway down the second, Kojo Asamoah says, 'You have the apartment for five days. I've reset the lock to your iris already.'

Lucasinho pulls himself up on to the bed and curls up like a pet ferret at Kojo's feet. Now he takes a brownie. The medical bots hum and swarm and register their patient's increasing level of stonedness. The two teenagers munch and giggle the sweet hours down.

The tall double doors open and the delegates rise from their sofas and drift away, conversation looping into conversation. The Pavilion of the White Hare is ended.

'So, Senhora Corta, what did you make of your first taste of lunar politics?' The banker Vidhya Rao slips in to Ariel's side.

'Surprisingly banal.'

'Attention to the banal keeps us alive,' Vidhya Rao says. The chef Marin Olmstead hurries to the elevator lobby, impatient to rez up his familiar and arrange his report to Jonathon Kayode. 'Of course politics doesn't have to be this banal.' E touches Ariel's arm, an invitation to linger, to conspire. 'There are councils within councils.'

'I've only just got my feet under the table at this one,' Ariel says.

'Your nomination was not universally welcomed,' the banker says. E beckons Ariel to sit with er. The touch of vat-grown leather has always made Ariel's flesh crawl. She can't forget its provenance: human skin.

'It would be impolitic to name names,' Ariel suggests.

'Of course. Some of us argued strenuously for your admission. I was one of them. I've followed your career with interest. You are an exceptional young woman, with a stellar career before you.'

'I'm far too vain to blush,' Ariel says. 'I hope so too.'

'Oh my dear, this is not wishful thinking,' Vidhya Rao says. Er eyes are bright. 'This has been modelled with a high degree of precision. The Rao forward is the least of my achievements. What every investment bank desires is the ability to see the future. To predict which prices will go long and which will short, that would give us a powerful advantage.'

'You said "us",' Ariel says.

'I did, didn't I? For the past seven years I have been developing algorithms to model the markets. In effect, I have created shadow markets running on quantum computers, from which it is possible to make educated guesses as to the movements of the real markets. The accuracy is surprising, though we find it's a less useful tool than we had imagined – acting on that information shows our hand, so to speak, and the market moves against us, abolishing any advantage Whitacre Goddard might enjoy.'

'Voodoo economics,' Ariel says. 'Black magic.' She snaps her vaper to full length and locks it rigid. She ignites, inhales, lets out a curl of vapour.

'We found a more useful application for the technique,' Vidhya Rao says. E leans forwards, demands Ariel meet er eyes. 'Prophecy. That's religious gobbledegook of course. I mean useful predictions based on highly-educated guesses derived from fine-scale computer modelling. Modelling the lunar economy and society. We have three independent systems, each running the model. Taiyang constructed three quantum mainframes, I developed the algorithms. We call them the Three August Ones: Fu Xi, Shennong and the Yellow Emperor. They seldom agree – one has to find patterns in their output, but they agree with a high degree of confidence on one person. You.'

Ariel's outward demeanour is calm and elegant – her court face – but she feels a shock of cold electricity run from her heart to the root of her brain.

'I'm not sure I like being the Chosen One to a cabal of quantum computers.'

'It's nothing so tendentious. We naturally modelled the Five Dragons. You are the major shapers of the economic and political society. You emerge as a significant figure in the Corta family. The significant figure.'

'Rafa is bu-hwaejang.'

'And Lucas is the power behind the throne. You do know he is planning to take over the company. Talented boys, but they are predictable.'

'And you've predicted my unpredictability.' Ariel looses another stream of vapour into the air. Effortless cool. Inside, she is electrically alert.

'The Three August Ones were unanimous. The Three August Ones are never unanimous. I shall be frank, Ariel. We want to make a bid for your potential.'

'You're not talking about Whitacre Goddard.'

'I'm talking about a movement, a ghost, a philosophy, a diversity.'

'If you give me good versus evil, this conversation is over.' But the small neutro has her attention. Curiosity conspires with vanity.

'Your mother built the moon.' Judge Reiko's voice. Ariel had not seen her reenter the lobby. 'But the political legacy of the LDC and the Five Dragons is essentially feudalism. Great Houses and the Monarchy, dispensing territories and favours, monopolising water, oxygen, carbon allowance. Vassals and serfs indentured to their sponsoring corporations. It's like Shogun Japan or medieval France.'

Reiko sits beside Vidhya Rao. Ariel begins to feel targeted.

'The Three August Ones agree that this model is unsustainable,' Vidhya Rao says. 'The Five Dragons have reached the pinnacle of their power – last quarter profits from derivatives trading exceeded those of the Five Dragons for the third quarter in a row. Financial entities like Whitacre Goddard are in the ascendant.'

Ariel holds Vidhya Rao's eyes until the banker looks away. Corta disdain.

'The woman in Hamburg plugging her car into the charge point on the street, the girl in Accra who recharges her familiar chip from the school touch-pad, the boy in Ho Chi Minh City playing his DJ set, the man in Los Angeles boarding the HST to San Francisco; what they plug into is Corta helium.'

'Eloquently put Senhora Corta.'

'It's more eloquent in Portuguese.'

'I'm sure. The fact remains, the future is financial. We are a resource-poor, energy-rich economy. It's obvious that our economic future lies with weightless, digital goods.'

'Weightless goods turn strangely heavy when they fall on you. Or have you learned nothing from the Five Crashes?'

'The Three August Ones...'

'We are an independence movement,' Nagai Reiko cuts in.

'Of course you are,' says Ariel Corta with a feline smile and a slow draw on her gleaming vaper.

'We have our own pavilion. The Lunarian Society.'

'More talking.'

'Words are better than blades.'

'And you want me.'

'The Lunarian Society draws from all Five Dragons and levels of society.'

'It is much more democratic than the White Hare,' Vidhya Rao interjects.

'I'm a Corta. We don't do democracy.'

Vidhya Rao can't disguise er scowl of distaste. Nagai Reiko smiles.

'You want to invite me to join your society,' Ariel says.

Vidhya Rao sits back, honest surprise on er face.

'My dear Senhora Corta, we don't propose to invite you. We want to *buy* you.'

With a bed under his back and money in his pouch, Lucasinho hits the party circuit. It's never hard for a Corta boy to find a party. He follows a chain of acquaintances of acquaintances to Xiaoting Sun's apartment up on Thirty Aquarius Hub. His reputation has preceded him. You skipped out on your father? I mean, no network, no carbon, no bitsies? Where are you sleeping?

Kojo Asamoah's. While he's growing a new toe. I saved him. But they roll straight with the next question: *Whatever are you're wearing?*

Xiaoting Sun has hired Banyana Ramilepe, the new narco-DJ. She mixes and prints custom highs and moods and loves into juice for a battery of vapers. Lucasinho drifts through the party, gorgeous in tight pink, inhaling empathy, religious awe, pleasure that's better than any sex, euphoria, golden melancholy. For twenty minutes he is in deep deep love with a short, wide-hipped serious Budiño girl. She is an angel, a goddess, love divine, every day he'll just sit and stare at her, sit and stare. Then the chemicals break up into nothing and they are sitting and staring at each other and he drops new juice into his vaper. By the end of the night a boy and a girl are drawing hallucination-creatures on his suit-liner with marker pens.

No one comes back with him to Kojo's.

At the party the next night in Orion Quadra there are two girls in suit-liners, fluorescent green and hi-visibility orange. He's still trying to work out if one of them was at the Sun party when a bubble-blonde white girl appears in front of him and asks, *Can I see the money?*

He flicks out the notes and fans them like a street magician.

And this is bitsies?

Five ten twenty fifty one hundred.

A crowd has gathered, the notes pass from fingers to fingers, feeling the textures, the crumple.

And if I just took it?

And if I tore it in half?

And if I set fire to it?

It would be dead money, Lucasinho says. *This stuff doesn't have insurance.*

A boy takes a five bitsie note and scribbles on it with a pencil. He's one of those moços whose tongue sticks out a little when they concentrate. He's not used to writing.

What about this?

He's changed the Five to Five Million.

Doesn't make any difference, Lucasinho says. The boy has left another message, written along the edge in a hand so bad Lucasinho can barely read it. A location in Antares Quadra, and a time.

Antares Quadra is eight hours behind Orion so Lucasinho has only enough time to stuff the suit-liner in the laundry, get his head down, shower and order in some carbs-for-cash before he finds himself at the top of West 97th, in sun-down dark, with riders on luminous bicycles blazing past him. It's a long climb when elevators and escalators don't take folding money. He's at a downhill; an urban bike race down five kilometres of precipitous city architecture. Zigzagging down ramps and stairways. Stupendous leaps, soaring high over roof tops to land in narrow alleys, and on and on, swerving around hairpin corners, accelerating up ramps to leap and fly again. On and on, hurtling down the dark, steering by night-vision lenses and luminous arrows sprayed on walls and the lamps of Antares West, blowing whistles to warn pedestrians and night-strollers. A girl's hand snatches Lucasinho into a doorway as whistles blare out of nowhere and two bikes streak past, leaving luminous after-imagines on his retinas.

Oh my God, is it you?

It's me, Lucasinho says. He's become a celebrity. He buys her mejadra from one of the stands at the top of the run not because she is hungry but because she wants to see cash at work.

You have to do all those sums in your head?

It's not so hard.

Together they watch the streaks of light race through the alleys and over the roofs and down the walkways, dipping in and out of sight as they duck under build-overs or round corners. Far below, on Budarin Prospekt, tiny luminous spirals wind around each other: bikes at the finish line. The times don't matter. The winner doesn't matter. The race doesn't even matter. What matters is the spectacle, the daring, the sense of transgression, that something wonderful has fallen out of the sky into safe, conventional lunar life.

117

There are a lot more suit-liners tonight. Two of the guys are decorating each other with the luminous paint the downhillers use on their bikes. Lucasinho's presence has somehow graced the downhill. Two girls come to Lucasinho through the crowd. They are dressed as nineteenth-century European males: tail coats, wing-collars, top hats and monocles. Kiss-curls and kill-you-deadly make-up. They carry canes in their gloved hands. Their familiars are little dragons, one green, one red. One of them whispers a time and a place in Lucasinho's ear. He feels her teeth tug on the metal spike in his earlobe. Pleasurable little pain. Abena Asamoah licked his blood at his moon-run party.

The girl who rescued him and shared his mejadra is Pilar. She is of no family but she goes back to Kojo's apartment with Lucas and falls straight asleep in the guest hammock. It's still light. Lucasinho sleeps to local morning and makes her fresh-baked muffins as a parting gift.

The rest of the batch he brings to this new party. It's in Antares Quadra, the morning side of the city, across seven rooms in a colloquium block. The two girls from the previous night receive him. They are still dressed as nineteenth-century aristo boys.

Oh baked goods, says one.

But this is old already, says the other, running a finger up Lucasinho's suit-liner and holding it a moment under his chin. Her lips are very full and red. *We will have to do something about you.*

The rest of the night is spent making Lucasinho Corta over. Lucasinho giggles as the girls strip him but he's vain enough to enjoy the exposure.

You see, it's not about who you do.

You're so bi, so spectrum, so normal.

It's about who you are.

What you are.

They paint him, cosmetic him, change his hair, spray him with temporary tattoos, play with his piercings, dress him up and down.

Clothes from all retros and none; inventions by fashion students; of all genders and none.

This is you.

A 1980s gold lamé dress, cinched waist, leg-of-mutton sleeves, power shoulders. Panty hose and red heels.

Absolutely you.

The crowd nod and yes and coo. At first Lucasinho thought he had come to a fancy-dress party: mini-bustles and tutus, hair woven with mirrors and bird-cages; hats and heels; ripped hosiery and leather; hi-cut leotards and kneepads. Everyone made-up in a hundred different regimes, all immaculate. Then he realised that this was a subculture where everyone was a subculture.

One of the boys has a mirror in his bag as a period accessory and Lucasinho studies himself in the glass. He looks stunning. He is not a girl, he is not trans-dressing. He is a moço in a dress. His quiff has been backcombed and gelled into a reef. The lightest touch of make-up turns his cheekbones into edged weapons and his eyes into dark murderers. He moves like a ninja in heels. Not a girl, not entirely a boy.

I think he likes it, says Top-Hat and Monocle.

I think he knows who he is, says Wing-Collar and Cane.

One of the girls catches him: *Hey, you're Lucasinho Corta, great dress, show me the cash.* Says, *Do you want to come to a party?*

Where?

She gives him a location and it's only when he's back in Kojo's on his own that Lucasinho realises that it's in Twé, the capital of the Asamoahs and that Abena Asamoah might be there. And that what he wants, what he really really wants, has only ever been the girl who put the spike through his ear.

'This is a strange room,' the musician says.

Lucas sits on a sofa. The room's only other piece of furniture is a chair, directly facing the sofa.

'It is acoustically perfect. It's designed for me but it will still be the best acoustic you have ever heard.'

'Where should I . . .'

Lucas indicates the chair in the centre of the room.

'Your voice,' the musician says.

'Yes,' Lucas says, quietly and without emphasis and his words fill the room. He doubts there is a sound room in the two worlds to match his. He had acoustic engineers flown up from Sweden to supervise its construction. Lucas loves its discretion. There are sonic marvels hidden in its micro-grooved walls, beneath its absorbent black floor and re-shapable ceiling. The sound-room is his only vice, Lucas believes. He controls his excitement as the musician opens his guitar case. This is an experiment. He has never tried the room with live music before.

'If you don't mind.' Lucas nods at the open case on the floor. 'It will interfere with the wave forms.'

The case removed, the musician bends over his guitar and picks a soft harmonic. The notes come as soft and clear to Lucas as if they were breathing.

'It is very good.'

'You should come over here and try it,' Lucas says. 'Except then who would play the guitar?'

Tuning, then the musician rests his hands on the wooden body of his instrument.

'What would you like to hear?'

'I asked you play a song at the party. My mama's favourite.'

'*Aguas de Marco.*'

'Play that for me.'

Fingers float across the board, a chord for every word. The boy's voice is not the strongest or the most refined Lucas has ever heard – an intimate whisper, as if singing only for himself. But it caresses the song, turns its dialogue into pillow-talk between singer and guitar. Voice and strings syncopate around the beat; between them it vanishes, leaving only the conversation: chords and lyrics. Lucas's breathing is shallow. Every sense is tuned as precisely as the strings of the guitar, harmonically alive and resonating, focused on the player and the song. Here is the soul of saudade. Here are holy mysteries. This room is his church, his tereiro. It is everything Lucas hoped.

Jorge the musician ends the song. Lucas composes himself.

'*Eu Vim da Bahia*?' he asks. An old João Gilberto song with difficult descending chord progressions and a heartbreaking turn. Jorge nods. *Lua de São Jorge. Nada Sera Como Antes. Cravo e Canela.* All the old songs his mother brought from green Brazil to the moon. The songs of his childhood, the songs of bays and hills and sunsets he has never seen and can never see. They were seeds of beauty, strong and sad, in the grey hell of the moon. Lucas Corta realised young that he lives in hell. The only way to transform hell, to even survive it, is to rule it.

Lucas feels a tear run down his face.

Por Toda a Minha Vida ends. Lucas sits silent and unmoving, letting his emotions settle.

'Thank you,' Lucas says. 'You play beautifully.' A thought sends the fee to Jorge's familiar.

'This is more than we agreed.'

'A musician argues about being overpaid?'

Jorge fetches the case and stores his guitar. Lucas watches the care and love with which he handles the instrument, wiping sweat from the strings, blowing dust from under the end of the fingerboard. Like laying a child in a cradle.

'This room is too good for me,' Jorge says.

'This room was made for you,' Lucas says. 'Come again. Next week. Please.'

'For that money, I'll come when you whistle.'

'Don't tempt me.'

And there it is, in the flicker of smile, the flash of exchanged looks.

'It's good to find someone who appreciates the classics,' Jorge says.

'It's good to find someone who understands them,' Lucas says. Jorge hefts the guitar case. Toquinho opens the door of the sound room. Even the muffled footfalls, the creak of the guitar case, sound perfect.

Shafts of light fall around the fighting figures. The Hall of Knives is a tunnel of bright, dusty pillars of sunlight. The two males, one tall, one short, lunge and dance, feint and follow, barefoot across the absorbent floor, now lit, now shaded. It is as beautiful as ballet. Rachel Mackenzie watches from a small spectators' gallery by the door. Robson is quick and brave but he is eleven years old and Hadley Mackenzie is a man.

There is no law on the moon, only consensus, and the consensus outlaws projectile weapons. Bullets are incompatible with pressurised environments and complex machinery. Knives, bludgeons, garrottes, subtle machines and slow poisons, the Asamoah's fancy of small, biological assassins: these are the tools of violence. Wars are small and eyeball close. Rachel hates to see Robson in the Hall of Knives. She hates more his love for and skill in the techniques Hadley teaches him. She hates most that it's necessary. The Five Dragons rest uneasy on their treasures. Hadley is the family's duellist. Rumours pass up and down Crucible that Robert Mackenzie has ordained it to keep Jade Sun's ambitions in check, and to preserve the inheritance line with pure Mackenzies. There is no one better to teach Robson the way of the knife, but Rachel wishes there were another, better bond between him and Hadley. Sport – like his father's handball obsession – would be healthy and wholesome and command Robson's energies.

Look at him, slight but sharp as the blade in his right hand. The fighting pants hang off his slender hips. His shallow chest heaves but his eyes take in everything in the long room. A cry. Robson kicks forward to break a kneecap, follows with a slashing cut, high left to low right. Aiming at the eyes, the throat. Hadley dodges the kick, steps inside the blade and twists the arm. Robson cries out. The knife falls. Hadley catches it before it reaches the floor. Another twist and a trip land Robson flat on his back. A knife in each hand, Hadley brings the blades hammering down towards Robson's throat.

'No!'

The blades stop a millimetre from Robson's brown skin. A drop of sweat falls from Hadley's brow into Robson's eyes. Hadley is grinning. He hadn't even heard Rachel's cry. She didn't stay his hand. It's just the two of them. Nothing else exists. The intimacy of violence.

'What's the rule, Robbo? If you take a knife...'

'You must kill with it.'

'This time – this time only – I'm letting you live. So what's the lesson?'

'Never lose the knife.'

'Never let go. Use their weapons against them,' says a voice from the door.

Rachel hadn't heard Duncan enter. Her father is in his early sixties but has the energy and bearing of a man twenty years younger. His suit is simple grey, conservative, single-breasted, immaculately cut but unflashy. His familiar Esperance is a plain silver sphere, its only ornament, liquid ripples that flow across its surface. Nothing in Duncan Mackenzie's practised minimalism and modesty advertises that he is CEO of Mackenzie Metals. Everything about Duncan Mackenzie declares it.

'Is he good?' Duncan Mackenzie asks.

'He could cut you up,' Hadley says.

Duncan Mackenzie gives a sour, twisted smile.

'Bring him along, Rachel,' he says. 'There's someone I want him to meet.'

'He'll be five minutes in the shower,' Rachel says.

'Bring him along, Rachel,' Duncan Mackenzie repeats. Robson looks to his mother. She nods. Hadley raises his knife: a fighter's salute.

*

Rachel Mackenzie has always been repelled by her Uncle Bryce. Robert is a horror, but Bryce Mackenzie, Director of Finance, is a monster. He is huge. Tall even for a second-gen, lunar gravity has allowed him to pile weight upon weight. He is a gross man-mountain balanced on strangely tiny feet. Not fat, vast. He moves with the lightness and delicacy that big men often possess.

Bryce Mackenzie looks Robson up and down, like a sculpture, like an account. 'Such a pretty boy.'

A young adoptee brings mint tea. The formality is that Bryce Mackenzie finds his boys at puberty and adopts them, afterwards finding them employment in the company. Many have married in or out, some have become fathers. Bryce is close to his former lovers, and supports them generously. There is never any scandal. Bryce is too dutiful for that. The teaboy is one of three amors currently serving Bryce. Fingers meet over the tea-glass. A look, a smile. Rachel imagines him on top of Bryce, man-mountain Bryce. Riding, riding. Ass pounding.

'Robson, meet your new husband,' Duncan says. Rachel's eyes open. 'This is Hoang Lam Hung.' A grown man, well built: twenty-nine, thirty years old.

'One of your boys,' Rachel says. Bryce's soft, full lips purse in offence.

'Rachel,' Duncan says. Hung shrugs away the insult, but there is a crack of hurt in the crease of his mouth.

'This is the nikah.' Bryce slides the print contract across the desk at the same instant it arrives on Cameny. A legal sub-AI kicks in and summarises the contract to bullet points.

'You're joking,' Rachel Mackenzie says.

'It's standard form. No alarms, no surprises,' Bryce says.

'Have you asked Robson about his preferences?' Rachel professes.

'Dad wants this,' Duncan Mackenzie says.

'What do you say?' Rachel asks her father. She wishes she hadn't formed that image of the teaboy riding Bryce's naked bulk. It leads her to imaginings so hideous she covers her mouth with her hands.

'Like Bryce says, it's standard.'

'I need a day or two.'

'What can there possibly be to think about?' Bryce says. Rachel is powerless. The will of Robert Mackenzie rules Crucible and she is at the heart of his power. There is no one to whom she can appeal. Jade Sun will always stand with her husband. Whether Hung is kind or cruel, the marriage makes Robson a hostage of the Mackenzies.

Duncan uncaps the pen. Cameny presents the digital signature panel on the virtual contract.

'I will never forgive you, Bryce.'

'So noted, Rachel.'

Two quick, decisive stabs of the pen and she would put Bryce's eyes out. But she signs, and Cameny imprints her digital yin. And it is done.

'Robson, son: go to your new husband,' Duncan says.

Hung stands with his arms welcoming. Rachel kneels and hugs Robson to her.

'I love you, Robbo. I will always love you, and I will never ever let you be hurt. Believe me.'

She leads the boy by the hand across the room. Three steps and the world changes: son to husband. Rachel stands close to Hung and whispers loud for all to hear.

'If you hurt him, if you even touch him; I will kill you and everyone you have ever loved in your life. Understand.' Rachel says it to Hung, but her eyes are on Bryce. Again, Bryce's wet, full mouth works with displeasure.

'I'll take care of him, Ms Mackenzie.'

'I'll make sure you do.'

Hung rests a hand on Robson's shoulder. Rachel wants to break every finger, one at a time. She slaps it away from her son.

'I warned you.'

A touch on her arm: her father.

'Come along, Rachel.'

The office door opens and two of Duncan's security enter.

'What do you think I'm going to do, Father?'

'Come along, Rachel.'

Rachel Mackenzie kisses her son, then turns away from him, fast so no one will see the look on her face. Never, ever again will she let her uncle, her father, her grandfather, see the marks of the nails they have driven through her heart.

'Mum, what's happening?' The door seals behind her but she can still hear the cries of her son. 'What's happening? I'm scared! I'm scared!'

Never let go, her father had said. Use their weapons against them.

The lock is vast, built for rovers and buses, but Marina feels a heart-clench of claustrophobia as the inlock closes behind her. While the lock chamber depressurises, Marina observes. Minute observation is her way of dealing with her fear of confining spaces. Lose herself in the sensory. The crunch of dust under her boots. The dwindling hiss as air is abstracted. The tightening of the sasuit's grip on her body as the smart weave adjusts to vacuum. Weird, the familiars hovering over the shoulders of her squad. They should be wearing virtual sasuits.

José, Saadia, Thandeka, Patience. Oleg is dead. Physics killed him. He mistook weight for mass, speed for momentum. A Joe Moonbeam error. He thought he could stop the moving freight pallet with one hand. Momentum had driven the bones of his outstretched arm through his chest and burst his heart.

Oleg, Blake up in Bairro Alto. As many people have died in Marina's short life on the moon as in all her years on Earth. Oleg's death has widened the rift between her and her squad-mates. José no longer speaks to her. Marina knows the squad blames her. She is a jinx, a storm-crow, a karma magnet. She's started to hear a new lunar word; apatoo: spirit of dissension. The moon is the mother of magics and superstitions.

Marina can't get the Long Run out of her head. She can't understand how hours and kilometres disappeared. She can't understand how she could lose herself in something so irrational. It was nothing more than endorphins and adrenaline, but in her bed she feels the rhythm of the feet, hears the heartbeat of drums. She can't wait to go back. Body paint next time.

Rotating red lights. *The lock is depressurised,* Hetty says. She and every familiar wink out and re-visualise as the name of the squaddies, hovering green over each head. Green for all systems normal. Yellow for alert: air supply, water, batteries, environmental warning. Red for danger. Flashing red: extreme danger, immediate risk of death. White for death.

'Coms check,' Carlinhos says. Marina says her name and the little tongue-twister of the day to check that she is not touched with oxygen narcosis. 'Copy,' she adds hastily. So much to remember. 'Outlock is opening,' Carlinhos says. His sasuit is a patchwork of stickers and logos and icons but in the middle of his back is Ogun, São Jorge, his personal orixa. On the wall beside the outlock is an icon of Lady Luna. The skull side of her face has been worn away by thousands of gloved fingers. Touch for luck. Touch to foil death. 'This is Lady Moon. She is drier than the driest desert, hotter than the hottest jungle, colder than a thousand kilometres of Antarctic ice. She is every hell world anyone ever dreamed. She knows a thousand ways to kill you. Disrespect her and she will. Without thought. Without mercy.'

One by one the Jo Moonbeams line up to touch Lady Luna. Deserts, jungles, Antarctica: those aren't words Carlinhos has ever experienced, Marina thinks. They sound like a old mantra. The duster's prayer. Marina brushes fingers across the icon of Lady Moon.

Through the soles of her boots Marina feels the outlock door grind up. A slot of grey between grey door and grey floor opens on to ugly machinery: laagers of surface rovers, service robots, coms towers, the upcurved horns of the BALTRAN. Dumped machinery, wrecked machinery, machinery under maintenance. An extractor, too tall for even this huge lock, roped off with chains of yellow service flashers: a Christmas tree of lights and beacons. Ranges of solar panels, slowly tracking the sun. Far distant hills. The surface of the moon is a scrapheap.

'Let's go for a walk,' Carlinhos Corta says and leads his squad up the ramp. Marina steps out on to the surface. There is no transition, no crossing from indoor to great outdoors, not even a particular sense of bare surface and naked sky. The close horizon is visibly curved. Carlinhos leads the squad around a kilometre loop marked out by rope-lights. Hundreds of Jo Moonbeams have walked this way, bootprints overlay bootprints overlay bootprints. Bootprints everywhere, wheel tracks, the delicate toe-tips of stalking and climbing robots. The regolith is a palimpsest of every journey made across it. It is very ugly. Like every kid with access to binoculars, Marina had turned the magnification on King Dong; a giant spunking cock a hundred kilometres tall, boot-printed and tyre-tracked into the Mare Imbrium by infrastructure workers with too much time on their hands. Fifteen years back it was already blurred and scarred by criss-crossing tracks of subsequent missions. She doubts anything now remains of its gleeful frat-boy esprit.

Marina looks up. And stops leaving footprints.

A half Earth stands over the Sea of Fecundity. Marina has never see a thing bluer, truer. The Atlantic dominates the hemisphere. She makes out the western limb of Africa, the horn of Brazil. She can track the swirl of ocean storms, drawn in to the bowl of the Caribbean where they are stirred into beasts and monsters, sent spiralling out along the curve of the Gulf Stream towards unseen Europe. A hurricane blankets the eastern terminator. Marina can easily read its spiral structure, the dot of its eye. Blue and white. No trace of green but Marina has never seen anything look more alive. On the VTO cycler she had looked down at the Earth from the observation blister and wondered at the splendour unreeling before her. The streaming clouds, the turning planet, the line of sunrise along the edge of the world. For the first half of the orbit out she had watched Earth dwindle, for the second half she had watched the moon wax. Marina has never seen the Earth from the moon. It squats in the sky, Planet Earth; so much bigger than Marina had imagined, so terribly far away. Bright and brooding and forbidding, beyond reach and touch. Marina's messages take one and a quarter seconds to fly down to her family. This is home and you are a long way from it, is the message of the full Earth.

'You staying out here all day?' Carlinhos's voice crackles on Marina's private channel and she realises, startled and embarrassed, that everyone is back at the outlock and she is standing like a fool, gazing up at the Earth.

That is another difference. From the cycler she had looked down on the Earth. On the moon, the Earth is always up.

'How long was I standing there?' she asks Carlinhos as the lock repressurises.

'Ten minutes,' Carlinhos says. Airblades blast dust from the sasuits. 'When I first went up I did exactly the same thing. Stood staring until São Jorge gave me a low oxygen warning. I'd never seen anything like it. Heitor Pereira was with me: the first words I said were, "Who put that there?"'

Carlinhos unlocks his helmet. In the few seconds when conversations can still be private, Marina asks,

'So what do we do now?'

'Now,' says Carlinhos Corta, 'we have a drink.'

'Did he touch you?'

The little rover bowls flat out across Oceanus Procellarum. It hits every bump and rock at full speed, bounds into the air, lands in soft detonations of dust. Speeds on, throwing great plumes of dust behind its wheels. Its two passengers are banged and bruised, jolted hard, snapped back and forth, to and fro in their safety harnesses. Rachel Mackenzie pushes the rover to the very limits of its operational envelope.

Mackenzie Metals is hunting her.

'Did he do anything to you?' Rachel Mackenzie asks again over the whine of the engines and the creak and thump of suspension. Robson shakes his head.

'No. He was real nice. He made me dinner and we talked about his family. Then he taught me card tricks. I can show you. They're real good.' Robson reaches into a patch pocket of his sasuit.

'When we get there,' Rachel says.

She thought she would have longer. She had been so careful with her decoys and deceptions. It was a skill of Mackenzie women. Cameny had booked a railcar to Meridian. Rachel had even hacked the lock to create the illusion of two people exiting. Robert Mackenzie had stopped the railcar on remote within twenty kilometres. At the same time, two rovers had set out from Crucible in opposite directions. The first rover took the obvious route, north-east to the Taiyang server-farm at Rimae Maestlin. A logical road to escape; the Suns were doggedly non-aligned in lunar family politics. The wrath of Robert Mackenzie held no fear for House Sun.

Rachel has taken the illogical road. Her course seems headed south-east to the old polar freight line. Power stations and supply caches are strung all along the track. By ancient tradition – ancient by lunar standards – the Vorontsovs must stop a train for anyone who flashes it down from the trackside. Everything after that is negotiable, but the tradition of support and rescue endures. Duncan Mackenzie will have contracted private security to meet trains at all the main stations – Meridian, Queen, Hadley. But those aren't Rachel Mackenzie's destination. Not even the rail line.

The rover is windowless, airless, unpressurised, little more than a transmission and power system. Automatic return and overrides have been disabled on this and the decoy, sent in the opposite direction. Rachel has always been a good coder. The family has never valued the talent; any of her talents. Her true destination is the isolated BALTRAN relay at Flamsteed. She has a series of jumps laid in. But Mackenzie Metals rovers are closing in from the extraction plants to the south and east. Cameny is shut down to a whisper: Rachel doesn't want to advertise her location through the network. She hopes the hunters will be trying to cut her off at the rail line. Journey times can be calculated with high precision. The equations are sharp and cold. If they guess the relay, they will catch her. If they guess the mainline, she will escape. But she has to go on to the network, which will advertise her position to the whole moon.

'We'll be there soon,' Rachel Mackenzie says to her son. Look at him, strapped in in his sasuit across the narrow belly of the rover, his knees touching hers: look at him. The helmet visor masks his hair, the shape of his face and draws all attention to the eyes, his eyes, his great green eyes. There is no world finer – not this grey world, not the big blue world up there – than those eyes. 'I have to talk to someone. I'm making Cameny active but don't switch on Joker. Not yet.'

The sense of opening as Cameny connects to the network is physical; like breathing from the bottom of the lungs.

Ariel Corta's familiar curates the call. Hold please. Then Ariel Corta herself appears in Rachel's lens.

'Rachel. What is happening?'

Ariel's dress, hair, skin, make-up are immaculate. Rachel has thought her sister-in-law snobbish, aloof, careerist. She possesses enough honesty to recognise envy – those Brazilians have all the gifts and graces. Ariel has defeated her family many times in court, but she needs her now.

Rachel summarises the escape. Cameny flicks over the nikah.

'One moment please.' Ariel is briefly replaced by Beijaflor, then back. 'It's a standard-form marriage contract committing my nephew to a ten-year marriage to Hoang Lam Hung. It's tight.'

'Get him out of it.'

'The contract is legal and binding. The obligations are clear. I can't release Robson from it under any of the clauses. I can get the contract voided.'

'Do it. He's eleven years old. They made me sign it.'

'Legally, there is no minimum age of wedlock or consent. Duress is not necessarily a defence in our law. I would have to demonstrate that by failing to consult Robson regarding his preferences before signing the sexual activity clause, you violated your parenting contract with him. That would nullify the nikah. I wouldn't be acting for you, I would be acting for Robson against you. I would be trying to prove that you are a bad mother. Lucretia Borgia degrees of bad mother. However, in taking out this action, by escaping with Robson, you are acting like a good mother. It's a Catch-22. There are ways around it.'

'I don't care how bad you make me look.'

Does she see Ariel Corta, perfect Ariel Corta, loose the smallest smile?

'There would be a lot of dirt.'

'Mackenzies built their fortune from dirt.'

'So did I. Robson would need to retain me and agree a contract. Yet again, only a good parent would advise him to hire me. I must advise you off the record that taking this to court means clear and open conflict between our families. It's a declaration of war.'

'It's a declaration of war if Rafa finds out that I let Robson go without a fight. He would tear Crucible apart with his bare hands to get him back.'

Ariel Corta nods.

'I can't think of a more intractable situation. It's almost as if your grandfather deliberately chose the most provocative act possible.'

The rover lurches. Rachel's safety harness snaps against the sudden acceleration. And again. Something is crashing against the rover,

132

again and again. She feels not hears the vibrations of cutters, drills. A sudden deceleration: the rover is slowing.

'What's happening?' Ariel Corta asks. Concern on her perfect mask.

'Cameny, show me!' Rachel shouts.

'I'm alerting Rafa,' Ariel says, then Cameny flashes the exterior cameras up on Rachel's lens. The maintenance drone clings to the rover like a little toothed nightmare. Manipulators and cutters hack at cabling and power conduits. Again the rover slows as the drone severs another battery. How can this machine be here? Where did it come from? Cameny pans the cameras: there are the upraised horns of the BALTRAN relay among the thicket of solar panels, not two hundred metres away. That's the answer: her family has retasked the relay's maintenance drone.

But they've forgotten the rover is a depressurised model. Two hundred metres of vacuum is a stroll in sasuits.

Rachel touches Robson on the knee. He starts; his eyes are wide with fear.

'When I say go, follow me. We're going to have to finish this on foot.'

The rover drops with a jarring crash to one side. Rachel is thrown hard against her restraints. The rover is immobile, capsized at a crazy angle. The drone has cut away a wheel. Then it takes out the final camera.

'Robson, my love: go.'

The hatch blows. Dust and hills and the flat black heaven. Rachel grabs the side of the hatch and propels herself out. She hits the regolith, runs. Glances over her shoulder to see Robson land light as a hummingbird and run. The drone is crouched over the wreckage of the rover. Rachel thinks of Bryce Mackenzie, of cancer, if cancer could walk and hunt.

Now the bot raises itself on its manipulators from the wreckage of the rover. Unfolds cutters and long sharp plastic fingers. Climbs down on to the surface, picks its way towards her. It's not fast, but it is inexorable. And there are operations Rachel needs to perform before she and Robson can catapult to safety.

'Robson!'

Step by step, the bot gains on the boy. He is slew-footed on the regolith. He doesn't know how to move in vacuum, how to avoid kicking up blinding sheets of dust. His father kept him too long in the coddled womb of Boa Vista. Should have taken him up to see the Earth at age five, the Mackenzie way. Should have could have would have.

The hatch is ready, Cameny says. The personnel lock will only take one person at a time. Out on the Mares, the BALTRAN system is rough and ready, prioritised for bulk transport.

'Get in!' Rachel shouts. Robson scrabbles at the lock. He is so clumsy.

'I'm in!'

Cameny closes the hatch. Now Rachel must rotate in the capsule. Slow. Why is it so slow? Where is the bot? She doesn't have time for even a glance behind. Breath hisses through teeth in supreme concentration as Cameny powers up the launch sequence.

The pain in her right calf is so sharp and clean Rachel cannot even cry out. Her leg won't hold her. Something has been severed. Helmet displays flash red; she gasps as the sasuit fabric tightens above the breach, sealing the suit, compressing the wound.

Your right hamstring tendon has been severed behind the knee, Cameny announces. *Suit integrity is compromised. You are bleeding. The bot is here.*

'Get me in,' Rachel hisses and then the pain comes, more pain than she imagined could exist in the universe and she screams; terrible, bellowing agonised screams. Screams that sound impossible from a human throat. A movement, a dart, a second clean slash, and she's down. The bot is over her, a shadow against the black sky. Her suit lights glint from three drills, descending on her helmet visor.

'Launch it, Cameny! Get him out of here!'

Launch sequence initiated, Cameny says. *The probability of your survival is zero. Goodbye Rachel Mackenzie.*

Drill bits shriek on toughened visor. And at the end Rachel Mackenzie finds only rage: rage that she must die, that it must be here in the cold and dirt of lonely Flamsteed, rage that it is always family fucks you. Her visor shatters. As the air explodes from her helmet she feels the ground shake, sees the flicker of the BALTRAN capsule from the mouth of the launch tube.

Gone.

Rafa Corta is ire and thunder, striding at the head of his security detail. João de Deus is his town; his face is familiar among the Corta Hélio workers and ancillary staff, but not like this: an icon of rage and joy. He is Xango the Just, São Jeronimo, judge and defender. His people glance away from his eyes and make way for him.

The boy has already exited the lock. He stands alone in the arrivals, still in sasuit and helmet, smeared with dust, his familar hovering over his left shoulder.

'He taught me a trick,' Robson says. Joker relays his words to the world beyond the helmet. 'It's a real good trick.' Gloved hands take a deck of playing cards from a thigh pocket. Robson fans them out. His voice is dead, flat, alien. Joker catches every tone. 'Pick one.'

The cards fall from his fingers. His knees collapse, he pitches forwards. Rafa is there to take him.

'Your mother.' Rafa shakes the trembling boy. 'Where is your mother?'

FIVE

Duncan Mackenzie storms through Crucible. Humans make way for him, machines accommodate him. The CEO of Mackenzie Metals is not to be kept waiting for trivial safety regimes. Not in his pale wrath. Duncan Mackenzie's anger is grey, like his suit, his hair, the surface of the moon. Esperance has hardened to a ball of dull pewter.

Jade Sun-Mackenzie meets him at the lock to Robert Mackenzie's private car.

'Your father is undergoing a routine blood-scrub,' she says. 'You'll appreciate the process can't be disturbed.'

'I want to see him.' Duncan Mackenzie's voice is cold as the metal above his head is hot.

'My husband is undergoing a delicate and important medical treatment,' Jade Sun restates. Duncan Mackenzie's grip is at her throat. He slams her head back against the lock. A fat drip of blood runs slowly down the white lock. *You have a scalp contusion and possible impact trauma,* her familiar Tong Ren says.

'Take me to him!'

I have images, Esperance says. The familiar overlays Duncan Mackenzie's lens with a high-angle view of the old horror in a diagnostic cot. Nurses, human and machine, surround him. Tubes and lines pulse red.

'That's not real. You could have fed that to Esperance. You fuckers are clever like that.'

'You. Fuckers?' Jade Sun whispers. Duncan Mackenzie releases his grip.

'My daughter is dead,' Duncan Mackenzie says. 'My daughter is dead, do you hear?'

'Duncan, I'm so sorry. A terrible thing. Terrible. A software error.'

'The recovery team found precise cuts in her sasuit. That bot hamstrung her.' Duncan Mackenzie covers his mouth with his hands to hold in the horror. After a moment he says, 'They found drill marks on her helmet. That's a very precise software error.'

'Radiation regularly causes soft fails in chips. As you know, it's an endemic problem.'

'Do not fucking insult me!' Duncan Mackenzie roars. 'Endemic. Endemic! What kind of word is that? My daughter was killed. Did my father order this?'

'Robert would never do a thing like that. You cannot possibly suggest that your father – my oko, my husband – would order his own granddaughter assassinated. That is ridiculous. Ridiculous and odious. I've seen the report. It was a terrible robotic accident. Be thankful that the boy is unharmed.'

'And the Cortas are parading him around like a newly signed handball star. When that idiot Rafa Corta isn't swearing that he'll cut the throat of every Mackenzie he sees. We're on the edge of war because of this.'

'Robert would never court the possibility of harm to the company. Never.'

'You put a lot of words in my father's mouth. I'd like to hear them from his lips. Let me through.'

Jade Sun takes a step forward. The only way to the lock is through her.

'What are you saying?'

'Like you say, Robert would never harm his own granddaughter.'

'Is this an accusation?'

'Why won't you let me see my father?'

Duncan Mackenzie takes Jade Sun by the shoulders, lifts her, hurls her hard against the lock. She crumples. Hands fall on his shoulders. Strong arms wrestle him away from the gasping, shaken woman. Duncan Mackenzie tears free to confront his assailants. Four males in suits as grey and corporate as his own. Big men, Jo Moonbeams, heavy with Earth-muscle.

'Leave us,' he orders. The four men do not budge. Their eyes flicker to Jade Sun.

'These are my personal blades,' she says, still pale and shaking on the floor.

'Since when?' Duncan Mackenzie bellows. 'By whose authority?'

'Your father's authority. Since I started to feel unsafe in Crucible. Duncan, I think you should go.'

The largest blade, a mountainous Maori with rolls of muscle down the back of his neck, lays a hand on Duncan Mackenzie's shoulder.

'Get your fucking paw off me,' Duncan Mackenzie says and slaps away the hand. But there are four of them and they are big and they are not his. He lifts his hands: no trouble here. Security steps back. Duncan Mackenzie straightens the fall of his jacket, the alignment of his cuffs. Jade Sun's blades place themselves between Duncan Mackenzie and his stepmother.

'I will see my father. And I'm ordering my own investigation into what happened out there.'

Duncan Mackenzie turns and stalks away, a walk of shame and humiliation through the shafts of light from the smelting mirrors, but there is time for last thrown-back word, à l'esprit de l'escalier. 'I am CEO of this company. Not my father. Not you fucking people!'

'My fucking people stand shoulder to shoulder with your fucking people,' Jade Sun shouts. 'Vorontsovs are barbarians, the Asamoahs are peasants and the Cortas are gangsters straight from the favela. Suns and Mackenzies built this world. Suns and Mackenzies own it.'

'She's never out of that dress.' Helen de Braga and Adriana Corta stand by the rail of the eighth-level balcony, between the stone cheekbones of Ogun and Oxossi. The cheeks are dry, the waterfalls have been shut down. Gardeners, robotic and human, dredge leaves from the ponds and stream.

'Every time it gets dirty, Elis just prints her a new one,' Adriana Corta says. In her beloved red dress, Luna runs barefoot through the puddles at the bottom of the pools, splashing the garden bots, skipping from stepping stone to stepping stone in a complex game: this one must be landed on left-footed, that right-footed, the other two-footed or skipped over entirely. 'You must have had a favourite dress when you were that age.'

'Leggings,' Helen de Braga says. 'They had skulls and crossbones on them. I was eleven and a proper little pirate. My mother couldn't get them off me so she bought me another pair. I refused to wear them because they weren't the same, but the truth was, I didn't know which were which.'

'She has little hiding holes and dens all over Boa Vista,' Adriana Corta says. Luna disappears into the stand of bamboo. 'I know most of them – more than Rafa does. Not all of them. I don't want to know all of them. A girl has to keep some secrets.'

'When will you tell them?'

'I thought about my birthday but it seems too morbid. I'll know the time. I need to finish with Irmã Loa first. Make a full confession.'

Helen de Braga's lips tighten. She is a good Catholic still. Mass in João de Deus weekly; saints and novenas. Adriana Corta knows that she disapproves of Umbanda, under the eyes of pagan gods every day. What must she think of Adriana making holy confession to a priestess, not a priest?

'Look out for Rafa,' Adriana says.

'Enough with that kind of talk.'

'I will become less able and competent. I feel it already. And Lucas has his eyes on the throne.'

'He has always had his eyes on the throne.'

'He's having Rafa watched. He's using the assassination attempt to destabilise Rafa. And after what happened to Rachel...'

Helen de Braga crosses herself.

'Deus entre nós e do mal.'

'Rafa wants an independent investigation.'

'That will never happen.' Helen de Braga and Adriana Corta are of a generation, the pioneers. Helen was moneyed, an accountant, a Tripeiro from Porto. Adriana was self-made, an engineer, a Carioca of Rio. Adriana reneged on her vow never to trust a non-Brazilian. More than nationality, more than language; they were both women. Helen de Braga has quietly directed Corta Hélio's finances for over forty years. She is as much family as any of Adriana's blood.

'Robson is safe,' Helen de Braga says. Adriana's children have always been her second family. Her own children and grandchildren are scattered across the moon in a dozen Corta Hélio facilities.

'That filthy nikah,' Adriana says. 'I've already had demands for compensation from Crucible.'

'Ariel will shred that in court.'

'She's a good girl,' Adriana says. 'I fear for her. She is so terribly vulnerable. Is it silly to want her here, at home, with us and Heitor and fifty escoltas between her and the world? But you never stop worrying, do you? The Court of Clavius, even the Pavilion of the White Hare, they won't protect her.'

'How did we get to be two old women standing on a balcony worrying about vendettas?' Helen de Braga says. Adriana Corta rests her hand on her friend's.

At the heart of the bamboo grove is a hidden place, a whispering special place. Natural dieback has exposed the soil and inquisitive hands and feet have picked and trodden it into an enchanted circle.

This is Luna's secret room. The cameras can't see it, the bots are too big to follow her path through the stems, her father knows nothing and she's pretty sure that Grandmother Adriana, who knows everything, doesn't know this one. Luna has staked her claim with scraps of ribbon tied to the the canes, print-ceramic Disney figures, buttons and bows from loved clothes, pieces of bot, cat's cradles of wiring. She crouches in the magic circle. The bamboo stirs and whispers above her head. Felipe the head gardener once explained to her that Boa Vista is big enough to have its own small winds but Luna doesn't want there to be a scientific reason.

'Luna,' she whispers and her familiar unfolds its wings. The wings open to fill her vision, then close to form her mother.

'Luna.'

'Mãe. Hi. When can I see you?'

Lousika Asamoah glances away from her daughter.

'It's not so easy, anzinho.' She speaks Portuguese to her daughter. 'It's not fun here any more.'

'Oh love, I know. But tell me, tell me; what have been doing?'

'Well,' says Luna Corta, holding up fingers to count off, 'Yesterday, Madrinha Elis and I played animal dress-up. We got the printer and the network kept showing us things and we kept printing out animal clothes. I was an anteater. That's an animal, from the other place. It's got a big long nose that touches the ground. And a big long tail.' She folds a finger, one transformation counted. 'And I was a bird with a big... What's that thing on their mouths?'

'Beaks. They are their mouths, coracão.'

'A beak and it was as long as my arm. And yellow and green.'

'I think that's a toucan.'

'Yes.' Another counted. 'And a big cat with spots. Elis was a bird, like Tia Ariel's familiar.'

'Beijaflor,' Lousika says.

'Yes. She liked that one a lot. She asked me if I wanted to be a

142

butterfly but a moth is really like a butterfly so I said she could be the butterfly, I think she liked that a lot too.'

'Well, that sounds fun.'

'Yessss,' Luna concedes. 'But . . . It's always Madrinha Elis. I used to go to play dates in João, but Papai doesn't let me do that now. He won't let me see anyone who isn't family.'

'Oh my treasure. It's only for a while.'

'Like you said you would only go away for a while.'

'I did, yes.'

'You promised.'

'I will come back, I promise.'

'Can I come to Twé and see real animals, not dress-up ones?'

'It's not so easy, my love.'

'Do you have ant-eaters? I really want to see ant-eaters.'

'No, Luna, no ant-eaters.'

'You could make me one. Real small, like Verity Mackenzie's pet ferret.'

'I don't think so, Luna. Your know how your grandmother feels about having animals around Boa Vista.'

'Daddy's been shouting a lot. I hear him. From my special place. Shouting and angry.'

'It's not you, Luna. Believe me. It's not me either, this time.' Lousika Asamoah smiles but the smile puzzles Luna. Now Lousika's smile vanishes and in its place she seems to be chewing her words as if they taste bad. 'Luna; your tai-oko Rachel . . .'

'She's gone.'

'Gone?'

'Gone to Heaven. Except there is no Heaven. Just the Zabbaleen who take you away and grind you down to powder and give you to AKA to feed to the plants.'

'Luna! That's a terrible thing to say.'

'Helen de Braga believes in Heaven but I think it's a silly thing. I've seen the Zabbaleen.'

'Luna, Rachel...'

'Dead dead dead dead dead. I know. That's why Daddy is upset. That's why he's shouting and smashing things.'

'He's smashing things?'

'Everything. Then he prints it out new and smashes it up again. Are you all right, Mamãe?'

'I'll talk to Rafa – your daddy.'

'Does that mean you're coming back?'

'Oh Luna, I wish I could.'

'So when will I see you?'

'It's Vo Adriana's birthday at the end of the lune,' Lousika says. Luna's face brightens like noon. 'Oh yes!'

'I'll be here for that. I promise. I will see you, Luna. Love you.' Lousika Asamoah blows a kiss. Luna leans forward to place her lips on her virtual mother's face.

'Bye Mamãe.'

Lousika Asamoah unfolds Luna into moth form. The familiar returns to its ordained place above Luna Corta's left shoulder. As she twists and twines back along the twisty path through the bamboo, Luna becomes aware of a change in the the air, a humidity, and a noise. The gardeners have completed their tasks and turned the cascades on again. Water drips, tears, gushes, then torrents from the eyes and lips of the orixas. Boa Vista is filled with the gleeful rush of playing waters.

The ball bends. It's a beautiful fast arc curving in from right to left, from the height of a throwing hand at the apex of a dive to the bottom left corner of the goal-line. The goalkeeper never moves. It's in the back of the net before Rafa hits the deck.

The elegance of LHL, what makes handball the beautiful game on the moon and an Olympic oddity on Earth, is its relationship with gravity. With and against. The size of the net, the dimensions of the court and the goal area constrain the advantages of lunar gravity, while gravity makes possible the tricks of spin and slice and ball bending that make spectators gasp at the magic skills of the top players.

'You're supposed to stop the ball,' Rafa Corta laughs. Robson sullenly picks it out of the back of the net. How competitive can a father be against his children? How much can he gloat when he scores against them? 'Come on.' He dances back across the court, feet barely brushing the wood. This handball court at Boa Vista is Rafa Corta's indulgence. The playing surface is perfectly sprung. The sound system was installed by the same engineer who built Lucas's listening room, though its acoustic is geared for rousing go-faster beats rather than the subtleties of old school bossa. There are concealed bleachers for private invitation matches between Rafa and his LHL rivals. It's the most perfect court on the moon, and Robson can't throw, can't catch, can't run, can't score, can't do anything on it. Rafa intercepts Robson's dribble, the boy scrambles back and in under a second he is picking the ball out of the back of the net again.

'What did those Mackenzies teach you, eh?'

Corta security rushed Robson straight from the BALTRAN capsule to the Boa Vista medical centre. His escape from Crucible had left no physical damage but the psych AIs noted a reluctance to speak and a compulsion to show a card-trick to any human who showed an interest in him. Psych recommended a prolonged course of trauma counselling. Rafa Corta's therapy is more robust.

'Didn't they teach you this?'

Rafa throws the ball hard and flat. It strikes Robson on the shoulder. He cries out.

'Didn't they teach you to dodge and weave?'

Robson throws the ball back at his father. There is venom in it but no skill. Rafa neatly picks it out of the air and curves it back at Robson. Robson tries to move but it strikes him on the thigh with a clear slap.

'Stop doing that!' Robson says.

'So what did they teach you?'

Robson turns his back and drops the ball. Rafa scoops it up and throws it at point blank range with all his strength. Handball game-suits are tight and thin and the smack of ball against ass is loud as a bone breaking. Robson turns. His face is tight with fury. Rafa catches the ball on the rebound. Robson lunges to slap the ball from his father's hand but it's not there: Rafa has dribbled it, turned and scooped it up again. He slams it hard. The court echoes with the boom of ball on flooring. Robson recoils from the ball bouncing up in his face.

'Afraid of a ball?' Rafa says and it's back in his hand again. Again Robson lunges. Again Rafa skips around him, a circle of bounces around his son. Robson turns, turns but he can't follow the ball. His head turns this way, that way. Boom! He turns into the bounce and it takes him in the belly.

'Once afraid of a ball, always afraid of a ball,' Rafa taunts.

'Stop it!' Robson yells. And Rafa stops.

'Angry. Good.'

And the ball is back, bouncing, hand to hand. Badam badam badam. Shoot. Robson yelps at the slap of weighty handball. He yells and throws himself at his father. Rafa is big but fast and light of movement. He dances effortlessly away from his son. The mocking ease with which Rafa outclasses Robson stokes the boy's anger higher.

'Anger is good, Robbo.'

'Don't call me that.'

'Why not, Robbo?' Dribble, shoot, sting. Catch and bounce, always a blink ahead of Robson's fingers.

'That's what they called me.'

'I know. Robbo.'

'Shut up shut up shut up shut up!'

'Make me, Robbo. Get the ball and I'll shut up.'

Robson doubles over at a point-blank impact to the stomach.

'Your mama is dead Robson. They killed her. What does that make you want to do?'

146

'Go away. Leave me alone.'

'I can't, Robson. You're a Corta. Your mamãe. My oko.'

'You hated her.'

'She was your mother.'

'Shut up!'

'What do you want to do?'

'I want you to stop!'

'I will, Robson. I promise. But you have to tell me what you want to do.'

Robson stands stone still in the centre of the court. His hands are held low, outstretched a few fingers' breadth from his body.

'You want me to say I want them dead.'

The ball smashes him in the back. Robson rocks but does not move.

'You want me to say I will get back at them for Mamãe, however long it takes.'

To the belly. Robson wavers but does not fall.

'You want me to swear like vengeance and vendetta on them.'

Belly, thigh, shoulder.

'And I do that and they do it back and I do more and they do more and it never ends.'

Belly. Belly. Face. Face. Face.

'It never ends, Pai!' Robson punches out. He hits the small, dense handball a glancing blow, enough to deflect it. In an instant it's back in Rafa's hand.

'What they taught me in Crucible,' Robson says. 'What I learned from Hadley.' Rafa can't clearly see what Robson does, but in a sly fast heartbeat he steps inside his father's reach and the ball is in the boy's hand. 'They taught me to take a man's weapon and use it against him.' He flings the ball the length of court and walks off to the sound of its slow, dying bounces.

Badam. Badam. Badam.

*

From its claw-hold on the inside of the Oxala's right eye, the spy-fly observes the board table of Corta Hélio.

The Serpent Sea floats in Lucas Corta's augmented vision. Socrates and Yemanja display identical maps to Rafa and Adriana Corta.

'A prospecting site at Mare Anguis.' Toquinho zooms in, rings the named areas. 'Twenty thousand square kilometres of mare-regolith.'

Lucas lifts a finger and taps the illusory map. Data from selenological surveys overlay the grey and dust. Rafa flicks over the information but Lucas sees his mother's eyes narrow with concentration.

'I've taken the liberty of running a cost-benefit analysis. Corta Hélio starts turning a profit in the third quarter after the claim is licensed. We can reposition extraction plant from Condorcet. Condorcet is eighty per cent mined out; we have materiel mothballed. Within two years we will be extracting half a billion dollars of helium-3 annually. We estimate the life of Mare Anguis at ten years.'

'This is thorough,' Rafa says. Sourness on his tongue and lips. Through his little fly Lucas knows of the private, furniture-smashing tantrums. The constant bodyguard, even among the waters of Boa Vista. The hesitation in Luna before her father scoops her up and throws her up into the air. Golden, affable Rafa is turning dark, ugly with sudden anger at parties and receptions. Berating his useless handball manager, his useless coaching team, his useless players. Lucas appreciates irony: the man who had no good word for his wife in life rages at her death. The news channels reported Rachel Mackenzie's death as a catastrophic depressurisation event. A delicate lie. The press won't press. Journalists who vex the Five Dragons suffer their own catastrophic depressurisation events. Report the smiles and the frocks, the affairs and the beautiful children, the marriages and the adulteries. Don't tug the Dragon's tail.

'How soon?' Adriana asks.

'Twelve ZMT on Muku.'

'Not long,' Rafa says.

'Long enough,' Lucas says.

'This is sound information?' Adriana asks. Lucas sees her eyes darting over her own virtual lunar terrain. She has the highest surface hours of any living Corta, even Carlinhos. She may not have locked a helmet for ten years but once a duster, always a duster. She will be analysing the terrain, the dust cover, the logistics, the electrical effect of the moon's transit of Earth's magnetotail, the likelihood of a solar storm.

'It comes from Ariel. A tip-off from someone in the Pavilion of the White Hare.'

'Hell of a tip-off,' Rafa says. Lucas hears an energy in his voice, an interest in his eyes. His muscles tighten, he draws himself up from his uncharacteristic stoop. The old gold light glows under his skin. It's game night. The teams are in the tunnel and the crowd is in full cry. But he is still suspicious. 'We have to act now.'

'Delicacy,' Adriana says. She presses the tips of her fingers together, vaults of a bone cathedral. Lucas knows this gesture well. She is calculating. 'Too fast, we expose Ariel and I spend the rest of my years fighting my way through the Court of Clavius for alleged claim-jumping. Too slow . . .'

The law on extraction rights is primitive: the steel law of placer stakes and gold rushes that shaped the North American West. Who-ever stakes out the four corners of the newly released territory has forty-eight hours to lodge a legal claim and the licence fee with the LDC. It's a straight race. Lucas has seen Rafa screaming, incoherent, transcendent at Moço games. This is the same thrill. This is what he loves: movement. Energy. Action.

'What assets have we?'

Lucas commands Toquinho to highlight extraction units around the target quadrangle. Orange icons lie at varying distance from north-west, north-east and south-east corners. The south-west vertex is dark.

'I have the north-east Crisium units in motion. It will be hard to disguise it as a routine redeployment or a scheduled maintenance.'

Lucas is jonmu: movement orders are not his to issue. Anger flickers; Rafa contains it. He passed the test.

'My concern are the vertices.' Toquinho zooms in the scale.

'We have nothing we can get there in less than thirty hours,' Rafa says, reading the deployment tags.

'Nothing on the surface,' Lucas hints. Rafa picks the ball up.

'I'll go talk to Nik Vorontsov,' Rafa says. He dips his head to his mother and is in motion: decisions to be made, actions to be taken.

'A simple call will save hours,' Lucas says.

'This is why I'm hwaejang, brother. Business is all about relationships.'

Lucas dips his head. Now is the time for a small acquiescence. Let his mother see that her boys are united.

'Bring this home, Rafa,' Adriana says. Her face is bright, her eyes clear. Years have rolled from her. Lucas sees the Adriana Corta of his childhood, the empire builder, the dynasty-maker; the figure in the doorway of the berçário. Madrinha Amalia's whisper: Say goodnight to your mother, Lucas. The smell of her perfume as she leaned over the bed. She wears it still. People are loyal to perfume in a way they are not to any other personal adornment.

'I will, mãezinha.' The most intimate term of endearment.

Unseen, the spying fly disengages from its cranny and floats after Rafa.

The bolt of electric blue hits Lucasinho square on the abs. Blue splat to join the red, the purple, the green, the yellow. Almost none of his bare body is unstained. He is a harlequin of colours, as bright as a reveller on Holi.

'Whoa,' Lucasinho says as the hallucinogen kicks in. He spins, gets a shot off from his splatgun and then the world unfolds into millions of butterflies. He turns, grinning like a fool, at the centre of a tornado of illusory wings.

The game is Hunting, played up and down and through the

Madina agrarium, with bare skins and guns that fire random bolts of coloured hallucinogens.

The butterflies open their wings and link and lock together. Reality returns. Lucasinho ducks under the fronds of a towering plantain. Rotting fronds mash to slime beneath his bare feet. He advances, gun at the ready, still wide-eyed and trippy after the blue. He has been shattered into diamond tiles, flown up the side of an endless skyscraper, watched the colours drip from the world into purple, been his left big toe for what seemed an eternity, chasing and being chased through towering cylinders of dappled light, sniped at from positions high among yams and dhal bushes.

Fronds rustle: movement. Splatgun muzzle next to his cheek, Lucasinho ducks under foliage into a small, damp clearing, heady with growth and rot, a hidden nest.

Something touches the nape of his neck.

'Splat,' says a female voice. Lucasinho awaits the sting of the ink-hit, the trip into somewhere else. He came to the party because it was at Twé and he might meet Abena Asamoah. Guerrilla games were not Abena Asamoah's fun. But it is exciting to chase and be chased, to be lost and a little bit scared at times, to beat people to the draw and shoot them, to snipe them so that they never knew what had hit them, and be hit in return. The gun against his neck is sexy. He's at the mercy of this girl. Arousing helplessness.

He hears the trigger click. Nothing.

'Shit,' the girl says. 'Out.'

Lucasinho rolls and comes up, splatgun levelled.

'No no no no!' the girl cries, hands held up in surrender. Ya Afuom Asamoah, an abusua-sister of Abena and Kojo. Leopard abusua. AKA kinship makes his head hurt. Her skin bears five colour-blots, right hip, left knee, left breast, left thigh, the right side of her head. Lucasinho pulls the trigger. Nothing.

'Out,' he says. The same call rings out across the tubefarm, down from the high terraces and the sniping positions in the solar array.

Out. Out. Faintly, down the tunnels that connect the agrarium tubes. Out. Out.

'You're lucky,' Lucasinho says.

'What do you mean?' Ya Afuom says. 'I had you on your knees.' She looks him up and down. 'You're covered, man. You need a bath. Come on. This is the best. You're not scared of fish, are you?'

'Why?'

'You get them in the ponds. Frogs and ducks too. Some people freak at the idea of being touched by a living thing that isn't human.'

'I think this game is broken,' Lucasinho says. 'The more you get hit, the easier it is to get hit.'

'It's only broken if you're playing to win,' Ya Afuom says.

The bar is set up on the decking. Drinks and vapers in plenty but Lucasinho has had so many chemicals through his brain that he doesn't welcome any more. The pools are already full. Voices and water-splash ring up the shaft of the tubefarm. Lucasinho lowers himself carefully into the water. Do fish bite, do they suck, can they swim up your dick-hole? Mildly hallucinogenic skin-paint dissolves into the water; halos of red and yellow and green and blue. What does that do to the fish? What does that do to the people who eat the fish? He can't imagine eating anything that's shared water with him. He can't imagine eating anything with eyes.

'Hey ha!' Ya Afuom splashes in beside him. Hips, butts touch. Legs entwine. Bellies rub, fingers walk.

'Was that a fish?'

Ya Afuom giggles and Lucasinho finds he has a breast in his hand and her fingers cradling his ass. His own hands dive deeper through the blood-warm water, seeking folds and secrets. 'Oh you!' She has the best ass since Grigori Vorontsov. Then he's hard and they're touching foreheads and looking on each other's eyes and she's laughing at him, because naked men are ridiculous.

'I always heard the Asamoah girls were polite and shy,' teases Lucasinho.

'Who told you that?' Ya Afuom says and pulls him in.

Abena. Glimpsed through tomato leaves. Moving from the bar towards the service tunnel.

'Hey! Hey! Abena! Wait!'

He surges up out of the pool. Abena turns, frowns.

'Abena!' He strides dripping towards her. His semi swings painfully. Abena raises an eyebrow.

'Hi Luca.'

'Hey Abena.'

Ya Afuom slips in beside him, puts her arm around him.

'Since when?' Abena says and Ya Afuom smiles and presses closer. 'Have fun, Luca.' She drifts away.

'Abena!' Lucasinho calls but she's gone and now Ya Afuom is gone too. 'Abena! Ya! What's going on?' Some game of abusua-sisters. Now the air is chill and the semi is gone and the hangover of the multiple hallucinogen hits makes him shivery and paranoid and the party has soured. He finds his clothes, begs a favour to get a ticket back to Meridian and finds the apartment very full of Kojo and his new toe. Lucasinho can stay the night but only the night. Homeless fuckless Abena-less.

Wagner is late into Meridian. Theophilus is a small town, a thousand lives on the northern edge of the great desolation of Sinus Asperitatis where only machines move. The rail link to the mainline went in three years ago, three hundred kilometres of single track; four railcars a day to the interchange at Hypatia. A micrometeorite strike took out the signalling gear at Torricelli, trapping Wagner – pacing, scratching his itchy skin, drinking glass after glass of ice tea, howling in his heart – for six hours until the maintenance bots slotted in a new module. The railcar was crowded, standing room only for the hour-long ride.

Am I changing before your eyes? Wagner thought. *Do I smell different, other than human?* He has always imagined he does.

The Torricelli strike has thrown out travel plans over much of the western hemisphere. By the time Wagner gets into Hypatia Station – little more than the junction of four branch lines from the southern seas and central Tranquillity with Equatorial One – the platforms are thronged with commuters and shift workers, grandparents on pilgrimage around their extended families. Tribes of children; running, shrieking; sometimes complaining at the long wait. Their voices grate on Wagner's heightened senses. His familiar has managed to book him on to Regional 37; three hours' wait. He finds a dark and quiet place away from the families and the discarded noodle cartons and drinks cups, sits down with his back against a pillar, pulls his knees up and puts his head down and redesigns his familiar. Adeus, Sombra: olá Dr Luz. The pillars shake, the long halls ring to the impact of fast-passing trains, up there. Zabbaleen robots sniff around him, seeking recyclables. Calls, messages, pictures from Meridian. *Where are you we want you it's kicking off.* Train trouble. *Miss you, Little Wolf.* None from Analiese. She knows the rules. There is the light half of life, and there is the dark half.

Dr Luz couldn't book Wagner his usual window seat so he can't spend the journey gazing up at the Earth. That's good: there's work to be done. He has to devise a strategy. He can't arrange a meeting. One whisper of Corta and Elisa Stracchi will run. He'll lure her with a commission, but he'll have to make it convincing and exciting. She will do due diligence. Companies within companies, nested structures, a labyrinth of holding bodies; a typical lunar corporate set-up. Not too complicated; that too will spark suspicion. He will need a new familiar, a counterfeit social media trail, an online history. Corta Hélio AIs can fabricate these but it takes time even for them. It's hard to be thorough when he can feel the Earth up there, tearing at him, quickening and changing him with every fast kilometre. It's like the first days of love, like being sick with excitement, like the moment of euphoria at the edge of being drunk, like dance hall drugs, like vertigo, but these are weak analogs; none of the moon's languages has a word for what it's like to change when the Earth is round.

He almost runs from the station. It's small morning hours when he falls into the Packhouse. Amal is waiting.

'Wagner.' Amal has embraced the culture of the two selves more fully than Wagner and has taken the Alter pronoun. Why should pronouns only be about gender? né says. Né pulls Wagner to ner, bites his lower lip, tugs with enough force to cause pain and assert ner authority. Né is pack leader. Then the true kiss. 'You hungry, you want anything?' Wagner's demeanour says exhaustion more eloquently than words. Change days burn human resources. 'Go on, kid. Jose and Eiji have still to arrive.'

In the dressing room Wagner peels off his clothes. Showers. Pads soft-footed to the bedroom. The sleeping pit is already full. He lowers himself in; the soft upholstery, the fake-fur lining caress him. Bodies grunt and turn and mutter in their sleep. Wagner slides in among them, cupping and curling like a child. Skin presses close to him. His breathing falls into rhythm. Familiars stand over the entwined bodies; angels of the innocent. The union of the pack.

The rover is lunar utility at its purest: a roll-frame open to vacuum, two rows of three seats facing each other, air plant, power, suspension and AI, four huge wheels between which the passenger frame hangs. Shit fast. Clamped in with her Surface Activity Squad, Marina jolts against the locking bars as the vehicle bounces up rilles, leaps crater rims. Marina tries to calculate her speed but the close horizon and her unfamiliarity with the scale of lunar landmarks gives her mathematics no anchorhold. Fast. And boring. Degrees of boredom: the high blue eye of Earth, the low grey hills of Luna, the blank faceplate of the sasuit opposite her – Paulo Ribeiro, says the familiar tag. Hetty flicks up in-suit entertainment. Marina plays twelve games of Marble Mayhem, watches *Hearts and Skulls* (a holding episode, as the writers maneouvre the series arc and characters towards the finale) and a new video from home. Mom waves from her wheelchair on the porch. Her arms are thin and blotched, her hair a grey straggle, but she smiles. Kessie and her nieces, and Canaan the dog. And there, oh there is Skyler her brother, back from Indonesia, and his wife Nisrina and Marina's other nephews and niece. Against a background of grey rain, grey rain cascading from the overwhelmed porch gutter, a waterfall, rain so loud everyone on the porch shouts to be heard.

Behind the blank mask of her faceplate, Marina cries. The helmet sucks up her tears.

A tap on her shoulder. Marina unblanks her faceplate: Carlinhos leans across the narrow aisle of the rover. He points over Marina's shoulder. The seat restraints allow just enough freedom to turn and take her first sight of the mining plant. Spidery gantries of the extractors reach up from beneath the close horizon. The squad mission is a scheduled inspection of Corta Hélio's Tranquillity East extraction facility. Moments later the rover brakes in a spray of dust and the harnesses unclamp.

'Stay with me,' Carlinhos says on Marina's private channel. She drops to the tyre-streaked regolith. She is among the helium harvesters. They are moon-ugly, gaunt and utilitarian. Chaotic, hard to comprehend in a glance. Girders house complex screws and separator grids and transport belts. Mirror arms track the sun, focusing energy on solar stills that fraction out helium-3 from the regolith. Collection spheres, each marked with its harvest. Helium-3 is the export crop but the Corta process also distils hydrogen, oxygen and nitrogen, the fuels of life. High-speed Archimedes screws accelerate waste material into jets that arc a kilometre high before falling in plumes of dust like inverted fountains. Earthlight refracts from the fine dust and glass particles, casting moonbows. Marina walks up to the samba-line. Ten extractors work a five-kilometre front, advancing at a crawl on wheels three times Marina's height. The near horizon partly hides the extractors at each end of the samba-line. Bucket wheels dig tons of regolith at a scoop, moving in perfect synchronisation: nodding heads. Marina imagines tortoise-kaiju with medieval fortresses on their backs. Godzilla should be fighting these things. Marina feels the vibration of industry through her sasuit boots, but she hears nothing. All is silence. Marina looks up at the mirror arrays and waste jets high above her head, back at the parallel lines of tracks, ahead at the ridge of Roma Messier. This is her workplace. This is her world.

'Marina.'

Her name. Someone said her name. Carlinhos's gloved hand grasps her forearm, pushes her hand gently away from her helmet latches. The latches: she had been about to open them. She had been about to remove her sasuit helmet in the middle of the Sea of Tranquillity.

'Oh my God,' Marina says, awed by the absent-minded ease with which she had almost killed herself. 'I'm sorry. I'm so sorry. I just…'

'Forgot where you were?' Carlinhos Corta says.

'I'm okay.' But she isn't. She has committed the unforgivable sin. She has forgotten where she is. Her first time out in the field and every word of training has fallen from her. She's panting, snatching for breath. Don't panic. Panic will kill you.

'Do you need to go back to the rover?' Carlinhos asks.

'No,' she says. 'I'll be fine.'

But the visor is so close to her face she can feel it. She is trapped inside a bell jar. She must be rid of it out of it. Free, breathe free.

'The only reason I'm not sending you back to the rover is because you said, *I'll*,' Carlinhos says. 'Take your time.'

He's reading her biosigns on his hud; pulse rate, blood sugar, gases and respiratory function.

'I want to work,' Marina says. 'Give me something to do, take my mind off it.'

Carlinhos's blank helmet visor is motionless for a long moment. Then he says. 'Get to work.'

The moon is almost as violent with robots as it is with human meat. Unfiltered radiation eats AI chips. Light degrades construction plastic. The monthly magnetotail, the event of the moon passing through the streaming coma of Earth's magnetic field, can short weakened electrical circuits and whip up brief but destructive dust devils. Dust. Chief devil of the Tranquillity East samba-line. Everywhere dust. Always dust. It coats struts and spars and spokes and surfaces like fur. Marina moves a finger gingerly over a structural truss. The fuzz of dust moves like hairs to the dance of the electrostatic charge of her sasuit. Over lunes dust grinds, wears, abrades, destroys. Marina's job is regaussing. It's simple enough for a Jo Moonbeam and fun to watch. A timer sets the magnetic and electrical reversal and she runs in great bounding moon-strides to the safe distance. The field reverses and repels the charged dust particles in a sudden cloud of silver powder. It is pretty and dramatic and very more-ish. Marina sees in terrestrial, biological similes: an ocean-wet dog shaking its coats; a forest fungus exploding a puffball of spores. The module team is at work even as the dust settles on their sasuits, swapping chipsets and actuators: work robots find hard. Marina's fingers trace graffiti hidden like heiroglyphs under the dust: the names of lovers, handball teams, imprecations and curses in all the Moon's languages and scripts.

Boof. Marina gausses off another soft explosion of dust. It should make a noise. The silence is improper. *Boof*, she whispers inside her helmet. She hears laughter on a private channel.

'Everyone does that,' Carlinhos says.

Under the dust are hieroglyphs. Generations of dusters have left their names, their curses, their gods and their lovers on the bare metal in a dozen colours of vacuum pens. Pyotr H. Fuck this shit. Moços HC.

She *boofs* with every extractor. There are tricks to moon-work. Maintain concentration. The sameness of the terrain, the closeness of the horizon, the uniformity of the extractors, the mesmerising weave on their scoop-heads; all conspired to sedate, to hypnotise. Marina finds her thoughts drifting to Carlinhos running, tassles and weaves and body oil. She shakes him out of her head. The second trick is also a seduction. Not all pressure suits are equal. A sasuit is not a diving suit. There is no water resistance, no air resistance on the surface. Things move fast. Oleg's head was crushed in training because he made that very mistake. Mass, speed, momentum. Concentrate. Focus. Check your suit reports. Water temperature air radiation. Pressure, coms, network. Channels, weather reports. The Moon has weather, none of it good. Magnetotail, solar activity. A dozen things to check every minute, and still do her work. Some squadmates are listening to music. How do they do that? By the fifth extractor Marina's muscles are aching. Focus. Concentrate.

So deep is her concentration, so sharp her focus, that Marina doesn't notice when alerts go off across the public channel as the name above Paulo Ribeiro's helmet goes red, and then white.

Rafa runs his hands over the burnished aluminium of the landing strut.

'She's beautiful Nik.'

The VTO transporter *Orel* stands bathed in kilowatt brilliance from twenty floodlights. The lifter's own search-spots highlight hull, thruster pods, the clustered spheres of the fuel tanks, the manipulator arms, the recessed pilot windows, the VTO eagle on the nose.

'Fuck off, Rafa Corta,' Nikolai Vorontsov says. 'She is not beautiful. Nothing on the moon is beautiful. You are such a shitter.' He laughs like a landslide.

Nikolai is everyone's idea of a Vorontsov, a wall of a man, as broad as he is tall. Bearded, long hair braided. Earth-blue eyes and a deep booming voice. He amplifies the accent. No follower of the current taste for retro fashion, Nik Vorontsov. Shorts with many pockets, workboots, T-shirt straining over heavy muscles slumping into slack flab. Like all his family, his familiar is the double-headed eagle, with his own personal heraldic device emblazoned on the shield. He is professionally Vorontsov.

'It's not how she looks,' Rafa says, 'It's what she is.'

'Now really fuck off,' Nik Vorontsov says.

Orel is a moonship. A point-to-point surface transporter. The most expensive and spendthrift means of travel on the moon. The hydrogen and oxygen in the spherical tanks are precious; the fuel for life, not rocket thrusters. It's the same insanity as burning oil for electricity, up on old Earth. On the moon, energy is cheap, resources rare. People and goods travel by train, rover, surface bus, decreasingly the BALTRAN, the orbital tethers, their own muscle power on foot and wheel and wing. They don't fly in the cargo pods of moonships.

VTO maintains a fleet of ten transporters stationed at widely dispersed locations around the moon. They are the emergency service, the ambulance, the rescue team, the lifeboat. Nowhere is more than thirty minutes flying time from a transporter hub. Nik Vorontsov commands the fleet and is occasional pilot, engineer and lover of his ugly moonships. They are dearer to him than any of his children.

'So, you come all the way from John of God to lick my ugly babies and tell me they are beautiful?' Nik Vorotnsov asks. He says the name of the city in Globo because he has always made a play about how impossible it is to pronounce Portuguese. He and Rafa are old university friends. They studied together, they gymmed together: weights and body culture. Nik went further up Muscle Road than Rafa, but Rafa has made it business to keep on top of the sport to be able to discuss supplements and training regimes with his former gym buddy when they meet at the Nevsky Bar in Meridian over vodka.

'I came all the way from João de Deus to hire one of your babies,' Rafa says.

'Any baby in particular?'

'*Sokol* at Luna 18.' Knowing the locations of the VTO lifeboats is core surface-work knowledge, as is an up-to-date rescue insurance.

'So sorry. That baby is rotated out for maintenance,' Nik Vorontsov says.

'What about *Pustelga* at Joliot?'

'Ah. *Pustelga*. Still waiting spaceworthiness certification. The LDC is so slow.'

'That's the entire Tranquillity-Serenity-Crisium sector without any cover.'

'I know. It's deplorable. Civil servants – hah. What can I do about it? Be careful out there.'

Rafa slaps *Orel*'s landing leg.

'This one.'

'When do you need her?'

'A forty-eight-hour wet lease, from now.'

Nik Vorontsov sucks in the air through his teeth and Rafa knows that *Orel* will not be available for that time, that no Vorontsov transporter will be available. Rafa's jaw and belly muscles tighten. Anger blisters hot across his face, his hands. The personal touch, he had assured Lucas. Business is all about relationships. Now he has come all this way in his stylish clothes and groomed hair and manicured hands to be made to look like a fool by this Vorontsov blockhouse.

'How much do you need?'

'Rafa, this is undignified.'

'Who got to you?'

'Rafa, this is not good talk.'

'The Mackenzies. Was it Duncan, or did the old man crank himself up to doing it personally? Family to family. Robert, it'll have been Robert. Tying up the transporter fleet, that's his sense of style. Duncan never had any style. Did he ask you personally, or did it ping up to old Valery and he told you to jump?'

'Rafa, I think you should leave now.'

Rage bursts inside Rafa, a surge of boiling blood. He is shouting in Nik Vorontsov's face, speckling him with spittle.

'You want to make an enemy of me? You want to make an enemy of my family? This is the Cortas. We can fuck you so many ways you will never get out from it. Who the fuck are you? Bus drivers and cabbies.'

Nik Vorontsov wipes the back of his hand across his face.

'Rafa—'

'Fuck you, we don't need you. We will get this claim, and then the Cortas will fucking deal with you.' Rafa petulantly kicks the transporter's landing leg. Nik Vorontsov roars in Russian and Corta security has Rafa's arms pinioned. They came out of nowhere, silent, well-dressed, strong.

'Senhor, let's go.'

'Let me fucking go!' Rafa shouts to his bodyguards.

'I'm afraid not, Senhor,' says the first escolta, wrestling Rafa away from Nik Vorontsov.

'I'm ordering you,' Rafa says.

'We're not on your orders,' says First Escolta.

'Lucas Corta's apologies for any slight to your family, Senhor Vorontsov,' says Second Escolta, a tall woman in a well-cut suit.

'Get your boss the fuck off my base!' Nikolai Vorontsov roars.

'At once senhor,' says Second Security. Rafa spits as he is man-handled towards the door. The gob flies far and elegantly in the lunar gravity. Nik Vorontsov dodges it easily but it isn't aimed at him. It's aimed at his ship, his baby, his precious *Orel*.

The Professional Handball Owners Club is small, comfortable, intensely private. It displays a flagrant discretion: leave your escoltas at the door. The clubs heavily-muscular security tap left forefingers to their pineal glands as you pass: *no familiars*. The staff will politely remind you until you comply. The club is sporty not luxurious; its ambiance recalls university colloquiums. It has two dozen members, all of them men.

Two dozen men, two dozen friends, and Rafa doesn't want to speak to any of them. Jaden Wen Sun calls from the depths of a club chair across the salon; Rafa waves an answer and strides for his room. He is charred with anger. He slams the door, lifts a chair and slings it effortlessly across the room. Table, lamps smash and fall. He kicks the shards high and hard. He rips the old-fashioned screen from the wall, how the owners watch their team in the so-discreet PHO Club, smashes it across the edge of the dressing table, smashes and smashes and smashes until it breaks in two. He wedges the broken screen halves into the output hopper of the printer, levers them until he has warped the printer into uselessness.

A tap at the door.

'Mr Corta.'

'Nothing.'

The rage has burned to embers. He breaks everything. This room, the deal with Nik Vorontsov – all the same rage. He spat on Nik Vorontsov's ship. He might have spat on his daughter. When he called João de Deus, Lucas's pauses and long silences were more eloquent condemnations that any outburst of anger. He has failed the family. He always fails the family. Everything he touches falls to ruin.

Rafa has been careful in his room-smashing red rage. The bar is intact. He sits on the bed, eyes the bottles like lovers across a crowded room. The club keeps Rafa's room stocked with his personalised gins and rums. It would be a fine night with them, drinking together. Drinking himself to maudlin regret; drunk-calling Lousika in the small hours.

Have some fucking dignity, man.

'Hey,' Jaden Sun calls again.

'I'm going out,' Rafa says.

The club staff will have the room rebuilt by his return.

Madrinha Flavia is as surprised to see Lucasinho at her door as he was to see her at the foot of his hospital bed.

Lucasinho opens the cardboard box he has carried so carefully from Kojo's apartment. Green fondant-frosted letters spell the word Pax.

'They're Italian,' he says. 'I had to look up where Italy is. They're really light. They've got almond in them. Are you okay with almond?

It says Pax. It's kind of like the Catholic word for paz.' A boy naturally speaks Portuguese to his madrinha.

'Paz na terra boa vontade a todos os homens,' Flavia says. 'Come in, oh come in.'

The apartment is cramped and dim. The only light comes from dozens of small biolights, arranged in every crevice and cranny and along every shelf and ledge. Lucasinho frowns in the green glow.

'Wow, it's kind of small in here.' Lucas ducks under the door lintel and tries to find a place to sit amid the paraphernalia.

'There's always space for you,' Flavia says, taking Lucasinho's face between her hands. 'Coração.'

When you need a roof, a bed, hot food, water and clean, your madrinha will always be there.

'I like your place.'

'Wagner pays for it. And my per diems.'

'Wagner?'

'You didn't know?'

'Um, my Dad doesn't...'

'Talk about me. Your mother neither. I'm used to that.'

'Thank you for coming to see me. In hospital.'

'How could I not? I carried you.'

Lucasinho squirms. No seventeen-year-old male can bear being told that he was once inside an older woman. He settles on the indicated spot on the sofa and surveys the apartment while Flavia flicks on the boiler and brings plates and a knife from her kitchen cubby. She shifts icons and biolamps to clear a space on the low table in front of the sofa.

'You've a lot of... Stuff.'

Icons, statues, rosaries and charms, offering bowls, stars and tinsel. Lucasinho's nose wrinkles at the collision of incense vapers, herbal mixes and stale air.

'The Sisterhood is big on religious clutter.'

'The...' Lucasinho catches himself before the conversation

descends into asking parrot-questions to his madrinha's every statement.

'The Sisterhood of the Lords of Now.'

'My vovo has something to do with that.'

'Your grandmother gives us money to support our work. Irmã Loa has been visiting her as a spiritual adviser.'

'What does vo Adriana need with a spiritual adviser?'

The boiler sings. Madrinha Flavia crushes mint leaves and infuses.

'No one's told you.' Flavia pushes more statues and votives to the end of the low table and settles on the floor.

'Hey, I should...'

Flavia waves away Lucasinho's offer to take her place.

'Now, this cake you've brought me.' She lifts the knife before her eyes and whispers a prayer. 'You must always bless the knife.' She cuts a tiny fingernail of cake and sets it on a dish in front of a statue of Saints Cosmos and Damiano. 'Unseen guests,' she murmurs then takes her own slice of Pax cake between fingers as thin and precise as porcelain chopsticks.

'This really is very good, Luca.'

Lucasinho blushes.

'It's good to be good at something, Madrinha.'

Madrinha Flavia brushes crumbs from her fingers.

'So tell me what brings you to your madrinha's door?'

Lucasinho lolls back on the patchouli-smelly upholstery and rolls his eyes.

On the train back from Twé he had thought his heart might explode. Heart, lungs, head, mind. Abena had walked away from him. He found his fingers straying to the metal spike in his ear. Abena had licked his blood at his party. At the Asamoah party she looked at him and stalked away. Five times he almost pulled the plug from his ear, to send back it back to Twé the moment the train arrived in Meridian. Five times no. *When you have no other hope,* Abena had said. *When you're alone and naked and exposed, like my brother; send the pierce.* He wasn't any of those things. To misuse the gift would make her hate him more.

'I need someplace to stay.'

'Obviously.'

'And I have this question I can't figure.'

'There's no guarantee I can figure it either. But go on.'

'Okay. Madrinha, why do girls do things?'

'He's making that wrong.'

The bartender freezes. The bottle of blue Curacao waits over the cocktail glass. The woman turns with granite slowness to stare from the other end of the bar.

'The lemon twist goes in first.'

Rafa Corta slides to the end of the bar beside the woman. Her clothes are immaculate, her Fendi bag on the stool beside her a classic. Her familiar is a rotating galaxy of golden stars. But she is a tourist. A dozen physical misco-ordinations and stiltednesses, mistimings and maladaptations declare her terrestrial origins.

'Excuse me.'

Rafa lifts the glass and sniffs.

'At least that's correct. The Vorontsovs insist on vodka, but a true Blue Moon must be made with gin. Seven botanicals minimum.' He lifts the orb of curled lemon peel with tongs and drops it into the glass. He nods at the Curacao bottle. 'Give me that.' A click of the fingers. 'Teaspoon.' He inverts the teaspoon and holds it twenty centimetres above the glass. The bottle he holds another twenty centimetres above the spoon. 'It's about sculpting with gravity.' He pours. A thin thread of blue liqueur falls slow as honey from the lip on to the back of the spoon. 'And two steady hands.' The Curacao coats the back of the spoon and drips from the rim in chaotic runnels and drops. Azure spirals like smoke into clear gin. The yellow marble of lemon peel is wreathed in ribbons of diffuse blue. 'Fluid dynamics does the stirring. It's the application of chaotic systems to cocktail theory.'

He slides the cocktail to the woman. She takes a sip.

'It's good.'

'Only good?'

'Very good. You make a sweet Blue Moon.'

'I should. I invented it.'

A group of four middle-aged customers toast some family business success in a corner booth. Corta security haunt a table a discreet distance from the bar. Rafa and the Earth woman are the only other clients. Rafa has stumbled into this bar because it was the closest to the club but he likes it. Old-fashioned up-light turning each drink into a jewel, tightening chins, sharpening cheekbones, shading eyes with mystery. Rare wood and square club couches in tank-leather. Mirrors along the back bar, muttered music, a terrace high on the central hub of Aquarius Quadra. Galaxies of city lights in every direction. He was two caipis down when the tourist woman entered the bar. His mind is made up. No more drinking alone. Blue Moon all the way.

Her name is Sohni Sharma. She is a New York-Mumbai post-graduate researcher finishing a six-month placement with the Farside Planetary Observation Array. Tomorrow the moonloop snatches her up to the cycler and back to Earth. Tonight she drinks the moon out of her mind and blood. She either doesn't recognise his name or her Mumbai hauteur is supreme. Rafa moves into the vacant social space.

'Leave these,' Rafa says, touching the cocktail paraphernalia. 'A bucket of ice for the gin. I'll let you know when we need glasses.'

She moves the Fendi. Rafa's invitation to sit.

'So did you invent these?' she asks after the third.

'Ask them at Sasserides Bar in Queen of the South. Do you know what the expensive part is?'

Sohni shakes her head. Rafa taps the lemon peel.

'It's the only bit we can't print.'

'Your hands are very steady,' Sohni says as Rafa performs the spoon and Curacao trick. Then she gasps as Rafa snatches up a glass, slings the gin across the bar floor and slaps it upside down on the bar. Inside, under-lit, buzzing: a fly. Rafa turns to the guards quiet at their tables.

'Do you know what is in this glass?'

His escoltas are on their feet.

'Sit down. Sit down!' Rafa bellows. 'Tell my brother I know his little spy has been buzzing around since Ku Lua.'

'Senhor Corta, we don't—' the woman starts but Rafa cuts her off.

'Work for me. Doesn't matter. You let it get close. You let it get close to me. You're fired. Both of you.'

'Senhor Corta—' the woman guard starts again.

'You think Lucas wouldn't fire you for that? You stay with me until I get replacements from Boa Vista. Socrates. Get me Heitor Pereira. And my brother.' He looks over at the family, sheepish at their table. 'Where are you going?'

They mumble the name of a restaurant, a song bar.

'Here's three thousand bitsies. Have the best night of your lives.'

Socrates transfers the money. They bow themselves out of the bar. The bartender rearranges the bottles while Rafa withdraws to speak with his head of security and then, in less reasoned tones, with his brother. Sohni rests her chin on the bar to stare at the fly.

'It's a machine,' she says.

'Half machine,' Rafa says. 'One of those things almost killed me. I'm sorry I scared you. You shouldn't have seen that. I'm not sure I can make it up to you.' He summons a clean glass and pours ice-chilled gin. Splash of lemon. Tendrils of dissolving Curacao. 'Not a tremor.' He slides the Blue Moon across the bar to Sohni. 'One wife has left me, my other wife is dead, my daughter is afraid of me and I hurt my son because I was angry at someone else. My brother spies on me because he thinks I'm a fool and my mother is halfway to believing him. I just lost a deal, my enemies have fucked me over, my security guards couldn't find their own asses in the dark, someone tried to assassinate me with a fly and my men's handball team is bottom of the league.' He raises his own glass. 'But I still invented the Blue Moon.'

'I could be an assassin,' Sohni says. 'I could pull out a knife and open you from here to here.' She runs a finger from chin to crotch.

Rafa arrests her hand.

'No you couldn't.'

'Are you sure of that?'

Rafa tilts his head at his former guards.

'I may have fired them but they still scanned everyone in the place.'

'You infringed my privacy.'

'I can compensate you.'

'Everything really is a contract with you people.'

'You people?'

'Moon people.'

Rafa still hasn't let go of her hand. Sohni still hasn't slipped it from his grasp.

'I know I should feel privileged to be working here, but I can't wait to get back home,' she says. 'I don't like your world, Rafael Corta. I don't like its meanness and tightness and ugliness and that everything has a price.' She lifts a finger to her eye. 'I can't get used to these. I don't think I could ever get used to these. You're rats in a cage, one look, one wrong word away from eating each other.'

'The moon is all I know,' Rafa says. 'I can't go to Earth. It would kill me. Not quickly, but it would kill me. None of us can go there. This is home. I was born here and I will die here. In between, it's people, all the way up, all the way down. At their best and at their worst. In the end, all we have is each other. You see contracts for everything; I see agreements. Ways we work out between us to live.'

'Okay then. Compensate me.' Sohni frees her hand to tap the gin bottle. Rafa seizes her hand, so firmly her lips part in small shock.

'Don't you ever pity me,' he says and in the same instant releases her. A click of mechanisms releasing: an awning unfolds from above the bar and extends over bar and drinkers.

'It's going to rain,' Rafa says, looking up. 'Have you seen it rain on the moon?'

'You haven't been to Farside Array, have you?'

'I'm a businessman, not a scientist.' Slug of gin, plash of peel, the trick with the spoon and the slow Curacao.

'It's tunnels and corridors and cubbyholes. I feel like I've been stooping for six months. I'm amazed I can straighten my spine.' She turns on her barstool to look out at the stupendous vistas of Aquarius Quadra. 'This is the furthest I've looked in six lunes.'

Sudden drumbeat on the canopy. Beyond its shelter, rain drops like glass ornaments, detonating softly on the terrace.

'Oh!' Sohni raises hands to face in delight.

'Come on.' Rafa extends a hand. Sohni takes it. He leads her out into the rain. Fat drops splash Blue Moon from their glasses, detonate around their feet. Sohni turns her face up to the rain. Within seconds they are soaked through, expensive clothes clinging, wringing. Rafa brings Sohni to the rail.

'Watch,' he orders. The vault of Aquarius hub is a mosaic of slow-falling, quivering drops, each a twinkling jewel in the night lights of Aquarius. 'See.' The skyline comes on, momentarily blinding. Sohni shields her eyes. When she can see again a rainbow spans the vast space of the quadra's hub. 'Look!' Down on Tereshkova Prospekt traffic has come to a standstill. Passengers, pedestrians stand motionless, arms outspread. From stores and clubs, bars and restaurants, others stream to join them. On the terraces and balconies children run out to cavort and yell in the rain. The rain hammers Aquarius Quadra, drumming, booming from every roof and awning, gantry and walkway.

'I can't hear myself think!' Sohni shouts and then the skyline fades to dark. The rain ends. The last drops fall and burst on her skin. The world drips and glistens. Sohni looks around her, dazed with wonder.

'It smells different,' she says.

'It smells clean,' Rafa says. 'This is the first time you've breathed air without dust in it. The rain scrubs out the dust. That's why we do it.'

'How can you afford to waste the water?'

'It's not wasted. Every drop is collected.'

'But the expense. Who pays for this?'

Now Rafa touches a finger under his eye.

'You do.'

Sohni's eyes widen as she reads the charge to her water account on her chib.

'But that's . . .'

'Nothing. Do you begrudge it?'

'No. Never.' She shivers.

'You're wet through,' Rafa says. 'I can print you something fresh at my club.'

Sohni smiles through the shivers.

'That's a pick-up line.'

'Yes it is.'

'Come on then.'

Socrates throws a big tip to the bartender and Sohni and Rafa dash back through the dripping city to the PHO Club. The spying fly remains, buzzing in its glass bell-jar.

Lucas returns to the listening room and sits on the acoustic centre of the sofa.

'Is everything all right?'

'Everything is in order. Please start *Expresso* again.'

'It's just that you don't take interruptions.' This is Jorge's third listening room session but the pattern is established. He plays for an hour unbroken, Lucas listens for an hour undivided. But in the third bar of *Expresso*, Lucas had risen abruptly from the sofa and hurried from the room. Jorge could not hear Lucas's business but he was gone several minutes.

'*Expresso*, please.'

But the disturbance has thrown Jorge and it takes him a few moments to work out the tension in his fingers and body and throat. Fingers find the chords, voice the syncopation. There are no further interruptions but the flow of energy from performer to audience and back to performer is disturbed. Jorge finishes *Izaura* with a muted cadence and packs away the guitar.

'Same time next week, Senhor Corta?'

'Yes.' A hand on Jorge's shoulder as he turns to go. 'Stay for a drink.'

'Thank you, Senhor Corta.'

Lucas guides Jorge, guitar in hand, to the lounge and brings him a mojito.

'I have got the proportions right?'

'It's perfect, Senhor Corta.'

'Taste it first.'

He does. It is.

Lucas takes his own drink to the window. João de Deus whirls past, movement and light, level upon level. Blue neon, green bio-lights, gold street lamps.

'I apologise for taking that call. I could see it threw you.'

'Being professional is not letting it throw you.'

'It threw me. I must still be an amateur audience. Do you have brothers, Jorge?'

'Two sisters, Senhor Corta.'

'I would say you're lucky, but in my experience, sisters can be as difficult as brothers. Differently difficult. The thing about brothers is, the rules are set in place at birth. Firstborn is always firstborn. Always golden. Are you firstborn, Jorge?'

'I'm in the middle.'

'That would be me and Ariel. Carlinhos is the darling. The youngest always is.'

'I thought there were five Cortas.'

'Four Cortas and a pretender,' Lucas says. 'I see you've finished.' Jorge gulped his mojito. Nervy drinking. 'Have another one. Try to enjoy it this time. The rum really is good.' He brings the second drink and with it lures Jorge to the window. 'My mother was a pioneer, an entrepreneur, a dynasty builder but in many ways quite traditional. Those things are not incompatible. The firstborn will run the company. The rest serve as their talents allow. I do. Carlinhos does. Even Wagner serves. Ariel. I envy Ariel. She chose her own career outside the company. Counsel Ariel Corta. Queen of the nikahs. The toast of Meridian.' Lucas raises his glass to the teeming, dusty street. 'She is a White Hare.'

'Anyone who says they're a White Hare—'

'Almost certainly isn't. I know. If Ariel says she is a White Hare, she is. What do you think of my rum, Jorge?'

'It is good.'

'My own personal brand. When you were a boy, did you have pets?'

'Only machine ones.'

'Us too. My mother wouldn't have anything organic about the place. All that shitting and dying. The Asamoahs gave us a flock of decorative butterflies for Lucasinho's moon-run. My mother complained about the mess for days. Wings everywhere. Machines are cleaner. But they still terminate. They die. They make them die, you know? To teach kids a lesson. And then someone has to put them into the deprinter. That was my job, Jorge.' Lucas takes a sip. Jorge is nearing the bottom of his second mojito. Lucas has barely tasted his first. 'The Golden Boy has made a dreadful mistake. He has managed to alienate the Vorontsovs. He let his feelings get the better out of him and has jeopardised not just our expansion plan but our shipping deal with VTO. We rely on VTO to ship helium containers to Earth. And it's up to me to repair the damage. Think of a solution. Upcycle the dead. Clean up the mess.'

'Should I be hearing this, Senhor Corta?'

'You're hearing what I want you to hear. Jorge, I fear for my family. My brother is an idiot. My mother... She's not what she was. She's keeping something from me. Helen de Braga and that fool Heitor Pereira will never tell me, no matter what levers I apply. The company will fall unless someone deals with the shit and the death. Do you have any children, Jorge?'

'I'm not on that spectrum.'

'I know.' Lucas takes Jorge's empty glass and sets a fresh one in his hand. 'I have a son. I find myself unexpectedly proud of him. He ran away from home. We live in the most enclosed, surveilled society in human history and young people still try to do that. I cut him off, naturally. Nothing fatal, nothing health-limiting. He lives by his wits. It seems he has some. And charm. He doesn't take after me in that. He's making some success of it. He's become a minor celebrity. Five days of fame and then everyone will forget him. I can pull him in any time I want but I don't want to. Not yet. I want to see what else he finds inside himself. He has qualities I don't. He's kind, it seems, and quite honourable. Too kind and honourable for the company, I fear. I fear a lot for the future. What do you think of this one?' Lucas tilts his glass towards Jorge's.

'It's different. Smokier. Tougher.'

'Tougher. Yes. That's my own cachaça. It's what we should be drinking when we make bossa. I find it a little uncouth. So, I must stage a board-room coup. I must fight my family to save my family. And I'm telling all this to a bossa nova singer. And you're thinking, am I his therapist, his confessor? His minstrel, his fool?'

'I'm not a fool.' Jorge snatches up his guitar. Lucas stops him three paces from the door.

'In old Europe the king's fool was the only one the king could trust with the truth, and the only one who could tell the truth to the king.'

'Is that an apology?'

'Yes.'

'I should still go.' Jorge looks ruefully at the glass in his other hand.

'Yes. Of course.'

'Same time next week, Senhor Corta?'

'Lucas.'

'Lucas.'

'Could we make it a little earlier?'

'When?'

'Tomorrow?'

'Mamãe?'

Adriana wakes with a small cry. She is in a bed in a room but she doesn't know where and her body will not answer her though it feels light as a dream, insubstantial as fate. A presence over her, close as breath, breathing in as she breathes out.

'Carlos?'

'Mama, it's all right.'

The voice is inside her head.

'Who?'

'Mama, it's me. Lucas.'

That name, that voice.

'Oh. Lucas. What time is it?'

'Late, Mamãe. Sorry to disturb you. Are you all right?'

'I slept badly.'

The light swells. She is in her bed, in her room, in her palace. The looming, breath-eating ghost is Lucas, rendered on her lens.

'I've told you to see Dr Macaraeg about that. She can give you something.'

'Can she give me thirty years?'

Lucas smiles. Adriana wishes she could touch him.

'I'll not disturb you then. Get some sleep. I just want you to know that we haven't lost Mare Anguis. I have a plan.'

'I'd hate to lose that, Lucas. I'd hate that more than anything.'

'You won't, Mama, if Carlinhos and those damn fool dustbikes of his are up to it.'

'You're a good boy, Lucas. Let me know.'

'I will. Sleep well, Mama.'

Marina rides back with the corpse strapped beside her. It's close enough to rub thighs and shoulders but that is better than it facing her in the opposite seat. The suit, the featureless helmet, the seat harness restricting movement; there is little to distinguish the meat from the dead. Knowledge, that's the horror. Behind that blank face is a blank face: dead.

Cause of death was a swift and catastrophic rise in body temperature that cooked Paulo Ribiero to death in his suit. Carlinhos sifts data, trying to discern what went wrong. If a duster with a thousand surface hours on his log can die inside three minutes, anyone can. So can she, Marina Calzaghe, strapped into an open, unpressurised roll frame; hurtling at one hundred and eighty kilometres per hour through hard, irradiated vacuum. Nothing between her and it but this flim-flam suit, this bubble of helmet visor. Even now, a thousand tiny failures could be conspiring, multiplying, allying. Marina Calzaghe bolts back panic like yellow bile. In the Sea of Tranquillity she had almost taken her helmet off.

'You all right?' Carlinhos on her private channel.

'Yes.' Liar. 'It's a shock. That's all.'

'You're fit to continue?'

'Yes. Why?'

'We've been redeployed.'

'Where?'

'I'm going to turn you into a drinking game,' Carlinhos says. 'Every time you ask a question, I take a drink. We're catching a train.'

Marina can't discern any change in the rover's course but an hour later it skids to a halt at the side of Equatorial One. Seat harnesses lift, the squad disembarks shaking stiffness out of their limbs.

Marina gingerly rests a foot on the track, feeling for the vibration of an approaching express. Nothing of course. And the outer rails are reserved for the Mackenzie mobile foundry – Crucible, Marina remembers from her briefings. The expresses runs on the inner four maglev tracks. She can see the adjacent power tracks. Touch a foot to those and your death would be clean and instantaneous and light up Carlinhos's hud like Diwali.

'It's coming,' Carlinhos says. An atom of light appears on the western horizon, becoming three blinding headlights. The ground is shaking. At maglev speed, with so tight a horizon, the train is on them before Marina can make sense of her impressions: size, speed, blinding light; oppressive mass and utter silence. Windows blur past, then slow. The train is stopping. Marina sees a child's face, hands cupped against the glass, peering out. The train comes to a halt. Two thirds of its kilometre-length are passenger carriages; freight and pallet cars take up the rear third. Carlinhos waves his crew across the tracks to the very last flatbed. Marina easily vaults up the sintered track-bed and hand-over-hands up the side of the open car. Motorbikes. Big, fat-tyred, studded with sensors and coms equipment, ugly and unaerodynamic, but unmistakably motorbikes.

Wha— she starts to ask but that would only gift Carlinhos another win in his drinking game.

'We're claim-staking,' Carlinhos announces on the common channel. Rumbles of approval from the old dusters, squad and those who have come with the bikes. 'Lucas tells us we're heading to Mare Anguis. There's a claim that Mackenzie Metals thinks only they know about. But we do, and we can steal it out from under them. They've got VTO's surface fleet in their pockets but we've got these.' He pats the handlebars of one of the motorbikes. 'Corta Dustbike Team will win it. First, we ride train.' A roar of approval. Marina finds her voice among them. Without lurch or jolt the train moves off. Marina watches the rover power up and swing away from Equatorial One, carrying its sole, dead passenger back to João de Deus.

Flavia makes food. It's substantial, entirely vegetable like most lunar cuisine but it tastes thin to Lucasinho, like music from a guitar missing bass strings.

'Is there something wrong with onions and garlic?' he asks. 'And chili?'

'They are theologically improper vegetables,' Flavia says. 'They raise passions and stimulate base instincts.'

Lucasinho picks at his food.

'Madrinha, why did you leave?'

Lucasinho was five when Flavia left Boa Vista. He remembers confusion more than hurt; an absence that filled quickly with grains of new normality. Amanda, his genetic mother, had quickly passed him to Elis, pregnant with Robson.

'Has your father never told you?'

'No.'

'Your father and grandmother dismissed me and forced me to leave you and Boa Vista. I carried Carlinhos and I carried Wagner and last of all I carried you, Luca. Do you know what we madrinhas do?'

'You are surrogate mothers.'

'We sell our bodies, that's what we do. We sell the very heart of our womanhood to someone else. It's prostitution. We spread our legs and take someone else's embryo into our wombs. You were conceived in a tube, Luca, and you were carried in a stranger's uterus, for money. A lot of money. But you weren't mine. You were Lucas Corta and Amanda Sun's baby. Carlinhos was Carlos and Adriana Corta's.'

'You were Wagner's madrinha too,' Lucasinho says.

'It's the cruellest profession. If you had been taken away from me after birth, maybe that would have been easier. But the contract is that we don't just gestate and birth you, we raise you. My life was dedicated to you, and Carlinhos. And Wagner. I was in every way a mother, except one.'

'You didn't have a baby of your own. I mean, one you made.'

'You can't imagine what it's like to spend every hour with children that you carried, that are yours in everything but genetics, but aren't yours, and never will be yours.'

'But you could...'

'You can't understand, Luca. You can't even begin. The contracts are exclusive. The only children I was allowed to have were Corta sons and daughters. I love you, Luca, and Carlinhos. And Wagner. I love you like you're my own.'

Lucasinho's head pounds. Pressure in the skull. Pressure behind the eyes. This is heavy stuff. Stuff he can't factor, stuff that doesn't play on any of the emotional processes he's learned. Flavia is right. He can't understand it. This is what adults feel.

'And Wagner,' Lucasinho says. 'You keep saying "and Wagner".'

'You always were smarter than your father gives you credit for, Luca.'

'Pai's always said he's not a Corta. Vovo can't talk to him. As soon as he was eighteen he left Boa Vista.'

'Leave, or was made to leave?'

'What did you do?'

'Wagner is half Corta. Half Corta, half Vila Nova.'

'That's you.'

'Flavia Passos Vila Nova. Madrinhas are very well paid. Enough to hire an obstetric gynaecologist to fertilise and implant a different set of embryos.'

'Vovo, Carlos's...' Lucasinho can't say the words. Eggs, sperm, embarrassing. Moreso when they make you.

'Carlos had been dead twenty years. There were still hundreds of sperm samples frozen. Carlinhos came from one. Then the gracious Adriana decided she wanted another child. A baby-toy, a last reminder of her dead husband. At the age of fifty-six she wanted another baby. And there was me, with nothing of my own! She didn't deserve another child, a little late-life boy-toy. And it was so very simple.'

The saints, the orixas, the exus and guias fix Lucasinho Corta with plastic eyes. He feels itchy and self-conscious. The green bio-light makes him nauseous. He's sure it's the green biolight. Not the immediate, terrible question he has to ask.

'Flavia. What about me?'

'Those are Sun cheekbones and Corta eyes, Luca. No mistaking.' Flavia reads his confusion. 'I said you couldn't understand it.'

'So you had Wagner...'

'A boy of my own. That was all I needed. You Cortas, your pride makes you blind. It's the first and greatest sin, pride. You would never have considered that Wagner might be the son of Carlos and Flavia and not Carlos and Adriana. Never. Arrogance and pride!' Flavia lifts her hands, as if in praise, or denunciation. 'And you would never have known except for Wagner going to hospital for that lung treatment. He developed a bronchial condition. Adriana was worried that it might be congenital, that Carlos's sperm and her eggs had curdled and gone sour over the years. The hospital ran genetic tests. My deception was revealed in an instant. I had broken my contract, but it would have been the scandal of the century if the news networks had found out that Adriana Corta's last child wasn't hers. I took Corta money to be quiet, and a threat.'

'Vo threatened you?'

'Not Adriana. Her agents came bearing gifts. Helen de Braga showed me the money, Heitor Pereira showed me the knife. Wagner stayed at Boa Vista to be brought up a Corta in every way. But Adriana couldn't love him. She looked at him and she saw something that was Carlos's, but not hers.'

'She's always been distant around him. Cold. But my father really hates him.'

'He's wise, your father. Wagner is a threat to the family, I am a threat to the family, me telling you this is a threat to the family.'

Lucasinho's heart leaps with panic.

'Would he, if he knew you'd – Hurt you?'

'He wouldn't run the risk of losing you forever.'

'Like that would bother him. I didn't see him sending security to find me when I ran out of Boa Vista.'

'Your father knows exactly where you've been and what you've been doing. He knows where you are right now.'

'I fucking hate being a Corta.' A sudden sweep of the arm clears the table of saints and votives. Flavia painstakingly replaces them.

'Listen to rich boy. You run away and your friends throw you parties, your aunt throws you cash and your lovers throw a sheet over your ass and a roof over your head. You hate being a Corta? You hate never having to sell the breath in your lungs and the piss in your bladder? You hate never having to steal from recycle bots, knifing someone for a bag of manioc fries? Close your mouth. Your brains might fall out. That cake you brought? I would have cut you open for it, boy. Your family always hired Jo Moonbeams for madrinhas because we've got Earth bones and muscles. I was six months off the cycler, working in robotics development for Taiyang in Queen of the South when a micro-recession threw me out on to the street. I slept up in the roof, I could feel the radiation hammering through my body like sleet. I stole and I maimed and I sold everything I had and then I said never again. Never again. So I went to the Sisters because I knew what they were doing with genelines and the Mãe-do-santo looked me up and down and checked my medical records five, ten, fifty times. Then sent me to Adriana Corta and she put Carlinhos in me and I was never hungry or thirsty or breathless again. You hate having all those things? Mother and saints, you fucking ingrate.' Flavia crosses herself and kisses her knuckles.

Lucasinho's face burns with anger and shame. He's tired of being told what he needs to do with himself. Wear this dress. Put on that make-up. Don't be with that girl. Be a thankful son. Madrinha Flavia gets up from the floor and boils water in her kitchen cubby. Pestle in mortar, then a thick green smell fills the small room.

Lucasinho's hand is on the door.

'Where are you going?'

'Does it matter?'

'No. But you won't go. You wouldn't be here if you had anywhere else to go. And I don't want you to go. Here.' Flavia hands him a glass of herbal maté. 'Sit.'

'Orders. Everyone gives me orders. Everyone is so clever about me and who I am and what I want.'

'Please.'

Lucasinho sniffs the brew.

'What is this?'

'Helps sleep,' Flavia says. 'It's late.'

'How do you know?' The apartment has no clocks. The Sisterhood does not countenance them: clocks are the knives of time, slicing the Great Now into finer and finer divisions: hours, minutes, seconds. Continuity is the philosophy of the Sisters: time whole and undivided, existing all at once in a fourth dimension, in the mind of Olorum the One.

'It feels late.'

'Don't like this,' Lucasinho says, sniffing the glass with a scowl of distaste.

'Who says it's for you?'

Lucasinho drinks. By the time Flavia comes back from washing the glasses in the kitchen, he is curled up asleep on the sofa.

Twelve lines of moon dust. Twelve riders in V formation, cutting across the Eimmart K crater. Marina Calzaghe is three hours into the ride. Her ass has long since turned to rock. Her neck aches, her fingers are numb with vibration, she can feel the cold gnawing her sasuit and she cannot tear her gaze away from the O_2 figure in the bottom right of her hud. It's all been calculated: air enough to reach the location plus an hour. That's time enough for the rovers from Mare Marginis to reach them and resupply. Three hours in, one hour to go, one hundred and eighty kilometres an hour – two hundred and twenty flat out but it chews battery life – and somewhere, up there, around the shoulder of the world, the Vorontsov fleet is barrelling towards Mare Anguis. The calculations say Team Corta will arrive at the furthest vertex five minutes before the Mackenzie/VTO transporters. Plus or minus three minutes. All worked out. Lucas Corta is precise in his calculations.

The first hour of the ride north from the rail stop is over jolting, jarring highland terrain; craters and ejecta and treacherous slopes that demand the focus of every sense, natural and cybernetic. The dustbikes' massive drive wheels take the smaller debris with ease but every rock is a judgement call; run it, steer it. Call it wrong, wreck the wheels and the transmission and you are alone among the craters watching your comrades draw long lines of dust away from you. The lifeboats won't come. They've been bought up by the Mackenzies. Marina grits her teeth at every rock and rille. Every rim sends a jolt of pain up her spine. Her back is a rod of molten pain. Her arms throb from holding the handlebars steady, steady as the bike bounds and bucks over the fearsome terrain. Her jaw is set rigid and she can't remember when she last blinked. Marina Calzaghe is deliriously alive.

'Motorbikes,' she'd said.

'Dustbikes,' Carlinhos had corrected.

Eleven bikes, corralled on the flatbed car. Magnificent, potent things that showed their veins and wires and bones and gears; brutally functional and beautiful for that. Each was different, handcrafted and bespoke, metal surfaces engraved with death's-heads, dragons, orixas, big-cocked men and mega-breasted women, flames and starbursts and swords and flowers. Biker aesthetic is changeless and eternal. Marina ran a gloved hand over a chromed flank.

'Have you ridden one of these before?' Carlinhos asked.

'Where would I...' Marina began and then remembered the game. 'Do you think you could?'

'How hard can it be?'

'Hard. If something goes wrong, you will be left behind.'

There was no bike for her. The Jo Moonbeam would ride to Meridian in pressurised warmth and comfort. But with Paulo Ribeiro heading back to autopsy at João de Deus Team Corta was down a rider and the plan required every bike. The Mackenzies might pull something out of their asses yet. The more riders, the more flexibility.

'Will you come?'

In Portuguese, it was an invitation, not a question. Already the train was slowing. Lucas's plan was simple. Marina remembered him as the dark, serious man who had spoken the words that had saved her life: *You work for Corta Hélio now.* He had remembered a detail that even Carlinhos had forgotten: they were dustbikers. Lucas's plan: rail all available dustbikes to the closest point to the claim, open the throttles and strike north for the Mare Anguis. Fire up a GPS transponder from each of the four corners of the territory. Four corners, eleven bikes.

'I will,' said Marina Calzaghe.

'Here's the contract.' Hetty flashed it up on Marina's lens. A cursory scan – so many clauses referencing accidental death – a yin and back to Carlinhos.

'Keep with me,' Carlinhos said on Marina's private channel. Eleven bikes, four corners. So it would be her and Carlinhos racing Mackenzie Metals and all their spaceships for the furthest, final point of the territory.

Riders mounted up. Marina's machine was a beast of twisted aluminium and crackling power cells. A chrome-etched Lady Luna regarded her from between the handlebars, her skull hemi-face grinning. The AI meshed with Hetty as Marina settled on to the saddle.

The bike came to life. The controls were easy. Forward, back. Twist for speed.

Before the train had even come to a halt Carlinhos gunned his engine and leaped off the flatbed, soaring high and beautiful, glinting in the earthlight, to land beyond the furthest rail track. By the time Marina craned her bike down to the surface and learned how to keep the machine from performing terrifying, deadly wheelies, Carlinhos was over the horizon.

She locked in the bearing, twisted the throttle and steered up the dust-trails. A burst of speed took her into the formation and there, to Carlinhos's left, was a gap in the arrowhead. Marina kicked into it. Carlinhos turned his blank face and nodded to her.

The bikers plunge down the long shallow crater rim of Eimmart K. Marina veers to avoid a corpse-sized chunk of ejecta. It's sat there for longer than life has existed on Earth, she thinks. Dumb grey in-the-way rock. Out on to the dead sea-floor.

Carlinhos raises a hand but familiars have already cued the riders. Three bikes peel off from the left trailing edge of the arrows and steer east-south-east. Marina watches their slow-settling dust plumes. They will strike the south-eastern vertex of the quadrangle. Nine bikes now, racing across the dark flatland; a lop-sided wing. The riding is easy and fast and monotonous and full of traps; the worst kind, the kind that come out of yourself, out of boredom and familiarity and monotony. Flat flat flat. Monotony monotony monotony. This can't be the fun of it. Flat flat flat fast fast fast. Why invent a sport just about going fast in a straight line? Maybe that is it. Men and their sports. Everything can be turned into a pointless competition, even going fast across a lunar sea-bottom. There must be more to it. Stunts, skills. What Marina understands of sports is they are all stunts, scores or speed.

At the designated way point Carlinhos again raises his hand and the trailing right wingtip peels off and cuts a westerly arc across the

Mare. The south-east corner of the claim is fifty kilometres distant. The five remaining bikes race on.

'Do you like Brazilian music?' Carlinho's voice startles Marina. She wobbles, recovers.

'Not really. It all sounds kind of elevator-y. Maybe there's something I'm just too norte to get.'

'I don't get it either. Mamãe adores it. She grew up with it. It's her link with home.'

'Home,' Marina says but it's not a question.

'Lucas is a big fan. He tried to explain to me once how it worked – saudade, bitter-sweet, all that, but I didn't have the ear for it. I'm very simple. I like dance music. Beats. Something physical, with weight.'

'I like to dance but I'm not a dancer,' Marina says.

'When we get back, when we've got this, we'll go dancing.'

At one hundred and ninety-five kilometres per hour across the Mare Anguis, Marina's heart leaps. 'Is that a date?'

'I'm taking everyone else in the squad as well,' Carlinhos says. 'You haven't seen a Corta party.'

'I was at the one in Boa Vista, remember?' Marina says, backing away, crestfallen. Flushing hot inside her sasuit.

'That wasn't a Corta party,' Carlinhos says. 'So, what music do you like, Marina Calzaghe?'

'I grew up in the Pacific Northwest so it's guitars all the way down. I'm a rock girl.'

'Ah. Metal. My squad, it's all they listen to: metal.'

'No. Rock.'

'There's a difference?'

'Big difference. Like your brother says, you have to have the ear for it.'

Forward radar paints an obstruction over the horizon. A detour would cost precious minutes.

'You know a lot about me Marina Calzaghe – I like dance music,

I follow the Long Run, I love my mother but I don't like my big brothers. I love my kid brother and my sister I don't understand at all. I hate business suits and having rocks over my head. But I still don't know anything about you. You rock, you're from the norte, you saved my brother: that's it.'

The obstruction is an outcrop of rough highland terrain marooned when ancient basalts flooded the Mare Anguis basin. The transition is abrupt for the gentle, eroded moon, but Carlinhos shows no hesitation and steers straight for the rocks.

'I kind of drifted here,' Marina says.

'No one drifts to the moon,' Carlinhos says and his bike hits a ridge and goes flying, ten, twenty metres before splashing down in an explosion of dust. Marina follows him. She is powerless, abandoned; her heart chokes in panic. Hold it steady. Steady. Then the rear wheel touches down, she fights to hold the bike upright, then both wheels. Steer true. Steer true. She gasps with exhilaration.

'So?' Carlinhos's voice on the private channel.

'My mom got sick. Tubercular meningitis.'

Carlinhos whispers a Portuguese invocation to São Jorge.

'She lost her right leg from the knee down and the use of both of them. She's alive, she talks and gets around but it's not her. Not the mom that I knew. Bits the hospital salvaged.'

'So you work for the hospital.'

'I work for Corta Hélio. And my mom.'

There are only two of them now. Carlinhos leads her down off the rocks and the Sea of Serpents is wide and open before them.

'I was born and grew up in Port Angeles, Washington State,' Marina says, because there are only two of them, alone on the plain that curves away from them in every direction, she talks about growing up in the house up by the edge of the forest that was full of bird calls and windchimes and the fluttering of flying banners and windsocks. Mother: reiki practitioner and angelic healer and reader of the cards and feng shui arranger, cat sitter and dog walker and horse trainer: all the many jobs of late twenty-first service employment. Father: faith-ful in gifts at birthdays and holidays and graduations. Sister Kessie, brother Skyler. The dogs, the fogs, the log trucks; the engine-throb of the big ships out in the channel, the parade of RV and motorbikes and trailers passing through to mountains and water; the money that always appeared just as desperation turned its wheels into the front yard. The knowledge that the whole dance was one pay-cheque away from collapse.

'I had this thing about the ships,' Marina says, realising as she does that Carlinhos may have no referent for the gigantic carriers that sailed the strait of San Juan de Fuca. 'When I was real small I imagined that they had giant legs, like spiders, dozens of legs and that they were really walking across the bottom of the sea.'

Thus engineers are built: from walking ships and a loved toy, an improving game for girls where the mission was to rescue imperiled animals using ribbons and pulleys and elevators and gears.

'I liked to make them really complicated and spectacular,' Marina says. 'I videoed them and stuck them up online.'

Her mother was nonplussed and delighted that her eldest daughter showed a flair for problem-solving and engineering. It was an alien philosophy in the ramshackle, last-minute lives of family and friends and associated animals but Ellen-May Calzaghe was fierce in her support even if she did not completely understand what Marina was studying at university. Computational evolutionary biology in process control architecture was a jabber of tech-talk that sounded most like regular pay-cheques.

Then the tuberculosis came. It blew in from the east, from the sick city. People had been moving out from the city for years now, but the house had thought itself immune, protected. The disease blew past charms and chimes and astral warders and into Ellen-May's lung and from there into the lining of her brain. One by one the antibiotics failed. Phages saved her, but the infection took her legs and twenty per cent of her mind. It left a bill for insane money. More money than any lifetime could earn. More money than any career; except black finance. Or one on the moon.

Marina never intended to go to the moon. She grew up knowing there were people up there, and that they kept the lights burning on the world below. Like every child of her generation she had borrowed a telescope to giggle at King Dong of Imbrium but the moon was as distant as a parallel universe. Not a place you could get to. Not from Port Angeles. Until Marina found that she not only could, but she must, that that world was crying out for her skills and discipline, that it would welcome her and pay her lunatic money.

'And that skill is serving Blue Moons at Lucasinho's moon-run party?' Carlinhos says.

'They found someone cheaper.'

'You should have read the contract closer.'

'It was the only contract on offer.'

'This is the moon...'

'Everything is negotiable. I know that. Now.' Then she had known nothing, only the surge of impressions and experiences, that every sense was yelling *strange, new, frightening*. Her training failed. Nothing could prepare her for the reality of walking out of the tether port into the crush and colour and noise and reek of Meridian. Sensibility rebelled. *Put this lens in your right eye quick. Move like this, walk this way, don't trip folk up. Set up this account, and this and this and this. This is your familiar: have you got a name, a skin for it? Read that? So: sign here here and here. Is that woman flying?*

'Word from the south-east squad,' Carlinhos interrupts. 'The Mackenzies have arrived.'

'How far are we?'

'Open her up.'

Marina has been hoping he would say that. She feels the engine leap between her thighs. The dustbike answers with a surge of speed. Marina bends low. She doesn't need to; there is no wind resistance to cut on the moon. It's what you do on a fast bike. She and Carlinhos race side by side across the Mare Anguis.

'And what about you?' Marina asks.

'Rafa's the charmer, Lucas the schemer, Ariel's the talker; I'm the fighter.'

'What about Wagner?'

'The wolf.'

'I mean, Lucas can't tolerate him. What's that about?'

'Our lives aren't simple. We do things differently here.' In those few words, Carlinhos says, we are still contractor and contractee.

'I'm at about twelve per cent O_2,' Marina announces.

'We're here,' Carlinhos says, brakes and swings the tail of the bike round in a doughnut of flying dust. Marina loops wide and slows to park up beside him. The dust settles gently around her.

'Here.' Dark, flat sea-bottom, as featureless as a wok.

'North-east vertex of the Mare Anguis quadrangle,' Carlinhos says. He unstraps the beacon from the back of the dustbike.

'Carlinhos,' Marina says. 'Boss . . .'

The horizon is so close, the Vorontsov ship so fast it is as if it has materialised in the sky above her, like an angel. It's big, it's half the sky; it's low and descending on flickers of rocket thrust from its engine pods.

Carlinhos swears in Portuguese. He is still snapping out the legs of the Corta beacon.

'Those things have built-in positioning. If it touches the ground . . .'

'I've an idea.' A bad mad idea, a clause not even a lunar contract would cover. Marina guns the dustbike. The Vorontsov ship pivots on its central axis. Its thrusters throw up pillars of dust. Marina accelerates through the dust and brakes directly under the belly of the ship. She looks up. Warning lights splash across her helmet visor. They wouldn't land on an employee of Corta Hélio. They wouldn't mash her and burn her, not in front of a Corta. They wouldn't. The ship hovers, then the thrusters glow and the transporter veers away from its landing zone.

'No you fucking don't!' Marina kicks the dustbike again and dashes in underneath the descending ship. Rocket thrust buffets her, threatens to tumble her. Lower this time. Belly cameras swivel to lock on to her. What arguments are going on in the cockpit of that ship? This is the moon. They do things differently here. Everything is negotiable. Everything has a price: dust, lives. Corporate war with the Cortas. The transporter hangs in the air.

'Carlinhos…'

The transporter darts sideways. It can't drift too far from the co-ordinates of the vertex which neutralises its advantage in speed. Marina can always catch up. But it's low; dear gods it's low. Too low. With a cry Marina throws the bike into a skid. The rear wheel goes out, bike and rider hit the dust and slide slide slide. Marina grabs dust to try and brake her speed. Winded, she comes to a halt under the landing pad. Engine-blast wraps her in blinding dust. The landing pad is crushing death bearing down inexorably on her. They've made the calculation.

'Marina! Out of there!'

With the last of her strength Marina rolls out from under the landing gear. The Vorontsov ship touches down. Pad and strut and shock absorbers are two metees from her face.

'I've got it, Marina.'

She rolls on to her other side and there is Carlinhos crouched, hand extended to help her up. Behind him the transponder beacon blinks. Those blinks are life. Those blinks are victory.

'We've got it.'

Marina struggles to her feet. Her ribs ache, her heart flutters, every muscle groans with exertion, she might throw up in her helmet, a dozen hud alerts are flashing from yellow to red and she can't feel her fingers or toes from the cold. But those lights, those little blinking lights. She puts an arm around Carlinhos and lets him help her hobble away from the ship. The transporter is beautiful and alien, a thing out of place, a child's toy, abandoned in the Sea of Serpents. Figures in the brightly lit cockpit; one of them raises a hand in salute. Carlinhos returns the gesture. Then the thrusters fire, blinding Marina and Carlinhos in dust and the transporter is gone. They are alone. Marina sags against Carlinhos.

'How long until that rover gets here?'

Jorge settles the guitar into its customary, comfortable position against his body. Left foot a step forward, weight balanced.

'What would you like me to play, Senhor Corta?'

'Nothing.'

'Nothing.'

'Nothing. I've brought you here falsely, Jorge.'

Sleep had come hard after practice with the band, sequences and chord progressions running silver through his musical imagination; ways of working a difficult syncopation with the drummer. Gilberto his familiar whispered in his ear: *Lucas Corta*. Three thirty-four. Jesus and his Mother. *I need you.*

'I don't want you to sing.'

Jorge's breath catches.

'I want you to have a drink with me.'

'I'm very tired, Senhor Corta.'

'There's isn't anyone else, Jorge.'

'Your oko; Lucasinho ...'

'There isn't anyone else.'

On the balcony, a mojito mixed to Jorge's taste. Lucas's personal rum. Heading four o'clock now but São Sebastião Quadra bustles, robots and shift workers, maintenance and materiel technicians. The air is still, electric with suspended dust. Jorge tastes it on his tongue, in his throat. He would slip on his kuozhao to protect his singing voice but the dust-mask might affront Lucas.

'I'm going to divorce my wife,' Lucas says.

Jorge struggles for an appropriate reponse.

'I don't know much about nikahs in the Five Dragons but I imagine it would be expensive to buy out of the contract.'

'Very expensive,' Lucas says. 'Ridiculously expensive. The Suns are used to fighting in court. They've been fighting the CPC for fifty years. But I am ridiculously rich. And I have my sister Ariel.' Lucas leans on the rail.

'If you don't love her...'

'If you think love ever had anything to do with it, you really know nothing about the way we marry among the Dragons. No, it was pragmatic, political, dynastic. They all are. First the marriage, then the love. If you're lucky. Rafa was and it's killing him. This is a celebration, Jorge.'

'I don't understand, Senhor – Lucas.'

'I have pulled off a singular victory. I had a brilliant idea, executed brilliantly. I have defeated my enemies and I have brought power and wealth to my family. I am the toast of Four Dragons. Tonight this is my city. And all I see is a man huddling in a cave in an empire of dust. I was born in this cave and I'll die in this cave and all my borrowed water and air and carbon will be taken back and paid out. I'll become part of a million lives. It's a mean sort of resurrection. And we never had a choice. My mother did. She traded the Earth for wealth. I didn't have that choice. None of us do. We can't go back – there is no back for us. This is all we have: dust, sunlight; people. The moon is people. That's what they say. Your worst enemy and your best hope. Rafa likes people. Rafa hopes for heaven. I know we live in hell. Rats in a tunnel, banished from beauty.'

'Should I sing for you, Lucas?'

'Maybe you should. Everything is clear, Jorge. I know exactly what I have to do. That's why I will be rid of Amanda. That's why I can't rejoice. That's why I can't hear you tonight. Jorge.' Lucas brushes a finger along the back of Jorge's hand. 'Stay.'

*

'Wake up.'

Hands grasp her under the shoulders and lift her. She was within a nod of sliding asleep into the water. Carlinhos crouches by the side of the water tank. He taps Marina's cocktail glass, sticky with the sapphire residue of a Blue Moon. 'Not a good mix. Drowning on the moon: it's not good on the autopsy report.'

'I felt owed a celebration.'

Marina had been on her last sips of oxygen when the relief rover dashed up over the horizon; shuddering with cold; anoxia blue as Carlinhos hooked her into the life support. The rover spun its wheel-housings and laid in a course at full speed for Beikou, a Taiyang server-farm on the rim of Macrobius. By the time Carlinhos bundled Marina through the outlock and the airblade had blasted her clean of dust she was slipping in and out of hypothermic unconsciousness. Fingers unsealing her sasuit. Hands peeling it from her. Intimate fingers unhooking her function tubes, the tug of caked lubricant and crusted body fluids. Hands lowering her into water, warm warm water what? Water surrounding penetrating caressing her. Water calling her back to life.

What is this?

'Just a tank.' Carlinhos's voice. Those hands: his hands? 'You nearly died out there.'

'They wouldn't have landed a ship on me.' She could barely force the words through chattering teeth. She was coming back to life and it was agony.

'That's not what I meant.'

'Needed doing.'

'I love the way you say that.' Carlinhos said. 'So *norte*. So righteous. *Needs doing.*' He trailed a finger across the surface of the pool. 'We'll cover the water charge.'

Beikou is as close and introverted as a convent: Suns, Asamoahs and minor clans twine together in chains of linked polyamorys. The narrow, stooping tunnels ring with the voices of children in five languages; the triple-breathed air smells of bodies and sweat, the peculiar dust of computer systems, sour urine. For Marina to inhale it, to wallow in this egg of water, clenched inside the moon, Corta Hélio struck contracts with Taiyang and AKA. Marina leans back, lets her hair swirl out in the warm water. She can reach up and touch the sintered glass roof. Ao Kuang, Dragon-king of the East Sea, painted manhua-style, glares down from the close ceiling. Water laps against her breasts. Something has disturbed the pool.

'What are you doing?'

She had blinked out again, blinks open to see Carlinhos shrug out of his sasuit.

'I'm coming in.'

He lowers himself into the water. *You look tired,* she thinks. *You're magnificent but bone tired. You move like an old crab.* Hetty's activity log reported twenty-eight hours on the surface. The sasuits were rated for twenty-four. *We should all be dead.* She flicks water in Carlinhos's face. He's so tired he hardly flinches.

'Hey.'

'Hey.'

'Did we get it?'

'The Court of Clavius recognised our claim and issued a licence. We've already put out construction tenders.'

She lifts a little, painful fist; gives a little painful *yay*.

'You know, maybe we are owed a celebration,' Carlinhos says. 'They make a really good potato vodka here.'

'What was that about drowning looking shit on your death cert?'

'Worse than a VTO moonship landing on you?'

'You.' She flicks water at him again. He can't or won't dodge. *Oh you man, you are so cute when you're tired and stinky and stubbly and hurting and I could so do you now and you're right in front of me, touching my knees, my shins, my feet and if I moved my hand just a few centimetres there and you moved your hand a few centimetres here we would, but I won't because I'm a wreck and you're a wreck and you're still my boss and a Dragon and Dragons have always scared me, but most of all because we are like twins in a womb, curled up next to each other in this warm water and that would be prenatal incest.*

She shuffles next to him and they lean comfortably, painfully against each other, like old people, skin to skin, enjoying each other's weight and presence. A long-limbed teen Sun – Marina can't make out their gender beyond skinny-gangly – ducks through the low door to serve Blue Moons. Laughter, pop music, children yelling, the burr of machinery, resound through the tunnels as it they were the pipes of a great musical instrument.

'Corta Hélio.' A toast.

'Sea of Snakes. If I do nod off...'

'I'll watch out for you,' Carlinhos says.

'And I'll watch out for you.'

The sex always begins the same way. One glass, cold-dewed. One measure chilled gin. Three drops of blue Curacao from a glass pipette. No music. Music distracts Ariel Corta from sex. Tonight she wears an exquisite Rappi ballerina-length dress with petticoats, a New Look Dior straw platter hat and gloves. Her lips are Revlon Fire and Ice red, and pursed in small concentration as she releases the drops of Curacao one at a time from the pipe. Tonight she uses the ten-botanical Dilma Filmus gave her. When the last drop has sent its ripples across the surface of the martini glass Ariel Corta steps out of her dress. Brassieres are unknown in lunar gravity and she eschews other underwear. Gloves, hat, lace-top hold-up stockings, Roger Vivier five-inch heels. Ariel Corta lifts the martini in her gloved hand and takes a sip.

The boys brought it home. Vidhya Rao's tip was sound. Ariel's short, secure conversation through private encryption with Lucas has proved three things. To Rafa, that she too has power. To her mother, that the Cortas truly are the Fifth Dragon. To Lucas, that she is always a Corta. *We want to buy you,* Vidhya Rao had said. Not bought; fee-ed. Hired, not owned. That is the difference between the trader and the consultant. You've triumphed. Ariel Corta raises a toast to herself and to all her clients and contractees and coterie. She takes another sip from her Blue Moon. Beijaflor shows Ariel herself through discreet cameras. Ariel poses to better admire her body. She is magnificent. Magnificent.

Before undressing she vapes a capsule of Solo. The Chemical Sisters, narco-designers to society, print it for bespoke, for these sessions. Hat on padded stand, gloves and stockings patiently and carefully rolled off. Ariel enters the sex room. Her skin, her nipples, her lips and vulva and anus crackle with sexual desire. Walls and floor are softly padded white faux-leather. The apparel awaits her, laid out in careful order, made to measure in white faux-leather. The boots first; high and tight and laced tighter still; tightest yet as she tugs in the lacing. She paces around the small room letting her thighs brush against each other, the tickle of the laces against her ass and vulva. She kneels, thrilling in the dig of the eyes and heels against her buttocks. Then the gloves, shoulder length and laced; pulled tight. She spreads her fingers, encased in tight white leather. The stiff, high collar. Ariel gasps as the laces tighten and she surrenders mobility and freedom. Last of all, the corset. A ritual, this; the exhalations, the carefully timed drawings-in of the laces until she can barely breathe. Her small breasts are proud and pert.

At age thirteen Ariel Corta orgasmed after pulling on a sasuit. She hasn't worn one since but its tightness, its unforgiving constriction and control of the body has permanently shaped her sex play. Ariel Corta has never told a soul about the sasuit come.

The gag. A classic red-ball gag, matching her lip-gloss. She buckles it tight, tighter. This is for those times when she wedged half a bedsheet into her mouth to stifle the noises of her fabulous masturbation. It keeps the bubbles in the champagne. Ariel Corta squeals and begs into her gag. Beijaflor is outside verbal command but the familiar has played this game many many times. The dressing is complete.

Ariel softly claps her gloves together. Haptics engage; she strokes each breast, hissing into her gag at the touch of thick soft fur. She circles each nipple, delirious with pleasure. The haptics realign and she squeaks at the touch of bristles. The gloves follow a random sequence: Ariel is down on her knees, drooling ecstatically as she introduces the soft sensitive folds of her vulva to bristles that become vinyl nubs, then gritty abrasives. Long slow strokes with her right hand; her left explores the terrain of bare skin between the tight-laced leatherwear. She is bursting; blood and bone and flesh and fluid held in check by taut leather. Now the haptics run different sensations on each hand. Ariel in on her knees, leaning back to allow her fingers access to her fierce little vulva. Sharp heels dig into her ass, she can feel her cheeks spreading on the padded floor. She is blaspheming piously into her gag. Beijaflor shows her herself, thighs spread, fingers working, face upturned and eyes wide. Her cheeks are streaked with saliva leaking from either side of the gag. Haptics switch to prickles: now Ariel's fingers move for her clitoris for the first time. She shrieks freely and joyfully into her gag. The Solo has hypersensitized her clitoris, her nipples, her vulva and the rosebud of her anus. Each touch is an agony and daring delight. Ariel Corta is bellowing mutely now. Beijaflor swoops the camera around her: close-up on her fingers, her eyes, the pillow of thigh-flesh over spilling her tight boots.

The foreplay lasts an hour. Ariel Corta brings herself to the edge of orgasm half a dozen times. But this is the foreplay. Sex is as ritualised as mass. A printer chimes, the haptics deactivate. Shaking, sleek with sweat and saliva flicked from her gag, Ariel crawls to the printer. Coco de Lune is the moon's greatest sex toy designer. Ariel never knows what she will get until the printer chimes. All that is certain is that it will be customised to her body and tastes and that it will take many hours to explore its subtleties fully.

Ariel opens the printer. A dildo, a set of polished anal balls. The dildo is long and elegant, a classic old school moon-rocket, complete with four stabilising fins at the bottom. Each fin control a different haptic field. A silver pussy-rocket printed to the dimensions of her vagina and vulva. Not a penis. Never a penis. Ariel Corta has never allowed a penis inside her.

You're beautiful, Beijaflor whispers to Ariel in Ariel's voice. *Love you love you love you.*

Ariel moans into her gag, lies back on the padded leather, opens her legs.

Put it up you, in you, kilometres in you, Beijaflor says. *Fuck yourself to death.*

Ariel works the self-lubing pleasure balls into her anus. Corset and collar hold her rigid, unable to see what she is doing to her orifices. Beijaflor shows her close-ups and whispers filth and insults in her own Portuguese. Ariel works the balls in, pushes them deep, hooks a finger through the handle. She tugs gently, feels the drag and grate inside her. At orgasm she will pull them out, perhaps slowly, perhaps all at once. Then one by one she will push them in again.

She holds the dildo up before her eyes, panting in dread and expectation as her own voice tells her exactly what she is going to do with it, how deep and how fast and how long, every position and stroke. It will take hours. Hours. At the end, Ariel Corta will crawl from a sex room soaking with sweat and saliva and body fluids and creamy lubrication and slowly release herself from her binding leather. No lover, no body, no flesh can compare with the perfect sex she has with herself.

Since the age of thirteen Ariel Corta has been joyously, enthusiastically, monogamously autosexual.

The man goes low, swinging for her knees with the wrench. Marina dives away. Her strength and momentum carry her high, far. High and far are vulnerable. Momentum kills. Marina comes down hard enough to knock the wind out of her, slides, slams into a girder. The Mackenzie man knows how to fight. He's on his feet, wrench raised to bring it down on her chest. Marina kicks out. Her boot connects with kneecap. The crunch of bone, the scream silences the dock for a moment. The man goes down, felled. Marina picks up the wrench.

'Marina!' Carlinhos's voice. 'Don't.'

The Mackenzie is tall, fit, male. She is short, female, but she is a Jo Moonbeam. She has the strength of three moon-men. She could crush this man's ribcage with a single blow of her fist.

How did the fight start? Like any fight starts: like a fire: combustible tempers, proximity, a spark, something to feed the ignition. Beikou Lock Control kept Team Corta in the holding bay while a Mackenzie Metals rover squadron docked and locked. The squad fretted: enough confining tunnels, foul air, old water. They wanted home. Patience frayed. The Mackenzie squad – all men, Marina observed – filed in from the outlock carrying the spicy smell of moon dust. As the squad leader passed Carlinhos: two words: *Corta thieves*. Patience snapped. Carlinhos roared and felled him with a head-butt and the holding bay exploded.

Marina has never been in a fight. She has seen them in bars, in student houses, at parties but she was never part of them. Here she is a target. These men want to hurt her. These men don't care if she dies. The Mackenzie man is down and out of the fighting, burbling faintly in shock. Marina crouches – low is strong – scanning the room. Real fights are not movie fights. Fighters go to ground, tug and claw and try to smash each other's heads in. Carlinhos is down, on his back. Marina grabs his attacker by the arm. The man screams. She has dislocated his shoulder. She picks him up by suit collar and belt and slings him across the dock as easily as if he were a piece of clothing. Marina spins, charges at the first Mackenzie she sees. She mashes the Mackenzie man against a stanchion. She stands, panting. She has superpowers. She is She-Hulk.

'Where are the cops?' she yells to Carlinhos.

'Earth,' he yells back, sweeps an attacker's legs from under him. Carlinhos drives fist into face. Blood sprays from the crushed nose; slow falling red.

'Fuck!' Marina cries. 'Fuck fuck fuck fuck.' She throws herself into the fight. The seduction of power is horrible and juicy. This is what it's like to be a man on Earth, to know that you will always have strength. She kicks, she grabs, she seizes and snaps, she smashes. And it's over. Blood on the sinter. Burbling sobbing. Dock control has arrived and are holding the parties apart with tasers and knives but fights have half-lives and this one has decayed into pointing and lunging and shouting. The argument now is over who pays, who compensates. The legal AIs fight now.

'You all right?' Carlinhos asks. Marina smells violence from him. Her gooseflesh rises: he fought without restraint or passion, as if violence were another tool of his business. Out on the dustbikes, he had said, *Rafa's the charmer, Lucas is the schemer, Ariel's the talker; I'm the fighter.* Marina thought he was speaking metaphorically. No. He is a fighter and a strong one. She is a little afraid.

Marina nods. Now the shaking comes, the physical and chemical release. She hurt people. She broke bodies, smashed faces and she feels as pure and euphoric and alive as she did after Carlinhos took her on the Long Run. Elated and intense; dirty, itchy, degraded: a blood-slut. She doesn't recognise herself.

'The bus is here. Let's go home.'

The cold perhaps, or the subtle realignment of weight, or the tiny, careful noises that night amplifies, but when Sohni Sharma wakes she knows Rafa isn't there. The sex had been almost an afterthought; cursory, due diligence. *Come back to my club,* he had said and perhaps she should have read the warning in those words. Loud men, some drunk, in their own place and space, looking her up and down, weighing and assaying and slipping sly looks and eyebrow-raises and smiles to Rafa. Men who own things. Then the news came through about the deal – some new extraction rights, territory claimed – that not only annihilated Rafa's bar-room darkness, but reversed it; turned it into golden light. The club was his. Drinks for everyone; all my friends, drink drink. Raucous and laddish and backslapping; crude and con- gratulatory: she was trophy and promise. To the victor the prize. Rafa's arm around her all night, into the vanishing hours. The Professional Handball Owners Club was not a safe space but she stayed.

Her eyes ache, her joints throb, she is as dehydrated as the surface of the moon. How bad is it to ride the moonloop hung over?

Time. Oh five twelve. The sunline is a strip of indigo along the top of the world. She should move, get her stuff, get things together. Where is Rafa? Not in the bedroom, nor the ensuite, the office or the generous living space she tiptoes through, bare-skinned. The air still smells clean, washed. He's on a chair on a shallow balcony, perched on the edge. The only thing he wears, against all club etiquette, is his familiar. He's talking, voice low, back turned, a conversation not meant to be overheard. Overhear it she must.

But Robson is perfectly safe. I swear to you. God and his mother. Robson's safe, Luna's safe; Boa Vista is safe. I don't want to have to fight you. I don't want to fight you. Think about Luna. She'll be in the middle. Come back. Back to Boa Vista, coracão. You promised me it would only be for a little time. Come back. It's not about the kids. It's about me...

Bare-skinned, barefoot, shivering with alcohol and a betrayal she expected but which still wounds, Sohni turns, walks away, dresses, picks up her few things, leaves the moon forever.

In the end, Adriana orders Paulo out of his own kitchen. He is her cook, he has studied the technique, and printers have already produced the flask, the mesh, the lid and plunger. But he has never prepared it, tested it, even smelled it. Adriana has. He leaves with poor grace. The aroma passes through Boa Vista's aircon. What is that thing?

I think it's coffee.

Staff are lined up outside Paulo's kitchen: what's Senhora Corta doing? She's measuring it. She's boiling water. She's taking the water off the boil. She's counting. She's pouring the water on to the stuff, from a height. What's that about? Oxygenation, says Paulo. She'll stir it too: the flavour develops fully through an oxidation reaction. Now she's waiting. How does it smell? Not like anything I'd want past my lips. What's she doing now? Still waiting. It's a bit of a ritual, this coffee.

Adriana Corta depresses the plunger. A bronze *crema* floats on the top of the French press. One cup.

Adriana sips her last cup of coffee. She pushes down the thought. This is a celebration, a small one, a private one, the true one before the gaudy carnival Lucas insists on for her birthday. *Not this time,* she whispers, to the Mackenzies and to death. But her life is filling with last things, like flooding water filling a tunnel. A rising level: or perhaps it is that her life is descending towards it.

The coffee doesn't taste the way it smells. For that Adriana is thankful. If it did, humans would never do anything other than drink it. Smell is the sense of memory. Each coffee would recall countless memories, boundless memories. Coffee as the drug of remembering.

'Thank you, Lucas,' Adriana Corta says and pours a second cup. The press is empty, only moist grounds. Coffee is precious stuff. *Rarer than gold,* Adriana whispers, a memory from her duster days. *The gold we throw away.*

Adriana takes the two cups out to the São Sebastião pavilion. Two cups, two chairs. One for her, one for Irmã Loa. Adriana takes another sip of coffee. How did she ever love this earthy, musky, bitter brew: how did anyone? Another sip. It is the cup of memories. As she sips this coffee, she sips again her previous cup: forty-eight years ago. That coffee too had been a memorial. Her boys have been magnificent; their achievement in stealing Mare Anguis from between the Mackenzies' grasping fingers will be moon legend for generations, but coffee will always bring her back to Achi.

SIX

I met Achi because free fall sex made me sick. It was all the talk during training. Freefall sex. It's all they do, it's all they want to do. It ruins you forever. After freefall sex, heavy sex is gross and ugly. Those Vorontsov Space people; they're sex ninjas.

They were matching us up even as we swam in through the lock. Those Vorontsov Space people. There was one guy: he looked and I looked back and nodded yes, I will, yes even as the tether snatched the transfer pod away from the cycler and cut our last connection with Earth. I'm no prude. I've got the New Year Barra beach bangles. I'm up for a party and a chance for life-changing sex; you don't pass on that. I wanted to try it with this guy. We went up to the hub. There were bodies everywhere, drifting, bumping into each other. The men had to use condoms. You didn't want to get hit by that stuff, flying. I said *be kind* and I did something worse than flying cum. I threw up all over him. I couldn't stop throwing up. That's not sexy. Zero gee turned everything inside me upside down. He was very polite and vacuumed it all up while I retreated to gravity.

The only other person in the centrifuge arm was this caramel-eyed girl, slender hands and long fingers, her face flickering every few moments into an unconscious micro-frown. She would barely meet my eyes; she seemed shy and inward-gazing. Her name was Achi

Debasso. I couldn't place the name; it was like nothing I had ever heard before, but, like mine, it was a name rolled by tide of history. She was Syrian. Syriac. That one letter was a universe of difference. Her family were Syrian Christians who had fled the civil war. She left Damascus as a cluster of cells in her mother's womb. London born, London raised, MIT educated but she was never allowed to forget – *you are Syriac*. Achi was born an exile. Now she was headed into a deeper exile.

Up in the hub our future co-workers fucked. Down in the centrifuge pod we talked and the stars and the moon arced across the window beneath our feet. And each time we met the whirling moon was a little bigger and we knew each other a little bit better and by the end of the week the moon filled the whole of the window and we had moved from conversationalists into friends.

She was a girl filled with ghosts, Achi. The ghost of having no roots. The ghost of being an exile from a dead country. The ghost of privilege: Daddy was a software engineer, Mummy came from money. London welcomed refugees like that. The ghost of guilt; that she was alive when tens of thousands were dead. Her darkest ghost was the ghost of atonement. She could not change the place or order of her birth, but she could apologise for it by being useful. This ghost rode her all life, shouting in her ear: Be useful Achi! All the way through grad at UCL, post-grad at MIT: Make things right! Atone! The ghost of useful sent her to battle desertification, salinisation, eutrophication. She was an -ation warrior. In the end it drove her to the moon. Nothing more useful than sheltering and feeding a whole world.

If these were her ghosts, her guiding spirit, her orixa, was Yemanja. Achi was a water girl. Her family home was near the Olympic pool – her mother had dropped her into water days out of the hospital. She had sunk, then she swam. She swam and surfed: long British summer evenings on the western beaches. Cold British water. She was small and slight but feared no wave. I grew up with the sounds of waves in my bedroom but never dipped more than a toe in the warm Atlantic. I come from beach people, not ocean people. She missed the ocean terribly, on the moon. She tuned the screens in her apartment to make it look like she lived on a coral reef. It always made me a bit sick. As soon as any new tank or pool was built and there was a chance for swimming, she would be there, stroking up and down through the water. The way she moved through it was so natural, so beautiful. I would watch her dive and push herself down through the water and I wanted her to stay down there forever, her hair floating around her, her breasts weightless in the water, her hands and feet making these tiny, beautiful movements that held her in position, or send her flashing across the tank. I see her still, in water.

She introduced me to her ghosts, I showed her mine: Outrinha: Average Jane: Little Lady Look at Me. Plain Jane and the Mermaid. They would need each other very much in the days and the months to come. The moon was a wild place then. Now she is old like me. But then, in the early days, she was the land of riches and danger, opportunity and death. It was the land of the young and the ambitious. You needed aggression to survive on the moon. She would try and kill you any way she could; by force, by trickery, by seduction. There were five men for every woman, and they were young males, middle class, educated, ambitious and scared. The moon was not a safe place for men, even less safe for women. For the women, it was not just the moon, there were the men too. And we were all scared, all the time. Scared as the moonlop spun up to meet us at the transfer capsule docked and we knew that the only way was forward. We needed each other, and we stuck, and we clung, in our suits, all the way down.

The freefall sex? Grossly oversold. Everything moves in all the wrong ways. Things get away from you. You have to strap everything down to get purchase. It's more like mutual bondage.

*

We came out of the moonloop dock – there was only one transfer tether then, in a polar orbit: one hundred and twenty Jo Moonbeams. It's an old word that, one of the oldest on the moon. Jo Moonbeam. It sounds bright and wide-eyed and innocent. We were all that.

Even before they officially welcome, the LDC planted the chibs on our eyeballs. We had ten inhalations free, then we started paying. We've been paying ever since. Air, water, carbon, data. The Four Elementals. You were born here, you won't remember a time when you didn't have those numbers in your eye. But I tell you, the first time you see the numbers change because the market has shifted, your breath catches in your throat. Nothing tells you that you are not on Earth any more than exhaling at one price and inhaling at another. Then they pushed us into medical. They wanted to look at my bones. You don't think about the bones. To Jo Moonbeams everything is new and demanding. You need to learn how to move – you need to learn how to stand. You need to learn how to see and hear. You learn about your blood, and your heart, and dust and how that's the thing that is most likely to kill you. You learn evacuation drills and depressurisation alarms and what side of a door to be on and when it's safe to open it. You learn when to help people and when to abandon people. You learn how to live on top of each other, breathe each other's air, drink each other's water. You learn that when you die LDC will take you and break you down and recycle you for carbon and calcium and compost. You learn that you don't own your body. You don't own anything. From the moment you step off the moonloop, everything is rented.

You don't think about the bones, but they tick away, under the skin, hour by hour, day by day, lune by lune losing mass and structure. Again, Sister, you were born here. This is your home. You can never go to Earth. But I had a window through which I could return. I had two years until my bone density and muscle tone deteriorated to a point where Earth gravity would be fatal to me. Two years. It was the same for all of us: two years. It's still the same for every Jo Moonbeam who arrives at Meridian looking for the land of opportunity. We all of us face our Moonday, when we have to decide, do I stay or do I go?

They looked at my bones. They looked at Achi's bones. And then we forgot about them.

We moved into barracks, Achi and I. The Jo Moonbeam accommodation was a warehouse with partitions to mark off your living space. Shared bathrooms, mess hall meals. There was no privacy, what you couldn't see you could hear and what you couldn't hear you could smell. The smell. Sewage and electricity and dust and unwashed bodies. The women naturally banded together: Achi and I traded to get cubicles beside each other, then merged them into one space. We held a little ritual that night and swore undying sisterhood over weird-tasting cocktails made from industrial vodka. Humans had been on the moon only five years and already there was a vodka industry. We made decorations from fabric scraps, we grew hydroponic flowers. We had socials and parties and we were the central point for the tampon trade. It was like a prison economy, with tampons instead of cigarettes. We had a natural social gravity, Achi and I. We drew the women, and the men who got tired of all the loud voices and the macho boasting: we're the world-breakers, the moon-busters: we're gonna take this rock and shake a million bitsies out of it. We're going to fuck this moon. I've never been in the military, but I think it might be a bit like the moon in those early days.

We weren't safe. No one was safe. Ten per cent of Jo Moonbeams died within three months. In my first week an extraction worker from Xinjiang was crushed in a pressure lock. Twenty-four launched from Korou on my OTV: three were dead before we even finished surface-activity training. One was the man who had flown up in the seat next to me. I can't remember his name now. We recycled their bodies and reused them and we ate the vegetables and fruit they

209

fertilised and never thought twice about the blood in the soil. You survive by choosing what not to see and hear.

I told you about the stink of the moon. What it stank of most was men. Testosterone. You breathed constant sexual tension. Every woman had been assaulted. It happened to me: once. An older worker, a duster, in the lock as I was changing into my training suit. He tried to slip the hand. I caught and threw him the length of the lock. USP Brazilian jiu jitsu team. My father would have been proud. I had no trouble from that man, or any other man, but I was still scared they would come as a gang. I couldn't have fought a gang. They could hurt me, they might even kill me. There were contracts and codes of behaviour, but there were only company managers to enforce them. Sexual violence was a disciplinary matter.

But Achi didn't know Brazilian jiu jitsu. She didn't know any fighting art, she had no way to defend herself when the man tried to rape her. He didn't succeed – a group of other men pulled him off. He was lucky. If I had caught him, I would have stabbed him. I was glad of those men. They understood that we had to find a way to live together. The moon couldn't be another Earth. If we turned on each other, we would all die. I did think about finding that man and killing him. Cortas cut. That's our name. Hard sharp fast. There are a million ways of killing cleverly on the moon. I thought about it long and hard: should it be secret vengeance, or should my face be the last thing he ever saw? I chose another way. I am many things but I am not a killer.

For Achi's attacker I used slower, subtler weapons. I found his surface-activity training squad. I made some adjustments to his suit thermostat. It would look like a perfect malfunction. I'm a good engineer. He didn't die. He wasn't meant to die. I count his frostbitten thumb and three toes as my trophies. Everyone knew it was me, but nothing was ever proved. I liked the legend. If it made men look at me with fear, that was good. Hanif was his name. He swore he'd rape me and gut me from his hospital bed. By the time he got out of med centre, Achi and I were out on contract.

Achi got a contract with the Asamoahs designing ecosystems for their new agrarium under Amundsen. My contract with Mackenzie Metals took me out on to the open seas. She would be a digger, I would be a duster. In two days we would be parted. We clung to the I and A barracks, we clung to our cabins, our friends. We clung to each other. We were scared. The other women threw a party for us; moon mojitos and sing-alongs to tablet music software. But before the music and the drinking: a special gift for Achi. Her work with AKA would keep her underground; digging and scooping and sowing. She need never go on the surface. She could go her whole career – her whole life – in the caverns and lava tubes and huge agraria. She need never see the raw sky.

I used all my charm and reputation but the suit hire was still cosmologically expensive. I contracted thirty minutes in a GP surface-activity shell. It was an armoured hulk next to my lithe sasuit spiderwoman. We held hands in the outlock as the pressure door slid up. We walked up the ramp amongst a hundred thousand bootprints. We walked a few metres out on to the surface, still holding hands. There, beyond the coms towers and the power relays and the charging points for the buses and rovers; beyond the grey line of the crater rim that curved on the close horizon and the shadows the sun had never touched; there perched above the edge of our tiny world we saw the full Earth. Full and blue and white, mottled with greens and ochres. Full and impossible and beautiful beyond any words of mine. It was winter and the southern hemisphere was offered to us; the ocean half of the planet. I saw great Africa. I saw dear Brazil.

Then my suit AI advised me that we were nearing the expiry of our contract and we turned our backs on the blue Earth and walked back down into the moon.

That night we drank to our jobs our friends, our loves and our bones. In the morning we parted.

It was six lunes before I saw Achi again. Six lunes on the Sea of Fecundity, sifting dust. I was stationed at Mackenzie Metals' Messier unit. It was old, cramped, creaking: cut-and-cover pods under bull-dozed regolith berms. Too frequently I was evacuated to the new-cut deep levels because of a radiation alarm. Every time I saw the alarm flash its yellow trefoil in my lens I felt my ovaries tighten. Day and night the tunnels trembled to the vibration of the digging machines, eating deep rock. There were eighty dusters in Messier.

There was a sweet man; his name was Chuyu. A 3D print designer. Kind and funny and talented with his body. After a month of laugh-ing and sweet sex, he asked me to join his amory: Chuyu, his amor in Queen, his amor in Meridian, her amor also in Meridian. We agreed terms: six months, who I would and would not have sex with, seeing others outside the amory, bringing others into the amory. We had nikahs even then. It had taken him so long to ask me, Chuyu confessed, because of my rep. Word about Achi's attacker had reached Messier. *I wouldn't do that to an amor,* I said. *Not unless severely provoked.* Then I kissed him. The amory was warmth and sex, but it wasn't Achi. We talked or networked almost every day but I still felt the separation. Lovers are not friends.

I had ten days furlough and my first thought was to spend it with Achi. I could see Chuyu's disappointment as I kissed him goodbye at Messier's bus lock. It wasn't a betrayal: I'd said in the contract that I would not have sex with Achi Debasso. We were friends, not lovers. Achi had come up to the railhead at Hypatia to meet me and all the way down the line to Queen of the South we talked and laughed. So much laughter.

Such fun she had planned for me! Messier was smelly and cramped, Queen of the South was intense, loud, colourful. In only six lunes it had changed beyond recognition. Every street was longer, every tunnel wider, every chamber higher. Achi took me in a glass elevator down the side of the recently completed Thoth Quadra and I reeled from vertigo. Down on the quadra floor was a small copse of dwarf tree – full-size trees would reach the ceiling, Achi explained. There was a café. In that café I first tasted and immediately hated mint tea.

I built this, Achi said. *These are my trees, this is my garden.*

I was too busy looking up at the lights, all the lights, going up and up.

Such fun! Tea, then shops. I had to find a party dress. We were going to a special party, that night. Exclusive. We browsed the catalogues in five different print shops before I found something I could wear: very retro – it was the 1980s then – padded and cinched but it hid what I wanted hidden. Then, the shoes.

The special party was exclusive to Achi's workgroup. A security locked rail capsule took us through a dark tunnel into a space so huge, so blinding, that I almost threw up over my Balenciaga. An agrarium, Achi's last project. I was at the bottom of a shaft a kilometre tall, fifty metres wide. The horizon is close at eye level on the moon; everything curves. Underground, a different geometry applies. The agrarium was the straightest thing I had seen in months. And brilliant: a central core of mirrors ran the full height of the shaft, bouncing raw sunlight one to another to another to walls terraced with hydroponic racks. The base of the shaft was a mosaic of fish tanks, criss-crossed by walkways. The air was warm and dank and rank. I was woozy with CO_2. In these conditions plants grew fast and tall; potato plants the size of bushes; tomato vines so tall I lost their heads in the tangle of leaves and fruit. Hyper-intensive agriculture: the agrarium was huge for a cave, small for an ecosystem. The tanks splashed with fish. Did I hear frogs? Were those ducks?

Achi's team had built a new pond from waterproof sheetings and construction frame. A pool. A swimming pool. A sound system played Ghana-pop. There were cocktails. Yellow was the fashion. They matched my dress. Achi's crew were friendly and expansive.

They never failed to compliment me on my frock. I shucked it and my shoes and everything else for the pool. I lolled, I luxuriated. Over my head the mirrors moved. Achi swam up beside me and we trod water together, laughing and plashing. The agrarium crew had lowered a number of plastic chairs into the pool to make a shallow end. Achi and I wafted blood-warm water with our legs and drank golden bison-grass vodka.

I woke up in bed beside Achi the next morning; shit-headed with vodka. I remember mumbling, fumbling love. Shivering and stupid-whispering, skin to skin. Fingerworks. Achi was curled on her right side, facing me. She had kicked the sheet off in the night. A tiny string of drool ran from the corner of her mouth to the pillow and trembled in time to her breathing. I see it still.

I looked at her there, her breath rattling in the back of her throat in drunken sleep. We had made love. I had sex with my dearest friend. I had done a good thing, I had done a bad thing. I had done an irrevocable thing. Then I lay down and pressed myself close to her and she mumble-grumbled and moved in close to me and her fingers found me and we began again.

My mother used to say that love was the easiest thing in the world. Love is what you see every day. That was how she fell in love with my father; every day she passed him, welding.

I did not see Achi for several lunes after the party in Queen. Mackenzie Metals sent me out prospecting new terrain in the Sea of Vapours. Away from Sea of Vapours, it was plain to me and Sun Chuyu that the amory didn't work for me. I had broken my contract, but in those days there were no financial implications of extra-contractual sex. All the amors agreed to annul the contract and let me leave the amory. No blame, no claim. A simple automated contract, terminated.

I took a couple of weeks' accumulated leave back in Queen. I called Achi about hooking up but she was at a new dig at Twé where the Asamoahs were building a corporate headquarters. I felt relieved. Then I felt guilty that I had felt relieved. Sex had made everything different. I drank, I partied, I had one-night stands, I talked long hours of expensive bandwidth with Mum and Dad back in Barra. The entire family gathered in front of the lens to thank me for the money, especially the tiny kids. They said I looked different. Longer. Drawn out. There they were, happy and safe. The money I sent them bought their education. Health, weddings, babies. And here I was, on the moon. Outrinha Adriana, who would never get a man, but who got the education, who got the degree, who got the job, sending them the money from the moon.

They were right. I was different. I never felt the same about that blue pearl of Earth in the sky. I never again hired a sasuit to go look at it, just look at it. Out on the surface, I disregarded it.

The Mackenzies sent me out to the Lansberg extraction zone and there I saw the thing that made everything different.

Five extractors were working Lansberg. Have you seen an extractor? Of course not, forgive me. You've never been on the surface. They are ugly things, with their insides exposed; they were no more elegant then. But to me they were beautiful. Marvellous bones and muscles. I saw them one day, out on the regolith, and I almost fell flat from the revelation. Not what they were made for – separating rare-earth metals from lunar regolith – but what they threw away. Launched in high, arching ballistic jets on either side of the big, slow machines.

It was the thing I saw every day. One day you look at the boy on the bus and he sets your heart alight. One day you look at the jets of industrial waste and you see riches beyond measure. The plan formed there and then, all at once in my head. By the time I made it back to the rover it was in place, every last detail, intricate and engineered and beautiful and I knew it would work straight out of the box. But for it to work, I had to put distance between myself and anything that might link me to regolith waste and beautiful rainbows of dust. The

Mackenzies could have no claim on any part of it. I quit Mackenzie and became a Vorontsov track queen.

I went up to Meridian to rent a data crypt and hunt for the leanest, freshest, hungriest law firm to protect the thing I had seen out on Lansberg. And there I saw Achi again. She had been called back from Twé to solve a problem with microbiota in the Obuasi agrarium that had left it a pillar of stinking black slime.

One city, two friends, two amors. We went out to party. And found we couldn't. The frocks were fabulous, the cocktails disgraceful, the company louche and the narcotics dazzling but in each bar, club, private party we ended up in a corner together, talking. Partying was boring. Talk was lovely and bottomless and fascinating. We ended up in bed again, of course. We couldn't wait. Glorious, impractical 1980s frocks lay crumpled on the floor, ready for the recycler.

I remember when Achi asked: *What do you want?* She was lying on the bed and inhaling THC from a vaper. I could never take that stuff. It made me paranoid. And she also said: *Dream and don't be afraid.*

And I answered: *I want to be a Dragon.* Achi laughed and punched me on the thigh, but I had never said truer words.

In the year and a half we had been on the moon, our small world had changed. Things moved fast in those early days. We could build an entire city in months. We had energy and raw materials and human ambition. Four companies had emerged as major economic forces. The four families. The Mackenzies were the longest established. They had been joined by the Asamoahs in food and living space. The Vorontsovs finally moved their operations off Earth entirely and ran the cycler, the moonloop, the bus service and were wrapping the world in rails. The Suns had been fighting the People's Republic's representatives on the LDC board and had finally broken free from terrestrial control. Four companies: Four Dragons. And I would be the Fifth Dragon.

*

I didn't tell her about what I'd seen out there on Lansberg. I didn't tell her about the data vault and the squad of legal AIs. I didn't tell her about the brilliant idea. She knew I was keeping secrets from her. I put a shadow in her heart.

I went to my new job, laying track. The work was good, easy and physical and satisfying. At the end of every up-shift you saw three kilometres of gleaming rail among the boot and track prints, and on the edge of the horizon, the blinding spark of Crucible, brighter than any star, advancing over yesterday's rails, and you said, I made that. The work had real measure: the inexorable advance of Mackenzie Metals across the Mare Insularum, brighter than the brightest star. So bright it could burn a hole through your helmet sunscreen if you held it in your eyeline too long. Thousands of concave mirrors focusing sunlight on the smelting crucibles. In ten years the rail lines would circle the globe and the Crucible would follow the sun. By then, I would be a Dragon.

I was sintering ten kilometres ahead of Crucible when Achi's call came. Ting ching and it all came apart. Achi's voice blocking out my work-mix music, Achi's face superimposed on the dirty grey hills of Rimae Maestlin. Achi telling me her routine medical had given her four weeks.

I hitched a ride on the construction car back down the rails to Crucible. I waited two hours, squatting in the shadows, tons of molten metal and ten thousand kelvin sunlight above my head. That's time to realise the irony. That's not a tradeable commodity here. I hid from the Mackenzies by working ahead of them; I lurked in the dark places of their capital. I rode a slow freight train to Meridian. Ten hours clinging on to a maintenance platform, not even room to turn around, let alone sit. I listened my way through my bossa nova collection. I played Connecto on my helmet hud until every time I blinked I saw tumbling, spinning gold stars. I scanned my family's social space entries offline. By the time I got to Meridian I was two degrees off hypothermic. I couldn't afford the time it would take to re-pressurise for the train, so I went dirty and fast, on the

BALTRAN. I knew I would vomit. I held it until the third and final jump. The look on the BALTRAN attendant's face when I came out of the capsule at Queen of the South was a thing to be seen. So I am told. I couldn't see it. But if I could afford the capsule I could afford the shower to clean it up. And there are people in Queen who will happily clean vomit out of a sasuit for the right number of bitsies. Say what you like about the Vorontsovs, they pay handsomely.

All this I did, the endless hours riding the train like a moon-hobo, the hypothermia and being sling-shotted in a can of my own barf, because I knew that if Achi had four weeks, I could not be far behind.

We met in a café on the twelfth level of the new Chandra quadra. We hugged, we kissed, we cried a little. I smelled sweet by then. Below us, excavators dug and sculpted, a new level every ten days. We held each other at arm's length and looked at each other. Then we drank mint tea on the balcony.

We didn't talk about the bones at once. It was eight lunes since we last saw each other: we talked, we networked, we shared. I made Achi laugh. She laughed like soft rain. I told her about King Dong, that the Mackenzie dusters and Vorontsov track-queens were stamping out in the dust, like boys would. She clapped her hands to her mouth in naughty glee but laughed with her eyes. So wrong. So funny.

Achi was out of contract. The closer you are to your Moonday, the shorter the contract, sometimes down to minutes of employment, but this was different. AKA did not want her ideas. They were recruiting direct from Accra and Kumasi. Ghanaians for a Ghanaian company. She was pitching ideas to the LDC for their new port at Meridian – quadras three kilometres deep; a sculpted city; like living in the walls of a titanic cathedral. The LDC were polite but they had been talking about development funding for two lunes now. Her savings were running low. She woke up looking at the tick of the Four Elementals on her lens. She was considering moving to a smaller space.

'I can pay your per diems,' I said. 'I have lots of money.'

And then we talked about the bones. Achi could not decide until I got my report. The guilt, the ghost of doing something wrong. She could not have borne it if her decision influenced my decision to stay with the moon or go back to Earth. I didn't want to do that. I didn't want to be here on this balcony drinking piss-tea. I didn't want Achi to have forced the decision to go to the medics on me. I didn't want there to be a decision for me to make.

Then the wonder. I remember it so clearly: a flash of gold in the corner of my vision. Something marvellous. A woman flying. A flying woman. Her arms were outspread, she hung in the sky like a crucifix. Our Lady of Flight. Then I saw wings shimmer and run with rainbow colours; wings transparent and strong as a dragonfly's. The woman hung a moment, then folded her gossamer wings around her, and fell. She tumbled, now diving heard-first, flicked her wrists, flexed her shoulders. A glimmer of wing slowed her; then she spread her full wing span and pulled up out of her dive into a soaring spiral, high above Chandra Quadra.

'Oh,' I said. I had been holding my breath. I was shaking with wonder. If you could fly why would you ever do anything else? It's commonplace now; anyone can do it. But back then, there, I saw what we could do in this place.

I went to the Mackenzie Metals medical centre and the medic put me in the scanner. He passed magnetic fields through my body and the machine gave me my bone density analysis. I was eight days behind Achi. Five weeks, and then my residency on the moon would become citizenship.

Or I could fly back to Earth, to Brazil.

That night the golden woman swooped through my dreams. Achi slept beside me. I had booked a hostel room. The bed was wide, the air was as fresh as Queen of the South could make and the taste of the water did not set your teeth on edge.

Oh, that golden woman, flying loops through my certainties.

Queen of the South hadn't gone to a three-shift society, so it never went completely dark. I pulled Achi's sheet around me and went out on to the balcony. I leaned on the rail and looked out at the walls of lights. Lives and decisions behind every light. This was an ugly world. It put a price on everything. It demanded a negotiation from everyone. Out at the railhead I had seen a new thing among some of the surface workers: a medallion, or a little votive tucked into a patch pocket. A woman in Virgin Mary robes, one half of her face a black angel, the other half a naked skull. It was the first time I met Dona Luna. One half of her face dead, but the other was alive. The moon was not a dead satellite, she was a living world. Hands and hearts and hopes like mine shaped her. Here there was no Mother Nature, no Gaia to set against human will. Everything that lived, we made. Dona Luna was hard and unforgiving, but she was beautiful. She could be a woman, with dragonfly wings, flying.

I stayed on the hotel balcony until the roof reddened with sun-up. Then I went back to Achi. I wanted to make love with her again. My motives were all selfish. Things that are difficult with friends are easier with lovers.

It was Achi's idea to make a game out of it. We must clench our fists behind our backs, like Scissors, Paper, Stone, and count to three. Then we open our fists and in them there will be something, some small object, that will say beyond any doubt what we have decided. We must not speak, because if we say even a word, we will influence each other. It was the only way she could bear it, if it was quick and clean and we didn't speak a word. And a game.

We went back to the balcony table of the café to play the game. Two glasses of mint tea. I remember the air smelled of rock dust over the usual electricity and sewage. Every fifth sky panel was blinking. A less than perfect world.

'I think we should do this kind of quickly,' Achi said and her right hand was behind her back so fast I caught my breath. Now, the time was now. I slipped my small object out of my bag and clenched it in my hidden fist.

'One two three,' Achi said. We opened our fists.

She held a nazar: an Arabic charm: concentric teardrops of blue, white and black lunar glass, like an eye.

In my hand was a tiny icon of Dona Luna: black and white, living and dead.

The last things were simple and swift. All farewells should be sudden, I think. I booked Achi on the cycler out. There was always space on the return orbit. She booked me into the LDC medical centre. A flash of light and the chib was bonded permanently to my eye. No hand shake, no congratulations, no welcome. All I had done was decide to continue doing what I was doing.

The cycler would come round the Farside and rendezvous with the moonloop in three days. Three days: it focused our feelings, it kept us from crying too much.

I went with Achi on the train to Meridian. We had a whole side row of seats to ourselves and we curled up like small burrowing animals.

I'm scared, she said. It hurt, going back. The cycler slowly spins you up to Earth gravity and then there's the gees coming down. She could be months in a wheelchair. Swimming, they say, is the closest a returnee can come to being on the moon. The water supports you while you build up muscle and bone mass again. Achi loved to swim. And then were the doubts. What if she had been mixed up with someone else and she was already past the point of no return? Would they try to bring her back to the moon? She couldn't bear that. It would kill her as surely as the Earth shattering her bones, suffocating her under her own weight. I understood then that she hated the moon. She had always hated it; the danger, the fear, but most of all, the people. The same faces looking into your face, forever. Wanting

221

something from you. Wanting and wanting and wanting. No one can live that way, she said. It's inhuman. I was the only thing that made the moon bearable for her. And I was staying, and she was leaving.

So I told her the thing I kept secret: the thing I had seen out in Lansberg, that would make me a Dragon. It was so simple. I just looked at something I saw every day in a different way. Helium-3. The key to the post-oil economy. Mackenzie Metals threw away helium-3 every day. And I thought, how could the Mackenzies not see it? Surely they must... I couldn't be the only one. But family and companies, and family companies especially, they have strange fixations and blindnesses. Mackenzies mine metal. Metal mining is what they do. They can't imagine anything else and so they miss what's right under their noses. I could make it work. That's what I told Achi. I knew how to do it. But not with the Mackenzies. They'd take it off me. If I tried to fight, they'd just bury me. Or kill me. It's cheaper. The Court of Clavius would make sure my family were compensated, but that would be the end of my hopes for dynasty. I would make it work for me, I would build a dynasty. I would be the Fifth Dragon. Mackenzie, Asamoah, Vorontsov, Sun: Corta. I liked the sound of that.

I told her this on the train to Meridian. The seat-back screen showed the surface. On a screen, outside your helmet, it is always the same. It is grey and soft and ugly and covered in footprints. Inside the train were workers and engineers; lovers and partners and even a couple of small children. There was noise and colour and drinking and laughing, swearing and sex. And us curled up in the back against the bulkhead. And, I thought, this is the moon.

Achi gave me a gift at the moonloop gate. It was the last thing she owned. Everything else had been sold. There were eight passengers at the departure gate, with friends, family, amors to see them off. No one left alone. The air smelled of coconut, so different from the vomit, sweat, unwashed bodies of the arrival gate. Mint tea was available from a dispensing machine. No one drank it.

Achi's gift was a document cylinder, crafted from bamboo. My instructions were to open it after she was gone. The departure was so fast, the way they say executions are. The VTO staff had everyone strapped into their seats and were sealing the capsule door before either I or Achi could respond. I saw her mouth begin a goodbye, saw her wave fingers, then the locks sealed and the elevator took the capsule up to the tether platform.

I tried to imagine the moonloop: a spinning spoke of M5 fibre twenty centimetres wide and two hundred kilometres long. Up there the ascender was climbing towards the counterbalance mass, shifting the centre of gravity and sending the whole tether into a surface-grazing orbit. Only in the final moments of approach would the white cable be visible, seemingly descending vertically from the star-filled sky. The grapple connected and the capsule was snatched from the platform. Up there, one of those bright stars was the ascender, sliding down the tether, again shifting the centre of mass so that the whole ensemble moved into a higher orbit. At the top of the loop, the grapple would release and the cycler catch the capsule. All engineering, all process, all technical. So I kept the terrible emptiness from me, like charms. I tried to put names on the stars: the cycler, the ascender, the counterweight; the capsule freighted with my amor, my love, my friend. The comfort of physics. I watched until a new capsule was loaded into the gate. Already the next tether was wheeling up over the horizon.

Then I went to buy coffee.

Yes, coffee. The price was outrageous. I dug into my savings. But it was the real thing: imported, not spun up from an organic printer. The importer let me sniff it. I cried. She sold me the paraphernalia as well. The equipment I needed simply didn't exist on the moon.

I took it all back to my hotel. I ground to the specified grain. I

223

boiled the water. I let it cool to the correct temperature. I poured it from a height, for maximum aeration. I stirred it. I made it like I made this coffee, for you, Sister. You never forget these things.

While it drew I opened Achi's gift. I unrolled drawings, concept art for a habitat the realities of the moon would never let her build. A lava tube, enlarged and sculpted with faces. The faces of the orixas, each a hundred metres high, round and smooth and serene, over-looked terraces of gardens and pools. Waters cascaded from their eyes and open lips. Pavilions and belvederes were scattered across the floor of the vast cavern; vertical gardens ran from floor to artificial sky, like the hair of the gods. Balconies – she loved balconies – galleries and arcades, windows. Pools. You could swim from one end of this Orixa-world to the other. She had inscribed it: *a habitation for a dynasty.*

This is Achi's gift, all around you.

When the importer had rubbed a pinch of ground coffee under my nose, memories of childhood, the sea, college, friends, family, celebrations flooded me. They say smell is the sense most closely linked to memory. When I smelled the coffee I had prepared, I experienced something new. Not memories, but a vision. I saw the sea, and I saw Achi, Achi-gone-back, on a board, in the sea. It was night and she was paddling the board out, through the waves and beyond the waves, sculling herself forward, along the silver track of the moon on the sea.

I plunged, poured and savoured the aroma of the coffee.

I drank my coffee.

It still doesn't taste the way it smells.

SEVEN

'Threw us around like fucking girls.' Twenty monitors on Robert Mackenzie's life-support chair peak into the orange. 'One of them was a fucking girl.'

The news had flashed down Crucible's spinal chord, familiar to familiar: *Duncan Mackenzie is leaving Fern Gully*. Unprecedented. Unthinkable. Unholy. Jade Sun oversaw the delicate loading of her husband's life-support unit into transit capsule. Her words were soft and kind and encouraging and left the ancillary staff pale with fear. The capsule sped along beneath the incinerating glare of smelting mirrors to Car 27. Duncan Mackenzie's private apartments.

'She was a Jo Moonbeam,' Duncan Mackenzie says.

'You offer any kind of excuse for this?' Jade Sun says, always one discreet step behind Bob Mackenzie's right shoulder.

'Don't be ridiculous.'

'It's not the fight, it's never a fucking duster fight,' Bob Mackenzie says. His voice is a rattle of respirators, his lungs half moon from years of inhaling dust. 'They bent us over and fucked it right up us. Have you see the social net? Asamoahs, Vorontsovs, even the Suns are laughing at us. Even the Eagle of the fucking Moon.'

'We would never laugh at your misfortune, my love,' Jade Sun says.

225

'Well you're a fool. I would if I were you. Fucking Brazilians on kids' bikes.'

'They got the jump on us,' Duncan says. 'It's a set-back.' *You smell vile*, Duncan realises. A sickly excremental tang, the sourness of urine, the thin disguise of sterilising swabs and anti-bacterial. His skin smells, his hair smells. Oils and caked sweats and exudations. His teeth smell; his vile hideous teeth. Duncan can't bear to look at those yellow stumps. How much better one fast, sharp punch and knock them out so he would never have to look at them again. That would kill the old man. Punch clean through packboard-soft crumbling bone into the soft pulp of his brain.

'A set-back?' Bob Mackenzie says. 'We've lost our entire north-west quadrant project. We'll be five years getting our helium operation out from under this pile of shit. Adrian had the tip-off directly from the Eagle. Adrian is a greasy little weasel but he knows how to protect a source. Someone leaked it. One of ours. We've a traitor. More than anything, I fucking hate traitors.'

'I've read Eoin Keefe's report. Our encryption is secure.'

'Eoin Keefe is a coward who's never put his balls on the block for this family.' One step behind Jade Sun's right shoulder; a lithe, intimidating presence, is Hadley Mackenzie. Duncan detests his father's presence in his private rooms, but he is patriarch, silverback, he has the right. Hadley he resents because his presence implies soft words and murmured decisions among the green fronds of Fern Gully, decisions to which Duncan is not party.

'Hadley has replaced Eoin Keefe,' Jade Sun says mildly.

'This is not your call,' Duncan says. 'You do not replace my heads of department.'

'I replace who the fuck I want when the fuck I want,' Robert Mackenzie says and Duncan understands the vulnerability of his position.

'This is a board decision,' Duncan murmurs.

'Board!' Robert Mackenzie shouts with all the spit he can summon. 'This family is at war.'

Does Duncan see a small smile flicker across Jade Sun's face?

'We're a business. Businesses don't fight wars.'

'I did,' Robert Mackenzie says.

'This is a whole new moon.'

'The moon doesn't change.'

'There is no profit in fighting the Cortas.'

'We'd have our pride,' Hadley says. Duncan stands close to him; eye to eye, breath-close.

'Can you breathe pride? Step out there and say that to Lady Moon: *I've got my Mackenzie pride.* We fight them the way we do best. We make money. Mackenzie Metals isn't pride, Mackenzie Metals isn't family; it's a machine for making money. It's a machine for sending profits back to all those investors; those fund owners and venture capitalists back on Earth who trusted you, Dad, to take their money to the moon and make it work for them. They're Mackenzie Metals. Not us.'

Robert Mackenzie growls in his stone lungs.

'My husband is very tired,' Jade Sun says. 'Emotions are exhausting for him.' Robert's LSU chair turns and Duncan knows it is against the old monster's will. The inlock to the transit capsule opens. Hadley nods to his half-brother and follows the slow-rolling entourage.

'We need peace with the Cortas!' Duncan shouts after them.

She sees Wagner in the chair and freezes.

'Everyone in this bar is a wolf,' Wagner says. She looks around. The two women at the near table, the group at the far table, the lone drinker at the bar, the handsome couple in the booth, turn and look at her. The bartender nods. Wagner indicates the seat opposite him.

'Please. Something to drink?'

She names a herbal cocktail unknown to Wagner. You were frightened before you entered this room, he thinks. But you became angry the moment you saw me. I can read this in the dilation of your pupils, the fixtures of your jawline, the lines on the back of your hand around the glass, the flare of your nostrils; a hundred micro-tells. Sometimes the heightened senses of his full-self overwhelms Wagner in barrage of impressions; sometimes their insight is as precise as a fighting knife. He can smell the components of her drink: a basil and tarragon spritzer with a dash of sours. The water is Peary ice-fresh.

'You set that up well,' she says.

'Thank you. I worked hard at it. I knew you'd run background checks. Did you like the social profile? Minor shareholder in the Polar Lunatics. I actually took a position in the team, in case you checked that. I sold it back when my people told me you were at the door.' He's over-telling. It's a danger in his light-self. Everything is there at once inside him: words fight for a place through the narrow doors of thought and voice. Mundanes are so slow.

'You were never that diligent in the colloquium.'

'Diligent. Diligent, yes. No. I've changed a lot since then.'

'So I've heard. That's your usual familiar?'

'Everything is different when the Earth is round,' Wagner says.

'I am scared of you,' Elisa Stracchi says.

'Of course. Yes. I had to make sure you wouldn't run. But I just want information, Elisa.'

'I didn't know what it was for.'

Wagner leans forward. Elisa Stracchi flinches at the intensity of his gaze.

'I don't think I believe that. No, I don't believe that at all. An assassination attempt on my brother? Bio-processors specifically designed for a fly-based neurotoxin delivery system? I don't believe that.'

'Would you believe me if I told you I have no idea who the client was?'

'I do believe that you would carry out the same due diligence on your client as you did on me. From which I can conclude that the real client was concealed by a similar nest of shell companies.'

'You sound like a fucking dick, Wagner,' Elisa says. Her foot jerks under the table. It does not take wolf senses to read that tell.

'Sorry. Sorry. Who did you deliver to?'

'Am I safe, Wagner?'

Wagner wishes he could stop reading her face. Every unconscious muscular twitch and tensing triggers empathies and anxieties in him. Sometimes he wishes that he could just stop perceiving so minutely, reading so deeply. To stop that would be to stop being Wagner Corta.

'We will protect you.'

She flicks Dr Luz the address of a corporate upload box. Dr Luz interrogates. A shell company, now closed down. She must have known this. The question for Wagner is how many other shell companies and dead drops the file went through before arriving at an assembler. His thoughts are already scurrying along a dozen different paths at once. Wagner thinks of his full mind as a quantum computer; exploring possibilities in many parallel universes at once, then collapsing the superimposed states to a single decision. He knows what to do next.

'Wagner.'

It's seconds before Wagner can refocus. Then, full seconds are instants to mundane folk.

'Fuck you forever. Once a Corta, always a fucking Corta. No one's ever said no to you, have they? You don't even understand the word.'

But she hesitates, just a second, just enough, when she turns to leave and finds the bar empty. Wagner doesn't have the authority to hire private security on the Corta account. He can hire a bar out of his own pocket. And he can crew it with his friends, his family, his pack mates.

That night he runs with his pack up into the roof of the city. Up there, as close as architecture allows to the light of the Earth, old service tunnels have been scraped out into chambers and vesicles. It's a bar, a club, a lair. It's like partying in a lung. The air is stagnant and stale. The bar smells of bodies and perfumes and cheap vodka with the polycarbonate tang of the manufactories. The light is blue,

Earthshine blue, the music real not piped privately through familiars and so loud it's physical.

The Magdalena pack from Queen of the South has come to Meridian. They're the oldest of the moon packs; from the dream-time they have been led by Sasha Volchonok Ermin. Né claims to be the oldest wolf on the moon; first to lift up ner eyes and howl at the Earth. First to claim the pronoun. Né's a First gen, a head shorter than any of ner pack, but ner charisma lights the bar like Diwali. Wagner finds ner intimidating; né has no regard for him, thinks him a soft aristocrat, no true wolf. Ner pack are rough and aggressive and believe themselves true heirs of the two natures. But they give good party. Already fighters are lining up in the pit, stripped to skins and hankering to wrestle. Wagner is a talker not a fighter and he finds a cavity in the warren of tunnels equally distant from the cheering and the DJ where he holds three conversations simultaneously with a roboticist with Taiyang Moongrid, a broker in physics-limited derivatives and an interior designer specialising in custom woods.

A Magdalena girl arrives on the edge of the conversations. When the Earth is round the wolves of the moon scorn mundane fashion: she is dressed in a lime-green suit-liner, be-scribbled by marker pens in the frenetic, spiralling, winding doodles of the Earth-lit visual imagination.

'You're small you're sweet you smell good,' she whispers and Wagner picks out every word from the weave of small talk.

'That's a look,' he says.

'It was a thing, then not a thing, so now a thing again,' she says. 'I'm Irina.' Her familiar is a horned skull with flames flickering from its eyes and nostrils. Another look that was a thing, then not a thing, then a thing again. Wagner has always wondered where the short-lived fad for graffitied suit-liners came from.

'I'm...'

'I know who you are, Little Wolf.'

She closes her teeth on his earlobe and whispers, 'I like to bite.'

'I like to be bitten,' Wagner says but before she can haul him away he puts a hand on her breastbone. He can feel every heartbeat, every breath, every surge of blood through her arteries. She smells of honey and patchouli. 'I have to go to my mamãe's birthday party tomorrow.'

'Then respect your Mom and don't show her too much skin.'

The two suits step in on either side of Lucasinho. He doesn't know who they are but he knows whose they are.

Lucas Corta sits on the couch where Lucasinho slept. Neat, precise, hands lightly resting on his thighs. Flavia crouches in a corner, among the saints. Her eyes are wide with fear. Her chest heaves, she visibly fights for every breath. Her hands flutter at her chest. Lucasinho has never seen this before but every moon-born know what it is. Her breath has been shorted. She is drowning in clear air.

'Give her her breath back!' Lucasinho yells. He crouches beside Madrinha Flavia, his arm around her.

'Of course,' Lucas Corta says. 'Toquinho.' Flavia takes a deep, rattling, whooping breath, breaks into coughing and choking. Lucasinho pulls her close. Her eyes are scared.

'Wagner pays for—'

'I made the LDC a better offer,' Lucas says. 'It seems a sensible precaution. If you don't breathe, you don't talk.'

'Fuck you,' Lucasinho says.

'You've been off the network so you may not know that we've scored a famous victory. Corta Hélio. Your family. We've staked out new helium-3 exploitation territories in Mare Anguis. The Court of Clavius has recognised our claim. I've secured the future for you, son. What do you say to that?'

'Congratulations.'

'Thank you.'

Madrinha Flavia's breathing is even now but still she cowers as if each breath might be her last.

'Oh, yes. I almost forgot. Switch on Jinji. Go on. You might as well.

Boot is successful, Jinji says. *Full access to your accounts has been restored.*

'Feels good to have money and carbon and network, doesn't it?' Lucas says. 'Toquinho.' The pattern of notes above Lucas's shoulder spin. There is a spray of virtual notes.

I've received a contract transfer, Jinji says. *It's the Four Elementals account for Flavia Vila Nova. Do you accept?*

'Your madrinha looked after you,' Lucas says. 'It's only proper that you should look after her.'

Do you accept? Jinji urges.

'Flavia,' Lucasinho says, 'It's your account. Pai wants me to take it over. I have to do that.' Then, to his father, 'I accept. It's still your money.'

'Yes. But I never did buy you a pet when you were a boy, did I?' Lucas stands up, brushes imaginary dust from his trousers. A nod, the security suits move to the door. 'One last thing. The important bit. The reason I came. You love parties. Everyone loves parties. I've a party invitation for you. Your grandmother's birthday. Bring a cake. You're good at cakes. I don't care if you keep your clothes on or off when you're making it, but it's eighty candles.'

Yemanja wakes Adriana Corta with music: *Aguas de Marco*: her favourite. Elis and Tom cover.

Thank you, she whispers to her familiar and lies under her light sheet, looking up at the ceiling, listening to the music, wondering why this tune, this morning. She remembers. It is her birthday. She is eighty years old today.

Yemanja has chosen birthday dresses: for itself the triple-crescent of the moon herself and for Adriana: Pierre Balmain, 1953, a wing-collared suit, long-sleeved, a tight pencil skirt and an outsized bow on the left hip. Gloves. Bag. Elegant. Flattering on eighty-year-old flesh. Before she dresses, Adriana swims for twenty minutes in the endless pool. She venerates the orixas outside her window with gin and incense. She takes her medication and gags as little as she does every day. She eats five slices of mango while Yemanja updates her on her family's business. A thousand concerns flock, but they will not land today. Not on her birthday.

First to greet her is Helen de Braga. A kiss, an embrace. Now Heitor Pereira wishes her congratulations for the day. In her honour he wears a fantastical uniform, braid and buttons and shoulder pads that would be ridiculous did he not bear it with such dignity. An embrace, a kiss.

Are you well? they ask.

I am joyful, she says. Death gnaws at her, a little more gone each day and her succession is uncertain but she woke this morning aflame with joy. Joy in the small things, the particular fall of the sunline across the faces of the orixas, the creep of the water up over her body as she lowered herself into the pool, the sweet-sour musk of the mangoes, the rustle of the fabric of her party clothes. Marvellous banalities. There are still new sensations to appreciate in this small world.

Now the grandchildren come running. Robson has a new card trick to show her: *in the shuttle, anzinho.* Luna brings flowers, a posy of blue that matches her dress. Adriana accepts them though her skin crawls at the touch of the once-living, now dead. She sniffs deeply – Luna giggles: *Violetas have no smell, Vo.*

Next the okos. There is only one remaining at Boa Vista. Amanda Sun embraces her mother-in-law and kisses her on each cheek.

The madrinhas now. Amalia and Ivete and Monica, Elis casting an eye over Robson, adjusting the knot of his tie, the set of his collar. Rafa, Lucas, Ariel and Carlinhos have long moved out of Boa Vista but their madrinhas remain. Adriana would never banish them from Boa Vista: Cortas honour their obligations. She would rather have them in one place, under her sky, rather than scattered across the world with their gossip and secrets. Like that other one. The faithless one. One by one the madrinhas embrace and kiss their benefactor.

Last in line are the staff. It's a long process, shaking the hands, acknowledging the good wishes for this auspicious day but Adriana Corta works assiduously; a word here, a smile there. Security falls in behind her at the entrance to the station. They form a dark-suited barricade between Adriana and her grandchildren, her oldest retainers, her people. Everyone, from her Director of Finance to her gardener, has reskinned their familiars in party shapes and colours.

The station out-door swishes open. Hands reach for knives: Heitor Pereira had balked at holding the party outside Boa Vista but Adriana insisted. Corta Hélio would not cower inside its fortress. The hands fall away. It's Lucasinho, with a small paper box.

'Happy birthday, Vo.' The box holds a cake, a green-frosted dome delicately decorated with a baroque lace of icing. 'It's Swedish Princess cake. I don't know what Swedish means.' Embrace and kiss. Lucasinho's pierces dimple his grandmother's skin.

'With or without clothes?' Adriana asks. 'I do hope without.' Lucasinho blushes. It's quite adorable on him. 'Are you wearing make-up?'

'I am, Vo.'

'That colour liner really brings out the gold in your eyes. Maybe highlight the cheekbones a little more. Play to your strengths.' He is a sweet boy.

The party will travel in two trams. Entourage first; Adriana, immediate family and security in the second shuttle. In the three-minute journey Robson shows his vo his new card trick – it's themed around people evacuating a leaking habitat: court cards all escaping from the top of the deck – and everyone gets their fingers a little green and sticky with Lucasinho's cake.

João de Deus is a working city and Adriana Corta would never sacrifice profit to declare a universal holiday, even on her eightieth birthday but many residents and contractees have taken a few minutes' leave and turned out to salute the First Lady of Helium. They watch the fleet of motos ferry the Cortas down Kondakova Prospect and up the ramp to the hotel where Lucas has arranged the birthday lunch. They applaud, some wave. Adriana Corta raises a gloved hand in acknowledgement. Blimps in the shape of cartoon animals manoeuvre on hushed micro-fans through São Sebastião Quadra like a divine circus. Adriana looks up as the shadow of M-Kat Xu falls over her. She smiles.

Heitor Pereira's people have been working for days, discreetly securing the hotel. Since mid-morning they have been discreetly scanning the guests. Applause; turning heads. Adriana arrives in the middle of a cocktail reception, whirled from face to face, party dress to party dress; kiss to kiss. Her boys, her handsome boys in their best suits. Ariel is late, Ariel is always late for family. Lucas is visibly annoyed but he is not his sister's keeper. This is a world without police, even family police.

Family close and far: a warm embrace from Lousika Asamoah, always Adriana's favourite among the okos. Cousins by blood and marriage; the Sores from Carlos's side of the family and minor clans; allies by nikah. Society next. An apology has been received from the Eagle of the Moon – no Eagle has ever accepted Adriana's birthday invitation. Adriana dances an elegant waltz among Asamoahs from Twé and immaculate Suns from the Palace of Eternal Light and Vorontsov grandees; houses lesser and petty, socialites and trend-setters, reporters and celebrities, amors and okos. Lucasinho's moon-run cohort are here, self-conscious and remaining in each other's social orbit. Adriana Corta has a word for each. Her social wake spirals off a hundred conversations and liaisons.

Politics last of all. LDC bureaucrats and Farside University deans. Soap stars and chart musicians, artists and architects and engineers. Adriana Corta has always filled her anniversaries with engineers. The media: social net reporters and fashion commentators; sharers and content-creators. The religious: Cardinal Okogie and Grand Mufti el-Tayyeb; Abbot Sumedho and, all in white, a Sister of the Lords of Now. Irmã Loa curtsies to her patron.

235

Ariel appears at her mother's side. A kiss and an apology, which Adriana waves away.

Thank you.

If I'd missed your eightieth, you'd never have forgiven me.

That's not what I'm thanking you for.

Ariel snaps her vaper to its full length and lets the party claim her.

Adriana looks up in delight at the sound of music. Bossa nova. The party parts before her as she is drawn to its source.

It's the same band we had at Lucasinho's moon-run, Adriana says. *How lovely.*

Lucas is at her side. He has never been more than two steps away from her through all the social turns and pirouettes of Adriana's progress.

All your favourites, Mamãe. The old tunes.

Adriana runs her hand over Lucas's cheek.

You are a good boy, Lucas.

Wagner Corta slips late into the restaurant, still trying to get comfortable in his print-fresh suit. The dimensions are right but it sits wrong, tight where it needs to be generous, rubbing where it needs to caress.

'Lobinho!' Rafa greets Wagner open-armed and effusive. Crushing embrace, heavy back slaps. Wagner winces. Man-breath. Wagner can identify the constituents of every cocktail his brother has thrown down his throat. 'It's Mamãe's birthday, could you not have shaved?' Rafa looks Wagner up and down. 'And your familiar isn't familiar.'

With a thought Wagner banishes Dr Luz and summons Sombra though everyone who knows he is of the two selves can tell he's the wolf from his fidgeting in his skin, the way he looks as if he is listening to several conversations at once, the generous stubble on his face.

'She missed you at the receiving line.' Rafa scoops a cocktail from a tray and slips it into Wagner's hand. 'Just make sure you get to her before you get to Lucas. He's not in a forgiving mood today.'

Wagner barely made the express; savouring every moment with Irina. She had bitten him. She had sucked his flesh so hard she left bruises. She had pinched and twisted and made him cry out. She had tugged his skin with gentle loving teeth. The sex had been the least part of it, perfunctory, obvious. She awoke sensations and emotions new to Wagner. His senses rang all night. He picked up the suit from the station printer, changed in the train washroom, gingerly pulling shirt and pants over still raw wounds and bruises. Each tiny pain was an ecstasy. She had obeyed Wagner's instruction and left hands, neck, face unmarked.

'I've found something,' Wagner says.

'Tell me.'

'I recognised one of the protein processors. You wouldn't be able to see it but, to me, it's like putting your name up in neon.'

'You're talking kind of fast, Little Wolf.'

'Sorry. Sorry. I met up with the designer – we went to university together. Same colloquium. She gave me an inbox address. Dead of course. But I got the pack to work on it.'

'Slowly slowly. You did what?'

'Got the pack to work on it.'

The Meridian pack are agriculturalists, dusters, roboticists, nail artists, bartenders, sports performers, musicians, masseurs, lawyers, club owners, track-engineers, families great and small; a diversity of skills and learning; yet, when they come together, when they focus on one task, something marvellous happens. The pack seems to share knowledge, to instinctively complement each other, to form a perfect team; a unity of purpose: almost a gestalt. Wagner has seen it rarely, participated in it once only but never called on it until now. The pack convened, minds and talents and wills blurred and merged and within five hours he had the identity of the engineering shop that built the assassin-fly. There's nothing supernatural about it; Wagner doesn't believe in the supernatural; it's a rational miracle. It's a new way of being human.

'It was a one-shot engineering house called Smallest Birds,' Wagner says. 'Based in Queen of the South. Registered to Joachim Lisberger and Jake Tenglong Sun.'

'Jake Tenglong Sun.'

'That doesn't mean anything. The company produced one item, delivered it and then dissolved.'

'Do we know who they delivered it to?'

'Trying to find that out. I'm more interested in who commissioned it.'

'And do you have any leads on that?'

'I may take this up with Jake Sun, personally,' Wagner says.

'Good work, Little Wolf,' Rafa says. Another agonising slap on the back. Every bite mark shrieks. Rafa has steered Wagner to the edge of Adriana's progress through the well-wishers.

'Mamãe, happy birthday.'

Adriana Corta's lips tighten. Then she leans towards him, an invitation to kiss. Two kisses.

'You could have shaved,' she says, to small laughter from her entourage, but as she wheels away into the party she whispers in his ear, 'if you want to stay a while, your old apartment at Boa Vista is ready for you.'

Marina hates the dress. It catches and itches, it's voluminous and uncomfortable. She feels naked in it; vulnerable, that one too-abrupt move and it will fall from her shoulders around her ankles. And the shoes are ridiculous. But it's fashionable and it's expected and while no one would whisper if she turned up in a pant-suit or men's tailoring, Carlinhos makes it clear to Marina that Adriana would notice.

Marina is trapped in a dull conversation whorl dominated by a loud sociologist from Farside U and his theories about post-national identities in second and third generation lunarians.

All this and you can't come up with a better name for moon-dwellers that Lunarians, Marina thinks. She runs phrases: *Moonfolk, lunarites, loonie moonie moonish loonish.* None good. *Rescue me,* she pleads to the orixa of parties.

She spies Carlinhos pushing through the press of bodies and festive familiars and cocktail glasses.

'My mother wants to meet you.'

'Me? What?'

'She's asked.'

He's already leading her by the hand through the party.

'Mãe, this is Marina Calzaghe.'

Marina's first impression of Adriana Corta had been coloured by a knife blade at her throat, but she seems to have aged more than the intervening lunes – no, not aged: withered, collapsed, become more transparent.

'Many happy returns, Senhora Corta.'

Marina's proud of her Portuguese now, but Adriana Corta flows to Globo.

'It seems once again my family is obliged to you.'

'Like they say, I was just doing my job, ma'am.'

'If I gave you another job, would you execute it as faithfully?'

'I'd do my best.'

'I do have another job. I need you to look after someone.'

'Senhora Corta, I've never been been good with small children. I scare them...'

'You won't scare this child. Though she may scare you.'

Adriana's nod directs Marina across the room, to Ariel Corta, a brilliant flame at the heart of a clutch of soberly dressed court officials and LDC technocrats. She laughs, she throws her head back, tosses her hair, weaves ideograms of smoke from her vaper.

'I don't understand, Senhora Corta.'

'I need someone to mind my daughter. I fear for her.'

'If you want a bodyguard, Senhora Corta, there are trained fighters...'

'If I wanted a bodyguard she would have one already. I have dozens of bodyguards. I want an agent. I want you to be my eyes, my ears, my voice. I want you to be her friend and her chaperone. She'll hate you, she'll fight you, she'll try to get rid of you, she'll shun you and snub you and be vile to you. But you will stay with her. Can you do this?'

Marina has no words. This is impossible, to do, to refuse. In her scratchy dress she stands in front of Adriana Corta and all she can think is *but Carlinhos won't be there*.

Carlinhos nudges her. Adriana Corta is waiting.

'I can, Senhora Corta.'

'Thank you.' Her smile is true, and the kiss on Marina's cheek warm but Marina shivers, chilled by the eternal waiting cold.

She leads him through the party, a dance in a red dress. She glances back to see if he is still looking, still following, moving on to keep her distance from him. Rafa catches her on the balcony. The balloon bestiary has flocked in around the restaurant, they wait, bobbing in the sky like prototype gods that never successfully auditioned for a pantheon.

Without a word, Rafa draws her to him. They kiss.

'You are the most beautiful thing in this world,' Rafa says. 'In both worlds.'

Lousika Asamoah smiles.

'Who's looking after Luna?' she asks.

'Madrinha Elis. She misses you. She wants her mamãe back.'

'Sssh.' Lousika Asamoah touches a carmine nail to Rafa's lips. 'It's always this.' They kiss again.

'Lousika, the contract.'

'Our marriage expires in six lunes.'

'I want to renew it.'

240

'Even though I'm living in Twé and and you're keeping my daughter and we only ever see each other at your family's social events.'

'Even so.'

'Rafa, I've been invited on to the Kotoko.'

Rafa admires and is at the same time baffled by AKA politics. The Golden Stool is a council of eight family members representing the abusuas. The Chair, the Stool, the Omahene, rotates annually through those members, as the Golden Stool itself moves from AKA habitat to habitat. It seems unnecessarily complex and democratic to Rafa Corta. Continuity is preserved by the Sunsum, the familiar of the Omahene which contains all the records and wisdoms of its preceding Omahenes.

'Does this mean you won't come back to Boa Vista?'

'It'll be eight years before I get to sit on the Golden Stool again. Luna will be fourteen. A lot can happen. I can't turn it down.'

Rafa steps back and holds his wife at arm's length, as if examining her for signs of divinity or madness.

'I want to renew the contract, Rafa. But I can't come back to Boa Vista. Not just yet.'

Rafa chews back furious disappointment. He forces himself to take time, swallow the words he feels.

'That's enough,' he says.

Lousika takes the lapels of his jacket and pulls him to her. Their familiars merge and mingle; inter-penetrating illusions.

'Could we not just sneak away from this party?'

Lucas spirals in from the edge of the party and cuts out Amanda Sun from among her laughing siblings and cousins. A touch on her elbow.

'A word. In private.'

He takes her by the elbow to the dining room, set out for the birthday feast around a ceiling-scraping ice-sculpture of birds taking flight. Through the swing doors to the kitchen.

'Lucas, what is this?'

Past the stoves and sinks and titanium work-surfaces, past the chillers and food-safes, the rise and fall of blades and choppers to a store room.

'Lucas, what is wrong with you? Let go of me. You're scaring me.'

'I'm going to divorce you, Amanda.'

She laughs. The small, almost irritated laugh that finds what has just been said ridiculous. Unthinkable. Like the moon crashing into Hudson Bay. Then, 'Oh my God, you are serious.'

'Have I ever been anything else?'

'No one could say that you weren't serious, Lucas. And I can't say that the idea doesn't appeal to me. But we aren't free in these things, are we? My father won't tolerate an insult to his daughter.'

'It wasn't me insisted on the monogamy clause.'

'You signed it. What is this really, Lucas?' Amanda studies his face, as if divining sickness or insanity. 'Oh my God. This is love, isn't it? You actually love someone.'

'Yes,' Lucas Corta says. 'Do you want me to break the contract, or will both parties agree to an annulment?'

'You're in love.'

'I'd appreciate it if you moved everything out of Boa Vista before the end of the lune,' Lucas calls back from the storeroom door. The restaurant staff work intently on placing and plating and glazing their sculpted amuse-bouches. 'There will be no question over Lucasinho. He's of majority.' Lucas stalks through the kitchen. In the store-room, Amanda Sun laughs and laughs, laughs until she has to rest to hands on her knees in exhaustion, then laughs again.

'Hey.'

'So hey.'

'So why were you bouncing my messages?'

Abena Asamoah twists the toe of a satin Rayne stiletto, looks away. She flicks the stud in Lucasinho's ear.

'You've still got it. That make-up really works on you.'

He has run her down here at the cocktail bar, edged her into a quiet corner. Part of him says, *This is stalkery, Luca.*

'My grandmother thinks so too.'

Lucasinho grins and sees it touch Abena and draw the smallest of smiles from her.

'So if I had a real emergency, I could go to you.' Lucasinho taps the spike.

'Of course. That's what it means.'

'It's just . . .'

'What?'

'When I was at the pool party at Twé, you wouldn't even look at me.'

'When you were at that pool party you were all over Ya Afuom, and you were out of your skull on gods-know-what.'

'Nothing happened with Ya Afuom.'

'I know.'

'And why would it matter to you if something had happened?'

Abena takes a deep breath, as if about to explain a hard truth, like vacuum, or the Four Elementals, to a child.

'When you saved Kojo, I would have done anything for you. I respected you. I respected you so much much. You were brave and you were kind – you still are. But when you go to see Kojo in Med Centre, all you want is to get his apartment. You used him. Like you let Grigori Vorontsov use you like a sex toy. I'm not a prude, Luca, but that was gross. You needed stuff and you used anyone who could get it for you. You stopped respecting other people, you stopped respecting yourself and I stopped respecting you.'

Lucasinho's face burns. He thinks of excuses, defences, justifications – I was angry at my father, my dad cut me off, I'd nowhere to go, I was off the network, it was all people I felt something for, I was exploring, it was a mad time, it was only for a little time, I didn't hurt anyone – not badly. They sound like whining. They can't abolish the truth. He didn't fuck Ya Asamoah, but if he had it would have been for a few nights in her apartment; a soft bed and warm flesh and laughing. Like Grigori, like Kojo. Like his own aunt. He is guilty. His only hope for repairing hearts with Abena is to admit it.

'You're right.'

Abena stands, arms folded, magnificently magisterial.

'You're right.'

Still not a word.

'It's true. I was vile to people.'

'People who cared about you.'

'Yes. People who cared about me.'

'Make me a cake,' Abena says. 'Isn't that what you do to make amends? Bake them a cake?'

'I'll make you a cake.'

'I want cupcakes. Thirty-two. I want a cup-cake party with my abusua-sisters.'

'What kind of flavour?'

'Every kind of flavour.'

'Okay. Thirty-two cupcakes. And I'll stream you the video of me making them, so you can see I'm making them right.'

Abena gives a little shriek of false outrage, slips off her right shoe and bangs Lucasinho none-too-gently on his chest.

'You are an insolent boy.'

'You tried to drink my blood.'

Security alert, Jinji says in Lucasinho's ear. *Remain calm, Corta Hélio security personnel are en route.* Across the room hands fly to ears, faces ask questions: *what where?* A woman in a Tina Leser frock vaults over the bar, pushes Abena away and puts herself between Lucasinho and the danger. She has a knife in each hand.

'What's going on?' Lucasinho says and then the movement of the guests away from the restaurant door shows him. With six corporate blades at his back, Duncan Mackenzie has crashed the party.

*

Heitor Pereira strides forward to confront Duncan Mackenzie. The CEO of Mackenzie Metals stops centimetres from the outstretched hand. He raises an eyebrow at the Corta man's flamboyant uniform. Behind both men are their armed retainers, hands on blades.

Rafa pushes through the line of security personnel. Lucas is a step behind him, on either shoulder Carlinhos and Wagner. Lucas flicks a glance to his son; Lucasinho pushes past his bodyguard to fall in with the men.

'What are you doing here?' Rafa says. The room is motionless. Not a cocktail supped, not a glass of tea sipped.

'I'm here to pay the compliments of the day to your mother,' says Duncan Mackenzie.

'We'll throw you out like we threw you out at Beikou,' a voice shouts from the line of security men. Rafa raises a hand: enough.

'Boys, boys.' Adriana touches Rafa on the hip and he drifts aside. 'You're welcome here, Duncan. But so many men?'

'Trust is a short market right now.'

Adriana extends a hand. Duncan Mackenzie stoops to kiss it.

'Happy birthday.' Then, in a whisper of Portuguese, 'We need words. Family to family.'

'We do,' Adriana replies in the same tongue, then, in command, 'Have another place set at my table. Beside me. Drinks for Mr Mackenzie's entourage.'

'Mamãe?' Lucas says. Adriana brushes by.

'You're not hwaejang yet. None of you.'

The food is exquisite, dish after dish, course after course of harmonious flavours and discordant textures, liquids and gels, geometries and temperatures but Adriana can only pick at it with her poison-sensing chopsticks. A scent, a taste to understand the theory and the skill. On her left hand Duncan Mackenzie eats with enthusiasm and many compliments; honouring the skill by not speaking until the last course is cleared.

'Congratulations on the Mare Anguis,' Duncan Mackenzie says. He lifts his glass of mint tea.

'You don't mean that,' Adriana says.

'Of course I don't. But it was cutely done and I admire that. You have fucked up our helium-3 development plan. How did you hear about the licence?'

'Ariel is in the Pavilion of the White Hare.'

Duncan Mackenzie chews over this aftertaste for a few moments.

'We should have known that.'

'How did you learn about it?'

'The Eagle of the Moon is a terrible pillow talker.'

'If I can find an advantage for my own people, I'll take it,' Adriana says.

'The Iron Law,' Duncan Mackenzie says. 'Served us well. I must have a word with Adrian. He needs some new tricks for the Eagle.'

'Why are you here, Duncan?'

Duncan Mackenzie has Lucas's place at Adriana's left hand; Lucas is banished to a low table from which he repeatedly glances with clear loathing. Adriana catches his glance: *This is not your business.*

'Birthdays are a time for looking forwards.'

'Not at my age.'

'Humour me. Five years, where will we be?'

'In this room, celebrating.'

'Or up in the Bairro Alto, selling our piss and clawing for food and water and fighting for every breath. The moon is changing. It's not the world it was when you and my dad fought. If we fight now, we will both lose.' Duncan Mackenzie speaks on a private channel, Esperance to Yemanja, subvocalising his words. Adriana responds in the same small voice.

'I have no desire to go back to the corporate wars.'

'But we are heading that way. The Beikou fight was only the start. There's been trouble at St Ekaterina and Port Imbrium. Someone will be killed. We caught one of your surface workers at Torricelli trying to sabotage a Mackenzie Metals rover.'

'What have you done with them?'

'We're holding her. There'll be a fee, but it's better than what Hadley wanted, which was to put her out the lock.'

'My grandson Robson is surprisingly good with a knife. Do you know where he learned that? From Hadley. He's over there. See him showing a card trick to Jaden Wen Sun? He's been doing that ever since he escaped from Crucible. If anyone's touched him—'

'I assure you no one has. But you have your son. My daughter is dead.'

'We had nothing to do with that.'

The silent speech is becoming impassioned, betraying itself in clenched jaws, tense throats, moving lips. Ariel looks across from her seat at the round table. Adriana knows her daughter is a talented lipreader. It's a useful courtroom skill.

'Who profits if we fight?'

'When Dragons fight, everyone burns,' Adriana says. It's a Sun proverb, of recent, lunar provenance.

'I'll rein my people in if you do the same for yours.'

'Agreed.'

'That includes your family.'

Adriana's mouth twitches with anger at the presumption. Rafa takes his hot temper from his mother, but she has a control, shaped over decades of corporate wars and board-room battles, investor pitches and legal tussles that he has never needed to learn. Anger is one of his many privileges.

'Rafa is bu-hwaejang.'

'I'm not saying demote him. I would never presume that. I'm suggesting maybe he could share responsibilities.'

'With whom?'

'Lucas.'

'You know my family too well,' Adriana says.

'We didn't try to assassinate Rafa,' Duncan says aloud.

'We didn't kill Rachel,' Adriana says. Heads are turning now. 'Excuse me, Duncan. I'll pass the word. I'm expected to make a speech now.' She taps her cocktail glass with her chopstick, a clear chime that silences the chattering room. Adriana Corta rises to her feet.

'My dear guests; friends, colleagues, associates, family. I am eighty years old today. Eighty years ago I was born in Barra de Tijuca in Brazil, on another world. For fifty of those years, over half of my life, I have lived on this world. I came to it as one of the first settlers, I have watched two generations grow up; my children's and my grandchildren's, and now it seems I am a Founding Mother. The moon has changed me in many ways. It has changed my body so that I can never go back to the world I came from. To you of the younger generations, that is a strange notion. You have never known anywhere other than this world, and though I talk about the changes the moon has worked on me, they are nothing compared to the ones I see in you. So tall! So elegant! And my grandchildren, why, I think I would need wings to be able to fly up to kiss you! The moon has changed my life. The girl from Barra, Outrinha, the Plain One is the owner of a powerful corporation. When I go up to the observation dome and look with my bare eyes at the Earth, I see those webs of lights across night on Earth and I think, *I light those lights*. That's another thing the moon changes in people: there is no gain from modesty.

'The moon changes families: I see friends and relatives and colleagues from all Five Dragons, I see retainers and madrinhas; but I am not like you. You came with your families, you Suns and Asamoahs and Vorontsovs, you Mackenzies, you of no great family. When I set up Corta Hélio I offered every member of my family back on Earth the chance to follow me to the moon and work with me. Not one took my offer. Not one had the courage or the hope to leave Earth. So, I built my own family; my dear Carlos and his family, but also dear friends who are as close to me as family; Helen, and Heitor. Thank you for your years of service, and love.

'And the moon has changed my heart. I came here as a Brazilian, I stand here as a woman of the moon. I gave up one identity to build another one. It's the same for all of us, I think; we keep our language and our customs, our cultures and our names, but we are the moon.

'But the greatest thing the moon changes is itself. I've seen this world go from a research base to a handful of industrial habitats to a full civilisation. Fifty years is a long time in a human life; it's even longer in the life of a new nation. We are no mean satellite; we are a world now. Down on Earth they say we've raped it, taken its natural beauty and despoiled it with our tracks and our trains and our extractors, our solar batteries and server farms and our billions and billions of eternal footprints. Our mirrors dazzle them, down there; our King Dong offends them. But the moon always was ugly. No, not ugly. Plain. To see the beauty of this place, you have to go under the surface. You have to dig down to the cities and quadras, the habitats and agraria. You have to see the people. I've played my part in building this wonderful world. More than my company, even more than my family, it's my proudest achievement.

'At the age of eighty, it's time to enjoy my achievements. My world is in good shape, my family are proud and respected, my company has gone from strength to strength, not least our recent successful acquisition of the Mare Anguis fields. So, for Adriana Corta, at last, a rest. I am stepping down from my position as hwaejang of Corta Hélio. Rafael will be hwaejang, Lucas will be bu-hwaejang. You'll find nothing changed: my boys have been effectively running the company for the past ten years. For me, I shall enjoy my retirement and the company of my family and friends. Thank you for your good wishes for this day; I shall treasure them in the days to come. Thank you.'

Adriana sits down to consternation. Around the room, around

her table, mouths are open in astonishment. All but Duncan Mackenzie, who leans close to Adriana and whispers, 'I sure picked the right party to crash.' Adriana answers with a small laugh but its bright, silvery; almost a girl's. An unburdened laugh. Ariel is leaning across the table, Rafa is on his feet, Carlinhos, Wagner; everyone asking questions at the same time, until a loud, steady handclap cuts through. Lucas stands, hands raising, applauding. Across the room another pair of hands replies; then two, then four, then the whole party is standing, raining applause on Adriana Corta. She stands, smiles, bows.

Lucas's is the last pair of hands to fall silent.

After the shock, the questions.

Helen de Braga slides in a whisper before Ariel's arrival.

'I thought you said it was too morbid for your birthday.'

'I only said I was retiring,' Adriana says. She squeezes her old friend's hand. 'Later.'

Ariel kisses her mother.

'I thought for one hideous moment you were going to give me a job.'

'Oh, my love,' Adriana says, then finds her tone of command to her entourage. 'I'm very tired. It's been a demanding day. I'd like to go home.'

Heitor Pereira summons security. They cordon Adriana from the inquisitions of her guests.

'Congratulations on your retirement Senhora,' Heitor says, 'but with respect to my position; it's no secret that Lucas wants rid of me.'

'I look after my own, Heitor.'

The guards part for Rafa. Behind him is Lousika Asamoah. Rafa embraces his mãe.

'Thank you,' he says. 'I won't let you down.'

'I've thought about the succession long and hard.' Adriana strokes his cheek.

'Succession?' Rafa asks but Adriana is already receiving a stiff embrace from Lucas.

'Whatever possessed you, Mamãe?'

'I've always been attracted to the dramatic.'

'In front of that Mackenzie.'

'He'd have found out. Whispers fly around the world in an instant.'

'The CEO of Mackenzie Metals. They tried to kill Rafa.'

'And I gave him my word that we would not go back to the old corporate war days.'

'Mãe, you're not hwaejang any more.'

'I didn't give him my word as hwaejang.'

'They'll break it. Duncan Mackenzie may give his word, but his father doesn't forgive. The Mackenzies repay three times.'

'I trust him, Lucas.'

Lucas purses his fingers, dips his head but Adriana knows he cannot concur. After him come Carlinhos, Wagner, the madrinhas and the children: Adriana progresses down an aisle of ringing applause and smiling faces. At the door she sees a figure among the ornamental trees.

'Let me through.'

Irmã Loa lifts her crucifix from among her beads. Adriana Corta bends to kiss it.

'When will you tell them?' Irmã Loa whispers.

'When the succession is secure,' Adriana says. Familiars are listening, they can hear whispers but they can't parse private code. Irmã Loa takes out a flask and sprinkles Adriana Corta with sacred water.

'The blessing of Saints Jesus and Mary, Jeronimo and Our Lady of Conception, Saint George and Saint Sebastian, Cosmos and Damian and the Lord of the Cemeteries, Santa Barbra and Santa Anne on you, your family and all your projects.'

Motos glide in to the lobby, silent and accurate.

*

Ariel's heels are glorious and impractical but they add elegance to her flounce to the lobby. But Marina is surface-fit, a Long-runner and she catches Ariel by the elbow.

'I don't like it either, but your mother ordered me—'

A hand, a grip, a twist and Marina follows the path that doesn't end in dislocated joints, snapped bones. The party spins and she's on her back, winded on the waxed wooden floor.

'When you can do this to me, maybe then I'll need a bodyguard,' Ariel says and steps into the moto that has opened up like before her like a hand.

'It's still my job,' Marina mutters as Corta security picks her up and sets her on her feet again but the moto is a half of Kondakova Prospekt away by now, a bright bauble of advertising, tracked by the balloon bestiary.

'Hey.'

'Hey.'

Abena's touch on Lucasinho's arm.

'You doing anything?'

'Why?'

'Just, some of us are going on to a club.'

She could have messaged him through Jinji, but she came in person, to touch him.

'Who?'

'Me, my abusua-sisters, Nadia and Kseniya Vorontsov. We're meeting up with some of the folk from the Zé Ka Colloquium. You coming?'

They're looking over at him, in their party clothes and coloured shoes and he wants more than anything to go with them, to be with Abena and look for chances; to redeem himself, to impress her. Two images won't leave his head: his father's two suits on either side of him. Flavia huddled among her saints, fighting to breathe.

'I can't. I really have to go spend some time with my madrinha.'

*

252

Parties decay by half-life. Conversations lose momentum. Topics are exhausted. It's tiring to talk. Everyone who should be cruised has been cruised. The hook-ups have hooked up, or failed and no one's listening to the music any more. The staff begin to clear. There is an evening service in an hour's time.

Lucas lingers, aware that he is in the way and that his presence is barely tolerated but wanting to bestow thanks here, a handshake there, a tip or a bonus. He has always appreciated work well done and believed it should be rewarded.

'My mãe was delighted,' he says to the restaurateur. 'I'm very happy.'

The band pack their instruments. They seem pleased with their performance. Lucas thanks them individually; Toquinho is generous with its tips. A whisper to Jorge: *A moment, if you would.*

A look from Lucas clears the balcony.

'Another balcony,' Jorge says. Lucas leans on the glass wall, looking down the length of São Sebastião Quadra. The birthday blimps have been flown down to ground level, puny humans struggle to wrangle the floating gods with ropes and grapples and deflate them.

'Thank you, Jorge,' Lucas says and there is a tone in his voice that kills every quip or levity in Jorge's conversation. A rawness, a choke.

'Thank you, Senhor Corta,' Jorge says.

'Senhor . . .' Lucas begins. 'You made my mamãe's day. No, this isn't what I want to say. I am bu-hwaejang of Corta Hélio, I argue strategy in the board, I talk for a living and I can't speak. I had a preamble, Jorge. All my justifications and realisations. All about me.'

'When my fingers freeze, when I can't get a line, when I feel the music wrong in me, I remember that I'm there because I'm doing something no one else in that room can,' Jorge says. 'I'm not like everyone. I'm exceptional. I'm allowed to be arrogant about that. You, Lucas; you've every right to say whatever you want, whatever you think.'

Lucas starts, as if realisation were a nail driven between his eyes. His hands grasp the glass rail.

'Yes. Simple.' He looks at Jorge. 'Jorge, will you marry me?'

This time, Duncan Mackenzie is summoned to the glasshouse. *The shuttle has arrived,* Esperance announces. Duncan adjusts the lie of his lapels, the fall of his trouser turn-ups, the length of his cuffs. He checks his appearance once more through Esperance. A whistle of breath through the teeth and he steps into the shuttle.

His father waits among the tree ferns. The air smells of damp and rot. Duncan can no longer read any emotion in his father's face. Everything is age, lines deep moon-carved. How easy to pull that plug, tug that line, rip out that tube and watch his father leak and gurgle himself to death all over the floor of his precious Fern Gully. Compost to compost. Food for plants. The medics would only bring him back to life again. They have done it three times already, catching that light in his eyes before it guttered out and using it to rekindle his ruin of a body. *This is what I have to look forward to.*

Behind Robert Mackenzie stands Jade Sun.

'Her birthday. Did you sing "Happy Birthday to you, dear Adriana"?'

'Not her.' Duncan flicks a look at Jade Sun.

'Whatever you say to Robert you say to me,' Jade Sun says. 'With or without familiars.'

'What she says,' Robert Mackenzie says. 'I thought we were a laughing stock before. Jesus God boy, you went to her birthday party.'

'I talked to her, Dragon to Dragon.'

'You talked to her pussy to pussy. You'll rein our people in? Our people? What kind of pussy deal is that? You'd tie our hands and let those thieves turn us out bare-ass naked on to the surface. In my day we knew how to deal with enemies.'

'Forty years ago, Dad. Forty years ago. This is a new moon.'

'The moon doesn't change.'

'Adriana Corta is retiring.'

'Rafael is hwaejang. Fucking clown. Lucas will run the show. That cunt has the right stuff. He'd never sign up to some kind of gentleman's agreement.'

'Ariel is a member of the White Hare,' Duncan says. The old man sheds spittle as he rages. In lunar gravity it flies in long, elegant, poisonous arcs.

'I fucking know that. I've known that for weeks. Adrian told me.'

'You didn't tell me.'

'And a good thing too. It would just have sent you running and hiding. She's much more than a White Hare, Ariel Corta.'

'Ariel Corta has been inducted into the Lunarian Society,' Jade Sun says.

'The what?' Duncan Mackenzie shakes his head with confused frustration. There is nothing he can hold in this fight, no grips on his father.

'A grouping of influential industrial, academic and legal talents,' Jade Sun says. 'They advocate lunar independence. Vidhya Rao has recruited her. Darren Mackenzie is a member.'

'You kept this from me?'

'Your father's political beliefs differ from ours. The Suns have always been staunch for independence, since we threw off the People's Republic. We believe it was the the Lunarian Society leaked the information about the claim release to Ariel Corta.'

'We?'

'The Three August Sages,' Jade Sun says.

'They're not real.' It is one of the legends of the moon; birthed as soon as Taiyang began to thread its AI systems through every part of lunar society and infrastructure: the computers so powerful, the algorithm so subtle, that it could predict the future.

'I assure you they are. Whitacre Goddard has been running a quantum stochastic algorithmic system we built for them for over

255

a year now. Do you really think we'd let Whitacre Goddard run our hardware without installing a back door?'

'Yeah yeah,' Robert Mackenzie. 'Quantum voodoo. White Hare and Lunarians: what matters is; we need to be able to wheel and deal. To do business our way. You've threatened our business model, boy. Worse, you've brought shame on the family. You're fired.'

The words are tiny, shrill as the bird whistles in this terrarium; heard but pushed to a distance.

'This is the most ridiculous thing I have ever heard.'

'I'm CEO now.'

'You can't do that. The board—'

'Not this again. The board—'

'I know about the fucking board. You can't because I resign.'

'You know, you always were a petulant little shit. That's why I did it five minutes ago. Your executive authorisations are revoked. I'm in sole possession of the codes.'

The shuttle has arrived, Esperance says.

'I'm back, son,' Robert Mackenzie says and now Duncan sees emotion where before there had only been rage and impotence. The body still pops and hisses, the stench is still sickly but that light that is Robert Mackenzie's life burns bright and hot. There is tension in his jaw, resolve in the set of his mouth. Duncan Mackenzie is defeated. He is sick with shame. The humiliation is absolute but not yet complete. The final humiliation comes when he turns the heel, walks away through the moist, rattling ferns to the shuttle lock.

'Do I have to call Hadley?' Jade Sun asks.

Duncan Mackenzie swallows bile-sick anger. He will never stop hearing the sound of his defeated heels on the deck.

'You've done this!' he shouts from the lock at Jade Sun. 'You and all your fucking family. I will punish you for this. We're the Mackenzies, not your fucking monkeys.'

EIGHT

Marina, running. Meridian is fine running terrain, under trees, up ramps steep enough to test her thighs, with staircases when she needs a tougher workout, over slender bridges with colossal panoramas on either side; over soft grass. She's never run anywhere better than Aquarius Quadra and she never wants to run there again. Her first run she went out in body paint, the tassels of Ogun around her arms and thighs. She ran for hours, listening for the chants of a Long Run, seeking the beautiful undulating wave of the bodies. The other runners she met smiled at her; some whispered to each other or giggled. She was gauche, she was clearly provincial. There was no Long Run here, no merging into a unity of breath and muscle and motion, into the body of a running god.

She bought less revealing shorts, a more decorous top. She put the coloured braids of São Jorge into vacuum storage.

Running was just running. Fitness. A regime.

I hate Meridian. I hated it the first time, I think I hate it even more than I did when I couldn't afford to breathe and was selling my own piss.

If I move this way; there, can you see that? That's the view from my apartment. West 53rd, Aquarius Hub. This is Aquarius Quadra's Hunt's Point. Come with me. Look. Separate dining area. See this? I don't have to pull the bed down. The shower isn't on a timer. Okay, it's like a rabbit hutch compared to your place but by moon standards, it's a palace. So, why should I hate it?

It's not really Meridian. It's Ariel Corta. She is a conceited, vain, clothes horse, has too many opinions and she's nowhere near as good as she thinks she is. And she has this, like, *entourage* of people around her whose only job is to tell her how clever she is, how fabulous she is, how fantastic that dress looks on her, how talented and clever and witty she is. Well, I see through you, all of you, and I'm telling you; you're none of that, Ariel Corta. You're Mama Corta's one and only little girl, you're spoiled rotten. You're the original Moon Princess; ooh, nothing nasty can ever happen to Princess Ariel! And that vaper? I want to take that thing and shove it up your ass.

Yes, it pays a fortune. It pays a lot more than I ever got up on the surface with Carlinhos. I wish I was back there. I wish I was back in Boa Vista. I knew where I was there. And yes, Carlinhos... But Boss Mama had a special job for me and you don't turn Adriana Corta down. But Ariel fucking Corta.

At least it's mutual. She hates me. Not so much hates me as disdains me. Is that a word? Well she does. It's like I'm not even alive. Even a bot is more useful. I'm a cheap and dirty João de Deus duster with no class and less taste, who's been forced on her against her will and who she can't get rid of. I'm like a genital wart.

The money'll be through in the next couple of days, I promise. It's some wrangle between our banks and yours. They've done something that makes them freer from Earth's economy and the Earth banks don't like it. But, money is money. It'll work through.

So, what do you think of the apartment?

'This simply will not do,' Ariel says, and taps Marina's shoulder, waist, thighs with the tip of her vaper. Tap tippy tap.

Marina thinks she might punch her charge's face through the back of her head. The seethe of blood in the forebrain. And release.

258

'What's wrong with my clothes?'

'You dress like an evangelical,' Ariel says. 'This is the Court of Clavius. My clients are the best of society – well, the richest. They have expectations. I have expectations. My zashitnik dresses better. So no no no.' Ariel forgoes the tap tippy tap. She sees the lava in Marina's eyes.

Za what? Marina wants to ask but the printer is already humming.

'I'm in court at eleven, an assets hearing at twelve, lunch with my old colloquium at thirteen,' Ariel says. 'Client meetings fifteen through to eighteen, the Akindele pre-legal at twenty. I'll be making an appearance at the Chawla wedding party about twenty-one, then on to the Law Society Debutante Ball at twenty-two. It's ten now so just put this on and try not to fall off the heels.' Ariel frowns.

'What now?'

'Your familiar.'

'You leave Hetty alone.'

'Hetty. And that is?'

'An orca.'

'That's an animal – a fish?'

'My totemic animus.' This is a lie but Ariel won't know. Hetty is a sneer too far. Hetty is inviolable; the relationship between a woman and her familiar is not subject to whim or fashion.

'I see. Religion. No religious objection to this, I presume?' Ariel hands Marina a bouquet of fabric, soft and fresh-laundry aromatic from the printer.

'What are you looking for?'

'Somewhere to change.'

Ariel's apartment is smaller and barer than Marina had imagined. White. Surfaces. Is it a minimalist refuge from the endless voices and colours and noise and rush of people, people, people? The only decoration is a wall-sized, bleached-out print of a face that must be iconic in a hagiography unknown to Marina Calzaghe. The closed eyes, the drooping mouth disturb Marina. Narcotic and orgasmic.

She puts a hand on a door.

'Not that one,' Ariel says with a speed that makes Marina determined to investigate later. 'Here.'

Marina wriggles into the dress. The mass of frill and lace is suffocating. The bodice is ridiculous. How do people move, breathe? Where can she hide the weapons? Taser down cleavage, knife in inner thigh holster. Don't spoil the line of the couture.

'Legs.'

'What?'

'Shave them. At some point we'll get you permanently depilated.'

'Fuck you will.'

Ariel holds up a pair of sheer stockings.

'Okay.'

As Marina opens the bathroom door she notices Ariel tipping her old clothing into the deprinter.

'Hey!'

'Daily print out. At least. My brother is a savage. He'd wear the same suit-liner for half a lune.'

Marina draws the stockings up her new smooth legs. She pulls on the shoes. Even in moon gravity she'll never stand more than an hour in them. They're weapons, not footwear.

Ariel looks Marina up and down.

'Turn.'

Marina manages a pirouette. The arches of both feet are already aching.

'You look as comfortable as a nun at a masturbation party but you'll pass. Here.' Ariel holds out a pair of soft ballet pumps. 'Society secret. Put them in your bag and any chance you get, slip these on. Just don't let anyone see you. Let's go to work.'

Marina does not imagine Ariel's small smile.

'Is that a real thing?'

'What?'

'A masturbation party.'

'Coração, you're in Aquarius Quadra now.'

I've been in court three days now and I still don't get lunar law. I get the principle – everyone gets the principle: there is no criminal or civil law, only contract law. I've done dozens of contracts – hundreds: Hetty deals with most of them without me even knowing. There are billions of contracts flying through air and rock and people every second of every day. It's a Fifth Elemental: contract. The Court of Clavius seems to be about avoiding law. The thing they hate most is making a new law, because that would tie things down and take away the freedom to negotiate. Lots of lawyers, not a lot of laws. Court cases are extended negotiations. Both parties haggle over which judges will preside and how much they're going to pay for it. They're more like movie producers than attorneys. The first sessions are all about compensating for bias – there's no assumption that judges are impartial, so contracts or cases take that into account. Sometimes judges have to pay to get to judge. Everything is negotiated. I have a theory that this is why the moon is so open sexually: it's not about labels like straight or gay or bi or poly or A. It's about you and what you want to do. Sex is a contract between fucker and fuckee.

The Court of Clavius; sounds real grand, doesn't it? All marble and Roman gear. I tell you, no. It's a maze of tunnels and meeting rooms and court spaces in the oldest part of Meridian. The air is stale and smells of moon dust and mould. But what hits you first is the noise: hundreds of lawyers and judges and plaintiffs and parties, all shouting their wares, hustling for work. It's like those old stock-exchange movies; men in ties jostling and shouting out bids and offers. It's a law market. So: you've hired your lawyers, your judges, your courtroom. Next you decide how you want to be tried – it's not just lawyers and judges on sale, it's legal systems too. So: I finally found out what a zashitnik is. A zashitnik is a big man – usually

261

a man, usually a Jo Moonbeam, because we're physically stronger. It's perfectly legal to settle your case in a duel, or, if you'd rather not fight yourself, hire someone to do it for you. That's a zashitnik. Apparently Ariel caused a big legal storm by calling a trial by combat and stripping down to her fighting pants in front of the whole court. I find that hard to imagine. Then again, she's a marriage and divorce lawyer, so maybe not so weird.

So, I'm in court with Ariel, which most of the time is her talking in a room with other lawyers and judges and me sitting outside playing games with Hetty. Or making posts for you guys. Or just trying to work out lunar law without my skull melting. You'd think the contracts would sew everything up tight, but even water-tight contracts go against the lunar principle that everything is negotiated, everything is personal. There must always be loopholes – every contract must have room to wriggle. Lunar law doesn't believe in guilt or innocence, or absolute right or absolute wrong. I say, isn't this blaming the victim? No, lunar law is about personal responsibility, Ariel says. I don't know. Seems like anarchy to me, but things get done. Cases are settled. Justice is done and people abide by it. They seem much more content with it than we do with our legal systems. No one ever appeals on the moon; that would mean there was a failure in negotiation and that's like a catastrophic culture shock here. So processes are long and there's endless talk-talk, but they seem sure. There's one point in common with terrestrial law: most of the work gets done over lunch.

Sorry. Nodded off there. It's two am, I'm at a reception – I think it's a reception, or maybe a launch – and Ariel is still talking. I don't know how she does it, day after day. Nothing more tiring than talking. It's relentless. I'm exhausted. I can't even run any more.

I can hear you, Mom; you're saying, is Marina maybe getting a little respect for Ariel Corta? Well, as a lawyer maybe. As a human being; well, let me say, it seems she's never had a partner or even a quickie lover. None. Ever. I can so believe that.

'It will cost you twenty million,' Ariel says.

'That's a lot for a Sun,' Lucas says. He has irritated his sister, haul-ing her out to Boa Vista but he will not suffer the indignity of the scrimmage of lawyers and judges and litigants howling through the corridors of the Court of Clavius. Corta affairs are conducted away from the commentariat, in intimate lounges over cocktails.

'They started at fifty.'

Toquinho floats the contract for Lucas's perusal. He scans a digest of main points.

'She gets access to Lucasinho.'

'I offered it as a sweetener. It always was and always will be Luca-sinho's choice whether to make contact.'

'Twenty million.'

'Twenty million.'

With a thought Lucas signs the divorce contract. With another he instructs Toquinho to transfer twenty million bitsies from his account to Taiyang's financial AIs at the Palace of Eternal Light. He has always admired the ponderous dignity of the name though he has only visited once, after the wedding when Amanda toured him through the convoluted layers of her family. The capital of the Suns was the oldest on the moon, carved out of the rim wall of Shackleton crater, a few kilometres from the moon's southern pole, clinging to the almost perpetual light above the eternal darkness of the crater's heart. Down there lay the permanently frozen gases and organics that seeded human presence on the moon. Lucas hated it. The contrasts were too stark, too unsubtle. High and low. Dark and light. Cold and heat. Amanda had taken him on the mandatory excursion to the Pavilion of Eternal Light, the tower built on the peak of Malapert Mountain. Eternal light blazed through the lantern at the top of the kilometre-high tower. Riding the elevator car with Amanda, Lucas had gritted his teeth, imagining radiation sleeting through the metal walls, sleeting through him, unsealing the chemical bonds of ceramics and plastics and human DNA. *Bask in it,* Amanda had invited as he stepped from the elevator car into the perpetual light that flooded the glass lantern. *The only place in the two worlds where the sun never sets.* Every surface, every sign or object was bleached by the light. Lucas felt shone through, rendered transparent, his skin turned pale and sick. He could smell the way it had scorched the air, lune after lune, year after year. Relentless light. *Come and see,* Amanda said but he would not follow her to the glass and the panorama of the whole south pole of the moon. He thought of the bleaching light, the cruel ultraviolet, picking at the molecules of the glass, one photon at a time. He imagined it bursting like a dropped cocktail. *Come and look at the light.* Humans are not made for endless light. Humans need their darknesses.

'Done,' Lucas says as Toquinho transfers a copy of the contract to Beijaflor. 'Free but broke.'

'Don't be ridiculous,' Ariel says. 'None of us will ever be broke.'

Jorge ends *Manhã de Carnaval* with a G Major Ninth, looks over to the drummer. The lightest susurrus of brushes. Set closer.

From his booth at the back of the club, in the blue bio light glow, Lucas applauds. G major Ninth is one of the classic chords of bossa, the very spirit of saudade, melancholy under the Rio sun. Incompletely resolved and therefore satisfying. Lucas's applause rings out. It's the only applause in the house. The club was never full, but Lucas's escoltas have been quietly emptying the bar during the set, a tap on the shoulder here, a whisper and a suggestion there. Jorge peers into the lights.

Lucas walks up to the stage.

'Might we?'

His band look at him; Jorge nods. Okay.

There's a mojito waiting in the booth, made to Jorge's taste.

'A good set. You're better solo. The band constrain you. Without them you'd fly. Is that why you're going to Queen of the South?'

'I've been wanting to go solo for lunes now. There's a market. Not a big one, but enough of one. Bespoke bossa.'

'You should.'

'You kind of inspired me.'

'I'm glad. I wouldn't want to think that you were running away from me.' Lucas touches Jorge's hand on the glass; delicate, almost fearful. 'It's all right, I'd guessed your answer when you didn't call.'

'I'm sorry. That was wrong. You caught me unawares – you scared me. I didn't know what to do. I had to get clear space, room to think.'

'I'm a single man again, Jorge. I'm free of that evil nikah. Cost me twenty million and the Suns are looking for another twenty for injury to their good name.'

'Don't say it, Lucas, please.'

'That I did it for you? No. Who do you think you are? No, I did it for me. But I love you. I think about you and I burn inside. I want you in every part of my life. I want to be in every part of your life.'

Jorge leans against Lucas. Their heads touch, their hands meet.

'I can't. Your life's too much. Your family – you're the Cortas. I can't be part of you. I can't be the one up at the top table, like your mother's birthday, siting next to you. I can't have them all looking and gossipping. I don't want their attention. I don't want to play and have people saying *that's Lucas Corta's oko. Oh, so that's how got the gig.* Marrying you, it would be the end of me, Lucas.'

Lucas forms a dozen replies but they're all barbed and cruel.

'I do love you. I loved you from the moment I saw you in Boa Vista.'

'Please don't. I have to go to Queen. Please let me go, let me have a life there. Don't look for me. I know you can do whatever you want, but let me go.'

'Did you ever...'

'What?'

These words too are barbed but the hooks catch in Lucas's throat.

'Love me?'

'Love you? The first day when I came to your sound room, I couldn't even tune the guitar, my hands were shaking so much. I don't know how I got the words out. When you asked me to stay, that night on the balcony, I thought my heart would burst. I kept thinking, what if he wants to fuck me? I want to fuck him. At home when I was jerking off, I got Gilberto to rez up an image of you, synth your voice. Is that creepy? Love you? You were my oxygen. I burned on you.'

'Thank you. That's not right. Thank you is too small and weak. Words can't say it right.'

'I can't marry you, Lucas.'

'I know.' Lucas stands, smooths out his clothes. 'I'm sorry about the audience. I sent them away. I'm far too used to getting my own way. If you go to Queen of the South, I promise I won't follow you.'

'Lucas.'

Jorge pulls Lucas to him. They kiss.

'I'll listen out for you,' Lucas says. 'You've brought me such joy.' Outside the club, he dismisses his guards and walks alone to São Sebastião Quadra. Long Runners cross Ellen Ochoa Prospekt on a tenth-level bridge. Drums and finger cymbals, chanting voices. Lucas customarily sneers at Carlinhos for his devotion to the Long Run but tonight the colour, the rhythm, the fine bodies strike a shard from his heart. To be able to lose yourself for a time and a space, to be somewhere that is not yourself, this casque of bone locked in this prison of stone. He's heard that some of the Long Runners now believe that they power the moon on its cycle around the Earth. A cosmic treadmill. Faith must be so comforting.

The apartment welcomes him and prepares a martini from Lucas's personal gin. He goes to the sound room. Those notes, those words and breaths, those pauses and harmonics, trapped in the walls and the floor. No ghosts on the moon, but if there were, those are the kind they would be: trapped words, whispers, stone memories. The only kind Lucas can believe.

Wordless with loss, Lucas hurls the glass to the wall. The room reflects the sounds of shattering glass, perfectly.

The codes are still valid. The elevator responds to his command. It waits in a little-used lobby by the main entry port to Boa Vista. He leaves footprints in the years-deep dust on the floor; he imagines the mechanisms give a groan as they return to work after long idleness. The dome is opaqued, a hemisphere of dust-grey but he knows he is on the surface. Systems come to life, touched by his familiar. He runs fingers over the tank-leather couches leaving trails in the dust; the chairs, awakened, swing towards him. He smells the human taint of old dust, the prickle of electricity, the slight scalded smell of surfaces blasted by years of light.

Slowly and with great formality, Wagner removes all his clothes. He stands naked under the apex of the dome, balanced lightly on the balls of his feet, a fighter's stance. His body is a mess, purple, scabbed, bruised. Wolf love is fierce love. He breathes deeply and steadily.

'Clear the glass.'

The dome turns transparent. Wagner stands naked on the surface of the Sea of Fecundity; the dust at his feet extends into the dusty regolith, marked with eternal footprints and tyre-tracks. Boulders that have stood in place from before life began. The distant rim of Messier A.

None of this is why Wagner has come. He throws his arms and wide and looks up. The full Earth shines down on him.

He has always known when the Earth was round. As a seven-, eight-, nine-year-old nestled deep in the walls of Boa Vista, he had lain in bed, staring at the ceiling, unable to sleep because the Earth light was shining inside his head. Ten, eleven, twelve, hyperactive and fractious and prone to dazzling flights of fantasy at full Earth. Doctors had prescribed ADHD medication. Madrinha Flavia had thrown it back into the de-printer. That child is Earth-touched, that's all. No medicine's going to put out the big light in the sky. Thirteen.

The full Earth had called him from his bed, through sleeping Boa Vista to this elevator, to this observation dome. He had closed the door, taken off his clothes. Thirteen was the age when everything changed, his body deepening and lengthening and filling. He was becoming a stranger in his skin. He stood naked in the Earthshine, felt it tugging him, tearing him, ripping him into two Wagner Cortas. He threw back his head and howled. The lock opened. Wagner had triggered a dozen security systems. Heitor Pereira found him, naked, curled on the floor, shaking and yelping.

Heitor never said a word about what he found in the observation dome.

Wagner basks in the light of the blue planet. He feels it cauterising his wounds, easing his bruises, healing him.

Fractal curls of white cloud stream across the Pacific. The blue of Earth's oceans never fails to tear Wagner's heart. Nothing is more blue. He can never go there. His is a distant, untouchable god. The wolves are the outcasts of heaven.

Night has already touched Earth's lowest limb, a hairline of darkness. Over the coming days it will climb the face of the world. The dark half of Wagner's life is drawing close. He'll leave this place, the pack will disperse, the nés become shes and hes. He'll find new powers of concentration and focus, analysis and deduction; he'll go back to Analiese and she'll see the healing marks all over his skin and she won't ask but the questions will always be there.

Wagner closes his eyes and drinks in the light of distant Earth.

Carlinhos has been hunting the raiders for thirty-six hours now across the Mare Crisium. They struck first at Swift: three extractors destroyed, five immobilised. The blast pattern of shaped charges was unmistakable. Even as Carlinhos led his pursuit bikes along their tyre-tracks, they struck again at Cleomedes F, three hundred kilometres north. A mobile resupply and maintenance base destroyed. Two deaths. Carlinhos and his hunters, his caçadores – crack dusters and bikers – arrived to find tractor and habitat punched through and through again with five-millimetre diameter holes. Entries and exits matched. Projectiles.

Two strikes, three hundred kilometres apart, in under an hour. No ghosts on the moon, but other entities can haunt a plugged and re-pressurised mobile base: rumours, superstitions, monsters. The Mackenzies are teleporting; they work deep Australian magic, they have their own private moonship.

'Not a private moonship,' Carlinhos says, flicking through satellite data. 'VTO lifter *Sokol*.' From orbit, the scatter patterns in the dust are clear. Carlinhos books time on the moonloop's cameras and, on the second pass of Ascender Two, São Jorge spot an irregularity in the shadows of Cleomedes H crater. Magnification resolves the speck into the unmistakable shape of a moonship. 'Mackenzie is flying them in.'

Carlinhos's hunters saddle up and ride out. São Jorge has predicted that the most likely target is the Eckert samba-line; a flotilla of six primary extractors moving to the south-western end of the Mare Anguis. The caçadores hammer the dustbikes for every drop of speed until they see the running lights of Corta Hélio gantries lift over the horizon. Carlinhos insinuates his team into the shadows of the slow-moving extractors. São Jorge's orbiting eyes report a moonship grounded just below the south-eastern horizon. Carlinhos grins inside his helmet and snaps off the safety locks on the knife scabbards he wore on each thigh.

Three rovers. Eighteen raiders.

'Wait until they're out of the rovers,' he orders. 'Nene, your team take out the rovers.'

'That'll leave them marooned,' Gilmar protests. He's a veteran biker, built the first trails along Dorsa Mawson. Abandonment is the violation of all morals and custom. Dona Luna is everyone's enemy. As you save, so you may be saved.

'They've got a ship, haven't they?'

The rover tags break into subtags. Raiders on the move.

'Steady,' Carlinhos says, crawling in the cover of Number Three extractor. 'Steady.' The tags are fanning out. Plenty of targets. Plenty of space. 'Take them!'

Six bikes power up; wheels kick up dust. Carlinhos banks around the excavator and hurtles down on the nearest tag. The figure in the sasuit freezes in shock. Carlinhos draws a knife.

'Gamma hutch,' says Lousika Asamoah.

'Hoosh,' says Rafa Corta. 'Gamma*hoosh*. It's French.'

'French,' Lousika says.

'For that,' Rafa says. 'Gamahuche.'

'I'm not sure I got that right. I learn better through practical experience. Hutch?' She rolls up over Rafa, tucks legs under his shoulders with a small *oof* of exertion, squeezes his head between her thighs.

'Huche,' Rafa says and she comes down on his tongue.

Rafa has always loved Twé. It's noisy and anarchic and its design makes no sense – a chaotic maze of habitats and agraria, where cramped tunnels open on to sheer drops of tube-farms and low-ceilinged apartments back on to glades of fruit bushes shivered with shafts of lights from sun-tracking mirrors. Water gurgles, the walls are moist with condensation, the air is rich with rot and nutrients and fermentation and the tang of shit. It is easy to get lost here; good to get lost. Ten-year-old Rafa, on his first trip to Twé, got gloriously lost. A quick turn took him away from crowds of tall people into places where only leaves and light lived. Corta and Asamoah security ran the tunnels, calling his name, bots scuttled along ceilings and through ducts too narrow for humans but all too enticing to kids. Software found him, lying on his belly trying to count the tilapia fish circling in an agrarium pond. He'd never seen living creatures before. Years later Rafa understood that the visit had been dynastic, Adriana feeling out a potential marriage between Corta Hélio and the Golden Stool. To Rafa it had been fish, all the way up, all the way down.

'Here,' Lousika had said.

'Here?' But she had already locked the door with her new Golden Stool protocols and wriggled off her dress.

The excuse had been João de Deus Moças against Black Stars Women's. Robson was a life-long João de Deus fan and it was time to get Luna into the game. And because it's Twé: we can see Tia Lousika, Rob; your mamãe, anzinho. Wouldn't that be great? Lousika met them at the station. Luna ran the length of the platform. Robson showed her a good card trick. Rafa snatched her up in his arms and held her so hard she gasped and he squeezed tears from his eyes. At half-time at the AKA Arena the children went with security to get doces and Rafa slipped his warm hand between his wife's thighs and he said, *I am going to fuck you until you want to die.*

Go on, she said.

So on the warm damp moss Lousika Asamoah straddles Rafa Corta's face and he eats her out. Gamahuche. With his tongue he circles the head of her clitoris, coaxes it out to play with long strokes. Caresses it. Torments it. She grinds her vulva into his face. Rafa splutters and laughs. He nuzzles, he explores, he penetrates and withdraws. He is fast, he is slow. Lousika dances with his tongue, matching his rhythms, finding off-beats and discords of shuddering pleasure. It lasts – seems to last – for hours. She comes four times. He doesn't even pressure her for a mouth-job in return. This time is a gift.

'I missed that so much.' Lousika rolls from Rafa and lies on her back in the leaf-light. Fat drops of warm condensation roll down the soft grooves of leaves, hang like a pearl, swell and fall slowly on to her body. 'Have you been practising?' Lousika catches drops in her hand and flings them into Rafa's face.

Rafa laughs. He was good. Fidelity was never in the nikah but there are rules. Never talk about lovers. Save the best for each other. After such a feast he's exhausted. His jaws ache. He needs to rinse and spit but that would be unforgivable. He needs a break between courses. An entr'acte. High above, mirrors slowly track the long sun, throwing shadow across Rafa's face .

'There's an hour until Madrinha Elis comes back with Luna and Robson, and even then, I could just call her and tell her to keep them out for another hour or two. If I had a reason to? You know?'

Rafa rolls on to his back and blinks up into the mirror-dazzle. Lousika slides on top of him.

'So what else have you been practising?'

Carlinhos holds the blade flat at arm's length. The Mackenzie saboteur throws hands up in defence. Carlinhos Corta knows how to take care of blades and such a blade, so honed and loved, with such momentum has taken the right arm clean through just beneath the elbow. It's not survivable.

Carlinhos puts a boot down and doughnuts the dustbike, lining up on his next target. São Jorge sprays vital signs all over his hud; breathing, blood pressure, adrenaline, heart rate, neural activity, visual acuity, salts and sugars and blood oh-two. Carlinhos doesn't need São Jorge's visuals. He's blazing.

His dustbike cavalry has completed its first charge. Five Mackenzies down, the rest fleeing. The rovers are coming up at speed to evacuate. The raiding party has been routed. Carlinhos circles his knife hand in the air: *round and at them again.*

'Leave them!' Gilmar shouts on the common channel. 'They're running.'

The rovers unfold, Mackenzie raiders dump sabotage equipment as they pile into the seats and harness on. The dustbikes can easily match them. São Jorge superimposes an icon of the Vorontsov ship lifting off from over the horizon, swooping in for rescue. Let it come. A moonship is a battle worth fighting.

Two rovers accelerate away in arcs of dust; one of the raiders kneels by the side of the third rover, aiming a long metal device. The kneeler jerks: recoil. And Fabiola Mangabeira's head explodes.

Her body flies from the dustbike; the machine careers on, the dead woman spins in a spray of glass and fibre, bone and flash-frozen blood. Her name turns white on Carlinhos's hud.

'They've got a fucking gun!' Gilmar cries. The shooter tracks another target. Silent recoil. Carlinhos's hud tracks an ejected red-hot thermal clip. The shot takes Thiago Endres through the shoulder. Not a clean shot, not a head-shot; but a killing shot all the same. Sasuits can heal, but not this much damage, not this fast. Thiago spasms on the regolith, thrashing as blood sprays into vacuum and freezes in a thick glossy ice. Another name goes white.

The gun swings on to Carlinhos. He throws the bike over into a skid, slides across the dust. Then he sees Gilmar pile full speed into the shooter. Gilmar strikes true and hard. The shooter goes down under the wheels, arms and legs flailing; the bike bucks high, Gilmar holds it down. The massive tread of the drive wheel rips open sasuit, skin, flesh, ribs. The gun spins away.

Carlinhos sprints to his still-running bike.

'After them, get after them!'

The third rover clamshells up and accelerates away. Carlinhos stands in the soft-settling dust, a knife in each hand, bellowing.

'Let them fucking go!' Gilmar yells.

Carlinhos walks to the corpse of the shooter. Fabric, bone, bowel. Carlinhos contemplates it for long heartbeats; the fragility of this goop and gore, the totality of the destruction. The moon makes any injury fatal. A woman, he guesses. They are often the best shooters. Then he raises his boot to stamp down through the helmet and crush the skull. Gilmar seizes his arm and whirls him away. Carlinhos leaps back, blades ready.

'Carlo, Carlo, it's over. Put the knives away.'

He can't see. Who is this? His signs are off the scale. Red all over his visor. What are they saying? Something about knives.

'I'm okay,' Carlinhos says. The dust has settled. The rest of his team wait on him, standing at a distance between respectful and fearful.

Someone has recovered his dustbike. The ground shakes; from over the horizon a moonship rises on diamonds of rocket-fire, lights flashing, three rovers clutched to its belly. Carlinhos stabs his knives at it; roars in two-bladed futility at the lights in the sky. It turns, it's gone. 'I'm okay.' Carlinhos puts the knives away, one at a time.

Carlinhos learned to love the knife young. His guards were playing a game; stabbing the point of the blade between outspread fingers. Carlinhos aged eight could see the stakes and the appeal at once. He understood the small lethality, the simple precision, how there was nothing complicated or unnecessary about knives.

Like his brothers and sister, Carlinhos Corta had been taught Brazilian jiu jitsu. *He won't apply himself,* Heitor Pereira reported to Adriana. *He jokes and play-acts and won't take it seriously.* Carlinhos didn't take it seriously because it could not be serious to him. It was too close up and undignified and he loathed the master-pupil discipline. He wanted a weapon fast and dangerous. He wanted elegance and violence; an adjunct to his body, an extension of his personality.

After Madrinha Flavia found him printing out fighting daggers, Heitor Pereira sent Carlinhos to Mariano Gabriel Demaria's School of Seven Bells in Queen of the South. All dark skills were taught here; thieving, stealth and assassination, confidence tricks and poisons, torture and excruciation, the way of the two knives. Carlinhos fell in among the freelance security and bodyguards like true family. He learned the way of one hand and two, of attack and defence and how to trick and blind; how to win and kill. He grew fast and lean, muscular and poised as a dancer. *Corta means cut in Spanish,* Mariano Gabriel Demaria said. *Now it's time to try the Bell Walk.*

The heart of the School of Seven Bells was a labyrinth of old service tunnels, kept in darkness and hung with the seven bells that gave Mariano Gabriel Demaria's academy its name. Walk the maze without sounding a single bell and you graduated. Carlinhos failed on the third bell. He raged for three days, then Mariano Gabriel

Demaria took him and sat him and told him, *You will never be great. You're the kid brother. You'll never command companies or budgets. You're full of anger, boy, swollen like a boil with it. An idiot would tell you to use that anger but idiots die in the School of Seven Bells. You're not the strongest, you're not the smartest but you are the one who will kill for his family. Accept it. No one else can do it.*

Four times more Carlinhos Corta took the Bell Walk. The fifth time he walked clear in silence. Mariano Gabriel Demaria gave him a pair of matched handcrafted lunar steel blades; balanced and beautiful and honed to an edge that would part a dream.

It has taken Carlinhos five years to understand Mariano Gabriel Demaria's truth. The anger will never go away. He will never find a way through it. That's therapy-talk. Accept it. Just accept it.

In the repaired base, Carlinhos plays with his knives, over and over, rolling them around his fingers, spinning them, tossing and catching them while outside vacuum-sealed corpses hang in racks, their carbon and water the property of the Lunar Development Company now. And he is angry, still so angry.

The Sisters have disappointed Lucas Corta. Toquinho has led him to an industrial unit on East 83rd of Hadley's Armstrong Quadra. Glass and sinter, full-height windows, standard-fit partitions, functional utilities, quick-print catalogue furnishings, generic reception AI. Soft white, discreet full-spectrum lighting. The air is scented with cypress and grapefruit. It could be a budget beautician or a hire-by-the-hour developer farm. Hadley always was a cheap place, a budget boon dock. But Toquinho insists that this is the Motherhouse of the Sisters of the Lords of Now; their terreiro.

And they keep him waiting.

'I am Mãe-de-Santo Odunlade Abosede Adekola.' The woman is a short, rotund Yoruba, all in Sisterhood whites, her neck hung with dozens of bead necklaces and silver charms. Her fingers are busy with rings; she extends a hand to Lucas. He does not kiss it. 'Sisters

Maria Padilha and Maria Navalha.' The two woman flanking the Mãe-de-Santo curtsy. They are younger and taller than the Reverend Mother; one Brazilian, the other West African. Their head scarves are red. Filhos-de-Santo of the Street Exus and Pomba Gira, Lucas recalls from Madrinha Amalia's teachings.

'We are a familiar-free community,' Sister Maria Navalha says.

'Of course.' Lucas banishes Toquinho.

'We are honoured, Senhor Corta,' Mother Odunlade says. 'Your mother is a great supporter of our work. I presume that's why you've come to us.'

'You're direct,' Lucas says.

'Modesty is for the children of Abraham. I deplore your callous treatment of our Sister Flavia. To leave that dear woman in fear of her breath...'

'The matter is out of my hands now.'

'So I understand. Please.'

Sisters Maria Padilha and Maria Navalha invite Lucas to an adjoining room. Sofas, more budget-print furniture, soft-focus white. Lucas is defiantly bi-chromatic in his dark grey suit. He doesn't doubt that there is a sanctum hidden deep behind these bland walls, and that no non-believer, and precious few believers, will ever see it.

A metal cup of herbal brew.

'Maté?'

Lucas sniffs, sets it aside. Mother Odunlade sips decorously through a silver straw.

'It's a mild stimulant and concentration aid,' she says. 'We develop and export spiritual tisanes and matés to Earth – printer files. Everything from mild euphoric to full-on hallucinogens that make ayahuasca look like lemonade. They're pirated the very moment they hit the network, but we feel it's our duty to give the world new religious experiences.'

'My mother has donated eighteen million bitsies to your organisation in the past five years,' Lucas says.

'For which we are very grateful, Senhor Corta. Religious orders face unique opportunities and challenges on the moon. Faith must breathe. Our funders include Ya Dede Asamoah, the Eagle of the Moon and, on Earth, União do Vegetal, the Ifa Pentecostal Church of Lagos and the Long Now Foundation.'

'I know.'

'She says you're diligent.'

'Do not patronise me.'

The attendant Sisters sit up, affronted.

'Forgive me, Senhor Corta.'

'Would there be any point in asking that this conversation continue in private?'

'None, Senhor.'

'But I am diligent. I'm the son who won't let his mother waste her money on hustlers and conmen.'

'It's her own money.'

'What do you do, Mother Odunlade?'

'The Sisterhood of the Lords of Now is a syncretistic Lunar-Afro-Brazilian religious order dedicated to the veneration of the orixas, the relief of poverty, the practice of spiritual disciplines, alms-giving and meditation. We also engage in genealogical research and social experiment. It's the latter that interests your mother.'

'Tell me.'

'The Sisterhood is engaged in an experiment to produce a social structure that will last for ten thousand years. It involves genealogies, social engineering and the manipulation of bloodlines. Europeans see a man in the moon; the Aztecs a rabbit. The Chinese see a hare. You see business and profit, the academics of Farside see a window on the universe, we see a social container. The moon is a perfect social laboratory; small, self-contained, constrained. For us it's the perfect place to experiment with types of society.'

'Ten thousand years?'

'How long it will take humanity to become independent from this solar system and evolve into a truly interstellar species.'

'That's a long-term project.'

'Religions deal in eternities. We're working with other groups – some religious, some philosophical, some political – but we all have the same aim; a human society so robust and yet so flexible it will take us to the stars. We're evolving five major social experiments.'

'Five.'

'That's correct, Senhor Corta.'

'My family are not your lab rats.'

'With respect, you are, Senhor Corta—'

'My mother would never degrade her children—'

'Your mother was fundamental to the experiment.'

'We are not an experiment.'

'We all are, Lucas. Every human is an experiment. Your mother is not just a great engineer and industrialist, she is a social visionary as well. She saw the damage nation states, imperial ambition and the tribalism of identity groups has done to Earth. The moon was a chance to try something new. Humans have never lived in a more demanding or dangerous environment. Yet here we are, a million and a half of us in our cities and habitats. We've survived; we've thrived. The very constraints of our environment forced adaptation and change on us. The Earth is specially privileged. The rest of the universe will be like us. You are an experiment, the Asamoahs are an experiment, the Suns are an experiment, the Mackenzies are an experiment. The Vorontsovs are an extreme experiment: what happens to human bodies and societies after decades in zero-gee? You experiment, you compete with each other. It's a kind of Darwinism, I suppose.'

Lucas bridles at the presumption. He is the manipulator, not the manipulated. But he can't deny that the Five Dragons have reached very different solutions to surviving and thriving on the moon. His colleagues among the Vorontsovs have never confirmed nor denied the legend that Valery Mikhailovitch Vorontsov, the old rocketeer of Baikonur, has, over decades of free-fall aboard his cycler *Saints Peter and Paul*, become something strange and inhuman.

'Why is one of your Sisters visiting my mother?'

'At your mother's request.'

'Why?'

'You spy on your brother but not your mother?'

'I respect my mamãe.'

The Sisters look at each other.

'Your mother is making her confession,' Mother Odunlade says.

'I don't understand.'

'Your mother is dying.'

The moto closes around Ariel Corta. She lifts a hand: the cab opens a crack for Ariel to be heard.

'Excuse me?'

'I almost lost a finger there!' The moto had closed fast and hard in Marina's face.

'We'd compensate you. Darling, we've been through this. You can't come with me.'

'I have to come with you,' Marina says. This morning the printer delivered a male flamenco-style suit into the hopper. Marina very much likes the pants though she can't stop tugging the jacket down to cover hips and ass. She's been hacking the shoes for some time now. Not the silly heels. They are unhackworthy. The real shoes; adding a line of code here for comfort, there for custom fit, rewriting the soles for grip and acceleration. Action pumps.

'I'm ordering you.'

'I don't report to you, lady. I report to your mother.'

'Then report to her.' Ariel seals the moto. Before she is a block away, Hetty has summoned a second cab and set it to follow Ariel.

Ariel smokes theatrically as Marina's moto unfolds. An old-dig unit up on Orion West 65th, smartly close to the hub but faded and easily overlooked. Deliberately so, Marina thinks. *The Lunarian Society,* Hetty informs Marina.

'This a private member's club,' Ariel says.

'Clubs let in security.'

'This club doesn't.'

'I will follow you.'

Ariel turns, hissing with fury.

'Will you for gods' sake just do what I ask? Just once?'

Marina swallows her satisfaction. A hit.

'Okay. Okay. But you need to know one thing.'

'What now?' Ariel splutters.

'You've got a ladder on the calf of your left stocking.'

For an instant Ariel might explode, eyes bulging as if in a sudden pressure-out. Then she collapses into helpless laughter.

'Be a dear and run off to the public printer and get me a pair,' Ariel commands. 'Beijaflor has transfered the print file.'

'What wrong with...' Marina begins. Don't finish. Hetty guides her to the nearest printer, a level down. Ariel assiduously examines the stockings, then peels on and replaces them.

'Shouldn't you find somewhere a little less public?' Marina offers. She has views no employee ever should.

'Oh for gods' sake don't be so Earthy.' Ariel straightens her dress, peering with the long look of a woman being shown herself through public cameras. 'I'll be back in an hour.'

Vidhya Rao waits for Ariel in the lobby. Ariel looks over the Lunarian Society with distaste. There is carpet. She despises carpet. This one is sickness-green, stained and mottled with decades of tread and insufficient care. Patched too the tank-skin leather sofas, of a design so outmoded it has served its time as knowing and retro and drooped into terminal obsolescence. Low lights. Collegiate, conformist, like an old colloquium house in a musty subject. There were pockets of air here Ariel suspected had circled like djinn for years.

'Please.' Vidhya Rao indicates a cluster of sofas around a low table. 'Something to drink?'

'Bloody Mary,' Ariel says and snaps out her vaper. A bot brings her drink, water for the banker. 'Will there be others?'

'Just me, I'm afraid,' Vidhya Rao says. E rests er hands on er knees, fingers arched, a lively pose. Ariel sips her Bloody Mary.

'A successful parley, then.' Vidhya Rao lifts er glass. Ariel returns the toast. 'Quite a feat. Your mother is well?'

'It's hard to tell anything about my mother. There's a new corporate structure.'

'I know.'

'Your Three August Ones predicted that?'

'I am an avid fan of the gossip channels.'

'Why am I here, Ser Rao?'

'You remember when we last met I said we wanted to buy you?'

'Name your price.'

'The Lunarian Society is producing a paper. We do this on a regular basis; outlining various cases for lunar independence; economic, political, social, cultural, ecological. We like endorsements.'

'What would I be signing up to?'

'It's a politics paper, drafted by me, Maya Yeap, Roberto Gutierrez and Yuri Antonenko. We posit three alternative structures for the abolition of the LDC and the establishment of lunar home rule. They run from full participatory democracy to micro-capitalist anarchism.'

Ariel finishes her Bloody Mary. No breakfast like it.

'Last time we met I believe I said I'm a Corta, we don't do democracy.'

'Those very words. It is only a paper. We're not asking you to sign a declaration of independence in your own blood.'

'Well as long as I don't have to read anything,' Ariel says and hands her empty glass to the waiting server bot.

*

Lucas's tram has arrived, Yemanja announces.

'Leave me,' Adriana says to Heitor Pereira and Helen de Braga. Helen rests a parting hand on Adriana's.

'It's all right,' Adriana says. Lucas won't rage like Rafa; there will be no shouting, no tantrums, no sulks. But he will be furious. Adriana waits in the Nossa Senhora da Rocha Pavilion, under the face of Oxum.

The two kisses, dutiful as ever.

'Why didn't you trust me?' Direct, of course. Open with the personal betrayal. A strong card. The dutiful son, lied to.

'I would have had to tell the others. I couldn't have borne it from Rafa.'

'I have always been discreet.'

'Yes, you have, Lucas. No one's been more discreet, or trustworthy.'

'Or done more for the company.' Adriana knows the high card he holds, but this is too early to play the Jack of Guilt. 'When were you going to tell us? Another family celebration? Luna's birthday?'

'Lucas, enough of this.'

'So when, Mamãe?'

'Get it over with Lucas. I can't bear this from you.'

Lucas bites back his anger, dips his head.

'How long, until?'

'Weeks.'

'Weeks!'

'I would have told you, before . . .'

'Just enough time for goodbyes. Thank you. What did you think we would do when we found out?'

'It would have changed everything. I see how you look at me now and you've known for what? Five hours? I'm not your mother, I'm not Adriana Corta. I'm death walking.'

Worse then the look of death was the look of pity. Adriana could not abide pity, its whinnying solicitudes, its patient smile over seething resentment. *You will not pity me.* This death was hers alone. She would have no cares or hurts encroaching on it. Her children would take her death away from her, shape it and manage it and control it until she was pruned back, an old woman dying in a chair.

'I haven't told the others.'

'Thank you.'

'I had to hear it from the Sisters of the Lords of Now.'

'You shouldn't have endangered their funding.' As Lucas's train left Hadley Central, Mãe Odunlade had contacted Adriana. Lucas knew the reason for Irmã Loa's visits. Lucas had extorted the information by threatening to cancel funding after Adriana's death. Adriana is furious at what Lucas did. He was always the silken bully. Whatever else she has done, she has the right to be furious about that.

'You shouldn't have played dynasties with our family.'

'Lucas, it's all dynasties, always dynasties. I wanted the best for you, for all of you. For the family.'

He'll concede that. It's always been the family for Lucas. He'll play his card now. Adriana has forced his hand.

'Is it for the family that you named Ariel as the heir to Corta Hélio?'

'Yes.'

'Not Rafa. Not—'

'You?'

'Rafa would choke this company to death. You know that. Ariel has her own life and career. Do you think she'll want to be be hwaejang of Corta Hélio?'

'Perhaps not, but that is what I have decided. After my death, Ariel will become head of the company. She won't be hwaejang. I've invented a new title and executive authority for her. You and Rafa will retain your positions and responsibilities. You'll all work together.'

'Is this some notion the Sisterhood whispered to you?'

'That's beneath you, Lucas.'

'What about us?'

'Us? You and Rafa?'

'Us; you and me, mamãe.'

'Lucas Lucas, this is why I wanted this all to wait until I'm safely dead.'

'I think I'm owed an explanation.'

'This is the moon. You're owed nothing. Ariel will be Choego of Corta Hélio.'

'As I said, I've told no one else. So far.'

Adriana knew he would do this in the end, but the manipulation, the oiled threat still makes her catch her breath.

'And that is why I've put as much distance as I could between you and the throne, Lucas.'

This is the knife. This is the wound beyond healing. The corners of Lucas's mouth twitch.

'I will fight you.'

'I'm not your enemy Lucas.'

'If you act against the best interests of Corta Hélio, then yes you are. Even you, mamãe. You've hurt me, mamãe. I can't think of a deeper cut. I can't forgive you for this.'

He stands, purses his fingers and bows to his mother. No parting kisses. The air shivers with rainbow, struck from spray of Boa Vista's tumbling waters.

'Lucas.'

He is halfway to the shuttle station.

'Lucas!'

Can I come in?

Lucas, please no. You're not going to persuade me.

I don't want to persuade you.

He stands before Jorge's door-camera as if every bone is shattered like sub-regolith and only his will holds them together.

Come in. Oh come in.

He doesn't speak, doesn't let leak any word of the devastation inside but Jorge pulls him to him, enfolds him, kisses him. Holds him. Holds him long, in the tiny smelly room, in the tiny bed.

Afterwards Lucas rests his head on Jorge's belly. He's fit for a musician, tuned and toned.

The apartment is miserable, high in the rafters of Santa Barbra Quadra, the rooms tiny and cramped, the air over-breathed. The bed takes up an entire room. The guitar hangs on the wall, watching like an icon or a different lover. It makes Lucas uneasy; the sound-hole a cyclops eye or a horrified mouth.

'Is your mother still alive?'

'No, she died in the Aristarchus quake.' Lucas feels the gentle rhythm of Jorge's words and breath and heart. 'She worked for you. Selenology. Moon rocks and dust.'

Mild quakes shake the moon regularly; tidal stresses, the aftershocks of impacts, thermal expansion as the cold crust warms in the new sun: gentle trembles, a long slow temblor to remind the humans who crawl through the wormholes in its skin that the moon is not a dead stone skull in the sky. Rattlers, dust-stirrers. Once every few lunes the moon is struck with more powerful quakes: seisms twenty, thirty kilometres deep, that stop people in their business in their underground cities, that crack walls and gas seals, bring down power lines and sever rails. That collapsed the Corta Hélio maintenance and research base at Aristarchus and buried two hundred people. The base had been cheap and rapidly constructed. Some compensation cases were still working through the Court of Clavius.

Lucas turns his head to look at Jorge.

'I'm sorry.'

'You're lucky,' Jorge says. 'You're lucky you have her.'

'I know that. And I'll look after her and I'll defend her and I'll be the one who sits with her and holds her hand.'

'Do you love her?'

Lucas sits up. There is anger in his eyes and for a moment Jorge is afraid.

'I have always loved her.'

'I shouldn't have asked.'

'You should. No one ever asked. Every week I go and see my mamãe and no one thinks to ask me, do I do this because I have a duty or because I love her? Rafa is the lover. Lucas Corta? The dark one. The schemer. My boy Lucasinho is everything to me. That boy is a wonder, a treasure. But when I talk to him, I can't say that. It twists up. It goes wrong. It comes out hard. Why is it so easy for the Rafas of this world?'

Lucas sits up on the edge of the bed. The room is so small his bare feet are in the living space.

'At least let me get you a decent apartment in Queen.'

'Okay.'

'You agreed to that too quickly.'

'I'm a musician. We never turn down free accommodation.'

'I'd like to come and listen to you. Sometime.'

'Sometime. Not yet. If that's all right.'

'I'll do that.'

Jorge pulls Lucas down beside him and Lucas curls up around him, belly to back, balls to ass, innocent and for a few moments empty of past and future, history and responsibility.

'Sing me something,' Lucas whispers. '*Aquas de Marco.*'

Chef Marin Olmstead is ill. Chef Marin Olmstead is not ill. Chefs are the unhealthiest trade. Their hours are sick, their workplaces cramped, uncongenial, filled with vapours and fumes. They are serial abusers of their bodies. But they never take a day off from their kitchen. Chefs never get ill. When Marin Olmstead asks Ariel take his place reporting the deliberations of the Pavilion of the White Hare to the Eyrie of the Eagle of the Moon because he is ill, Ariel Corta knows a fatted lie. Jonathon Kayode wants words with her.

Security is discreet and begins the moment Beijaflor summons the moto to the Eyrie. Ariel and Marina have been throughly scanned and checked by the time the cab attaches to the ascender and climbs the south-west wall of Antares Hub. An elegant butler in a bolero suit and hat asks Ariel to follow her please, up through the terraced gardens.

The Eagle of the Moon takes tea in the Orange Pavilion. His Eyrie is a series of sinter-glass kiosks and belvederes set among tiered gardens, each themed around a colour. The Orange Pavilion is set at the edge of formal citrus trees; orange, kumquats, bergamot, all dwarfed to human scale by AKA geneticists. The view is stupendous; the Eyrie sits half up the central rotunda where Antares Quadra's habitats meet, high enough for panorama, low enough to be aristocratic. The breath catches in Ariel's chest. This is stepping out on to the edge of forever. Antares Quadra is eight hours behind Aquarius Quadra and the sunline wakes, casting golden light the length of the five Prospekts. Lights shine in the gloaming, dusty as stars. This is the Eagle's preview and the Eagle's alone.

'Counsel Corta.' Jonathon Kayode plucks a bergamot. He digs his fingernails into the green rind, releases a spray of aromatic oil. 'Smell.' Ariel bends to the fruit.

'I can't describe it.'

'No, it's impossible, isn't it? Sensations and emotions, there is no way to express them except in terms of themselves.' He throws the fruit away. Ariel doesn't see where it falls. It could have gone over the edge. 'Will you?'

The Eagle indicates a small domed pavilion at the very edge of the central rotunda, big enough for just a low table and two benches. Ariel settles her layered petticoats. A Dior circle-dress today, floating and cinch-waisted; its flagrant femininity intentional deception. The butler brings mint tea for the Eagle, a spanking dry martini for Ariel. It's always cocktail hour in some Quadra. Ariel flicks out her vaper.

'Do you mind?'

'You're my guest.'

287

The sky is already busy; cable cars swing across the canyon; bicycles and scooters skim across the flyovers; high above, in the poor town, Ariel can make out figures running the rope-bridges. Drones and fliers flash through the golden space.

'My sincere apologies for not making it to your mother's birthday. The world will miss her at the head of Corta Hélio.'

'My mother kept her distance from the world, so I very much doubt there will be weeping on the Gupshup network.'

'Unlike you,' Jonathon Kayode says. For the first time Ariel feels his physical mass: Earth-born weight and muscle. He intimidates her a little.

'So tell me what you want,' Ariel says. 'What you really want.'

Jonathon Kayode's smile could dazzle worlds. He sets down his tea glass and claps his hands in delight.

'So forward! I want a wedding.'

'It's a day out for everyone.'

'I want a Corta-Mackenzie wedding.'

'I annulled the nikah between Hoang Lam Hung Mackenzie and Robson Corta on grounds on parental neglect of his sexual rights and Luna is only five.'

'I mean Lucasinho, with Denny Mackenzie.'

'Another one of Bryce's little orphans.'

'Yes.'

'Do you want me to tell you what Lucas will say?'

'Lucas will say yes, after you've explained to him that if he declines, I will instruct the LDC to review the Mare Anguis licence for procedural irregularities.'

'Corta Hélio has deep pockets.'

'But not bottomless ones. How rich is your war chest when we impose an interim embargo on your helium-3 exports, until the investigation is concluded?'

'How long will you stay in this lovely palace when Earth goes dark?'

Jonathon Kayode leans forward and takes Ariel's hands in his. His skin is soft and very warm.

'But none of this has to be, Ariel. Lucasinho marries Denny Mackenzie. You even get to draw up the nikah. And we have peace between Cortas and Mackenzies. A dynastic marriage. I want peace, Ariel. I want a quiet moon. I know what you and Mackenzie Metals have been doing out in Mare Anguis. I will not have corporate war on my world. A simple union of houses. Two beautiful princes. I'd even provide them with an apartment right here at Antares Rotunda, so that neither side would have a claim on them.'

'Two beautiful hostages.'

'Ariel, this is disingenuous of you. How many nikahs have you drawn up?'

Ariel takes a long draw on her vaper. Her martini is untouched on the low table.

'Are you threatening Mackenzie Metals with similar sanctions?'

Full morning now, another glorious day in Antares Quadra.

'I sometimes forget how new your family is to real politics.'

Ariel slowly exhales a spiral of blue vapour. It curls out over the stupendous drop down through tiers and platforms, buttresses and pillars to glittering Han Ying Plaza.

'Fuck you, Jonathon.'

'I want you to take this message to your mother.'

'I'm not my mother's tell-tale.'

'Really? I think you're quite the cunning little spider.'

'If I can find for my people I will.'

'Of course. You acted ethically. But I do know that the Mare Anguis tip-off didn't come through the Pavilion of the White Hare.'

Ariel coolly takes her first sip of her martini. She wants it to restart her stone heart. He knows. Plead guilty. Bargain. Her gloved fingers set the glass down without a ripple.

'There's no law against the Lunarian Society. Gods save that there ever should be. Too many laws make bad justice. It's not even a conflict of interests.'

'But it does conflict with my interests, the interests of the LDC. You are not citizens, you're clients. Never forget that. That tract you put your name to: fascinating. Quite fascinating. Quite irrelevant: political theory? We're pragmatic people up here. It'll be read by the usual chatterati. But if you started attaching your name to subjects that really affect people, like the Four Elementals. Well, that might cause unrest, even panic. The LDC couldn't overlook that. You aspire to the judiciary. Don't deny it, Ariel. Your ambition is admirable but, never forget, appointments to the Court of Clavius are made by the Lunar Development Corporation.'

'Jonathon, once again...'

'Fuck me. Yes. Talk to your mother. Persuade your brother. Invite me to the wedding. Make it big. I do so love a big wedding.'

The butler arrives. The audience is ended. Jonathon Kayode plucks a second bergamot from his tree and presents it to Ariel with the delicacy of a baby or a heart.

'Do take this. Place it at the heart of your home and its fragrance will fill every room.'

The event may be the Modi reception or the Colloquium '79 reunion but it's the tenth in five days and it's one thirty and Marina wants her home, her bed, so much she could weep. She sits in a Jacques Fath dress at the bar with her glass of tea, tracking Ariel as she moves from group to group, conversation to conversation. The same faces, the same talk. The banality is crushing. It's a skill, Marina supposes. It can't be what's said; it's who it is said by, and to whom. Marina tries to find a millimetre of forgiveness inside her red stiletto-heeled opera shoes. Marina squeezes off the heels. The pleasure is so great and immediate it's pain. Her feet are swollen, agonised, her muscles relax from their taut ballet and she almost cries out. She winces as she pulls on each soft heel-less ballet slipper.

Ariel wafts through her entourage.

Marina looks up from pulling in the glorious kind shoes and sees the knife. The suggestion of knife; the movement of the hand, the tucking back of the clothing, the flash of metal from within the entourage. Knife. The draw.

The lunge.

Jo Moonbeam muscles. Marina launches from the chair. The dive carries her a quarter the length of the room. She piles into the attacker as he drives the knife at Ariel Corta's heart, knocks him so the strike goes awry. The knife goes through layers of Givenchy lace and bodice into Ariel's back. Blood. Blood sprays high and slow on the moon. Ariel is down. The attacker reels and comes up for another strike. He's moon-born, tall, light, fast; faster than Marina. He shifts his grip on the knife. Marina's weapons are locked inside her stupid clothing. She looks for a killing thing to hand, finds it. The attacker comes up, knife-ready. With all her strength, Marina drives the vaper up under his chin. The full length. Her fists jerk against his chin-stubble. Crunch of bone. The tip punches through the top of his skull. The assailant spasms. Marina holds the vaper, holds it firm, holds him impaled on it, holds his gaze until she knows there is no life in it. She lets go of her spear. The body slumps on to its side. Blood has run down the titanium spike of the vaper over her hands. Blood from Ariel's wound has sprayed across her face and dress. Ariel lies in dark blood, panting, twitching. The entourage stands in its eternal circle, looking down. We are aghast. We are concerned. We don't know what to do.

'Medics!' Marina screams. She kneels beside Ariel. Where to press, where to hold, how to staunch the flow? So much blood. Flaps of skin and flesh. 'Medics!'

NINE

He's been here all along, sitting waiting for me to call him in, listening to all my stories and digressions and smiling because I'm the engineer, I'm the one who's supposed to be no nonsense, get-to-the-point. He always was patient to a fault. Carlos, you'll have to wait a little longer. But not much longer.

Achi left and I never saw her or talked to her again. I worked. I had things to do. No time to miss people. Look at my productivity! I didn't miss her at all. It was a good thing she had gone; love would only have been a distraction. I had a business to build.

I was so busy, I missed my Moonday.

That's a lie. It's a lie too that I didn't miss Achi. I missed her so hard the loss was an ache in me; a vacuum. I missed her sweet seriousness; her tiny kindnesses like tea by my bed every morning or laying out my surface suit neat and right; her tidiness where I was a slob, her attention to detail, the way she would straighten things if we were in the apartment or a hotel or a pod; set things square to the walls of the room. Her inability to get my jokes or pronounce Portuguese. So many things! I pushed them all down in my memory, did not think of them because thinking of her made me think of all the things I would lose forever on the moon. Breathing free. Sunlight on my naked face. Looking up into an open sky. The far horizon; the moon at the edge of the world laying a silver path out across the ocean. Oceans of water not dust. The wind: listen!

I worked like the devil; modelling and designing and planning. It would work. It was simple. But you can only work so much before it eats your stomach and soul. I took a break. An Adriana Corta break. My old mining school mates from DEMIN would have been proud. I worked the twelve bars of Orion Quadra. I fell in through the door of the ninth. By the tenth I was taking bets on how high a tower of shot glasses I could build on the bar – fifteen. By the eleventh I was in an alcove touching foreheads with this sweet big-eyed Santos boy and burbling all my plans and ambitions with his big eyes wide and pretending he was interested. I never made it to bar twelve. I was in bed with the Santos Big-eyes. I was a lousy lover. I cried all night. He was sweet enough to cry along.

I didn't call my family for a long time after Moonday. I was afraid I would realise I had made a terrible decision, one that I could not reverse. Then I thought, for most of human history, migration has been a one-way trip. Old Portuguese families would hold funerals for children going off to a new life in Brazil. Agency is a comforting fairy story. Life is a series of doors that only open one way. We can never return. This is the world and we must live in it the best we can. But I did listen to a lot of music from the old world, the music my mother loved and sang around the house, and it was as if it floated up from that blue planet down there and settled itself over a new landscape, not the grey hills and scarps and rilles and all that ugliness, but the people. The only beautiful thing on the moon is the people.

So, I was a woman of the moon now. I had committed myself to a new world and a new life. I had an idea and I had money – if you emigrate, the return part of your fare, minus any outstanding balance and the inevitable fees, is refunded to you. I bought convertible LDC bonds. Safe, solid, with a high return. I had a stable of legal and design AIs and a model I was itching to test out in the real world.

What I didn't have was a clue. More specifically, I had no idea how to turn all this into a business. I didn't have a plan. It was engineering of a kind different from any I knew; how to plan a company and make it work.

Then I met Helen. I had cast a dark net for potential finance directors – none of my people was ever any good with money and I was no exception. It was all deliciously clandestine; encrypted messages – this was before we had familiars – and secretive meetings in teahouses that shifted location at the last minute. I could not risk Mackenzie Metals discovering my plan. You think we live in a wild world now; it's nothing like the frontier days. But there she was, this woman from Porto and she knew all her stuff and she knew which questions to ask and which not to ask but, can I tell you? What really decided me to take her on was that she spoke Portuguese. I learned English and I was learning Globo – it was beginning to take over as the common language, especially because the machines understood the accent – but there are things you can only say with your own words. We could talk.

I have worked with her every day since. She is my oldest and dearest friend. She will never disappoint me, though I know I have disappointed her many many times. She said, you don't talk money. Ever. You don't pay anything unless I tell you to. Ever. And you need a Project Engineer. And I happen to know one, a Brazilian boy, a Paulistano, three months up.

And that was Carlos.

Oh but he was an arrogant bastard. Tall and good looking and funny and knew it. He had that Paulistano sense of superiority: better educated, better food, better music, better work ethic. Cariocas lived on the beach and sat around drinking all night. Never did a stroke of work. We met in a bar, we ate shirataki noodles. You wonder that I remember we ate shirataki noodles. I remember everything about that meeting. 1980s casual was the look then and he wore chinos and a Hawaiian shirt. He treated everything I said as if it was the most ridiculous thing he had ever heard. He was arrogant and annoying and sexist and he made me so mad. I was a little in hate with him.

I said, 'Is it all women you have a problem listening to, or just this one?'

Then he spent the next hour laying out the business plan that would become the foundations of Corta Hélio.

Oh but it was fun, that year when we chased our ideas all over the moon. Gods know how we managed to keep breathing. A fare refund is significant money but it runs from you like dust, even when your Finance Director and Project Engineer are only taking for the Four Elementals and sleeping on friends' floors. The meetings, the pitches, the prospectuses, the promises. The rejections, the realisation that a quick no is better than a long maybe. The thrill when we pinned down an actual, real investor and tasted her bitsies. I was clear: I didn't want Earth-based investors and equity funds, I didn't want to be like the Suns, constantly fighting their way out of control from Beijing. I wanted to be like the Mackenzies. There was a proper lunar corporation. Bob Mackenzie had sold his entire terrestrial operation, transferred the funds to the moon and said to the rest of his family: Mackenzies are moon people now. Move up or move out. I had committed to the moon: I could never go back to Earth, I didn't want Earth coming to me. They would be customers, not owners. Corta Hélio would be my child. Helen de Braga is my dearest friend, she's a board member but she has never been an owner.

Helen and I worked on the money while Carlos developed the prototype and the business. The moon was a much smaller place then, we couldn't have built and trialed an extractor without word running round the Farside and back again before we'd even locked helmets. So we went to the Farside and hired a couple of units from the faculty. It wasn't the university then, it wasn't much more than an observatory and outpost for research into lethal pathogens. If anything went wrong, it was as far as you could get from Earth and you could dump, DP and irradiate the entire site. The tunnels were far too close to the surface; every night I imagined the radiation sleeting through my ovaries. We coughed all the time. It could have been the dust but we suspected it was some little souvenir from the pathogen lab.

Carlos built the prototype extractor. I say built, I mean, he hired the contractors, the bots, the quality control teams. He showed it to me and I said no no no, that's not going to work, that's not robust enough, that process is inefficient; what about maintenance access? We fought like crazy. We fought like a married couple. Still I didn't love him. I told Helen this. Over and over and over. I must have driven her mad telling her how stupid and arrogant and obstinate he was but she never once told me to just shut up and sleep with the guy. Because I was crazy about him. He could not have been more different from Achi. She went from friend to lover. He could be a lover but never a friend. The attractions were all different, all wrong, and real real real. I thought about him in bed. I thought about him naked, I thought about him doing something stupid and uncharacteristic and romantic like bending over the schematics to see what this annoying woman was on about and now and then kissing me. I flicked off to him. I think he heard. What is it about attraction?

I'll tell you where I first kissed Carlos: in a little dome on the Mare Fecunditatis that he built for me. Not even a dome, it was a couple of rover pods bermed over with regolith that we used as a base for the field trials. We broke the prototype down and shipped it from Farside in anonymised crates by BALTRAN, jump after jump after jump so it looked random, yet they all ended up where we wanted them, when we wanted them. Then we ran them out by rover to our little base and our team put them all together, in the ass-end of nowhere, where no one would ever look.

We were burning money like oxygen by now. We had enough left for one field test, one tweak and our VIPs. It had to work. We all huddled in our pod and watched the extractor rumble out across the mare. I fired up the extraction heads, the separator screws. Then I hit the switch on the separator and the mirrors swivelled and caught the sun and turned it on the separator and I burst into tears. It was the greatest thing I had ever seen in my life.

We got our first reading after an hour. I don't think I breathed once those entire sixty minutes. Gas spectrometer read outs: Hydrogen. Water. Helium 4. Carbon Monoxide. Carbon dioxide. Methane. Nitrogen, argon, neon, radon. Volatiles we could sell to AKA and the Vorontsovs. Not what we wanted, not what we were looking for: that tiny spike on the graph, so much smaller than all of the others. I magnified the axes. We all crowded around the display. There. There! Helium-3. Exactly where we thought it would be, in the proportions we expected. Sweet sweet little spectrograph spike. We were in helium. I screamed and danced up and down. Helen kissed me and then she burst into tears. Then I kissed Carlos. I kissed Carlos again. I kissed Carlos again and did not stop.

We drank cheap VTO vodka all huddled together in our tiny pod and got stupidly, dangerously drunk and then I pulled Carlos into my bunk and we made silent, furious, giggling sex while everyone else slept around us.

We conceived a city in that bunk. Those two pods, that shroud of regolith, over years and decades, became João de Deus.

I didn't marry Carlos right away. I had to get the nikah right and anyway, after Mare Fecunditatis, there was too much to do. I made the calls to our VIPS and booked the tickets. Return trips, Earth-moon, for six people. Two from EDF/Areva, two from PFC India, two from Kansai Fusion. I had been working them for months; telepresence conferences, presentations, sales pitches. I knew they wanted to escape the US-Russian duopoly on terrestrial helium-3 that was keeping the prices of fusion power high and stifling development. It was the oil age again.

It was our biggest risk. Executives from three of Earth's smaller fusion companies all arrive on the moon at the same time? Even the Mackenzies could work that one out. The question was when they would move, not if. Our sole advantage was that they didn't know who we were. Yet. If we could could finish the demonstration, negotiate the deal and sign the contract before Bob Mackenzie loosed his blades, then we could defend the contract in the Court of Clavius.

We put them all up in Meridian's best hotel. We took care of their Four Elementals. We bought the French delegates wine, the Indian delegates whiskey and the Japanese whiskey too. As I said, we were burning money like oxygen.

The night before we were due to ship the VIPs out to Mare Fecunditatis, Mackenzie Metals discovered us. I got a message from our Fecundity base. Dusters with Mackenzie Metals logos had blown up the prototype extractor. They were destroying the volatile storage tanks. They were coming for the base. They were at the base ... I heard no more.

I remember I sat in my room and I had no idea what to do. I sat in my room and did not know what to feel. I was numb. I was falling. It was like free fall. I wanted to vomit. The extractor; all our work, but more, so much more, the lives. People I had laughed with, drunk with, worked with; people who were more my family than my family. People who had trusted me. They were dead because they had trusted me. I had killed them. We were children, I realised. We had been playing at businesses. The Mackenzies were adult and they did not play. We were a children's crusade, marching into our own ignorance. I sat in my room and imagined Mackenzie blades in the elevator, at the door, outside the window.

Carlos saved me. Carlos pulled me down, Carlos was my gravity. *We win by getting that output deal,* he said. *We win by building Corta Hélio.*

299

That was the first time I had ever heard that name.

With his own money Carlos hired freelance security for our people and materiel. With my own money I booked the VIPS on to the moonloop and told them of our change of plan. We would be spinning them around the moon on a tether to Farside, where we stationed the second prototype of the helium-3 extractor.

Carlos had made the stipulation on the first day of his project management: never build just one prototype.

We put our VIPs into a capsule, slung them around the moon, followed in the next and showed them what our extractor could do. Then we took the extracted helium and fired it up in the University of Farside's LDX reactor.

With the last of our money, we contracted legal AIs to draft the output deal and signed it that night.

Not quite the end of our money. With the very end of it, Carlos and I had the AIs draw up a marriage contract. With the very very end of it, we threw a wedding.

Oh but it was cheap and blissful. Helen was my bridesmaid, the only other attendee was the witness from the LDC. Then we went and had eggs and sperm frozen. There was no time for romanticism, or a family. We had an empire to build. But we wanted children, we wanted a dynasty, we wanted to safeguard the future, once we had built a future safe for them. And that could be years, decades.

Creating Corta Hélio was nothing compared to building Corta Hélio. I went for lunes without seeing Carlos. I slept, ate, exercised, made love when I could, which was little, rarely. We need allies, Carlos said. I tried to build relationships. The Four Dragons had heard the name of Corta Hélio. The Suns were aloof, engaged on their own projects and politics. The Vorontsovs had their eyes turned up to space, though I secured favourable moonloop launch rates from them. The Mackenzies were my enemies. The Asamoahs – maybe because our business did not threaten theirs, maybe because we both came to the moon with nothing and made something, maybe because they identified with the underdog – they became my friends. They are still my friends.

With a secure and steady supply of cheap fuel, my terrestrial customers soon achieved a market position that forced their competitors to negotiate with us or go bankrupt. Shortly after that the US and Russian helium-3 markets collapsed. I beat America and Russia! At the same time! Within two years Corta Hélio had moved into a monopoly position.

See? There's no talk more boring than money and business talk. We built Corta Hélio. We turned the little hut where we made love into a city. High times. The highest times. We were breathless with excitement. A point came where our success bred its own success. We were making money just by existing. The extractors scooped up the dust, the moonloop sends the cannisters flying Earthwards. We stood on the surface with our helmets touching and looked at the lights of planet Earth. It was ridiculously easy. Anyone could have thought of it. But I did.

See how it hardens you? In all the rush and excitement and work work work, I forgot about the people who died out on the Sea of Fecundity; my team, the ones who gave to me and never got to see the success or share in it. People say the moon is hard; no, people are hard. Always people.

I was still sending money to my family. I made them rich, I made them celebrities. They were in *Veja* magazine: the sister, the brother of Our Lady of Helium. The Iron Hand, the woman who lit the world! They had a wonderful apartment and big cars and pools and private tutors and security guards and one day I said, *Stop*. You've taken taken taken, you've dined out and partied and grown fat on my money and name and not one word of thanks, not one acknowledgement of what I have done up here, not one glint of gratitude or appreciation. Your children, my nephews and nieces don't even recognise my face. You call me the Iron Hand, well, here's an iron judgement. The final gift from the moon. I have placed in a secure account fares for a one-way trip to the moon. If you want Corta Hélio money, work for Corta Hélio money. With Corta Hélio. Commit, or I will never send you so much as a single decima again.

Come to the moon. Come and join me. Come and build a world and a Corta dynasty.

Not one member of my family took up the offer.

I cut them off.

I haven't spoken to any of them in forty years.

My family is here. This is the Corta dynasty.

Do you think that was harsh? The money; that's nothing, none of them would ever be poor again. Do you think I was wrong to cut them off without a word, or even a thought? I could give you all the old excuses: everything is negotiable; if you don't work you don't breathe, the moon makes you hard. It's true, the moon changes you. It changed me so that if I ever went back to Earth, my lungs would collapse, my legs would fold under me, my bones would flake and splinter. And those three hundred and eighty thousand kilometres count. When you talk to home and you hear that two and a half second delay before the reply comes, that pushes you away. You can never bridge that gap. It's built into the structure of the universe. It's physics that's hard.

I haven't thought about them in forty years. But I think about them now. I look back a lot; things come up from my past without my calling them. I tell myself I have no regrets, but do I?

I can't help thinking that it was all those years putting the company together; more in a sasuit that out of one, in and out of rovers, up and down extractors, snuggling up with Carlos in that pod, the radiation shining through me...

It's more advanced than I've told you, Sister. The only one who knows is Dr Macaraeg. I know Lucas went to the Motherhouse: he knows my condition but he doesn't know its full extent. Listen to me: the euphemisms. Advanced, full extent. I can feel death, Sister, I can see its little black eyes. Sister, whatever Lucas says, whatever he threatens, don't tell him this. He would only try and do something and there is nothing he can do. He always has to prove himself. And I've hurt him, oh I've hurt him so terribly. So much to put right. The light is running out.

But I haven't even told you the story of the knife fight with Robert Mackenzie!

It's legend. I'm legend. Maybe you haven't heard it? I sometimes forget there are generations after me. Not forget – how could I forget my grandchildren? More that I can't believe the time that has passed since those days; that people could forget them. Such days!

The Mackenzies stopped physical attacks on our materiel as soon as we had enough money to hire our own security. There was this Brazilian ex-naval officer; laid off whenever Brazil decided it couldn't afford a navy any more. He had been in the submarines and his theory was that warfare on the moon was all submarine warfare. All vehicles under pressure, in a lethal environment. I hired him. He's still my head of security. We decided one bold strike would end the war. We attacked Crucible. The Mackenzies and VTO had just completed Equatorial One; now Crucible could refine rare earths continuously. It was – it still is – a magnificent achievement. I forget I played a part in it, when I quit Mackenzie Metals and became a Vorontsov track queen on my way to founding Corta Hélio. Carlos conceived the plan: *We shall breach Equatorial One and paralyse Crucible.* I remember the faces around the table: there was shock, amazement, fear. Heitor said it can't be done. Carlos said, *It will be done. Your job is to tell me how we do it.*

We did it with six rovers: two teams of three. We timed the attack just as Mackenzie Metals was to deliver on an important new rare-earths contract with Xiaomi. Carlos went with the first team.

I rode with the second. It was so exciting! Two rovers full of big brawny escoltas, one with the demolition team. It was really quite simple. We hit Crucible on the eastern Procellarum. The escoltas formed a periphery; the demolition teams struck simultaneously three kilometres up line and down line from Crucible. I watched the charges blow. The rails flew up so high I thought they would go into orbit. I watched them tumble away, catching the sunlight, and it was the closest we can get to fireworks on the moon. Everyone cheered and whooped but I couldn't because I hated to see fine, brilliant engineering destroyed in a flash. Track I might have laid myself. I hated it because no sooner had we built a thing to be proud of, we destroyed it.

The clever part was, even as we ran with Mackenzie Metals rovers on our tails, our secondary attacks went in twenty kilometres up and down the line. The VTO repair teams would have to bridge those breaches before they could rebuild the ones closer to Crucible. Even if VTO got teams out within the hour, Crucible would be in darkness for a week. They would miss the delivery deadline.

We lost their blades in the chaotic terrain of Eddington.

After the battle of East Procellarum, Mackenzie Metals moved their attacks to the Court of Clavius.

I think I would have preferred the war of blades and bombs.

Their tactics varied but their strategy was clear and simple: bleed Corta Hélio to death through legal fees. They hit us with suits for breach of contract, breach of copyright, personal injury, corporate damages, plagiarism, damages suits for every single crew person on Crucible on the day of the attack. Suit after suit after suit. Most of them were swept away by our AIs as soon as they were served but for every one we dismissed their AIs created ten more. AIs are prolific, and AIs are cheap but they're not free. The judges we had agreed upon finally ruled against any further frivolous suits and that Mackenzie Metals lay a solid suit with a reasonable chance of success.

They did. It named Adriana Maria do Céu Mão de Ferro Arena

de Corta in forty separate instances of breach of Mackenzie Metals patent in my designs for the extractor.

AIs, lawyers, judges settled in for a long trial.

I didn't.

I knew this could drag and drag and Mackenzie Metals would file injunctions against our exports and for each one we dismissed, they would file another. They wanted us soiled goods. They wanted my name and reputation dust. They wanted our terrestrial clients leery of us, leery enough to consider investing a little seed money in a helium-3 extraction venture with an established company, of good standing, who could deliver the goods: Mackenzie Fusion.

I had to end this hard and fast.

I challenged Robert Mackenzie, in name and person, to trial by combat.

I didn't tell any of my legals. I didn't tell Helen, I didn't tell Heitor, though he may have guessed because I asked him to teach me something of the way of the knife. I didn't tell Carlos.

There is angry, and there is furious, and there is a deeper rage beyond those for which we don't have a name. It's pale and very pure and very cold. I imagine it's what the Christian god feels at sin. I saw it in Carlos when he found out what I was going to do.

It ends it, I said. *Once and for all.*

And if you get hurt? Carlos said. *And if you die?*

If Corta Hélio dies, then I'm dead too, I said. *Do you think they'll just let us walk away? The Mackenzies repay three times.*

Half the moon was in the court arena that day, or so it seemed to me. I came up on to the fighting floor and I just saw faces faces faces, all around me, going up up up. All those faces, and me in a pair of running shorts and a crop top, with a borrowed escolta knife in my hand.

I wasn't afraid, no not a bit.

The judges called for Robert Mackenzie. The judges called again for Robert Mackenzie. They instructed his lawyers to approach them.

I stood in the centre of the court-arena with another woman's knife in my hand and looked up at all the faces. I wanted to ask them: *Why have you come here? What have you come to see? Is it victory, or is it blood?*

'I call on you, Robert Mackenzie!' I shouted. 'Defend yourself!'

In a heartbeat, there was absolute silence in the arena.

Again I called on Robert Mackenzie.

And a third time, 'I call on you, Robert Mackenzie, defend your self, your name and your company!'

I called him three times and at the end I stood alone on the fighting floor. And the the court erupted. The judges were shouting something but no one could hear over the uproar. I was lifted shoulder high and carried out of the Court of Clavius and I was laughing and laughing and laughing with my knife still gripped in my hand. I didn't let go of it until I got to the hotel where Team Corta had set up headquarters.

Carlos didn't know whether to laugh or rage. He cried.

You knew, he said.

All along, I said. *Bob Mackenzie could never fight a woman.*

Ten days later the Court of Clavius established a process to allow proxy fighters in the case of trial by combat. Mackenzie Metals tried to launch a new suit. No judge on the moon would touch it. Corta Hélio won. I won. I challenged Robert Mackenzie to a knife fight, and won.

And now no one remembers it. But I was legend.

Death and sex, isn't that it? People make love after funerals. Sometimes during funerals. It's the loud cry of life. Make more babies, make more life! Life is the only answer to death.

I defeated Bob Mackenzie in the court-arena. It wasn't death – not that day – but it did focus my mind most wonderfully. Corta Hélio was secure. Time to build the dynasty now. I tell you this; there is no greater aphrodisiac than being carried out of the court-arena with your knife in your hand. Carlos couldn't keep his hands off me. He was possessed. He was a big dick-machine. I know, it's not seemly for an old woman to say such things. But he was: a fuck-bandit. He was deadly. And relentless. And it was the best time in my life, the only time I could lie back and say, I'm safe. So of course I said, *Let's make a baby.*

We started interviewing madrinhas immediately.

I was forty years old. I had drunk a lot of vacuum, swallowed a lot of radiation, snorted a sea-full of dust. Gods know if things were still working in there, let alone if I was capable of carrying a normal healthy pregnancy to term. Too many uncertainties. I needed engineered solutions. Carlos had agreed with me: host mothers. Paid surrogates, who would be so much more than just rented wombs. We wanted them to be part of the family, to take on those elements of infant care that we simply didn't have the time or, to be honest, the taste for. Babies are tedious. Kids only start to become human on their fifth birthday.

We must have interviewed thirty young, fit, healthy, fecund Brazilian women before we found Ivete. This is how I came into contact with your Sisterhood. The Brazilian community said, talk to Mãe Odunlade. She has family trees and genealogies and medical histories on every Brasileiro and Brasileira who comes to the moon, and a fair few Argentinians and Peruvians and Uruguayans and Ghanaians and Ivorians and Nigerians too. She will set you right. She did, and I rewarded her for her services, and, well, you know the rest of the story.

We drew up the contract and her legal systems looked over it and Mãe Odunlade advised her and we agreed. We had already started a number of embryos; we picked one and then asked Ivete how she wanted to do this. Did she just want to go to the med centre for implantation or did she want to have sex with me, or Carlos, or both of us? To make it personal, with affection, and connection.

We spent two nights in a hotel in Queen of the South and then we had the embryo implanted. It took right away. Mãe Odunlade had selected her madrinhas well. Ivete came to João de Deus with us and we gave her her own apartment and full-time medical support. Nine months later, Rafa was born. The gossip networks were full of pictures and excitement – picture rights were part of Ivete's remuneration package – but the cheers were not warm. I could smell the disapproval. Surrogate mothers; rent-a-womb. They all had a weekend of wild sex together in a hotel in Queen. A threesome, you know.

Rafa was hardly off the teat before I was already planning the next in the succession. Carlos and I started looking for a new madrinha. At the same time I had my first visions of this place. João de Deus was no place to bring up a family. There are children there now, but back then it was a frontier town, it was a mining town, it was raw and rough and red-blooded. I remembered Achi's parting gift to me. I found the bamboo document tube easily – ten years since she had left. So fast! Waterfalls and stone faces; a garden carved into the heart of the moon. It was as if she had seen the future, or the insides of my heart. I commissioned selenologists; found this place, hidden away in the rock like a geode for billions of years. A palace, a child, another one coming together in the Meridian Medical Facility. A business and a name. Finally I was the Iron Hand.

Then Carlos was killed.

Did you hear what I said? Carlos didn't die. He was killed. There was intent in it. There was purpose and ill will. Nothing was ever proved, but I know he was killed. He was murdered. And I know who did it.

I'm sorry. I get over-emotional. It's been so long – half my life without him, but I see him so clearly. He comes and stands so close to me: I can see the texture of his skin – he had terrible skin; I can smell him – he had a very distinct, very personal smell; sweet like sugar. Sweet-smelling sugar-man. His children have it too: the sweet sweat. I can hear him, I can hear the little whistle he made when he breathed through his nose. His chipped tooth. I see it all in such detail and yet it doesn't seem real. It's as unreal to me as Rio. Did I ever live there? Did I waggle my toes in the ocean? We were together so short a time. I have lived three lives: before the moon; Carlos; after Carlos. Three lives so different they don't feel like me.

I still find it hard to talk about. I haven't forgiven. I don't even understand the concept; why should I stop feeling what I honestly feel, why should I pardon the injustice? Why should I take all the hurt that's been done to him and say, *None of that matters Carlos? I have forgiven.* Pious nonsense. Forgiveness is for Christians, and I am no Christian.

He was out on a five-day inspection run across the new Mare Imbrium fields. His rover underwent an uncontrolled depressurisation in the Montes Caucasus. Uncontrolled depressurisation – you understand what that means? An explosion. It was forty years ago and our engineering was not as good as it is now, but even then, rovers were sturdy; rovers were tough. They did not undergo *uncontrolled depressurisations*. It was sabotaged. A small device, internal pressurisation would do the rest. I went out on a Vorontsov lifeboat. The rover was scattered over five kilometres. There wasn't even enough to recycle for carbon. Do you hear my voice? Do you hear how I keep it flat and focused, how I choose my words like tools, precise and practical? This is still the only way I can talk about Carlos. I put a marker there; a pillar of laser-cut titanium. It will never rust, never discolour, never grow old and dusty. It will stand there for aeons. That's right, I think. That's long enough.

You killed Carlos Matheus de Madeiras Castro, Robert Mackenzie. I name you. You waited, you took your time and you worked out how to hurt me most. You destroyed the thing I loved dearest. You paid me back three times.

Three months later Lucas was born. I never loved him as I loved Rafa. I couldn't. My Carlos was taken, Lucas was given back. It didn't seem a fair trade. And that's not right, that's not just, but human hearts are seldom just. But it was Rafa who heard the name of his father's killer whispered over his bed; he was the one grew up in that shadow, with hate in his heart. Cortas cut. We begin and end with our names.

Rafael, Lucas, Ariel, Carlinhos: little Carlos. Wagner. I couldn't be kind to that boy. We get notions into our heads and then we look around and a lifetime has gone past and they become dogmas. And Ariel... Why didn't I... No point. Once an engineer, always an engineer. It has taken me a lifetime to realise that lives are not problems to be solved. My children are the achievements that make me most proud. Money – what can we spend money on here? A faster printer, a bigger cave? Empire? It's dust out there. Success? It has the shortest half-life of any known substance. But my children: do you think I've built strong enough to stand ten thousand years?

Yemanja laid a silver path out across the ocean and I walked up it until I came to the moon. What I like about the orixas – their particular wisdom: they don't offer much. No holiness, no heaven, just one opportunity, once given. Miss it and it will never come again. Take it and you can walk all the way to the stars. I like that. My mamãe understood this.

My story is finished now. Everything else is just history. But do you know? I wasn't average. I wasn't Jane-outside. I was *extraordinary*.

Sister, excuse me. Yemanja has an emergency call.

TEN

You pass the first line of security twenty kilometres out from João de Deus. You may be on the train, a bus or rover, perhaps you fall towards the Fecunditatis 27 catcher in a BALTRAN capsule, but your vehicle, your passenger manifest and you will have been interrogated by Corta security AI. The first trip-line is so subtle you won't even know you've crossed it. Unless you trip it.

The second line of security is not a line but a level, a field that covers every prospekt and level, every crosswalk and elevator, every duct and pipe and shaft of João de Deus. Bots, crawling and climbing and flying, from massive tunnel diggers and sinterers to insect-sized inspection drones. Eyes and ears and senses only bots possess turned outward, alert and engaged.

The third circle is the security personnel, women and men in sharp suits with sharper blades and other, longer-range weapons that can take down an assassin, biological or machine, before it closes to killing distance. Poisons, air-drones, tasers, targeted insects. Heitor Pereira has spent freely and widely. His arsenal is the finest on the moon.

At the centre of these rings of security lies Ariel Corta in an induced coma in the intensive care unit of the Nossa Senhora Aparecida Medical Facility.

The Cortas have come from the four quarters of the moon. The doctors are firm in their refusal to allow the family access to the ICU. There's nothing to see. A handsome woman in a life-support cot, tubed and wired, bot sensors and scanners weaving over her body like mudras from a Hindu dance. Beijaflor hovers above her head. Adriana has moved her court to João de Deus. Corta Hélio has requisitioned a suite of rooms on the level above the ICU. Occupants have been well-compensated; where necessary, they have been booked in other medical facilities, transported at Corta expense with the best available care, upgraded. Boa Vista staff print out furniture and fabrics and broadcast catering tenders. Press and gossip sites camp outside the med centre. Heitor Pereira has caught thirty spy drones already.

Their familiars have told them the details of the attack and the damage but the Cortas find comfort and reassurance in repeating, rehearsing, renewing them to each other. An assassin's litany.

'A bone knife,' Adriana Corta says.

'He carried it straight past the scanners at the party,' Rafa says. He's arrived directly from Twé; three jumps by BALTRAN. He's unruffled; groomed, clothes, shoes, hair immaculate despite the indignities of ballistic transport. 'They never saw it.'

'The pattern is widely available on the network,' Carlinhos says. He's come twelves hours by rover from the small war on the Sea of Crises, itchy in an unfamiliar shirt and suit. He tries to loosen the confining collar. 'Half my crew carried them. They were fashionable a couple of years back. You'd use your own DNA as the template.'

'A litigant with a grudge,' Adriana says.

'Not so short a commodity,' Lucas says.

'Ridiculous,' Adriana hisses. 'If you're on the sharp end of the bad divorce, you don't take it out on the lawyer, you take it out on the ex.'

'The story is credible,' Lucas says. 'Barosso vs Rohani. The Court of Clavius has the case file. He backed out of negotiations and went for a court settlement. Ariel took him to pieces.'

'Yet he was a guest at this party,' Adriana says. Ridiculous. Ridiculous.'

No one has yet named the obvious, nor will they until Ariel is out of danger. The rest of the moon can work up rumours and frenzies and network indignation. It feeds the Corta well, but not so well as their dignity in distress.

'And where is Wagner?' Adriana asks.

'Queen,' Carlinhos says. 'He's found something.'

'If he wants to be one of us, he needs to be here.'

'I'll try him again, Mamãe.'

But Lucas's eyebrow is raised and he flicks a look at his brother that says *we'll talk about this*.

Dr Macaraeg is here, everyone's familiar announces.

Ariel's physician hesitates in the open door, intimidated by the phalanx of Cortas facing her. She sits at one end of the conference table. The family congregate around the other end.

'It's not good,' Dr Macaraeg says. 'We've stabilised her though she's lost a lot of blood. A lot of blood. There has been nerve damage. The knife has severed part of the spinal cord. There has been a loss of function.'

'Loss of function?' Rafa blusters. 'What's that? You're not talking about a bot here. My mother needs to know what's happened to Ariel.'

Dr Macaraeg rubs her eyes. She's exhausted and needs nothing less than Rafael Corta's futile temper.

'The knife caused a category B lesion in the region of the L5 section of the spinal cord. With a category B lesion motor function is lost. Sensory function remains. The L5 region is associated with motor control in the feet, legs and pelvic region. That's been lost. There's also a loss of bowel and bladder control.'

'What do you mean, bowel and bladder control?' Rafa says.

'Incontinence. We've fitted a colostomy system.'

'She can't walk,' Carlinhos says.

313

'It's a paraplegia. Your sister is effectively paralysed from the hips down. We're also concerned about potential brain damage from the heavy blood loss.'

Carlinhos murmurs an umbanda invocation.

'Thank you, Doctor,' Adriana Corta says.

'What can you do?' Rafa asks.

'We'll begin stem cell therapy as soon as Ariel is stabilised. It has a good success rate.'

'I don't understand: good success rate? Kojo Asamoah had a new toe in two months,' Lucas says.

'There's a big difference between growing a new toe and repairing spinal nerves. It's a delicate process.'

'How long?' Adriana asks.

'It can take up to a year.'

'A year!' Rafa says.

'Maybe eight months, if the grafts take first time. Then there's the recuperation process, learning to use the motor systems all over again, imprinting the neural pathways. We cannot rush this. It's precision work. Any mistakes can't be rectified.'

'A year, in total,' Lucas says.

'Anything you need, we'll get it for you,' Adriana says. 'Equipment, new techniques from Earth, anything. Ariel will have it.'

'Thank you, but our medical technology is in advance of anything on Earth. We'll do everything we can, Senhora Corta. Everything.'

'Of course. Thank you, Doctor.' The second *thank you* is the dismissal. Adriana turns to her sons. 'Rafa, Carlinhos, if you please? I need a word with Lucas.'

'I'd be a fool and a liar if I said this didn't work for me,' Lucas says when the suite is empty.

'You expect me to admire that?'

'No. It's reprehensible but it is good business. But it's not the issue uppermost in my mind. The wedding, Mamãe. Without Ariel negotiating the nikah, the MacKenzies will eat Lucasinho alive.'

Lucas sees his mother try to take in this new perspective, like a piece of extraction plant that requires whole landscapes to make a turn, a train that must begin to brake before it's over the horizon. She would have spun like a dancer once. Quick of wit and apprehension. This dynastic marriage will not be the long trap he shared with Amanda Sun. Ariel will broker a deal. The best marriage contract of her career. Lucas still hasn't told Lucasinho. He had not intended to until the contract was prepared. Now the boy is on his way up from Meridian and Lucas dreads the coming conversation.

'What can we do?' Adriana asks and Lucas hears exhaustion and indecision in his mother's voice.

'Play for time.'

'The MacKenzies will never allow that.'

'I'll see who I can find. Beijaflor manages Ariel's contacts.'

'Yes,' Adriana says but Lucas can see that her thoughts are turned to the room below. 'We'll do our best for Lucasinho.'

'Mamãe, I feel for Ariel, I truly do, but the company...'

'Tend to the company, Lucas. I'll tend to Ariel.'

'Hey.'

'Hey.'

He's reeling up and down corridors trying to find food, tea, something to pass the waiting time with which medical facilities are so generous. She's stumbling out of a room where she has been debriefed by Heitor Pereira; question after question, questions, three hours of questions. Details. Memories. Tell me again, again, again. Any glimpse or peripheral detail that might be an insight into the attack. She is tired and sick.

The attacker was dead dead dead by the time the rest of the bodyguards arrived. Someone prised her fists off the vaper. Someone pulled her away from the pooling blood. Bots arrived first; scuttling across the ceiling, floating on fans. They assayed Ariel Corta, already blue from blood loss, ran lines and tubes into her arms, compressed and stapled the gaping flaps of flesh, printed up artificial blood, put her into recovery position and called human medics. A freelance security team, crash-contracted by Beijaflor, cleared the party. Now Corta Hélio brought its resources to bear. A Vorontsov moonship was arriving at Aquarius Quadra's surface lock. Ariel was to be taken to João de Deus. No questions. The security mercenaries escorted gurney and med team up into the hold of the moonship. Marina drifted in their orbit, a bloodstained satellite. She had never been in a moonship before. It was noisy. Everything shook. She felt much less safe than she ever had on Carlinhos's dustbikes. She was nauseous the entire twenty-minute flight, then understood as she threw up quietly in the corner of the elevator down into Nossa Senhora da Gloria Hub that it was from the stench of blood from her dress.

Heitor Pereira seized her at the gate and hurried her away from the emergency team. She glimpsed mother and brothers over shoulders, between milling bodies.

Tell me everything.

The cameras were swarming.

We need to know. Everything.

I saved her fucking life.

'Your, ah, dress.'

Marina's still wearing the Jacques Fath. It's rigid with dried blood, reeking of iron and death.

'They wouldn't let me . . .' Now she has stopped moving and the momentum of events and voices and faces threatens to topple her. Marina is dizzy with fatigue, shocky and vertiginous.

'Come on, we'll get you something.'

The big printers are tied up with medical parts or Corta Hélio furnishings but there is a small public unit behind the med centre teahouse. Customers stare, at the blood, at the Corta.

'Stop staring at me!' Marina shouts. 'Stop fucking staring at me!'

The deprinter refuses to accept Marina's dress. *Contaminated material*, Hetty informs her. *Please recycle by contracting Zabbaleen.*

'Here.' Carlinhos offers tea as Marina waits for the printer. Casual, classic: hoody and leggings. Pumps.

'Do you mind?' Marina peels the straps from her shoulders.

'I've seen you before,' Carlinhos jokes.

'Could you just give me a moment?' There are no possible jokes, no levities here.

The dress has stuck to her skin. Marina dabs the fabric with cooling tea to loosen the scabbed blood. Her underwear is soaked through. She peels it all off, there in the kiosk behind the teahouse; all of it, off her. She can smell herself. Marina gags. If she throws up now she'll never stop. Print-fresh, the leggings, the hoody feel religiously clean against her skin.

'Come on.'

Carlinhos takes her arm and she lets him guide up to a quiet room on the ninth floor. Sofas, fake fur throws, space to lounge and curl.

'Drink?'

Carlinhos holds a Blue Moon in either hand.

'How can you...' Marina cries. 'Sorry. Sorry.'

Carlinhos sits down beside her, sprawls. Marina huddles, arms around knees.

'You did good.'

'I just did. That's all. I didn't think about it. There was nothing to think about. Just do it.'

'Something takes over. It's not body, not spirit, something else. Instinct, maybe, but we're not born with it. I don't think we have a word for it. Something instant and pure. Pure action.'

'It's not pure,' Marina says. 'Don't call it pure. I can see him, Carlinhos. He looked so surprised. Like this was the last thing he expected. Then, annoyed. Frustrated, that he was going to die and wouldn't see if his plan had worked. I can still see him.'

'You did what you had to do.'

'Shut up, Carlinhos.'

'You do what you have to do. That's what I mean about it being pure. It's necessity.'

'I don't want to talk about it, Carlinhos.'

'You did good.'

'I killed a man.'

'You saved Ariel. He would have killed her.'

'Not now, Carlinhos!'

'Marina, I know how you feel.'

'You don't know anything,' Marina says and then her breath catches because truth lies in the eyes, the muscles, even the scent of the sweat; unconscious truths we read intimately. 'You do. Oh God you do. Get away from me, get away. I smell blood on you.'

Marina pushes Carlinhos away. Moonbeam muscles shove him hard into the wall, hard enough to bruise.

'Marina...'

'I'm not like you!' Marina screams. 'I'm not like you.' Then she runs.

The wolf is not a lone hunter. Wagner Corta is. He has realised a truth about his two natures that his pack mates haven't, for all their identities and arguments over pronouns and nés: he doesn't change from mundane to wolf and back again. There are two Wagner Cortas, light and dark, each a separate and distinct self, with unique personalities and characteristics, skills and talents. Mundane Wagner Corta died twelve years in the sun-dome of Boa Vista. Survived by the wolf and the dark one.

He folds himself into the post-match crowds shouldering along Falcon West 73rd. His familiar is likewise folded deep into the Queen of the South security grid. He worked for hours coding the hack that allows him to follow Jake Sun. He has spent days observing the man, his habits and his rituals, his patterns and his predictabilities. Rafa has called, again and again: Ariel; Ariel has been critically injured in a stabbing. Come to João de Deus. Now. He must push that aside, focus. Concentrate on the hunt.

Jake Sun is one block ahead, a level down, winding back from the game in the Taiyang Arena. Tigers 34, Moços 17. Another kicking. A terrible result for Rafa's Boys. Rafa has more to think about. The fans are in the best of humours. Jake Sun jokes with his friends; he is happy, relaxed, unsuspecting. Wagner can take him easily. The friends suggest a drink, dinner. Jake will refuse. He has an engagement lined up with Zoe Martinez, his Queen of the South amor. And here is where he will take the elevator down to 33rd. Wagner rides the parallel car down, one level behind. Zoe Martinez's apartment is down a side street off 33rd, shadowy and discreet. Wagner tightens step and closes on his victim. The prey turns in to the quiet district.

'Jake Tenglong Sun.'

Jake turns and sees the knife in Wagner Corta's hand. There is a flash, more pain than Wagner has ever known and he is on the ground, rigid. Hands have reached inside his body to shred every muscle. He rolls on to his back to see a ring of knives pointing down at him. Sun security.

'You're far too predictable, Little Wolf.' The taser sparks in Jake Sun's hands. 'The August Ones saw you coming a week back. And you're getting far too close. Sorry about this.'

The narrow street explodes with howls. For an instant the Sun killers are distracted. The instant is enough. Figures drop from balconies, whirl out of doors, vault up over the rail from the level below. Bodies fall, a boot comes down on the side of a head. Wagner rolls clear as a knife stabs for his eye. The tip jams in the soft surface of the street. In the split second it takes the security guard to wrench it free a woman in sports gear has run a blade through his neck. Hands grab Wagner's wrist, pull him clear, drag him upright. Two Sun assassins are down, the rest, outnumbered, cover Jake Sun's retreat.

'You okay?'

Wagner is gripped in an agony of pins and needles, but his eyes can focus and he can speak. Irina, who likes to bite. Sasha Ermin. The Magdalena pack.

'Come on go go,' Sasha Ermin. Er pack rushes Wagner down the street. He's numb, itchy, he's pissed himself.

'You cubs have a lot of learn about being a pack,' Irina says. 'You're way too used to having the Earth over your heads all the time. You don't stop being a wolf when the Earth goes dark.' But she looks different, smells different, wears her hair differently, dresses in standard sports gear; a thousand differences that say she isn't a wolf.

'We'd heard tenders were out for a hit on you,' says a tall, muscled man in sports tights and running shoes. Wagner saw him swing over the rail one-handed and take a hit-woman straight down with a kick to the kidneys.

'Thanks,' says Wagner. Lame but no word more true.

'There's got to be some better way than everyone for themselves, all the time,' Sasha says. 'We'll get you fixed back at the Packhouse.'

'I need to get to João de Deus,' Wagner protests. 'I need to see my family.'

'We're your family now,' Irina says. She hands him his lost knife.

Marina brings the tea from her living room to sit and sip and watch the man sleep. Sex has always rewarded her with insomnia. The men have snored or grunted or mumbled their way into the night while she pulls an arm from under a belly, repositions a leg, slips out from under a shoulder and there is no sleep until sun-up.

Marina drinks her tea. The darkened room, lit only by accidental light from the bathroom, the street, turns Carlinhos's skin to velvet. He has the most beautiful skin. Like all dusters he has shaved his body hair. It's a particular agony, peeling a sasuit off over back hair. She touches his skin gingerly, afraid to arouse him; enough to catch the nap, feel the living electricity. The light casts fine shadows across the landscape of his back, like low sun exposing the memories of old craters and rilles. His side, his hip and the sculptural curve of his ass are covered in a faint network of lines. Scars.

The charmer, the schemer, the talker, the fighter.

He breathes like a baby.

How good it is to have a muscled man. A tall, muscled man; moon-tall, big enough to scoop her up and enfold her and overpower her, which she likes. A big man to roll over on to his back and ride. The other men had been collegiate: geeks and engineers, dice-rollers and occasional runners; snowboarders and skateboarders. Board boys. One jock once; a swimmer. He had been a good shape. Earthmen. This is a moonman. Marina has seen Carlinhos naked, freshening up after the Long Run, suiting up, suiting down, in that precious pool at Beikou under the eyes and claws of Ao Jung, but she has never seen him as a man of the moon until now; on his belly, head turned to one side, in her bed. And he is so different, this moonman. A head and some taller than her, though he's reckoned not tall among the second generation, and below average by the slender trees of the third gen. His skin lies close over a different musculature, a landscape, like all landscapes, governed by gravity. His toes are long and flexible. You grip with your toes. His calves are round and tight: Marina's calves ached for a whole lune while she learned how to walk like a moon girl. Carlinhos's thigh muscles are defined and long from running, but underdeveloped by terrestrial standards. Thigh muscles are too powerful for the moon: they can send you slamming into walls and people, or soaring up to crack open your skull on the roof. His ass is magnificent. Marina wants to bite it. Calves and ass get you around, give you that Gagarin Prospekt swing. That's why 1950s retro is so hot this season; those skirts and petticoats, these box jackets move like seduction on the streets.

His belly is turned from her but she knows it's tight and packed. His spine runs in a deep valley of muscle. The upper body by contrast is overdeveloped. Heavy shoulders, massive pecs, biceps and triceps bulging. He's top heavy. On the moon you need upper body strength more than lower. He lies sprawled on her bed like a defeated cartoon superhero. Mouth-breathing.

Strange man, beautiful man. You're fit for this world and fitness is beauty. But I'm as strong as you, I pushed you into a wall at the hospital, when you scared me. I grabbed you when you came down on me and turned you over and you laughed because no amor has ever done a thing like that with you and then I came down on you.

Marina's tea has grown tepid.

She had run, corridor to corridor, unable to escape the hospital, the city, the moon, until she found a tiny corner. There she curled up, arms around knees, and felt the stone sky press down on her; billions of tons of sky. He found her there. He sat across the corridor from her, not speaking, not touching, not doing anything except being there. Up in Bairro Alto, in the desperate sky, a man with a knife had taken her fog-catcher and drunk her water before her eyes. The knife had won, the knife would always win. The knife was a reproach to her until fear and fury and adrenaline sent her to face the knife, and drive a titanium spike through a man's brain and through the top of his skull.

'Carlinhos,' she said. 'I'm scared.'

Scared?

'I am like you.'

In her room under the same stone sky she lays her cheek against the hollow of Carlinhos's spine. She feels the movement of his breath, the rhythm of his heart and blood. The impossible texture of his skin. She can't feel the scars at all.

'Oh man, what do we do now?'

'How old is he?' Lucasinho asks.

'Twenty-eight,' Lucas says.

'Twenty-eight!'

At Lucasinho's age, that's death. Lucas remembers seventeen. He hated it. Rafa's shadow fell long on him; his few friends had all moved away, he had slipped off contact with them and felt too gauche and uncertain to make new ones. Nothing felt right around him; friends, lovers, clothes, laughter and what seventeen understands as love. It came to Rafa like rain, soaked him through with charm, cleansed him. Alone then, alone now.

He's jealous of his son; Lucasinho's easy sexuality, his charm, his comfort in his own body. The Dona Luna pin on his lapel.

Lucas met his son at the station. The kid wore all his piercings – a formal occasion – and clutched a cardboard cake box. Lucas almost smiled at the cake box. Where had he learned this kindness? Escoltas cleared a way through the press of celebrity spotters. On the moon, nothing was as gossip-worthy as an assassination attempt. Lucasinho held the cake box like a baby while drones swooped overhead.

They stood together ten minutes by the window to the ICU. Familiars could have shown Ariel in every detail, overlain with schematics and medical notes, but that would just have been image. The glass made it physical. Ariel lay in her coma; Beijaflor performed slow topological involutions. Then Lucas took Lucasinho up to his room. Jinji had transfered schematics to the hospital printers: the Boa Vista staff had built a comforting replica of Lucasinho's colloquium room in Meridian. There Lucas told him about the wedding. He had planned it carefully. Lucas's own room would have been indecent, his office too formal, too overbearing.

'Your mother was twenty-nine when I married her. I was twenty.'

'Look how that worked out.'

'It worked out with you.'

'Don't make me do it.'

'We're not free in these things, Luca.' The intimacy, the nick-of-a-nickname: he had rehearsed it on the way down to the station, trying to get used to its discomfort in his throat. He had feared he would stumble over it but when he had to say it, the word slipped free. 'The Eagle of the Moon has ordered it.'

'The Eagle of the Moon, the rat of the moon – that's what you say.'

'He has us, Luca. He can wreck the company.'

'The company.'

'The family. I didn't want to marry Amanda Sun. I never loved her. Love wasn't in the contract.'

'But you bought you way out. Buy me out of this.'

'I can't. I wish I could, Luca. I would do anything to be able to do that. It's political.'

In the box are macaroons, glossy and perfect, arranged in a spectrum of colours. Those are the things that make Lucas feel the greatest traitor. They are innocent and kind and gentle and betrayed.

'I have a first-draft nikah,' Lucas says.

'Ariel is on life-support.'

'It's not one of Ariel's,' Lucas says. Lucasinho's cheek twitches.

'What?'

'It's a first draft. Luca, I could order you. For the family, all that. I'm asking you; will you marry Denny Mackenzie?'

'Paizinho...'

Now Lucas is rocked, a small quake: he can't remember the last time Lucasinho used the familiar, the contraction. *Daddy.*

'For the family?'

'What else is there?'

'How long have you been there?'

The voice wakes Marina from her warm, antiseptic doze. Intensive Care Units are hugely conducive to sleep. Their warmth, the hum and mesmerising dance of the machines, the perfume of gentle botanicals that reminds her of forests, of mountains and home.

'How long have you been awake?'

'Too long,' Ariel Corta says. Beijaflor brings up the head of the ICU bed. Her hair hangs loose, limp, unclean around her face. Her skin is dull and waxen, grey; her eyes sunken. Tubes and cannulae run from her wrists to the smooth white arms of the medical machines.

'I don't think you're supposed to—'

'Fuck *supposed* sideways,' Ariel says. She turns the bed to face Marina. 'What are you doing here?'

'I watch over you, remember?' After Ariel was brought out of her artificial coma her family had buzzed around her. There hadn't been an hour when one or more hadn't been at the bedside, holding hands, smiling, there even when she slipped back into the long healing sleeps the medical team had programmed for her. Over the hours, the days, the demands of the company drew them away. The vigils became visits. The media mob at the door flew away, the entourage dissolved. In the end, Marina sat the hours in the ICU. She feared the solitude, that would not be able to escape from the face of the man impaled on the spike but she found the watch peaceful, healing. Time away from people and their wants. She could accommodate what she had done to the man who tried to kill Ariel. In time she might justify it.

'Well you look like shit,' Ariel says. 'And what are you wearing?'

'Clean stuff. I like it. It's comfortable. And you can talk.'

Ariel's laugh is a dry, bitter bark.

'God yes; be a dear and get me some make-up? I'm not facing the moon like this.'

'Already ahead of you.' Marina hooks the zip-case out from under her chair and sets it on the bed. It's only a Rimmel Luna travel-pack, one upgrade from budget, but Ariel opens it with the impatience and excitement of a New Year present.

'You are a treasure.' Ariel's eyes soften as she regards her face through Beijaflor and surveys the restoration work. Abundant thanks for the cosmetics, not a word for saving your life, Marina thinks. 'And where is my ever-loving family?'

'Planning a wedding,' Marina says. Ariel jerks upright, then collapses back in pain. 'Are you all right?' Lipstick rolls from Ariel's fingers.

'No I'm not fucking all right. I think I tore something. Where's the doctor? I want a human. Get me some pain relief.'

'Easy.'

A nurse arrives at speed and bustles Marina away from the bed. Marina catches glimpses of Ariel's exasperated face as the bed is reset, the monitors checked, the dosage administered. The cosmetics are repacked and parked on a table out of reach.

'Give me those,' Ariel commands when the nurse is gone. She applies foundation, eye shadow and liner; mascara in careful, precise strokes. Ariel's ritual transformation of her face is a reclaiming of her body, a degree of control in an environment, a body outside her command. Finally, the lips. Ariel turns her head from side to side to catch every angle of her restored face.

'So: my nephew. Who's looking after the nikah?'

'Lucas.'

'Lucas! The kid's fucked. Get him over here. Now. Has he signed anything? Gods save us from amateur matchmakers.'

'The doctors say you're still very frail.'

'Then I'll fire those doctors and hire ones who have a bit of respect. What am I supposed to do, lie here and gaze up at the ceiling and have Beijaflor play me womb-music? It's my legs don't work, not my brain. This is therapy. Beijaflor, get Lucas over here.'

External communications have been restricted on medical grounds, Beijaflor says on the common channel. Ariel shrieks in exasperation. The nurse returns and is driven from the room in a fluster by Ariel's bellow. Marina turns away to hide her delight.

'Marina, coração, can you get Lucas for me?'

'Already done, Senhora Corta.'

'I keep telling you: Ariel.'

The cry wakes Marina. She's in the corridor, running while Hetty is still informing her of the alarm in Ariel Corta's room. Ariel has been moved from the ICU to a private room up on the former Corta floor. The level is airy and quiet and secure. Machines walk or flit by, sniff Ariel's vital signs, drift on. Marina's momentum carries her into the room and hard into the wall beside the bed. Medical bots reach out from their hatches in the walls to examine her. Superficial bruising, no lasting trauma.

'Are you all right?'

'Nothing.'

'I heard – Hetty alerted me.'

'Nothing!'

The bed again brings Ariel Corta into a sitting position. Hetty displays diagnostics but Marina can see the fear in Ariel's wide eyes, the tightness of her breathing, the resentment in the set of her mouth that she should be found like this: unseemly.

'I'm not going.'

'Nothing. No. I saw him.'

'Barosso...' Marina begins. Ariel holds up a hand.

'Don't say it.' She gives an exasperated sigh, fists clenched. 'I see him all the time. Every time anything moves; the bots, someone in the corridor, you; it's him.'

'It takes time. You've had a trauma – a serious trauma, you need to heal the memories...'

'Do not give me that therapy-speak, healing shit.'

Marina bites back her words. She grew up in the vocabulary of well-being, of balancing and aligning and rebirth. Crystals turned, chakras glowed. Hurts crippled, traumas wounded, offences maimed. She realises she has never examined its principles and beliefs. It is all analogies. But healing, practical healing, might be a thing of the body only, not the emotions. A different process might apply to the emotions – if what is wounded are emotions at all, if *wound* isn't just another analogy for a realm that has no names or words beyond the experience of the emotion itself. Or perhaps no process at all, except time and the decay of memory.

'I'm sorry.'

'Self-help shit,' Ariel growls. 'What I need: I need to be able to walk, I need to be able to take a piss or a dump without feeling something warm in a bag next to my hip. I need out of this bed. I need a bloody martini.'

You're angry, Marina makes to say. No. 'My brother-in-law, Skyler, was in the military.'

'Really?' Ariel props herself up on her elbows. The bed catches up with her. A human story. People doing things; those interest her.

'He was working down in the Sahel. That was when they brought the army in on any kind of emergency; some multiple-resistance outbreak or refugees or famine or drought.'

'What you people get up to down there, I don't understand any of it.'

A spike of fury stabs through Marina. Who is this lofty rich bitch lawyer? A rich bitch lawyer on the moon. Stabbed and paralysed. Let the emotion go. Calm. Heal.

'He was in information support. Every crisis needs information support. But he still saw things. Kids. They were the worst. That was all he'd say. He wouldn't talk about it. They never do talk about it. He was diagnosed as a PTSD victim. No, he said. I'm not a victim. Don't make me a victim. That's all people will see. That will become everything about me.'

'I am not a victim,' Ariel says. 'But I want to stop seeing him.'

'So do I,' Marina says.

'What do you mean, you don't do other people?'

Two o'clock and Marina and Ariel are insomniac again in a med centre room. They've talked people and politics, law and ambition; unspooled their stories and histories and they've come round to sex.

'I'm not sexually attracted to other people,' Ariel says. She lies propped up in bed vaping. Dr Macaraeg has given up her admonitions and warnings. *Who pays for your breathing, darling?* The vaper is new, longer and more deadly than the one with which Marina stabbed Edouard Barosso. Its flowing tip mesmerises Marina. 'I can't be bothered with them. All that neediness and attention seeking and having to think about them when they're not thinking about you. All that having to negotiate sex, and the falling in and out of sex, and then there's love. Spare us that. It's so much better to have sex with someone who's always available, knows what you want and who loves you more deeply than anyone else ever can. Yourself.'

'That's, um, wow,' Marina says. When she arrived as a print-fresh Jo Moonbeam, Marina explored the moon's sexual diversity but there are niches in the ecosystem – a sexual rainforest – she has never imagined.

'You're so terrestrial,' Ariel says with a flick of the vaper. 'Sex with other people is always compromise. Always barging and shoving and trying to get it all to fit and who comes first and who likes what and you don't like what they like and they don't like what you like. Always something held back; that secret thing you love or want to try or that makes you lose everything and scream yourself sick that you can't say because you're scared they'll look at you and say, *you want to do what?* and see not their lover but a monster. Nowhere is as dirty as the inside of your head. When you're with yourself, when you're jilling off, flicking the bean, fishing for pearls, playing women's handball, cutting a siririca; there's no one else to worry about, nothing to hold back from. No one's judging you, no one's comparing you, no one's got someone else in their head they're not telling you about. Me-sex is the only honest sex.'

'Me-sex?' Marina says.

'Self-sex sounds grubby, auto-sex is bots fucking and anything with the word "erotica" in it is by definition un-erotic.'

'But what do you—'

'Do? Everything darling.'

'That room you wouldn't let me into, in your apartment...'

'That's where I go fuck myself. The things I have in there. The fun I've had.'

'Is this an appropriate employer/employee conversation?'

'As you keep reminding me, I'm not your employer.'

'Goodness,' Marina says; an old grandma expression, but the only one she can think of that adequately expresses her sense of wonder and shock. It is as if she opened that locked door in the small, bare apartment and found an endless wonderland of meadows and rainbows, oiled skin and soft flesh and orgasmic choirs.

'Who are you thinking about?' Ariel asks.

'I'm not—'

Ariel cuts her short.

'Yes you are. When you tell anyone you're A, they immediately start comparing the best they've done solo with the best they're doing with their current other. Every time. Who is it?'

It's the dark, it's the smallness of the hour, it's the click and whirr of lunar machinery, always present but in this room on this level loud and present; it's the feeling that there is only her and Ariel in this whole world that gives Marina the courage to say, 'Your brother.'

A grin of delight spreads across Ariel's face.

'Oh you ambitious girl. One of the family. That's why I do like you so very much. Carlinhos? Of course it's Carlinhos. He's gorgeous. Really looks after himself. Doesn't talk too much either. If I were the kind of girl who fucked other people, I'd want to fuck him.' Ariel's vaper freezes on its way to her lips. Her eyes widen. She sits forward and grasps Marina's hands in her own. The gesture is startling, the skin still hot and dry from medications.

'Oh mi coração,' Ariel says. 'You have, haven't you? Please don't tell me you love him. Oh you silly woman. Did my mother not tell you this about my family? Don't get close to us, don't care for us; above all, don't love us.'

With a huff of effort, a bite of the lower lip in pain, Ariel Corta swings herself on to the edge of the bed. Marina watches in agony.

'Can I?'

'No you fucking cannot,' Ariel says. She pushes herself to the very edge of the bed, legs dangling, pulls the petticoats and skirts of the full-length dress up around her thighs. 'Come legs.'

In the corner of the room legs whirr and stir. Corta Hélio roboticists designed and built them in under a day: all other projects suspended to the imperative of making Ariel Corta walk. The legs stride across the floor to the bed. Their gait is natural, easy, human and quite quite horrifying to Marina. They're like bones a body has stepped out of. They'll be stalking through her nightmares for lunes. They nuzzle against Ariel's hanging legs, open like traps and lock from foot to thigh. 'I need your help now,' Ariel says. Marina gets an arm around Ariel's waist, a shoulder under her arm and holds Ariel up as the neural links spider up her spine seeking the socket the surgeons have set into her back. The woman is as light as thought; bone and air, but Marina feels her tight-wired strength. The spiders scuttle over skin beneath bunched fabric and sink connectors into the socket. Ariel hisses in discomfort. Two drips of blood.

'Let's try this.'

Marina steps away. Ariel drops down to the floor. The machine legs buckle, for an instant she might topple, then the gyros and servos mesh with her intentions and she stands firm.

'Hold the dress up.'

Ariel takes a step forward. There is no hesitation or faltering in it. She takes a tour of the room, Ariel holding up the train of her dress like a courtier.

'How does it feel?'

'Like I'm seven years old and wearing Mamãe's shoes,' Ariel says. 'All right. Make me presentable.'

Marina lets fall the dress and straightens out the folds and layers. It gives no flash of the prosthetics beneath. Ariel examines herself through Beijaflor.

'It'll do for now.' The grafts have already restored some control to bladder and bowel but the voluminous dress conceals discreet colostomy equipment. 'I'm not wearing floor-length frocks for the rest of my life. Unless I set a new trend. Please keep behind me. I want to make an entrance.'

Lucas is first to applaud as Ariel waltzes through the door into the reception room but Marina marks the momentary flicker of sour across his face. Kisses. Then Adriana embraces her daughter, stands back to admire what Corta engineers have wrought.

'Oh my love.'

'It's temporary,' Ariel chides. 'Purely cosmetic.'

The third member of the family to have come to the med centre is Wagner. He is the most intriguing Corta to Marina. Since the party in Boa Vista, Marina has seen him only once, at the birthday celebration. Like Carlinhos he serves the family outside the board room but Marina senses this is through politics not temperament. He is dark-eyed and -skinned, long-lashed and high cheekboned, his familiar is a sphere of oily black rubber spikes and he is here when Rafa and Carlinhos are not.

Ariel sits, crosses her legs, flicks out her vaper. Marina stands behind her, enjoying the show.

'Lucas. A proper nikah.' Familiars flicker with data transfer. 'That'll keep the boy safe and happy. Don't read it, just sign it and don't mess around with things you don't understand again.'

'Have the Mackenzies agreed?'

'They will or they'll be years renegotiating every clause and Jonathon Kayode is very impatient for a glam wedding.'

Lucas dips his head but again Marina reads resentment.

'Wagner has something to report to us,' Adriana says.

'Ariel, your bodyguard,' Lucas says.

'Marina stays,' Ariel says. 'I trust her with my life.'

Lucas looks to his mother.

'She has saved the lives of two of my children,' Adriana says.

'I know I don't have a position at the centre of this family,' Wagner says. 'I made an arrangement with Rafa, after the attack at the moon-run party. I'd make some investigations. My special . . . situation . . . means I can see things the rest of you can't.'

Ariel catches Marina's puzzled frown.

He's a wolf, Beijaflor whispers on Marina's private channel.

What? Hetty whispers back. Marina remembers when he had quizzed her at Boa Vista. Carlinhos had asked her whether she had any surface experience. Wagner had asked her about her engineering specialism. She sees the dark intelligence here, and the sense of something lonely, feral, vulnerable. *Wolf.*

'I caught a scent of something I recognised in one of the protein processors and tracked down the designer. She led me to the people who commissioned her. It was a one-shot disposable shell company but one of the owners was Jake Tenglong Sun. I went to talk to Jake Sun in Queen of the South. He knew I was coming. He tried to kill me. The Magdalena pack saved me.'

Magdalena pack? Hetty whispers to Beijaflor but Ariel has a question.

'He knew you were coming?'

'His words were "You're far too predictable, Little Wolf. The August Ones saw you coming a week back." '

'Gods,' Ariel says.

'Ariel,' Adriana says.

'I'm a member of the Pavilion of the White Hare. I'm also a member of the Lunarian Society.'

'Why was I not informed of this?' Lucas says.

'Because you're not my keeper, Lucas,' Ariel snaps. She vapes deep and long. 'Vidhya Rao is also a member.'

'From Whitacre Goddard,' Lucas says.

'E told me about an AI analytics system Taiyang designed for Whitacre Goddard. Three quantum mainframes, designed to make highly accurate predictions from detailed real-world modelling. E called it prophecy. Fu Xi, Shennong and the Yellow Emperor: the Three August Ones.'

'The Suns are our allies,' Adriana says.

'With respect Mamãe,' Lucas says, 'the Suns are their own allies.'

'Why would the Suns commission a device to try to kill my son?' Adriana says.

'To bring us to exactly where we are, Mamãe,' Lucas says. 'The edge of war with the Mackenzies.'

Lucas is awake the instant before Toquinho calls him. The present is an illusion. He had read that as a child. Human consciousness lags half a second behind every decision and experience. The finger moves unconsciously, the mind approves the action and imagines it initiates.

Helen de Braga, Toquinho says. Esperança Maria, her familiar, appears in the dark before him.

'Lucas, your mother asked me to call you.'

It's time then. Lucas feels no fear, no dread, no anxiety. He has prepared for this moment, rehearsed his emotions again and again.

'Can you come to Boa Vista?'

'I'm on my way.'

Helen De Braga meets Lucas on the tram platform. They kiss formally.

'When did you find out?'

'I called you as soon as Dr Macaraeg told me.'

Lucas has never had much regard for Dr Macaraeg. Hers is an unnecessary profession. Machines do medicine so much better; cleanly, impersonally.

'Your mother's condition has deteriorated.' Dr Macaraeg says. Lucas turns the full chill of his stare on her and she flinches. Another thing the machines do better: truth.

'Since when?'

'Since before her birthday. Senhora Corta instructed us...'

'Do you have ambitions, Dr Macaraeg?'

The doctor is taken aback. She flusters.

'I'm not ashamed to say it, but yes, I have ambitions to further private consultancy.'

'Good. Modesty is a vastly overrated attribute. I hope you're able to achieve them. My mother must have told you about her condition. Yet you kept the full degree of it secret from me. How do you think I should respond to that?'

'I am Senhora Corta's private physician.'

'Of course you are, yes. Is there any medical reason why I can't see my mother?'

'She is very weak. Her condition is—'

'Very good then. Where is she?'

'She's in the surface observatory,' Dr Macaraeg says and slips away from Lucas's attention. Boa Vista's staff have turned out under Nilson Nunes on the tailored lawns. Their questions Lucas Corta can't answer, but he is a Corta, he is authority. He nods acknowledgement to each of them. Good faithful people. Next the madrinhas, a word for each.

'How long does she really have?' Lucas asks Helen de Braga.

'Days at the most. Maybe only hours.'

Lucas leans a moment against the polished rock lintel of the elevator lobby.

'I can't blame her doctor for obeying her.'

'She asked for you and you alone, Lucas,' Helen de Braga says.

'You!' Lucas shouts. His eye has been caught by a movement of white: Irmã Loa blowing like paper between the pillars of the lobby. 'Out of my house!'

'I'm your mother's spiritual adviser.' Irmã Loa faces Lucas Corta.

'You are a liar and a parasite.'

Helen de Braga touches Lucas's arm.

'She's taken great comfort from the Sisterhood,' Irmã Loa says.

'I've called security. They're not under any orders to be gentle.'

'Mãe Odunlade warned me about your manners.'

335

Heitor Pereira and a smart security suit arrive. She flicks away the arresting hands.

'I'm leaving.'

'This woman is banned from Boa Vista,' Lucas says.

'We're not your enemies, Lucas!' Irmã Loa calls.

'We're not your project,' Lucas calls back and, before Helen de Braga can ask what he means, steps into the elevator.

The Earth's last quarter stands over the Sea of Fecundity. Adriana has arranged her seat to look full on it. Wheel tracks in the dust hint at discreet medical bots concealed in the walls. The only thing attending Adriana is a side table with a cup of coffee.

'Lucas.'

'Mamãe.'

'Someone's been up here recently,' Adriana says. Her voice is light and weak, a husk of will and Lucas hears in it the truth that her disease is very much more advanced than he or even Dr Macaraeg suspects.

'Wagner,' Lucas says. 'Security saw him.'

'What was he doing?'

'The same as you. Looking at the Earth.'

The lightest of smiles crosses Adriana's profile.

'I was too hard on that boy. I don't understand a thing about him but I never tried. It's just that he made me so angry. Not anything he did; just that he *was*. Just him *being* constantly said, You're a fool, Adriana Corta. That was wrong. Try and bring him in to the family.'

'Mamãe, he's not—'

'He is.'

'Mamãe, the doctor told me—'

'Yes, I've been keeping secrets again. And what would you have done? Rallied the family? Pulled in every Corta from every quarter? The last thing I see is all of you standing looking at me all big eyed and solemn? Hideous. Hideous.'

'At least Rafa—'

'No, Lucas.' Adriana's voice can still find the snap of command. 'Hold my hand, for gods' sakes.'

Lucas cups the thin kite of skin between his two hands and is shocked at its dry heat. This is a dying woman. Adriana closes her eyes.

'Some final things. Helen de Braga will retire. She's done enough for this family. And I want her away from us; safe. She's not a player. I'm afraid for us, Lucas. This is a terrible time to be dying. I don't know what will happen.'

'I'll take care of the company, Mamãe.'

'You all will. That's the way I've arranged it. Don't break it, Lucas. I chose this, I chose this.'

Adriana clenches her fist inside Lucas's hands and he releases it.

'I'm afraid for you,' Adriana says. 'Here. A secret just for you. Only you, Lucas. You'll know when you need it. In the early days, when it looked like the Mackenzies would wipe us out, Carlos commissioned a revenge weapon. He planted a trojan inside Crucible's smelter control systems. It's still there. It's a clever piece of code; it hides, it adapts, it self-updates. It's very simple and elegant. It will redirect Crucible's smelter mirrors, turn them on to Crucible itself.'

'Dear gods.'

'Yes. Here, Lucas.'

The briefest flicker of data between Yemanja and Toquinho.

'Thank you, Mamãe.'

'Don't thank me. You'll only use it when everything is lost and the family is destroyed.'

'Then I'll never use it.'

Adriana grasps Lucas's hand with startling strength.

'Oh, would you like some coffee? Esmeralda Geisha Special from Panama. That's a country in Central America. I had it flown up. What else am I going it spend my money on?'

'I never got the taste for it, Mamãe.'

'That's a pity. I'm not sure you could learn it now. Oh, can't you see what I'm doing? Sit with me Lucas. Play me some music. You have such good taste. That boy you wanted to marry; it would have been good to have a musician in the family.'

'The family was too much family for him.'

Adriana strokes the back of Lucas's hand. 'Still, you were right to divorce Amanda Sun. I never liked her sneaking around Boa Vista. I never liked her at all.'

'You agreed to the nikah.'

Lucas feels Adriana's hand start.

'I did, didn't I? I thought it was necessary for the family. The only thing that's necessary for the family is the family.'

Lucas has no right words so he orders Toquinho to play.

'Is that?'

'Jorge. Yes.'

Tears soften Adriana's eyes.

'It's all the little things, Lucas. Coffee and music. Luna's favourite dress. Rafa telling me the results from his handball teams, whether they were good or bad. The sound of water outside my bedroom. The full Earth. Wagner's right; you could lose yourself looking at it. It's so dangerous: you daren't look because it will snatch your eye and remind you of everything you've given up. This is an awful place, Lucas.'

Lucas hides the flinch of hurt from his mother. He grasps her hand again.

'I'm afraid, Lucas. I'm afraid of death. It looks like an animal, like a dirty, sneaking animal that's been hunting me all my life. That's lovely music, Lucas.'

'I'll play his *Aguas de Marco*.'

'Let it run, Lucas.'

Adriana opens her eyes. She had drifted off. That fills her with cold vertigo. It could have been the last sleep, with things unsaid. The cold shaking her heart is relentless now. Lucas sits with her. From his face Adriana guesses he is working; Toquinho a vortex of files and contacts and messages. The music has ended. It was very good. That boy can sing. She would ask Lucas to play it again but she doesn't want to break this moment; aware without being noticed.

She turns her eyes to the Earth. Traitor. Yemanja showed her the shining path, drawn across the sea, out from that world to the moon. She followed it. It was a trap. There is no path back. No line of light across this dry sea.

'Lucas.'

He looks up from his work. His smile is a delight. Small things.

'I'm sorry.'

'For what?' Lucas says.

'For bringing you here.'

'You didn't bring me here.'

'Don't be so literal. Why must you always take against things?'

'That's not my world up there. This is my world.'

'World. Not home.'

'You have nothing to be sorry for, Mamãe.'

Adriana reaches for the coffee on the table but the cup is cold.

'I'll have fresh made up,' Lucas says.

'Please.'

The terminator of the crescent Earth sweeps down across the Atlantic; the whorl of a tropical cyclone spinning north by north-west, the paisley-pattern cloud-avenues of the inter-tropical convergence zone disappearing silently into night. An edge of green, the tip of north-eastern Brazil, draws over the horizon. The night-side of the planet is edged in a lace-work of lights. Clusters and whorls; they mirror the patterns of meteorology. Those lives down there.

'Do you know what happened to them?'

'Who, Lucas?'

'I know when you look at Earth like that, you're thinking about them.'

'They failed like everyone fails down there. What else could they do?'

'It's no easy world, this,' Lucas says.

'Neither is theirs. I've been thinking about my mãe, Lucas. In the apartment, singing; and Pai in the dealership, polishing his cars. They were so brilliant in the sun. I can see Caio. None of the others. Not even Achi clearly any more.'

'You had courage,' Lucas says. 'There is only one Iron Hand.'

'That stupid name!' Adriana says. 'It's a curse, not a name. Play me that music again, Lucas.'

Adriana settles into the chair. Jorge's whispering voice and agile guitar surround her. Lucas watches his mother drift down through the words and chords into shallow sleep. Still breathing. *The coffee is here,* Toquinho says. Lucas takes it from the maid and as he sets it on the table he sees that his mother is not breathing.

He takes her hand.

Toquinho shows him vital signs.

Gone.

Lucas feels his breath tremble in his chest, but it is not as terrible as he imagined; not so terrible at all. Yemanja slowly fades to white and folds in on itself. The crescent Earth stands eternally on the eastern horizon.

Luna, in a red dress, picking barefoot over the boulders and through the empty pools of Boa Vista. The streams have run dry, the water no longer falls from the eyes and lips of the ten orixas. Rafa can't express why he shut down Boa Vista's waters but no one except Luna objected. The only way he could articulate it was that Boa Vista needed to say something.

The memorial was ramshackle and disappointing. The guests could not outshine the Cortas in their eulogies, the Cortas had no valedictory tradition so their tributes were sincere but stumbling and poorly stage-managed and the Sisterhood, who understood religious theatre, had been barred from attending. The words were said, the handful of compost that was all the LDC would permit of Adriana Corta's carbon for private ceremonials was scattered, the representatives of the great families made their way to the tram. Throughout the short ceremony, Luna wandered blithe as water, exploring her strange dry world.

'Papai!'

'Leave him, oheneba,' Lousika Asamoah says. Like her daughter she wears a red dress; a funeral colour among the Asamoahs. 'He has to get used to things.'

Rafa takes the stepping stones over the dry river, enters the bamboo. He looks up at the open-lipped, wide-eyed faces of the orixas. Small feet have drawn a path between the canes: Luna's feet. She knows this place and all its secrets better than he. But it is his now, he is Senhor of Boa Vista. There is a universe of difference between living somewhere and owning it. Rafa runs the long, rough-edged bamboo leaves through his fingers. He had thought he would cry. He had thought he would be disconsolate, sobbing like a child. Rafa knows how easily his emotions are stirred, to anger or joy or exultation. *Your mother has died.* What he felt: shock, yes; the futile paralysis of needing to do something, a hundred things, knowing that none of them can change the truth of death. Anger – some; at the suddenness, at the revelation that Adriana had been sick for a long time, terminal since the moon-run party. Guilty that the whirlpool of events after the assassination attempt had drowned any signals Adriana might have given about her condition. Resentment that it was Lucas who had spent the final hours with her. Not disconsolate; not overwhelmed: no tears.

He stands a moment in São Sebastião Pavilion, its streams now dry; their sediments caking and cracking into hexagons. This had been her favourite of Boa Vista's pavilions. There was a pavilion for drinking tea, a pavilion for meeting social guests and one for business guests, a pavilion for receiving relatives and one for reading, the morning pavilion and the evening pavilion but this one, at the eastern end of Boa Vista's main chamber, was her working pavilion. Rafa has never liked the pavilions. He thinks them affected and silly. Adriana built Boa Vista selfishly; the palace of her particular dreams. It's Rafa's now but it will never be his. Adriana is in the dry ponds and watercourses, the bamboo, the domes of the pavilions, the faces of the orixas. He can't change a leaf or a pebble of it.

'Water,' Rafa whispers and feels Boa Vista tremble as waters stir in pipes and pumps; a gurgle here, a trickle there; pouring from freshets and faucets; runnels merging into streams, channels filling, water chuckling around rocks, drawing eddies and foam and dead leaves; water gathering in the eyes and mouths of the orixas; a slow swell into great teardrops quivering with surface tension then burst into slow waterfalls; showers and trickles first, then bounding cascades. Until he silenced them, Rafa had never realised how the splash and trickle of moving waters filled Boa Vista.

'Papai!' Luna exclaims, dress hitched up and calf-deep in running water. 'It's cold!'

Boa Vista is Rafa's now but still Lousika won't share it with him.

'Do you think you'll move back?' Rafa asks.

Lucas shakes his head.

'Too close. I like my distance. And the acoustics are terrible.' A touch on the sleeve of Rafa's Brioni jacket. 'A word.'

Rafa wondered why Lucas had sought him out at the far end of the garden, risking wet trouser cuffs and stained shoes among the stepping stones and pools.

'Go ahead.'

'Mamãe and I talked a lot in the last hours.'

Rafa's throat and jaw tighten with resentment. He is eldest, hwae-jang, golden. He should have had these last words.

'She had a plan for the company,' Lucas says. The play of falling water masks his words. 'Her will. She's created a new position: Choego. She wanted Ariel to fill it.'

'Ariel.'

'I've been through this but she was quite obdurate. Ariel will be Choego. Foremost. Head of Corta Hélio. Above me and you, irmão. Don't argue, don't make suggestions. I have this already planned. There's nothing we can do about the will. That's set, locked in.'

'We could fight...'

'I said don't argue, don't make suggestions. It would be a waste of our time and money fighting through the courts. Ariel knows the courts, she would tie us up forever. No, we do this constitutionally. Our sister was badly wounded in a knife attack. She is effectively paraplegic. Her recovery will be slow, and by no means certain. The constitution of Corta Hélio contains a medical competency clause. The clause allows for a board member to be retired from office in the case of sickness or injury that would prevent them from fully discharging their duties.'

'You're suggesting—'

'Yes I am. For the company, Rafa. Ariel is a supremely competent lawyer, but she knows nothing about helium mining. It wouldn't be a board-room coup. Just placing her powers and responsibilities in temporary abeyance.'

'Temporary until what?'

'Until such time as we can restructure the company more in line with what it needs, rather than our mother's whims. She was a very sick woman, Rafa.'

'Shut the fuck up, Lucas.'

Lucas steps back, hands help up in appeal.

'Of course. I apologise. But I tell you this; our mother would never have survived her own medical competency clause.'

'No, fuck off, Lucas.'

Lucas backs off another step.

'All we need are two medical reports, and I have those. One from the João de Deus medical centre, the other from our very own Dr Macaraeg, who is very pleased to have been retained as our family physician. Two reports, and a majority.' Lucas calls back through the spray. 'Let me know!'

Luna goes splashing down the stream, kicking slow-settling sprays of silver water into the air. They catch the light of the sunline and diffract it: a child crowned with rainbows.

The door of the tram closes, the door opens. Ariel looks out.

'Well, are you coming?'

There is no one other than Marina on the platform that Ariel could intend, but she still frowns, mouths, *Me?*

'Yes you, who else?'

'I'm technically out of contract...'

'Yes yes, you didn't work for me, you worked for my mother. Well, you work for me now.'

Hetty chimes: incoming mail. A contract.

'Come on. Let's get out of the fucking mausoleum. We've got a wedding to arrange.'

ELEVEN

Meridian loves a wedding and there is no wedding bigger than the marriage of Lucasinho Corta and Denny Mackenzie. The Eagle of the Moon has donated his private gardens for the ceremony: the trees have been dressed with bows and biolights and twinkling stars. The bergamots and kumquats and dwarf oranges have been sprayed silver. Paper lanterns are strung between the branches. The path will be strewn with rose petals. AKA has donated a hundred white doves for a spectacular, wing-clapping release. They've been engineered to die within twenty-four hours. The vermin laws are strict.

The contracts will be signed in the Orange Pavilion. Behind the happy boy and boy a squadron of aerialists will perform a winged ballet high in Antares Hub, weaving ideograms in the air with streamers attached to their ankles. The Eagle of the Moon has made small grants available for the residents of Antares Hub to decorate their neighbourhoods. Banners hang from balconies, streamers festoon the crosswalks and the bridges drip strings of Diwali biolights. Balloons in the shape of manhua bats and butterflies and ducks navigate the hub's airspace. Space rental on those balconies with the best views has hit six hundred bitsies. The finest vantages on the bridges and catwalks were tagged and bagged long before. Exclusive image rights have been signed to Gupshup after a ferocious auction: the access agreement is stern: media drones must keep a respectful distance and no direct interviews with either oko will be entertained.

The four hundred guests will be waited upon by twenty catering staff and eighty servers. Cultural and religious diets will be accommodated, and all manner of dietary intolerances. There will be meat. A joke is running around that Lucasinho made the wedding cake, in his signature style. Not true: the Ker Wa bakery has the longest established tradition of oko cakes and moon cakes. Kent Narasimha from the Full Moon bar of the Meridian Holiday Inn has created a celebratory cocktail: the Blushing Boy. It involves a designer one-shot gin, foams, cubes of jelly that dissolve and send spirals of colour and flavour up through the gin and flakes of gold foil. Virgin cocktails and herbal waters for non-alcohol drinkers.

The security screening started a week ago. LDC, Corta and Mackenzie security have liaised on an unprecedented level. The gardens of Jonathon Kayode are being scanned down to the level of dust-motes and dead skin-flakes.

Three days to the wedding of the the year! What will the boys wear? Here are spreads of Lucasinho Corta's latest looks. The preppy colloquium boy. His moon-run party tweed and tan pants. His two weeks as a fashion icon, when everyone pulled on suit-liners and drew on them with marker pens. His grandmother's eightieth party; his grandmother's memorial, so sad, so soon. His return to the fashion flashlight: who does his make-up? So very defining of this season. Heads up, boys! You're all going to be wearing this look. Denny Mackenzie: oh who cares? When was a Mackenzie ever fashionable? But who will design the wedding suits. We simply can't leave it to the familiars. Design AIs we're loving include Loyale, San Damiano, Boy de la Boy, Bruce and Bragg, Cenerentola. Who will get the contract? And the cosmetics . . .

Two days to the wedding of the year! What makes the Dragons so much better than any of us: class. The Cortas have shown sheer class throughout the matrimonial process. It's less than a month since the terrible attack on Ariel Corta, but not only is she as mobile as ever on her bot legs, she arranged the nikah from her hospital bed! And only two weeks ago, the whole moon was rocked and saddened by the news of the death of Adriana Corta. But what better way for the Cortas to show their courage than chin up, dress up, glam up: the wedding of the year! Class tells.

One day to the wedding of the year. The sure social signifier of the now is: are you on the guest list, or aren't you? No one's telling, but Gupshup has called in a few debts, dealt out a few threats, lavished kisses and micro-kittens and we can exclusively tell you who's on the guest list! And who's not! Prepare to be shocked...

The day of the wedding of the year. It starts with a small row; the celebrity spotters with berths booked on the best viewing stations versus the blimp bats and butterflies and beasts of good omen. At the prearranged time, the residents of Antares Hub all flick their banners over their balcony rails and let them slowly unroll into a tapestry of blessings and wedding charms. Security takes up positions as the guest elevators arrive. Invitations are scanned, guests directed to the reception and given their special Full Moon bar bespoke Blushing Boys. Jonathon Kayode and Adrian Mackenzie are delightful hosts. Drone cameras flit and jockey at the prescribed range, battling for celebrity close-ups. Half an hour before the signing, the guests are guided to the Orange Pavilion. Choreography is subtle and tight, the seating plan rigorously enforced. Wedding ushers sends fountains of rose petals into the air. Twenty minutes: the families arrive. Duncan Mackenzie and okos Anastasia and Apollinaire Vorontsov. His daughter, Tara, her okos; their rambunctious sons and daughters. Bryce Mackenzie, lumbering with determination on two sticks, accompanied by a dozen of his adoptees. Hadley Mackenzie, poised and very handsome. Robert Mackenzie is unable to leave Crucible and sends his apologies and congratulations to the happy couple, with all best hopes for a peaceful settlement between the great houses of Mackenzie and Corta. He is represented by Jade Sun-Mackenzie.

The Cortas: Rafa and Lousika, Robson and Luna. Lucas alone. Ariel and her new escolta, who takes a place among the family to flurries of murmurs through the guests. Carlinhos, filling his suit well. Wagner and oko Analiese Mackenzie, looking nervous, and his pack mates; thirty of them in dark colours, a wedding party in themselves, adding a spice of danger to the silver and ribbons of the wedding garden.

They take their seats, a small ensemble performs *Blooming Flowers and Full Moon Night*.

Now all that is necessary for the wedding of the year is the groom and groom.

A man should undress from the bottom, Lucasinho has heard, so to dress he should reverse the order. The shirt, fresh from the printer. Silver cuff links. Gold is trashy. The necktie is dove grey with a Seikai-ha pattern, tied in an elaborate five-strand Eldredge knot Jinji showed Lucasinho and which he has practised every day for an hour. Underwear: spider silk. Why are all clothes not made from this? Because no one would ever do anything else than adore the feel. Socks also, mid-calf. No visible ankle: a terrible sin. Now the pants. Lucasinho dithered for days before deciding on Boy de la Boy. He turned down five designs. The fabric is grey, a shade darker than the tie, with a ghost of a floral damask pattern. Pants: no turn-ups, sharply creased, two pleats. Two pleats is on trend for now. Two of everything is on trend: for the jacket, two buttons at the front, two buttons at the cuff, cut away at the front. Four centimetre lapels starting high. Buttonhole for a buttonhole. A pocket square; folded into two triangular peaks. The square in-line fold has been old for a lune. Matching stingy-brim fedora, two-centimetre silk band and bow, which Lucasinho will carry, not wear. He doesn't want it to interfere with his hair.

'Show me.'

Jinji shows Lucas himself through the hotel room cameras. He turns, preens, pouts.

'I am so freakin' hot.'

Before the hair, the make-up. Lucasinho tucks a towel into his collar, sits at a table and lets Jinji close in on his face. The cosmetic pack is also a bespoke commission from Coterie. Lucasinho enjoys the rhythm of the ritual; the layers of application, the refining and blending, the fine touch and nuance. He blinks his kohled eyes.

'Oh yeah.'

Next, at the same table, his hair. Lucasinho carefully builds up the quiff, reinforcing it with back combing and strategic applications of spray, mousse, gel, hair-concrete. He shakes his head. His hair moves like a living thing.

'I'd marry me.'

Last thing. One by one he inserts his pierces. Jinji gives him one last look at himself, then Lucasinho Corta takes a deep breath and leaves the Antares Home Inn.

The waiting moto opens to accept Lucasinho Corta. A command from Jinji sends it whirring away into the traffic on Hang Yin Plaza. The hotel is centrally located, an elevator ride from the Eagle's Eyrie. Nothing left to chance. The people on the plaza glance, double-take, recognise. Some nod or wave. Lucasinho straightens his tie and looks up. The hub is a waterfall of coloured banners; manhua-balloons wallow and nudge each other. The bridges are fuzzy with humanity, he can hear their voices echoing down the great well of Antares Hub.

Up there is the wedding of the year. Across the plaza from the front door of the Home Inn is an AKA commissary, an up-market affair for recreational cooks. Lucasinho steps out into the street and walks towards it. The traffic detours around him, ripples of self-organisation running from the plaza out along the five prospekts. Trays of bright vegetables in the window, a prominent meat locker with hanging lacquered ducks and poultry sausage; fish and frogs on ice; at the back of the store, freezers and bins of beans and lentils, bouquets of salad under a freshening mist. Two middle-aged women sit at the counter, rolling and lolling together with a secret shared laughter. They wear adinkra familiars in the Asamoah manner: the goose of Sankara, the asterisk of Ananse Ntontan.

Their laughter stops when Lucasinho enters the shop.

'I'm Lucas Corta Junior,' he announces. They know who he is. The society channels have been filled with nothing but his face for a week. They look afraid. He sets his fedora on the counter. Lucas takes the metal spike from his left ear and sets it beside the hat. 'Please show this to Abena Maanu Asamoah. She'll know what it means. I claim the protection of the Golden Stool.'

We're Earth and moon, Lucas Corta thinks. Bryce Mackenzie a gravid planet, I a small svelte satellite. Lucas takes pleasure in the analogy. Another pleasure; this is the same hotel from which Lucasinho absconded. Two small smiles. That will be the extent of the pleasure in this meeting.

Bryce Mackenzie stamps his way to the sofa, stick, foot, other stick, foot, like some antiquated quadruped mining machine. Lucas can hardly watch. How can the man bear himself? How can his many amors and adoptees bear him?

'Drink?'

Bryce Mackenzie grunts as he lowers himself to the sofa.

'I'll take that as a no. Do you mind if I do? The staff from the Holiday Inn are on hourly contracts and, well, you know me. I like to extract the maximum value from any situation. And these Blushing Boys really are rather good.'

'Your levity is not appropriate,' Bryce Mackenzie says. 'Where is the boy?'

'Lucasinho should be arriving in Twé even as we speak.'

The guests, the families; then the celebrant. The role was nothing more than witnessing the signatures on the nikahs, but Jonathon

Kayode had brought the full magnificence of the Eagle of the Moon to the role. When Ariel has suggested he celebrate, he had feigned surprise, even coyness. *No no, I couldn't possibly, well, oh all right then.*

Jonathon Kayode had arrayed himself in formal agbada, adorned with golden regalia he had commissioned for the occasion. 'Is he wearing built-up shoes?' Rafa whispered to Lucas. Once noticed, it shaded everything. Without the elevator shoes, the Eagle would have been a head shorter than the couple he was marrying. Rafa caught his own joke. He squeezed his eyes shut, clenched his mouth, but Rafa quaked with suppressed laughter.

'Stop that,' Lucas hissed. 'I have to get up there and hand him over.' The infection was irresistible. Lucas swallowed a tight giggle and discreetly wiped tears from his eyes. The orchestra stuck up *The Blooming of Rainy Night Flowers*. Bryce Mackenzie rose and took his position by the Orange Pavilion. Every head turned. Denny Mackenzie walked the rose petal path. His walk was clumsy, self-conscious, half-hearted. He had no idea what to do with his hands. Bryce Mackenzie beamed. Jonathon Kayode opened his arms like a summoning priest.

'Show time,' Rafa whispered to his brother. Then every Corta familiar whispered simultaneously *call from Lucasinho*.

Within thirty seconds Gupshup had sent the news around the moon. *Lucasinho Corta: runaway groom.*

'You've been in touch with your son?' Bryce Mackenzie asks.

'I haven't heard from him.'

'Pleased to hear that. I was under the impression that this was something you had knocked up between you.'

'You're being ridiculous.'

Bryce Mackenzie shakes his head, a tic of annoyance.

'The question now is how do we repair the damage?'

'There's damage?'

Another tic: a flare of the nostrils, an audible breath.

'Damage to the image of my family, the reputation of Mackenzie Metals; our compensation for the suit Gupshup will bring against us.'

'The drinks bill must be pretty high too,' Lucas says. He has met Bryce Mackenzie twice, both times social occasions, never in business, but Lucas has worked out the man's trick, his malandragem. Physical intimidation, not by muscle, but by mass. Bryce Mackenzie dominates a room as if by gravity; a trip, a fall will break you. I know how the trick is done, Lucas thinks. But you are the Earth and I am the moon. He feels lightheaded with potential. Everything is clear, clear as never before.

'Flippant,' Bryce Mackenzie says. He is sweating, big sweaty man. 'Neither your family nor mine are intimidated by threats of litigation. What's your proposal?'

'The wedding is re-staged. We'll split the costs. Can you give me a guarantee that your son will actually be there?'

'I offer no guarantee,' Lucas says. 'I can't speak for my son.'

'Are you his father or not?'

'As I said, I can't speak for Lucasinho. But I stand by his decision with all my heart,' Lucas says. 'For me, I say, fuck you, Bryce Mackenzie.'

A third tic: a chewing in of the top lip. Those others had been irritation. This is fury.

'Fine.' Bryce's blades enter from the lobby and help the man from the sofa, steady him on his stick and surprisingly neat feet. He stalks past Lucas, click by click. There is a third pleasure, Lucas realises, a small, mean but very sweet one, in discommoding Bryce Mackenzie.

At the door, Bryce turns, one finger raised, his stick dangling from its wrist-loop. 'Oh yes. One final thing.' Bryce takes a step forward and slaps Lucas across the face. There is little weight in the blow; Lucas reels from the shock, the daring, the implication. 'Name your seconds and your zashitnik if you are to be represented. Time and location to be decided by the court. The Mackenzies will have blood for this.'

One by one the familiars of the Kotoko appear around Abena Maanu Asamoah. Her breath catches. She is more awestruck than she thought. The adinkras glow in her lens, every second a new one appears. She is ringed by shining aphorisms. Abena prepared her room respectfully. The board's members may be the people you meet in the tunnels, in the tubefarms, on the streets and in the compounds, but the Kotoko is more than its individuals. It's continuity and change, lineage and diversity, abusua and corporation. Anyone may consult the Kotoko; the implied question is, why do you need to? Abena has tidied away her few things, folded up the furniture, set biolights, black, red and white in a triangle on the floor and put herself at the centre of them. She's showered.

Last to appear is the Sunsum, the familiar of the Omahene. Abena shivers. She has summoned powerful forces.

'Abena,' says Adofo Mensa Asamoah. The familiars speak with the voices of their clients. 'How are you? Greetings from the Golden Stool.'

'Yaa Doku Nana,' Abena says.

'Oh you've tidied, lovely,' says Akosua Dedei from Farside.

'Nice touch with the lights,' says Kofi Anto from Twé.

'So, what do you need to ask us?' says Kwamina Manu from Mampong. The hidden question.

'I made a promise,' Abena says, her fingers unconsciously twisting the chain of her Gye Nyame necklace. 'And now I've had to honour it, but I don't know if I had the right to promise anything.'

'This is about Lucasinho Corta,' says the familiar that Abena knows is Lousika Asamoah.

'Yes. I know we owe the Cortas for Kojo on the moon-run, but what if the Mackenzies turn on us like they turned on the Cortas?'

'He asked for sanctuary,' Abla Kande from Cyrillus agrarium says.

'But was it mine to offer?'

'What would the moon think of us if we failed to honour our

promises?' Adofo Mensa says. Voices whisper in chorus around the ring of familiars: *Fawodhodie ene obre na enam.* Independence comes with responsibilities.

'But the MacKenzies, I mean, we're not the biggest family, or the richest or the most powerful...'

'Let me tell you a little history,' says Omahene Adofo. 'That's true. AKA is not the richest or the oldest of the Five Dragons. We're not exporters; we don't keep the lights burning up there like the Cortas, or Earth's tech industries fed like the Mackenzies. We're not industrialists or IT giants. When we came to the moon we didn't have political backing like the Suns or wealth like the Mackenzies or access to launch facilities like the Vorontsovs. We weren't Asians or Westerns; we were Ghanaians. Ghanaians going to the moon! Such presumption! That's for the white people and Chinese. But Efua Mensah had an idea, and saw an opportunity and worked and fought and argued her way all the way up to the moon. Do you know what she saw?'

'You may become rich by shovelling the dirt, but you will become rich by selling the shovel,' Abena says. Every child learns the proverb as soon as they're socketed, lensed and linked for a familiar. She's always thought it dull and worthy, old people's wisdom. Storekeepers and greengrocers; not glamorous like the Cortas and the Mackenzies with their handsome dusters or the Vorontsovs with their exquisite toys.

'We bought our independence dear,' Adofo Mensa says. Her familiar is made from the Siamese Crocodiles and Ese Ne Tekrema, the adinkras of unity and interdependence 'We don't surrender it. We will not be bullied by the Mackenzies.'

'By anyone,' Kwamina Manu adds.

'Are you answered?' Omahene Adofu asks.

Abena dips her head and purses her fingers in the accepted lunar way. One by one the familiars of the Kotoko wink out. Last to shine is Lousika Kande Asamoah-Corta.

'You're not, are you?'

'What?'

'Answered.'

'I am, I'm just not...'

'Reassured?'

'I think I put the family in danger.'

'How many people are there on the moon?'

'What? About a million and a half.'

'One point seven million. That seems a lot but it's not big enough that we don't have to worry about the gene pool.'

'Inbreeding, accumulating mutations, genetic drift. Background radiation. I did this in school.'

'And each of us has a differed mechanism for dealing with it. We refined the abusua system and all those regulations about who can't have sex with you. You're a, what?'

'Bretuo. Aseni, Oyoko, and of course my own abusua.'

'The Suns intermarry everyone and anyone, half the moon is a Sun; the Cortas have their weird madrinha system, but they're all ways to keep the gene pool open and clean. The Mackenzies, they're different. They keep the family close and tight, they have a fear of polluting the gene line, about diluting their identity. They intermarry among themselves and backcross: where do think all those freckles come from? But it's risky – very risky, so they have to make sure they breed true. They hire us to engineer the gene line. We've been doing it for thirty years. It's our secret, but it's the reason we're safe from the Mackenzies. The fear of the two-headed baby.'

Abena whispers a prayer to Jesus.

'The Asamoahs keep everyone's secrets. But look out for Lucasinho, Abena. The Mackenzies won't daren't touch us, but they hold long grudges and long knives.'

Zabbaleen carefully pick up and take away the dead doves that litter the gardens of Jonathon Kayode. The release had been timed; the cages sprang open, the birds beat upwards in an applause of wings and whisked out over the heads of the departing guests. Ariel picks her careful, purring path through the rotting rose petals. She doesn't trust her bot legs on the slippery slime. She shares her mother's distaste for living matter. Organic turns so nasty so fast.

Jonathon Kayode receives her in his apartment, overlooking the garden. Ribbons and silvered fruit still adorn the citrus trees, food scraps litter the lawns. The bots are diligent but four hundred guests shed a load of party.

'Well, this is a mess,' Jonathon Kayode says, greeting Ariel.

'We hire people to clear up our messes,' Ariel says.

'I didn't get the opportunity to mention it at the "event", but it's wonderful to see you so mobile. That lower hemline suits you. I've been around a few places. The wedding of the year flops but the groom's aunt sets a fashion trend. How is the boy?'

'The Asamoahs have given him sanctuary.'

'You always were close, Cortas and Asamoahs.'

'I want you to stop this Jonathon.'

Jonathon Kayode shakes his head, touches a finger to his forehead.

'Ariel, you know as well as I . . .'

'If the LDC wants a thing to happen or not happen, the LDC finds a way.'

They sit on either side of a low table. A bot brings two Blushing Boys.

'You know, I really got a taste for these,' the Eagle says. Ariel does not have the taste this afternoon. The Eagle takes a sip. He is a noisy drinker.

'It's two years since the Court of Clavius settled by combat,' Ariel says.

'Not quite.' Jonathon Kayode sets his glass down. 'Alayoum versus Filmus.'

'It would never have gone to blades. I knew that. Malandragem. It's how I win. And the two cases are different. That was a divorce case. This is an old-fashioned calling-out, a trial of honour.'

'Bryce Mackenzie did rather get the drop on your brother.'

'You can call it off Jonathon,' Ariel says.

'Are you sure you don't want anything to drink?' The Eagle of the Moon says, lifting his glass. Over its rim his eyes catch Ariel's. His glance darts to the rear of the apartment; once, twice, three times. Ariel's eyes widen.

'It's still a little too early for me, Jonathon.' It had been a standard joke among the court and legal circles that Adrian MacKenzie had the Eagle of the Moon trussed up like a piece of exhibition shibari. No joke.

They want blood, he mouths. 'Who's representing Lucas?'

'Carlinhos.'

Jonathon Kayode's mouth opens in shock. *Your oko didn't tell you that the blood they want is the heart blood.*

'They nominated Hadley Mackenzie as zashitnik. We had to match status.'

She won't let the Eagle of the Moon look away. *You can stop all this, save two young men.*

'Jonathon?'

'I can't help you, Ariel. I am not the law.'

'I seem to be making a habit of this, but fuck you.' Ariel wills her legs to stand her upright. She lifts her clutch bag. She raises her courtroom voice to hit the back wall of the drawing room. 'And fuck you too, Adrian. I hope my brother cuts yours to pieces.'

He's gone back to Boa Vista for the fight. I couldn't do that, Ariel thinks. Even in the deep dark, when she felt opened and reached into and violated, when she feared her fine legs would never carry her again, when she saw the knife every time she closed her eyes, she refused to let her mother carry her back to Boa Vista. You see the knife too, Carlinhos. Every time. It's behind me, it's ahead of you. I would be paralysed with fear.

He lies on his belly on a table in the Nossa Senhora da Rocha

Pavilion. Spray from the Oxum waterfall gathers and drips from the lip of the dome. A masseur works his body, fingers deep in the muscle fibres. Carlinhos moans, little cries that sound like sex. It repulses Ariel: another touching your body so intimately. Another has touched her body, more intimately than massage, or sex.

Carlinhos turns his head to one side, grins at his sister.

'Ola.'

'My silver tongue let me down this time, Carlo.'

Carlinhos's face twitches sad. He grimaces to another deep working by the masseur. You are magnificent, Ariel thinks, and I think of knives slicing that perfect skin and I am filled with cold horror.

'I'm sorry.'

'Nothing to be sorry for,' Carlinhos says.

'I can try . . . No I can't do anything. I've reached the end of words. They will have their duel.'

'I know.'

Ariel kisses the back of her brother's neck.

'Kill him, Carlo. Kill him slowly and painfully. Kill him in front of their eyes so they can see every last thing they hoped to do to our family bleed out in front of them. Kill him for me.'

'Can I come? Can I?'

'No!' Rafa thunders. Robson trots at his father's heel.

'I want to support Carlinhos.'

'No,' Rafa says again.

'Why not? You're going. Everyone is going.'

Rafa turns to Robson.

'It's not handball. It's not a game. It's not a thing you support. We're going because Carlinhos does not fight alone. I don't want to go. I don't want him to go. But I will go. And you will not.'

Robson shuffles, frowns.

'Then I want to see him now.'

Rafa sighs in exasperation.

'Okay.'

The gym is the least used of Boa Vista's chambers. Bots have cleared years of dust, slowly warmed it from the chill of the eternal deep rock. Carlinhos has hung ceramic bells on ribbons from the ceiling. Seven bells. In a pair of fighting trunks he feints and dodges, cuts and pivots across the floor.

'Irmão.'

Carlinhos comes panting to the rail. He sets the knife on the ledge, rests his chin on his folded arms.

'Hey, Robson.'

'Tio.'

'Did you ring any?' Rafa nods at the hanging bells.

'I never ring any bells,' Carlinhos says. A movement, so fast and unexpected Carlinhos has no answer to it. Robson presses the tip of the knife to the soft skin under Carlinhos's right ear.

'Robson...'

'Hadley Mackenzie taught me, if you take a man's knife, you must use it against him. Never let go of the knife.'

Carlinhos is liquid action; he ducks away from the knife point and in the same flow of movement twists Robson's wrist firmly enough to teach pain. Carlinhos scoops up the dropped knife.

'Thank you, Robson. I'll watch for that.'

All the bells chime, a gentle tintinnabulation. Another small quake.

Carlinhos comes out of the bathroom, eyes wide.

'There's a whirlpool in there. I didn't even have a whirlpool in Boa Vista.'

'It's the least I can do, Carlo.'

Lucas's preparation of Camp Carlinhos has been unusually difficult. The wedding fiasco still taints the social atmosphere. Should news of a duel between enemy Dragons leak, even the threat of litigation from Cortas and Mackenzies would not stay the gossip networks. Handsome boys fighting in not many clothes. Even better than handsome boys marrying. The exclusive apartment on Orion hub was hired through shell companies; the printer designs commissioned through another and the masseurs, physiotherapists, psychologists, cooks, dietitians, knife-smiths, discreet security hired anonymously through agency AIs. A training room has been built and Mariano Gabriel Demaria brought secretly from Queen of the South and set up in the adjoining apartment. Last of all, Carlinhos's fighting knives, of lunar steel, have been carried from João de Deus and installed in the dojo.

'This is the bedroom.'

'I can walk right round this bed.'

Carlinhos collapses back on to the bed and folds his arms behind his head. His glee is bright. Lucas's mouth tightens.

'I'm sorry.'

'What?'

'I'm sorry. This. I should never have asked...'

'You didn't ask. I offered.'

'But, if I hadn't held out on Lucasinho...'

'Ariel came to see me in Boa Vista. Do you know what she said? That she was sorry she couldn't stop it. And you're sorry because you think you're the cause of it. Luca, I always knew this would come. I printed out my first knife, and I looked at it and I saw this. Not Hadley MacKenzie, but a fight where the family would depend on me.'

It's a forgiving.

'Hadley Mackenzie is fit and very fast.'

'I'm fitter.'

'Carlinhos...'

Lucas looks at his brother, sprawled on the bed, happy on real cotton. In twenty-four hours you could be dead. How can you bear that? How can you bear to waste an instant to anything that is trivial? Perhaps that's the fighter's wisdom; the trivia, the immediate physicality of high thread-count imported cotton, the felt things are the vital ones.

'What?'

'You're faster.'

Wagner picks up the knives, instinctively finds the balance. He looks at the things in his hands. He's just past full dark and his focus and concentration are at their most intense. He could spend hours obsessing of the line of the edge, the metallurgy.

'You do that too comfortably,' Carlinhos says.

'Scary things.' Wagner sets them back in the case. 'I'll be there. I don't want to be, but I will.'

'I don't want to be either.'

Brothers hug. Carlinhos had offered a room in the apartment but Wagner has called on the pack. The Packhouse is a cold and dim place when the Earth is dark. He came up from Theophilus the night before and slept fitfully in the pack bed, tiny and spread across as much space as he could, but still one man; troubled by recurring dreams of standing naked in the middle of the Ocean of Storms. Analiese doesn't believe his story about going up to Meridian on family business but she can find no obvious lie to get purchase on.

'Is there anything I can do?' Wagner asks. Carlinhos's laugh startles him.

'All the others, they all say how sorry they are, how guilty they feel. Not one has asked if they can do anything for me.'

'What can I do for you?'

'I should like very much to eat some meat,' Carlinhos says. 'Yes, I'd like that.'

'Meat.'

'You can eat that?'

'Not usually in this aspect, but for you, irmão...'

Sombra locates a churrascaria, vainly expensive. It boasts rare-breed pork and gin-massaged, music-soothed beef from dwarf

Kuroge Washu cattle. Glass-fronted meat safes display the hanging carcases, small as pets. The prices are vertiginous. Carlinhos and Wagner take a booth and they talk and dip their wafers of exquisite beef into the sauces but most of the time they keep companionable silence together, as close men do, and find they have communicated everything.

Run with me, he said.

Marina and Carlinhos drop on to the back of the Long Run. In five breaths they have matched the rhythm of the ritual. Marina is not afraid to sing this time. There is only one Long Run. It hasn't stopped, day or night, since she last dropped out of it. Then her heart, her blood, her muscles tune to the unity.

Yes, I will, yes, she said. Marina had come to Carlinhos's call expecting sex, hoping for something else. Something to take them out of this apartment that stank of the close presence of death. Carlinhos wanted to go home and run. João de Deus was only an hour away on the fast train. She and Carlinhos travelled in their Long Run kit. They drew admiring smiles and glances. *They are handsome together. You know who they are? Oh, really?* Marina's kit was smaller and tighter than she had ever dared before; her body paint more aggressive. *I'm tighter and more aggressive,* she thought. She had retrieved the green tassels of Ogun from vacuum storage and wore them with pride.

Marina kicks forward to the head of the run. Carlinhos laughs and comes up on her shoulder. *Restless blade, Ogun's knife cuts out-of-doors. Restless blade. Ogun's knife goes for the kill.* Then time, self, consciousness vanish.

They fall on to the train home, sweet and sweaty, fall into the seats as the train accelerates on to Equatorial One, fall together. Marina curls up against Carlinhos. He is so good, he brings out her inner cat. She loves the otherness of men; they are as unknowable as animals. She loves them as things different from and marvellous to her self.

'Will you come?' Carlinhos mumbles.

She has been expecting and dreading this question so her answered is prepared.

'I will, yes. But...'

'You won't look.'

'Carlinhos, I'm sorry. I can't see you get hurt.'

'I won't die.'

Ten minutes to Meridian.

'Carlo.' This is the first time Marina has ever called Carlinhos by his most intimate name; his family-and-amors name. 'I'm going to leave the moon.'

He says, 'I understand,' but Marina feels Carlinhos's body tighten against hers.

'I've got the money and my mum will be all right and your family has been wonderful to me, but I can't stay. I'm scared every day. Every single day, all the time. I'm afraid all the time. That's not a way to live. I have to leave, Carlinhos.'

Passengers are already rising and collecting their children, luggage, friends in anticipation of arrival. On the pressurised side of the platform Marina and Carlinhos kiss. She stands on tiptoe. Train travellers smile.

'I'll be there,' Marina says. They go to their separate apartments and in the morning Carlinhos walks out to fight.

The bots finish dusting the courtroom moments before the combatants arrive. It hasn't been used in a decade. The air has been scrubbed; no taint, real or imagined, of old blood. The courtroom feels cold though it has been brought up to skin-temperature. It is small and very beautiful, panelled and floored in wood. Its heart is the fighting ring, a five-metre sprung floor, good for dancing or fighting. Witness docks and judges' benches are narrow galleries around the ring. Adversaries and judges sit close enough to be hit by arterial spray. This is the morality of the combat court: violence touches everyone.

In the Mackenzie dock; Duncan Mackenzie, Bryce Mackenzie. He can barely fit in the narrow gallery. Again in lieu of Robert Mackenzie, Jade Sun-Mackenzie, mother of the zashitnik. In the Corta dock, Rafa, Lucas, Wagner and Ariel Mackenzie. With Ariel, her escolta, Marina Calzaghe. Ariel defeated a last-minute subpoena attempt by the Mackenzies' legal team to compel Lucasinho, Robson and Luna to attend. Judges Remy, El-Ashmawi and Mishra preside, none of whom have ever worked with Ariel Corta.

Judge Remy calls the court to order. Judge El-Ashmawi reads the offence. Judge Mishra asks if any reconciliation or apology will be made. None, says Lucas Corta.

The formalities calm, the formalities order, the formalities distance you from what will happen in this wooden ring.

Seconds in. For the Mackenzies, Denny Mackenzie and Constant Duffus, deputy head of security. For the Cortas, Heitor Pereira and Mariano Gabriel Demaria. Each side presents the fighting knives to the judges. They inspect them minutely, though none knows about blades, and approve one from each case. Mariano Gabriel Demaria kisses the hilt as he lays the lunar steel knife in its cradle.

The combatants come up from their stables beneath the court. Both look up as they step into the court, then around as they size up the space and its limitations. Smaller than they thought. This will be close, fast and savage. Carlinhos wears cream trunks, Hadley grey. Both trunks contrast with their skins. They are digitally naked, without familiars. Jewellery is a weakness but Carlinhos wears a single green cord around his right ankle; the favour of São Jorge. Carlinhos's seconds close around him.

Marina covers her face with her hands. She can't look at Carlinhos, she must look at Carlinhos. He's a boy, a big smiling boy who has wandered from one room to another not realising that behind him each door is locked, each room smaller than the one before it until he

364

ends here, on the killing floor. She feels sick; a nausea of every bone and sinew. Carlinhos kneels, Heitor and Mariano huddled over him, and murmurs. Across the ring Hadley Mackenzie skips, bounces, sniffs, stares, a gyre of energy and intention. He will cut Carlinhos apart, Marina thinks. She has never known fear like this, not when Mama was diagnosed, not when the OTV rolled into its launch run at White Sands.

The Court summons the combatants to the bench. At two metres ten Carlinhos is taller than Hadley but heavier. The Mackenzie is wire and steel. Judge Remy addresses the fighters.

'We would inform you that though this combat is entirely lawful, the Court of Clavius deplores this action. It is barbarous and unbecoming to your families and corporations. You may continue.'

Mariano Gabriel Demaria presents Carlinhos with his knife. He feels its weight, finds his grip, locates it balance and speed. He tries it for heft and punch, dancing its tip through the nine directions. Grip, firm but floating. Effort/no effort. To feint, to lunge, to pivot is not to cut. All effort is to cut. Live at the ultimate extension of each sense, feeling for the invisible bells hanging in the dark maze.

'Seconds out.'

Heitor and Mariano retire to their ringside stall under the witness gallery. There are no rounds, there is no recovery or moments of advice in the corner in the court arena. You fight until there is a winner.

Carlinhos dips his head to his family. Slow fat tears roll down Marina Calzaghe's face.

'Approach.'

Carlinhos and Hadley meet in the centre of the ring, raise blades in salute.

'Fight.'

The fighters drop into stance, weight balanced, arm raised. And they clash. Carlinhos pivots, trying to draw Hadley, put him out of phase but the Mackenzie is sharp and fast, so fast that Carlinhos loses tempo for an instant. Carlinhos recovers. Marina has never seen a knife fight. It is ugly and violating and harsh. There is nothing glorious about it; no skill of cut and thrust, parry and riposte, blade as attack and defence like the way of the sword. In the way of the knife the first contact will be the last. Any hit will be final. Slash, disarm, stab, immobilise. The speed is dizzying. Faster than thought. Hadley wears a skull grin on his face; his concentration is total. And he is faster, lighter, quicker. Feint, pivot, recover. She glances over at the other Cortas. Rafa's eyes are closed. Ariel's hands are over her mouth. Wagner is a mask of utter concentration. Lucas's face is like a skull. The expressions are the same on the Mackenzie side of the ring.

She can't look. She can't look away.

No one can keep up this killing pace. She can see that Carlinhos's balance is off. His reactions are a fraction slow. Sweat gleams on his skin. His eyes are hard, his face is closed. It's a dance, a killing two-step. Tight, fast, blazing slashes and stabs: the knife hand, the tendons of the leg. High, low. Carlinhos feints, Hadley blocks with his blade, cuts a gash down Carlinhos's bicep that rotates into a slash across his abdominals. Carlinhos is already dancing away from the blade, it draws a line of blood on his belly. He doesn't notice. He is burning adrenaline, beyond pain, beyond anything except the unity of the fight. But the gash to the biceps is heavy. He's losing blood. He's losing control. He's losing the duel. Carlinhos swivels and skips back, putting distance between himself and Hadley. Hadley moves to close the gap but in that instant Carlinhos shifts knife from right to left hand. It's a surprise for an instant, but enough to force Hadley into retreat. Hadley shakes his head like he's shaking out a crick from his neck and shifts the blade from right hand to left.

Bare feet slide in a slick of Carlinhos's warm sweet blood.

Carlinhos sees all the ways that Hadley Mackenzie can come at him in the next attack, all of them simultaneously and in every one of them the knife opens the tendons of his hand, disarms him, tears his leg tendons and sends him down and guts him.

He dies here.

And then he sees the other way, that is not the way of the knife. The way of malandragem. Who brings Brazilian jiu jitsu to a knife fight? Carlinhos throws away his knife. It embeds in the wooden walls of the court, quivers. Hadley's eyes follow it and in that instant Carlinhos steps inside his guard, blocks his swing with his hands and snaps his elbow joint.

The crack resounds around the court arena. The knife falls.

Carlinhos twists the broken arm behind Hadley's back. The two men are as close as lovers. Carlinhos scoops up the dropped knife and in the same motion drives it into Hadley Mackenzie's throat and out through the interior jugular.

The court is on its feet.

There is a look of mild surprise on Hadley's face, then disappointment. Blood gushes from the hideous wound, his hands flap uselessly at death. Carlinhos lowers him to lie gurgling and flapping in the pooling blood.

Carlinhos roars. Throws back his shoulders, balls his fists, roars. He kicks the wood of the gallery, again and again, smashes a fist into the walls. Roars. He faces his family, shakes sweat from his hair and bellows his victory.

Marina hides her face in her hands. She can't bear what she sees. This is Carlinhos. This always was Carlinhos.

Hadley is still now and there is a second voice in the courtroom; a long, keening wail, so uncanny and inhuman its source is not obvious until Jade Sun lunges for the rail. Duncan Mackenzie grabs her, holds her. She cries on, incoherent with loss and desolation. The Mackenzie seconds cover the body.

'The case is satisfied,' Judge Mishra shouts over the roaring and the keening. 'The Court is dismissed.'

Heitor Pereira and Mariano Gabriel Demaria try to escort Carlinhos down to the under court. He shakes them off and crosses the fighting floor to bellow in front of the Mackenzies. His body drips with sweat-smeared blood. He jabs an accusing finger at Jade Sun, at Bryce Mackenzie.

Marina is dying.

'Seconds, control your zashitnik!' Judge Al-Ashmawi shouts. Heitor and Mariano seize Carlinhos, one on each shoulder, and fight him to the gate. Jade Sun spits. Spit flies far on the moon. The gobbet of saliva strikes Carlinhos on the shoulder. He turns, kicks a spray of blood from the floor at her. Blood rains in her face, speckles the Mackenzies.

'Get him out of here!' Rafa yells.

Marina has already fled the court arena. She presses the back of her head against the wall, hoping that its solidity and cool will press down the pulses of nausea. Escoltas rush past her to escort the Cortas to their waiting transport; a glass partition separates the Corta side of the corridor from the Mackenzie. Their blades huddle around the Mackenzie court party but Marina can see Duncan Mackenzie wipe blood from his mother-in-law's face.

'Oh Carlinhos,' she whispers. 'I could have loved you.'

The first Corta Hélio extractor goes dark within ten minutes of Carlinhos Corta's victory in the Court of Clavius. Thirty seconds later, the second goes offline. Within three minutes the entire North Imbrium samba-line has gone dark.

In the passenger pod of VTO moonship *Pustelga*, Rafa, Lucas, Carlinhos and Heitor Pereira's familiars light up. On the train back to Hypatia Junction, Sombra alerts Wagner Corta. In the moto to the Meridian apartment, Beijaflor and Hetty key in their clients.

Corta Hélio is under attack.

The hire of a VTO moonship is hefty even for a Dragon but Rafa knew that whatever the result on the killing floor of the Court of Clavius he would need to get the family to safety fast. By the time the ship drops on to the pad at João de Deus, West and East Imbrium and Central Serenity are all down.

'We've just lost West Serenity,' Heitor Pereira says as the ship lowers the pod on to the tractor. 'I have South Serenity, I'll link you in to it.'

Helmet feed appears on everyone's lenses: a devastated samba-line. The camera pans across wreckage and scrap, metal and plastic shards strew far across the regolith; five extractors dead, a rover smashed open like a skull by falling construction beams.

'Are you getting this?' a woman's voice shouts. Her familiar-tag identifies her as Kiné Mbaye: Mare Serenitatis. 'They're killing us.' Behind her a flash in the sky, a blast of light. An entire structural truss spins towards the camera. The woman swears in French. The camera goes dead. The name tag turns white.

'Carlinhos!' Rafa shakes his brother. After the explosive rage and madness of the court-arena Carlinhos collapsed into catatonia. His seconds wrestled him down to the zashitnik stables where a medical bot patched up his abdominals, his biceps and shot him full of tranquiliser. His seconds showered off the blood, shoved him into street clothes, bundled him on to the *Pustelga*. 'What's happening?'

Carlinhos tries to focus on his brother's face.

'We've lost the entire South Serenity samba-line,' Heitor Pereira says. His face is grey. Airlocks link and equalise, the passengers enter the elevator lobby. 'Thirty lives.'

'Carlinhos! You're the duster.'

'Show me,' Carlinhos says. He reviews Kiné Mbaye's footage three times as the elevator arrives. 'Stop all the samba-lines.'

'What's happening—' Rafa begins but Lucas cuts him off.

'I've given the order.'

'It won't hold them off for long. They'll just recalculate the trajectories.' Carlinhos looks at each of the faces in the elevator car in turn to see if any of them have worked it out. 'They're firing BALTRAN capsules at us. You can see one in the South Serenity report if you slow it right down, just before the impact. That flash, it's not a flash, it's a BALTRAN capsule impact.'

'There's nowhere we can hide,' Rafa says.

'This isn't something you just make up on the spur of the moment,' Lucas says. 'You have to plot the locations of every single one of our extractors, book the capsules, target the launchers. They've had this planned for a long time.'

'Who?' Heitor Pereira asks. Lucas rounds on him.

'Who do you think, you old fool?'

São Sebastião Quadra Kondakova Prospekt, the elevator says.

'What can we do?' Rafa says.

'Outbid them,' Lucas says. 'No one beats General Money.' He issues commands to Toquinho. There is a pause. There has never been a pause before.

Access to Corta Hélio accounts is temporarily unavailable, Toquinho says.

The elevator doors open.

'Explain,' Lucas says.

Our bank systems are under a denial of service attack, Toquinho says.

The elevator lobby rocks. All the lives on Kondakova Prospekt look up, the instinct of people who live in caves.

'What we need right now,' Rafa says. 'A quake.'

'Not a quake,' Carlinhos says. 'Shaped charges.'

One woman, one man, smartly dressed in the fashion of the moment, disembark from the 28 express and pass through the airlocks into Twé Station. They move through the press of passengers with poise and direction; they seem to have a clear destination through Twé's notorious labyrinth. They are guided. At a public printer they pick up two pre-ordered plastic knives; notched and edged and keen to harm. This woman and man are assassins, hired to locate Lucasinho Corta and gut him. Their familiars lock on to Jinji. The boy is public and exposed. They track him through the tunnels and agraria, across high walkways over precipitous farm tubes; along the ramps that spiral up through the residential zones, every step closing the distance between them.

Lucasinho Corta has spent the morning in his room waiting for news from the Court of Clavius, shredded by guilt. His father has told him time and again that it's not about the wedding. It's about the slap. The calculated insult, the call to duel. This is between him and Bryce Mackenzie. The wedding was the pretext.

I'm coming, Lucasinho said.

You're not, Lucas ordered.

I need to see, Lucasinho said.

No one needs to see, Lucas said. *Stay in Twé. You're safe in Twé. I'll let you know.*

Lucasinho tried to sit, tried to walk about, tried to play games, tried to scan the social networks, tried to bake something. He couldn't settle. He couldn't concentrate. He felt sick with dread. Then Jinji lit with a message from Lucas. *Carlinhos won.* Nothing more.

Carlinhos won. Lucasinho feels light. He feels released. He feels elated. He has to tell someone, has to see someone. A familiar message won't do. *Abena meet me.* He almost runs through the tunnels of Twé. The assassins flicker information between their familiars. The target is moving. So much simpler than having to hack apartment security. They'll cut him off at Nkrumah Circle and take him there, in public. They imagine their channels are secure. There. Their hands close on their concealed knives. They move to bracket Lucasinho.

Danger, Jinji says. *Danger, Lucasinho Corta!* Lucasinho freezes, spins in the middle of Rawlings Plaza trying to see which of those hundreds of people wants to kill him. He sees the man step towards him, the hand on the knife. He's close. He doesn't see the woman behind him.

But the robot in the roof sees her. AKA AIs saw patterns in the arrival of these two passengers, the activity of the Kuffuor Street printer and the evolving events on the surface. They tasked a security bot, a clever spider that scuttled unseen through the cluttered ceilings of Twé's crowded tunnels, tracking the assassins as they tracked Lucasinho Corta. The bot targets locks and attacks. It leaps on to the woman assassin's neck and sinks a neurotoxin needle into her neck. Even as her lungs lock rigid the bot springs from her, somersaults over Lucasinho's shoulder into the face of the male assassin. His hands never even make it to cover and protect before the thing is clinging to his face. AKA BTX toxin has been engineered to be fast and sure. The bodies drop on either side of Lucasinho Corta as the spider scuttles away into the under-architecture of Rawlings Plaza. AKA does not like to involve itself in the politics of the other Dragons but when it must the policy of the Golden Stool is to act quickly and decisively.

You're safe now, Jinji says. *Help will soon be here.*

Wagner has developed an affection for the quiet pillar at the end of the platform in Hypatia Junction. It's a place between worlds – the full world and the dark world; now it's become a place between times: past and future. Every Dragon, even a half-Dragon like him, lives under the shadow of violence but he never saw a human die at the hand of another. He can still smell the blood. He always will. He imagines he reeks of it and that everyone on the train could smell it. Wagner knows the wolf in him, but in the court-arena he saw a thing inside Carlinhos beyond wolves, a thing Wagner does not know and which scares him because it has always lived there inside Carlinhos and he never saw it. It makes every moment and experience they've shared as brothers false.

When Dragons fight, where does the wolf stand?

Sombra lights: a call from Analiese.

'Wagner, where are you?'

'Hypatia.'

'Wagner, go back to Meridian.'

'What's wrong, Ana?'

'Go back to Meridian. Don't come here. Don't come home.'

The low urgency of her voice, her hushed pitch, the secrecy in her sibilants, all these rasp his concentration and stand the hairs up on Wagner's arms and neck.

'What is it, Ana?'

Her voice drops to a whisper. 'They're here. They're waiting for you. Oh God they made me promise...'

'Ana, who...'

'The Mackenzies. They made me, they said you're either family or you're not. Don't come back, Wagner. They want every Corta dead.'

'Ana—'

'I'm family. I'm all right. I'm all right, Wagner.' He hears a fearful, stifled sob. 'Go!'

I've lost the connection, Sombra says.

'Get her back.'

I'm not able to do that, Wagner.

Families mill on the platforms. Children's voices echo and the echoes encourage them to shout louder. Noodle cartons blow in the strange winds of the under croft, evading trash bots. Up there, Cortas and Mackenzies battle. Down in the station, people change trains for work, family, friends, love, pleasure. If they saw the man huddled against the pillar with his knees pulled in to his chest, would they ever imagine that he's fighting for his life?

Analiese is back there. He doesn't know what's happened to her. *Go,* she said.

Wagner gets up from his pillar and crosses the platform to the opposite track. Exile then, in the company of wolves.

Kondakova Prospekt trembles again. Dust dislodged from the high roof drops in sparkling clouds as soft as grace. The street comes to a standstill. The people look up first, then at each other.

Breaches at Santa Barbra and São Jorge main locks, each familiar relates to its client. *Elevator security is compromised.*

'They're coming through the roof,' Rafa says.

Armed and hostile units at the main station.

'Show me,' Carlinhos orders. São Jorge shows him bodies in anti-stab body-armour disembarking from the train locks and forming up into squads on the platform. They wear crossed blades and taser holsters. A mundane invasion, on the 87 Limited. Passengers frown in confusion: is an episode of *Hearts and Skulls* being filmed? Train passengers and civilians are not legitimate targets. 'How many?'

Fifty. Ten in the Santa Barbra lock and the São Jorge lock. Five each in the São Sebastião elevators. São Sebastião Quadra shakes to another blast. *We've lost integrity on the emergency lock. My cameras are down.*

The sunline flickers. The sunline never flickers. A terrible fearful moan washes up and down Kondakova Prospekt. The greatest fear is to be trapped in the dark, and the air leaking away. *Enemy personnel in São Sebastião Quadra. Enemy personnel advancing on Kondakova and Tereshkova Prospekts.*

'They'll slaughter us down here,' Carlinhos says. 'Heitor, I want two escoltas on Lucas and Rafa. Rafa...'

'I need to be with my kids. They could be in Boa Vista...'

'You can't access the station from this side of the quadra. Take the perimeter tunnel and come out at West 12th. Use the Serova Prospekt entrance. Lucas.'

'I'm sounding the general evacuation alarm.'

'Good man. But you need to get out of here too.'

'I stay with the family.'

'You're not the fighter here, Luca. They will cut you apart, man.'

'They tried to kill Lucasinho, Carlo. They tried to kill my boy.'

'You're Corta Hélio now. Sorry Rafa. Save the company. You have a plan?'

'I always have a plan.'

'Go on go go.'

The skyline flashes. Seven short flashes, one long. General evacuation. The thing you fear worst; it just happened. Radiation, unconfined fire, depressurisation, roof-fall, breach. Invasion. Get safe, get to the refuges, get out. A thousand familiars on Kondakova Prospekt and on every level and prospekt and quadra of João de Deus echo the alarm. The quadra keeps a moment of shocked stillness then explodes into movement. Motos swerve and steer their passengers to the nearest muster point. Pedestrians breaks into runs; fliers swoop down to the safety points shown to them by the familiars. Shops, cafés, bars, clubs empty. Panicked drunks stare at the sky as if it is falling. School teachers gather their classes and hurry their weeping charges to the refuges. Where's Mãe, Pai? Parents call out for their children, lost children cry in panic, bots locate the waifs and lost and shepherd them to safety. Families will be reunited after, if there is an after. In the noche and semana quadras, the sleepers, the early morning people, the shift folk are shocked awake. Fear, fire, fall! Offices, apartments empty; feet pound on levels and walkways. Bodies pour down staircases, drop from the lower levels in low-gravity leaps.

Figures in combat armour advance up Kondakova Prospekt, ignoring the people fleeing around them. Behind them, the offices of Corta Hélio explode, one after another, sprays of construction plastic, cheap wood and soft furnishings.

'São Jorge, print me my armour.'

Available at West Fifteen public printer in three minutes.

'Heitor, give me my knives.'

Heitor Pereira opens the ceremonial case. The light of the sunline flashes from Carlinhos Corta's lunar steel blades. A squad of Corta Hélio security arrive breathless; unequipped, confused, too few.

'You, you, with Rafa and Lucas. Heitor, take five escoltas and fall back.' Carlinhos can't afford five escoltas. But he's seen the bodies among the flying debris of the exploded offices. The Mackenzies are destroying Corta Hélio substance and soul. 'Put a general call out: every Corta Hélio employee musters with you. Get them to the East Sebastião refuge. The Mackenzies won't touch them there.'

'You think?'

'Refuges are sacred. Not even the MacKenzies would blow a refuge. Go.'

Heitor Pereira beckons his troops to him. They lope up Konda-kova Prospekt, hands on hilts. They are a brave sight and a hopeless one. João de Deus is too big, too diverse, spread across too many timezones and the Mackenzies are already all through it. João de Deus is lost.

'Rafa!'

Lucas is already a level up, climbing steep ladders with his two bodyguards against the downpour of refugees. For the schemer, the man is handy.

'Get out of here!'

'Carlo!'

Lucas calls down from two levels up. The streets and prospekt are emptying now; abandoned motos crowd the refuge locks, purpose-less bots scurry back and forth.

'I can burn them. The Mackenzies. Robert, Jade, Duncan, Bryce: all of them. I can burn them all.'

'We're not like them, Luca.'

Lucas nods, then he is swooping hand over hand up the ladders. Rafa takes a last look and ducks down a cross-street. Carlinhos straps on his impact armour. He slides the knives into magnetic scabbards.

'We buy time,' Carlinhos tells his squad. Eight escoltas. The Mac-kenzie blades are twenty abreast, sweeping up Kondakova Prospekt. 'A fighting withdrawal. Buy that time dear. Okay, with me.' He breaks into a jog. His fighters form a wedge. Carlinhos cries a howl of defiance and his voice rings from the walls of empty São Sebastião Quadra.

Rafa runs. His jacket and tie flap. His shoes are all wrong. Emergency lights pulse-rotate yellow. The floor of the orbital tunnel is littered with discarded water bottles and drums and tassels in the colours of the orixas. The Long Run has finally come to an end.

Before they leave the apartment Ariel stuffs her and Marina's bags with cash.

'Lucas said the accounts were locked,' Ariel says. 'This works anywhere.'

'On the train?'

'I booked the tickets ten minutes ago.'

Corta Hélio is collapsing. João de Deus is under attack. Carlinhos is fighting, Rafa is trying to get to Boa Vista. No one knows where Lucas is. Wagner is in Meridian, Lucasinho in Twé. Ariel and Marina are going to join him there and seek sanctuary. Marina can't believe how fast it all came apart.

Twenty levels, one kilometre to Meridian Station. A hundred deaths could be waiting out there. Motos are fast but motos can be hacked. Elevators and escalators can hide a dozen blades. Any or all of the hundreds on the street could be hired knives. Right now, drones could be targeting this apartment, assassin bots and neurotoxic insects climbing up the ductwork.

'Get your legs,' Marina says. 'We walk.'

Ariel freezes halfway to the ladeira.

'Come on,' Marina shouts.

'I can't,' Ariel says. 'My legs won't work.'

Marina had covered every threat and hack except the most personal and debilitating.

'Get them off.' The very next hack could command the legs to walk Ariel straight into a ring of blades.

'I can't disconnect them.' Ariel hisses with effort and fear. Marina pulls her knife.

'Sorry about this.'

The first cut sends the skirt to the ground. The second and third sever the flex cables to the power supply. Servos unpowered, the legs buckle. Ariel flails, falls, Marina catches her.

'Get them off me, get them off me,' Ariel cries, fumbling at the dead prostheses.

'I don't want to cut you.' Marina works carefully, quickly with the point of the knife, nicking plastic locks and catches. The concentration is furious. 'Keep still!' Two connectors to go. Ariel's apartment is off a quiet side alley but it can only be a matter of moments before those who hacked the bot legs come looking to see why their plan has not succeeded. And this is a blind alley. 'Got you.' Marina prises the legs open. Ariel drags herself clear.

'Can you climb?' Marina asks.

'I can try,' Ariel says. 'Why?'

Marina nods at the service ladder at the back of the access alley.

'I don't know if I could make it all the way down,' Ariel says.

'We're not going down. There'll be a Mackenzie a metre all the way to the station. We're going up.' Up into the poor places, the high places, the Bairro Alto. The city of the unregarded. Where the moon's greatest matrimonial lawyer and her bodyguard can disappear into the roof of the world. 'I'll help you. First though...' Marina touches a forefinger between her eyes. Familiars off. Beijaflor vanishes an instant after Hetty. 'You go first.'

'Give me a hand,' Ariel orders, wrestling with the jacket of her suit. Marina helps her off with it. Ariel is stripped down to Capri tights and sports bra: her fighting garb.

'Give me my bag,' Ariel says. Marina kicks it away from her reach.

'How are you going to carry that? In your teeth?'

'The cash could be useful.'

'More useful than keeping your throat intact?'

Ariel hauls herself up two, three, four rungs of the ladder.

'I'm not going to be able to get very far.'

'I said I'd help you.' Marina ducks in close to the ladder under Ariel's hanging body. She drapes the paralysed legs on either side of her neck. 'Lean forward and put your weight on my shoulders. We're going to have to co-ordinate this. Left hands. Right hands. My right foot, then my left foot.' Piggyback, Ariel and Marina climb the ladder. Jo Moonbeam muscles and lunar gravity reduce Ariel's weight but they don't abolish it. Marina guesses Ariel's perceived weight at about ten kilogrammes. How long can she climb straight up ladders with a ten kilogramme weight on her shoulders? One level and she's aching already.

Two levels. Three. Sixty to go to the roof of the world. What Marina will do there she doesn't know. Whether the Cortas live or die, whether their empire stands or falls, she doesn't know. If she'll find a place in Bairro Alto, if she'll survive, if the Mackenzies will be waiting for her, she doesn't know. All she knows is left hands right hands, left foot right foot. Left hands right hands, left foot right foot, rung by rung, level by level, Marina and Ariel climb into exile.

The sound room burns; sheets of flame lick and lap across the walls, the acoustically perfect floor. The perfect mechanisms beneath crack and pop. Smoke swirls, stirred by the air-conditioning system into ghosts and devils, flicked with fire. The ball of vapour and smoke ignited in a fireball. The fire prevention systems click in, seal the room and douse it with halon.

The first taser takes Carlinhos in the back. He locks rigid. Every muscle spasms. Carlinhos cries out with effort as he fights to keep grip on his knives. He slashes down, jolts as he severs the wires that connect the barbs to the tasers. Spins, slashes out. Blades step back. He is alone now. All his squad lie awkward in their blood along Kondakova Prospekt. Mackenzie blades dance around him but Carlinhos Corta battles on. His armour is slashed and gouged, jagged with barbs where tasers have struck Kevlar not flesh. Five Mackenzies have fallen to him but every second more arrive.

Carlinhos has fought step by step, Mackenzie by Mackenzie, back to the lock of East refuge. Heitor Pereira is dead, his escoltas with him, but the refuge is full and sealed and safe.

Blades pile in around Carlinhos, taunting and jabbing. He cannot get out. He cannot get out. The second taser drives him to his knees. The third disarms him. The fourth turns him to a jerking puppet of flesh, webbed with the sparking lines of taser barbs. His strength, his agility, his knives are gone. He will die on his knees in a cave on the moon. All that remains is the rage. A blade steps towards and removes their helmet. Denny Mackenzie. He picks up one of Carlinhos's fallen knives and admires the finesse of line and edge.

'This is nice.'

He pulls Carlinhos's head back and slashes his throat through to the windpipe.

When the corpse is drained the blades strip it naked. They drag Carlinhos Corta to the West 7 crosswalk and hang him by the heels from the bridge.

Five minutes later, the contracts go out. To all surviving employees, subcontractors and agents of Corta Hélio. Terms, conditions and remuneration rates for the transfer of allegiance to Mackenzie Metals. The money is more than generous. The Mackenzies repay three times.

The rover races north across the Sea of Fecundity.

It is a fool who only has one escape plan.

Lucas first devised his exit strategies when he ascended to the board of Corta Hélio. Every year he reviews and revises them against such a day as this. They are all based on the same insight: there is nowhere to hide on the moon. He realised that when he took his seat at the board table and touched his hands to the polished wood and felt the fragility of the elegant table, the spindly chair on which he sat, the weight of the rock above him, the cold of the rock beneath him. No hiding place, but there is a way out. The last instruction Lucas gave Toquinho before he shut it down was to lay in the course to the Central Mare Fecunditatis moonloop terminal.

Ten million in gold, deposited in the Mirabaud Bank in Zurich,

Earth, five years ago. The Vorontsovs adore gold. They trust it when they can't trust their machines, their ships, their sisters and brothers.

Save yourselves, he'd ordered the escoltas at the lock. *Throw away the knives, drop the armour, go dark. I'll go from here.*

He didn't want them to know his true escape plan. He hopes they made it. Lucas has always appreciated true service. So do the Mackenzies, so they won't senselessly waste good labour, over and above the necessary bloodletting. It's what he'd do. Lucas has had to run fast and silent to avoid Mackenzie detection. João de Deus will have fallen. Carlinhos will be dead. He can only hope that Rafa made it to Boa Vista, that the madrinhas got the kids to safety. The Mackenzies will eradicate his family, root and branch. It's what he'd do. Wagner is on the run. Ariel. He has no idea about Ariel. Lucasinho is safe. The Asamoahs have asserted their independence in two dead Mackenzie assassins. That warms Lucas in his plastic environment bubble clutched to the belly of the Corta Hélio rover. His boy is safe.

Five minutes to Central Fecunditatis Terminal, the rover says.

'Ready the capsule,' Lucas instructs. The curving screen shows him the terminal, a kilometre-tall girder work tower attended by a long row on tether-transfer pods. Loading and docking facilities, a solar farm, a siding from the close-by Equatorial One: Central Fecunditatis Terminal is a major cargo hub for Corta helium-3 canisters and pallets of refined Mackenzie rare earths. Today it will heft a different cargo.

'Operate docking sequence,' Lucas says. The nimble rover scuttles in to a ring of flashing blue lights: the outlock. And stops dead.

'Rover, please dock with the terminal.'

The rover stands on the Sea of Fecundity five metres from the flashing lock.

'Rover...'

'It's not going to work, you know.' The voice breaks in on the com channels. A face appears on the screen: Amanda Sun.

'Isn't this a little excessive for post-divorce vindictiveness? Couldn't you just have cut up a few jackets?'

Amanda Sun laughs deeply and truly.

'I have to hand it to you, Lucas, you're a professional. But, you know, jackets? Deprinter? No, what's going to happen here has nothing to do with our divorce. But you know that. And I am going to kill you. This time, I will succeed. Unless you have a resourceful and plucky cocktail waitress tucked away in there somewhere? Didn't think so.'

'We always wondered how that fly got through security.'

Amanda Sun taps an earlobe.

'Jewellery, darling. You half-brother would have got there eventually. He's thorough. You Cortas are ridiculously easy to manipulate. All that Brazilian machismo. The Mackenzies hardly needed prodding at all. But it's far too easy when you can predict your enemy's next move. That's why we knew you'd try and get off the moon. And so here I am, in your software. But we're wasting time. I need to kill you. I have several options here. I could blow you up but you're a little close to the moonloop terminal. I could depressurise the rover. That would be fairly quick. But I think I'll just order the rover to drive and keep driving until your air runs out.'

Depressurise the rover. The human hide is an excellent pressure skin. The human body can operate for fifteen seconds in vacuum. Moonrun. He needs to keep her talking while he checks the cabin for what he needs to save his life. Vanity was always her vice.

'I have a question.'

'Yes, it is customary to grant a last request. What is it, darling?'

'Why?'

'Oh, that would be no fun at all. The villain gives away her entire master plan? I tell you what though, I'll give you a hint. You're a smart boy, Lucas. You should be able to work it out. It'll give you something to do rather than watching the air gauge run down. From day one my family has been taking out options on surface terrain adjacent to Equatorial One. Two lunes ago we started to exercise them. There. That should provide you with some distraction.'

'I'll give it my undivided concentration,' Lucas says and launches himself across the capsule. He slaps the emergency hatch release. The hatch blows. Lucas screams as needles are driven through his eardrums. Every sinus is filled with boiling lead. The scream is good. The scream saves his lungs from rupturing. The scream dies as the blast of air blows Lucas in his jacket and pleated pants and tie out on to the Sea of Fecundity. He hits the regolith in a cloud of dust and rolls. Eyes. Keep the eyes open. Close them and they freeze shut. Blind is disoriented. Disoriented is dead. He hauls himself to his feet. On the edge of his vision he sees the rover spin its wheels. It's moving. She wants to run him down. One step, two steps. That's all. One step, two. But everything is dying. He is tearing apart inside. Lucas lurches forward on his two-tone loafers and hits the outlock panel. The flashing lights lock solid blue. The lock slams open. Lucas hauls himself in. The lock seals. Lucas's lungs and eyes and ears and brain are about to burst. Then he hears the roar of air flooding back into the lock. Over it he hears his own voice. He never stopped screaming. A bang, the lock shakes. Amanda has rammed the rover into the lock. The Vorontsovs build tough but assault by a possessed lunar rover is not in their design parameters. Lucas gasps down air and crawls to the inlock. The door opens, he falls through. The door closes. Central Fecunditatis Terminal rocks again. Lucas presses his cheek to the cold, solid, wonderful floor mesh. On the wall in his direct line of sight is an icon of Dona Luna. He reaches out to stroke a finger down Lady Moon's bone face.

Still it is not over.

'Corcovado, Dorolice, Desafinado.' Lucas croaks the code.

Welcome Lucas Corta, the terminal says. *Your capsule is ready for you. Moonloop rendezvous and orbital transfer in sixty seconds.*

With the last of his strength Lucas staggers to the capsule.

Please be informed that maximum acceleration will momentarily peak at six lunar gravities, the capsule says as it lowers safety bars over his chest and clasps his waist in a padded hug. The locks seal. *Terminal ascent.* A different jolt shakes Lucas in his capsule and he almost weeps with relief: the capsule undocking and climbing the terminal tower to the tether platform. *At ascent. Moonloop lift in twenty seconds.*

He imagines the moonloop wheeling towards him along the equator, sending counterweights climbing up and down its length to dip lower into the moon's gravity well to snatch this parcel of life. Then Lucas cries out as the grapple connects. The capsule with the screaming Lucas Corta huddled inside it is snatched up into the sky, and flung away from the moon, into the big dark.

Bodies lie strewn like surface scrap along the platform of Boa Vista tram station. An entire Mackenzie blade squad taken down. Dart throwers swivel and lock on Rafa with a speed and accuracy that makes the breath catch in his throat. The guns hesitate. If the Mackenzies have hacked security, Rafa will be dead before he can reach the gate. The dart throwers snap up and away. Pass friend.

Socrates tried to raise Robson and Luna but Boa Vista's network is down.

Rafa steps out of the station expecting horrors. The long valley is deserted. Water cascades between the impassive faces of the orixas, gurgles through streams and pools and falls. Bamboo stirs, leaves flicker in the subtle breezes. The sunline stands at early afternoon.

'Ola Boa Vista!'

His voice returns in a dozen echoes.

They might have made it out. They might be dead in their own blood among the columns and in the chambers.

'Ola!'

Room after empty room. Boa Vista has never felt less his palace. His mother's apartment, spacious rooms open to the gardens. The reception rooms, the board room. Staff quarters. The old apartment he shared with Lousika, the crawlspace where Luna used to hide and spy and thought no one knew. Deserted. He steps through the door to the service area and an arm grabs him, swings him, slams him into the wall and throws him to the ground. Madrinha Elis stands over him, a knife-tip a centimetre from his left eyeball. She snatches the blade away.

'Sorry, Senhor Rafa.'

'Where are they?'

'In the refuge.'

Boa Vista shakes. Dust drops from the ceiling. There is no mistaking the flat thud of breaching charges.

'Come with me.'

Madrinha Elis takes Rafa's hand. Room after room, through the labyrinth of Boa Vista's ever-growing corridors. The refuge is a tank of steel and aluminium and pressure-glass; striped yellow and black, the universal dress of danger. Madrinhas and Boa Vista staff huddle nervously on the benches; Robson and Luna rush to the window, press their hands against the glass. Familiars can speak through the local network, Rafa goes down on his knees and presses his head to the pane.

'Thank gods thank gods thank gods, I was so scared.'

'Papai, are you coming in?' Luna says.

'In a minute. I need to see if there's anyone else out there.'

Boa Vista rattles again. The refuge creaks on its vibration-damping springs. It is designed to keep twenty people safe and breathing against the worst the moon can drop on it.

'I can do that, Senhor Rafa,' Madrinha Elis says.

'You've done enough. You get in. Go.'

The lock cycles open. Madrinha Elis gives Rafa a last questioning look; he shakes his head.

'I'll be back before you know it,' Rafa says to Luna. They touch hands to the glass.

He's checked the south wing but the company offices and ancillary areas are on the north side of the gardens.

'Ola!'

Another blast. He needs to hurry. The air plant, water recycling, power, thermal. Clear. A fresh explosion, the most powerful yet, shakes leaves from the trees. Masonry falls from the São Sebastião Pavilion. A crack runs down the face of Oxossi the hunter.

Clear.

Utterly clear. He was a fool to have come here. Luna and Robson didn't need him to save that. The madrinhas looked after them, calmly, efficiently. He is the liability, he's the danger. If he goes to the refuge, the Mackenzies will cut it apart to get him. They're up there blasting a path down to him. Boa Vista is a trap. Another explosion, the heaviest yet. The crack down Oxossi's face widens into a fissure. The dome of the São Sebastião Pavilion collapses into the water. Rafa runs.

The tram service is not currently available, the lock AI says. *The tunnel is blocked by a roof fall at kilometre three.*

Rafa stares dumb at the lock, as if it has committed some personal affront. All ideas have fled. The surface lock. He can steal out the way Lucasinho did, in a hard-shell emergency suit. João de Deus is lost, but there's a depot at Rurik; two hours run at full shell-suit speed. Pick up a rover, get out to Twé. Regroup and recover. Gather the family, strike back.

He runs for the surface lock elevator. Is blown off his feet by a staggering detonation that lifts Boa Vista and drops it like a fighter breaking an enemy's spine. The front of the elevator lobby disintegrates in a wall of debris. Deafened, stunned by the pressure wave, Rafa understands the meaning of the flying debris. They've blown the surface lock. Boa Vista is open to vacuum.

The pressure wave reverses. Boa Vista vents its atmosphere. The gardens explode. Every leaf is stripped from every tree, every loose object is syphoned towards the surface lock shaft and blasted out in a fountain of litter, leaf, garden furniture, tea glasses, petals, grass clippings, lost jewellery, debris from the explosion. Doors and windows buckle and shatter. Boa Vista is a tornado of glass splinters and shredded metal. Depressurisation alarms shriek, their voices weakening as the air pressure drops. Rafa clings to a pillar of the São Sebastião Pavilion. The killing wind tears at him. His clothes, his skin are lacerated by a thousand cuts of flying glass. His lungs blaze, his brain burns, his vision turns red as he draws the last oxygen from his bloodstream. He gasps in a shallow, airless final breath. He dies here but he won't let go. But his vision is darkening, his strength failing. Synapses fuse and die one by one. His grip is weakening. He can't hold on any longer. There is no point, no hope. With a final silent cry Rafa slips from the pillar into the storm.

The moonloop capsule flies out beyond the far side of the moon. If he had cameras or windows Lucas Corta could have gazed on the wonder of a half-Farside, diamond-bright, filling his sky. He has no windows, no cameras, little in the way of communications or entertainment or light. Toquinho is offline: everything is sacrificed to keeping Lucas breathing. There is not even enough power for a call to Lucasinho, to let the boy know Lucas is alive. The calculations are tight but they are accurate. They require no faith; they are equations.

Lucas's tie has worked loose from his jacket and floats in free-fall.

The Taiyang plan is child-like in its straightforwardness. Lucas has time to think about it in his capsule and he deduced it in instants from Amanda's confession. Never confess. That's a mistake he will repay three times. She never esteemed him. The Suns always treated the Cortas as a lesser, dirty class. Ludicrous gauchos. Jumped-up favelados. Mackenzie Metals destroys Corta Hélio. Planet Earth watches and fears for its helium fusion plants. Mackenzie Metals has a helium-3 stockpile from its attempts to muscle into Corta Hélio's market but the long game lies in Taiyang's exercising its long-bet options on the equatorial belt. Pave the moon's equator sixty kilometres on either side of Equatorial One with solar panels sintered from lunar regolith and beam the power to Earth by microwave. Taiyang has always been information and power. The moon as non-depletable permanent orbital power station. It is humanity's most expensive and largest infrastructure program but in the paranoia following the fall of Corta Hélio and the shrinking of the lunar helium-3 supply, investors will stab each other in the throat to bang cash on Taiyang's table. It will be the Sun's final victory in their long war with the PRC. It's a magnificent plan. Lucas admires it nakedly.

Its magnificence is its simplicity. Set a few simple motivators working and human pride will do the rest. The assassin fly was brilliant; a simple obfuscation that cast shadows between the Cortas and Asamoahs but pointed to the Mackenzies. Lucas has no doubt that the software malfunction that killed Rachel Mackenzie was sourced in a Taiyang server; or that the knife attack that disabled Ariel came out of the Palace of Eternal Light. Little triggers. Feedback loops. Cycles of violence. Conspire for your enemies to destroy each other. How long had the Suns been scheming? They worked in decades, planned for centuries.

It's far too easy when you can predict your enemy's next move, Amanda had said. Wagner had mentioned, Ariel had confirmed, that Taiyang had designed a quantum computing system for Whitacre Goddard. The Three August Ones. Highly accurate predictions from detailed real-world modelling. What serves Whitacre Goddard serves the Suns better.

They had not predicted Lucas would survive.

Toquinho powers up, a low-rez basic interface that allows Lucas to mesh with the capsule's sensors and control systems. The capsule has pinged, and the destination has pinged back. It was all calculation. Out there, close to the far end of its loop around the back of the moon into its return orbit to Earth, VTO cycler *Saints Peter and Paul* has locked on to the capsule and assumed control. Lucas's tie falls as the capsule jerks to micro-accelerations; thrusters burping to push it into a rendezvous orbit. Now the cycler is within range of the capsules' cameras and Toquinho shows him the breath-taking sight of the sun-lit ship: five habitat rings arranged up and down the central drive and life support axle, a crown of soar panels.

Ten million in Zurich gold will buy Lucas sanctuary here, for as long as he needs to calculate out his return and revenge.

Thrusters pop and belch, docking arms reach out to grasp the capsule and draw Lucas Corta in.

The moonship comes in low over the debris field. The ejecta of Boa Vista has fallen in a rough disc five kilometres across, graded by size and weight. The lighter material – the leaves, the grass clippings – forms the outer rings; then the glass shards, the pieces of metal and stone and sinter. The largest and heaviest items, the most intact ones, lie closest to the wreckage of the lock. The pilot brings her ship in manually, hunting for a safe landing zone. She plays the manoeuvring thrusters like a musical instrument: ship-dancing.

In the surface activity pod, Lucasinho Corta, Abena and Lousika Asamoah suit up with the VTO rescue team and the AKA security squad. There has been no sign of activity from Boa Vista for two hours now, except the pulse of the refuge beacon. Refuges are tough but the destruction of Boa Vista is well beyond design parameters. Green lights. The ship is down. The pod depressurises. Lucasinho and Abena bump helmets, a recognition of friendship and the anticipation of fear. Familiars collapse down into name tags over their left shoulders.

VTO had protested that diverting to Twé to pick up Lousika Asamoah would add perilous minutes to their rescue mission. 'My girl is down there.' VTO had still demurred. 'AKA will pay for your extra fuel, time and air.' That had settled it. 'There will be three of us.'

Pod depressurised, Jinji says. *Doors opening.*

Abena squeezes Lucasinho's hand.

Lucasinho has never flown in a moonship. He anticipated excitement: rushing over the surface faster than he ever travelled before, rocket-powered, riding to the rescue. His experience was a seat in a windowless pod, a series of unpredictable jolts and thumps and accelerations that threw him against his restraint harness and much time to imagine what he would find down there.

The VTO rescue squad strike through the debris field to the lock. They rig winch tripods and lights. Lousika, with Abena and Lucasinho and her guards, descend the ramp to the surface. The moonship's searchlights cast long, slow-moving shadows of warped garden furniture, twisted construction beams, shards of reinforced glass stabbed into the regolith, smashed machinery. Lucasinho and Abena pick a path through the wreckage.

'Nana.'

Lousika's guards have found something. Their helmet lights play across tweed, the curve of a shoulder, a hank of hair.

'Stay there, Lucasinho,' Lousika orders.

'I want to see him,' Lucasinho says.

'Stay there!'

Two guards seize him, turn him away. Lucasinho tries to wrench free but these are fresh workers six months up from Accra and they outmuscle any third gen moon-boy. Abena stands in front of him.

'Look at me.'

'I want to see him!'

'Look at me!'

Lucasinho turns his head. He glimpses Lousika on her knees on the regolith. Her hands are pressed to her faceplate, she rocks back and forth. He glimpses something smashed and distorted, burst open and freeze-dried to leather. Then Abena claps her hands on either side of his helmet and turns his head to her. Lucasinho returns the gesture. He pulls Abena's helmet to touch his, a duster kiss.

'I will never ever forgive the people who did this,' Lucasinho swears on a private channel. 'Robert Mackenzie, Duncan Mackenzie,

Bryce MacKenzie, I name you and claim you. I put down a marker. You're mine.'

'Lucasinho, don't say this.'

'You don't tell me that, Abena. This is mine, you don't have a say in it.'

'Lucasinho . . .'

'This is mine.'

'Ms Asamoah-Corta.'

Lousika starts at the call on the common channel from the VTO rescue squad.

'We're ready.'

She rests a hand on Lucasinho's shoulder. Sasuit haptics communicate the nap of the terrain, the touch of a hand.

'Luca, it will kill you.'

He only caught a glimpse; he was not allowed to see what Lousika saw; his uncle, her oko; but what he did see he will never stop seeing.

'Nana, they're waiting for us,' says one of the guards. She carefully steers Lucasinho to keep his back turned to the dead thing. The moon kills ugly.

The Vorontsov team hook first Lousika, then Lucasinho, last Abena to the winches. Lucasinho swings out over the black gullet of the lock shaft. He glances down, his helmet beams splash around the wall of the pit. The enormous blast of Boa Vista's depressurisation has scoured the shaft clean of anything that might snag and tear a sasuit. Still, it is a descent into dread and darkness. The refuge has been beaconing constantly but it could have shifted, become jammed, failed, ruptured.

'Lowering.'

It must have been likewise when Adriana first descended into the lava tube she would sculpt into her palace. Light on rock, the vibration of the winch through the drop line. *You came up this when you stormed out on your pai,* Lucasinho thinks and feels a brief burn of embarrassment. *How differently you make the return trip.*

Then Lucasinho's proximity sensors beep and his feet touch down. Crunch and texture of wreckage under his boots. He unsnaps the harness and steps out into Boa Vista. The Vorontsov team has rigged working lights; they hint at more than they reveal: dark shadows in the eye sockets of Xango. Pavilions fallen and strewn like unsuccessful card tricks. Leafless trees, frozen to their hearts, eerily underlit. The full, sensual lips of Iansa. Hints and glints of ice: the frozen tears of the orixas; Lucasinho's helmet beams playing across dead lawns rigid with frost, lenses of black ice in the dry pools and watercourses. What water wasn't blown away in the DP has flash frozen in a frosted glaze.

Lucasinho blunders into a lost object and sends it skidding across the tiled pavement. His helmet beams locate it: the wreckage of the old Corta Hélio board table; cracked, missing a leg. He sets it upright. It keels over immediately. Through broken door frames and smashed chairs, under trees draped in shredded bedding. His boots crunch vacuum-frozen twigs and crumbs of glass. Not a pavilion stands. He plays his helmet lights across the faces of the orixas. Oxala, Lord of Light. Yemanja the Creator. Xango the Just. Oxum the Lover. Ogun the Warrior. Oxossi the Hunter. Ibeji the Twins. Omolu, Lord of Disease. Iansa, Queen of Change. Nana the Source.

He never believed in any of them.

'I will bring this back,' he whispers in Portuguese. 'This is mine.'

A second pair of helmet beams strike out and fix him in a pool of light, a third: Lousika and Abena have arrived, but he walks ahead of them, down the dead river bed between the orixas, down to where the rescuers are waiting.

Glossary

Many languages are spoken on the moon and the vocabulary cheerfully borrows words from Chinese, Portuguese, Russian, Yoruba, Spanish, Arabic, Akan.

Abusua: Group of people who share a common maternal ancestor. AKA maintains them and their marriage taboos to preserve genetic diversity

Adinkra: Akan visual symbols that represent concepts or aphorisms

Agbada: Yoruba formal robe

Amor: Lover/partner

Anzinho: Little angel

Apatoo: Spirit of dissension

Banya: Russian sauna and steam bath

Berçário: Nursery

Bu-hwaejang: Korean corporate title: vice-chair. See also, hwaejang, jonmu

Caçador: Hunter

Chib: A small virtual pane in an interactive contact lens that shows the state of an individual's accounts for the Four Elementals

Choego: Korean corporate title: Foremost

Churrasceria: Brazilian/Argentinian barbecue

Coracão: My heart. A term of endearment

CPD: Social identity number in Brazil, necessary for a number of important social and financial transactions

Craque: Sports superstar

Escolta: Bodyguard

Four Elementals: Air, water, carbon and data: the basic commodities of lunar existence, paid for daily by the chib system

Gaye Nyame: Adinkra symbol meaning 'Except God, (I fear None)'

Globo: a simplified form of English with a codified pronunciation comprehensible by machines

Gupshup: The main gossip channel on the lunar social network

Hwaejang: Korean corporate title: President

Irmã/Irmão: Sister/brother

Jo/Joe Moonbeam: new arrival on the moon

Jonmu: Korean Corporate title: Managing Director

Keji-oko: Second spouse

Kotoko: AKA council, of rotating memberships

Kuozhao: Dust-mask

Ladeiro: A staircase from one level of a quadra to another

Madrinha: Surrogate mother, literally 'Godmother'

Malandragem: The art of the trickster, bad-assery

Mamãe/Mae, Papai/pai: Mother/Mum, Father/Dad

Manhua: Chinese manga

Miudo: Kid

Moto: Three-wheel automated cab

Nana: Ashanti term of respect to an elder

Nikah: A marriage contract. The term comes from Arabic

Norte: A person from North America

Oheneba: 'Little Princess' – term of endearment

Oko: Spouse in marriage

Omahene: CEO of AKA, on an eight-year cycle rotation

Onyame: One name for a Supreme being in Akan traditional religion

Orixa: Deities and saints in the syncretistic Afro-Brazilian umbanda religion

Patrão: Godfather

Sasuit: Surface Activity suit

Saudade: Melancholy. Sweet melancholy is a sophisticated and essential element on bossa nova music

Shibari: Japanese rope bondage

Ser: Form of address used to a neutro

Siririca: Brazilian slang for female masturbation

Terreiro: An Umbanda temple

Tia/Tio: Aunt/uncle

Yin: Digital signature

Zabbaleen: Freelance organics recyclers, who then sell on to the LDC which owns all organic material

Zashitnik: A hired fighter in trial by combat: literally defender, advocate

Hawaiian Calendar

Lunar society has adopted the Hawaiian system of naming each day of the lune (a lunar month) after a different moon-phase. Thus the lune has 30 days and no weeks.

1: Hilo
2: Hoaka
3: Ku Kahi
4: Ku Lua
5: Ku Kolu
6: Ku Pau
7: Ole Ku Kahi
8: Ole Ku Lua
9: Ole Ku Kolu
10: Ole Ku Pau
11: Huna
12: Mohalu
13: Hua
14: Akua
15: Hoku
16: Mahealani
17: Kulua

18: Lāʾau Kū Kahi
19: Lāʾau Kuū Lua
20: Lāʾau Pau
21: ʾOle Kū Kahi
22: ʾOle Kū Lua
23: ʾOle Pau
24: Kāloa Kū Kahi
25: Kāloa Kū Lua
26: Kāloa Pau
27: Kāne
28: Lono
29: Mauli
30: Muku

137b736

SF McDonald